Dexter & Sinister
DETECTING AGENTS

KEITH W. DICKINSON

HAMMERSMYTH PRESS

For all the dreamers
From one who never stopped

CHAPTER 1

FRIDAY

An ill wind blew through the cobbled streets of Hammersmyth. It guttered the gas lamps, whispering a warning to those with wit enough to hear it. It was not safe to be abroad that night. Something bad was going to happen. Somebody was going to die.

In a poorly lit street on the edge of town, two men – one big as a bull, the other skinny as a rat – stood before a large wrought iron gate. They were examining the old iron chain and brand new steel padlock that had been bought to replace the night watchman, dismissed just two weeks previous in a misguided attempt to save money.

"I reckon I can pick that," said the Skinny Man.

"We don't need to—"

"Here, watch." The Skinny Man knelt by the lock, jammed a bent piece of wire into the keyhole, and started fiddling about. The big guy beside him sighed. That was the problem with looking like the unholy union between a shire horse and an angry gorilla, no one ever listened to you.

"Look, just let me have a go will you."

"Just a sec, I almost got—" *Ping!* "Damn it!"

"What?"

"The wire broke."

"Right. Get out of the way."

"Why? What do you think you can—"

The Big Guy inserted a crowbar through the loops of the chain. With a quick twist, he snapped it like a dry twig. "New lock, old chain," he said, stepping back.

The Skinny Man glared at him. Barging his way through the factory gates, he stormed off into the darkness.

The Big Guy took his time stowing his crowbar. He didn't like his current associate very much. He was a nasty piece of work and no mistake. He always had a knife on him in case he ever needed it, and he always seemed to need it. They'd only been working together a couple of weeks and already he'd had to step in to stop him from cutting someone who didn't deserve it. It was just a matter of time before the two of them had Words, and then things would get really messy – for the Big Guy, at least. Getting rid of a dead body was a right pain. It took all night, and it always got on your shoes.

As the two men crossed the cobbled courtyard they saw the silhouette of a huge airship in the field beyond the factory, distinctive in the way it blotted out the stars in the sky.

"Well would you look at that," said the Skinny Man. "Maybe we could—"

"No."

"No what? What did I say? Did I say anything?"

"I know what you were gonna say, and I said no. We're not here for that."

"And what if I am, eh? What then?"

"Then you gets to explain yourself to the boss, that's what."

Inside the factory the darkness was tangible. What little moonlight that came in through its high windows did nothing to illuminate the factory floor. Lighting a lamp each the two men went in opposite directions, doing a full circuit of the factory floor before coming together again, empty-handed, by the giant building's big main double doors.

"See anything?" said Skinny.

"Nope. Nothing."

"Right. Then we'll just have to look again then, won't we? You go that way this time, and I'll go the other."

"What about the workshop?"

"What workshop?"

"The one next door."

The Skinny Man's lamp danced with rage. He charged up toe-to-toe with the Big Guy, although not nose-to-nose as he had hoped. Even at full stretch he still barely came up to the big man's chest. "Why didn't you mention that before?!" he growled, flecks of enraged spit flying all over the place.

The Big Guy wiped something unpleasant out the corner of his eye. "I said so now, din' I?" he replied, watching the other man's hands in case they made a move he didn't like.

For a few seconds, neither of them moved. Then slowly, deliberately, the Skinny Man lowered his heels to the floor. Keeping his eye on the Big Guy as he backed out of reach, he turned and stormed out of the building, his lamp swinging wildly with each furious step.

The Big Guy took a moment. *Maybe this is it,* he thought. *Maybe tonight's the night.* He felt the back of his belt where he'd stashed the crowbar, before following his associate out the factory.

He found his homicidal friend in the workshop next door, admiring a strange, four-wheeled contraption.

"That's her, I reckon. Has to be. Ain't she a beaut?"

The Big Guy nodded. "Y'know what, I ain't usually one fer new-fangled tecnollergy, but that there is one nice lookin' bit of kit."

"She sure is. Hey, did you hear what the boss plans to do wiv 'er?"

"No. And I don't want to neither." The big man tried to sound final about that, but his skinny accomplice couldn't contain himself.

"Suffice to say, someone's gonna be real surprised when they see that comin' down the street towards 'em. The shock could even kill 'em, you might say." He giggled like a little boy who'd just seen a flash of someone's knickers.

The Big Guy watched him out the side of his eye. "You need to stop listenin' at keyholes, mate. You're gonna get in trouble," he warned, but his associate simply swatted away his concerns. "Anyway, come on, let's get her going. I'll drive."

"I'll drive!" the Skinny Man hissed. "I'm the coachman around here."

Considering the device, and its utter lack of horses, the Big Guy couldn't see how that was a factor. But he couldn't be bothered to argue about it either.

"As you wish," he said wearily.

In a study worthy of a gentleman of means, in front of a small fire that crackled and popped with comforting regularity, the owner of the freshly-burgled airship factory sat with a cat balanced on one knee and a ledger of accounts balanced on the other. His brow furrowed, he ran his finger down a column of numbers, mumbling to himself as he totted them up in his head. When he reached the bottom of the page he pursed his lips, shaking his head.

"No. It's no good. I still don't see it."

The cat, a grey tortoiseshell tabby with yellowy-green eyes, turned to look up at its master. "What's that then?" it said.

The factory owner tapped the ledger. "These numbers. There's something not right about them. I mean they *look* right, and indeed they *do* balance out, but I've seen enough dodgy accounting to know when someone is trying to pull the wool over my eyes.

Someone's playing silly buggers, I can feel it. I just don't see how. Whoever it is, they're very good at it."

"Yeah?" said the cat. "So what are you thinking? Is it Peter, do you reckon? Do you think he's up to something?"

The factory owner shook his head. "No, I do not think that is the case."

"But it could be though, eh? It could be Peter. I mean, he's always been a bit..." The cat pulled a 'you know what I mean' kind of face.

"Yes, thank you," said the man, glowering at the accusing kitty. "Your opinion of my youngest son is duly noted."

With a shrug, the cat turned away and began cleaning itself. "So, what's the plan? What're you gonna do?"

"I've asked Henry to look into it, to see what he can find," the factory owner said, putting the ledger to one side. "Hopefully he will succeed where I have not."

The cat frowned up at its master. "Henry? Are you sure? I mean he's a nice lad and all that, but let's be honest, he wouldn't know a balance sheet from a bottle of rum. How's he going to find out anything?"

"I have no idea. I'm hoping he will come up with a way to get to the bottom of things that isn't all invoices and ledgers and accounts payable. My son is a smart lad, in his own way. I'm sure he'll think of something."

The cat wasn't convinced, but he knew better than to argue. Once his master's mind was made up, a dozen determined pit-ponies couldn't make it change direction.

Settling in to enjoy the fire, the cat let his mind wander to bigger, more important, more cat-related issues; like snoozing, and napping, and what he was going to do to that curly-tailed little monster, Mr Nibbles, the cheese thief... when he finally got his paws on him that is.

A few miles east of the airship factory, and several miles south of its owner, on a dockside bathed in the orange glow of the ironworks on the south side of the river, Hammersmyth's nightly street theatre of the unwashed and the unholy was already well under way. Hawkers and barrow boys as trustworthy as your average politician vied with painted flower girls and penny showmen for what little trade there was to be had, trying to entice the passing sailors and visiting top hats with the sort of delights and diversions you didn't get in the more respectable parts of town. Hammersmyth's docks were a playground for the bad, the lonely, the desperate, and the idle rich. They were where desire met fulfilment, where supply met demand, and they were a great place to get stabbed if you weren't careful.

Off to one side of the main drag, a young man in well-worn shoes and a faded blue jacket danced three cups back and forth on a cracked wooden board balanced between two upturned crates.

"Roll up, roll up! Come try your luck. Find the ball and win it all. Tuppence wins a groat, a groat wins a shilling, a shilling wins you half a crown!" A couple of passing sailors slowed their walk to watch. The young man flashed them the dried pea under one of the cups. "Watch close, watch close. She's on the move." He swished the cups left and right; fast, yes, but still slow enough to follow if you paid attention. He flashed the pea again, right where the sailors thought it would be. The two men stepped a little closer.

Swish, swish, pea, swish. The young man looked up. "What do you say gentlemen? Wanna try your luck? Tuppence wins a groat. A groat wins a shilling." The two sailors considered the three cups. Fresh off one of the North Sea tramp steamers, with a gut full of grog and a month's pay burning a hole in their pockets, they were sober enough to be suspicious but drunk enough to think they could win. Just how the young man liked them. He could make half a guinea off these two if he played it right. "I tell you what, gents, how about just a penny to get you started? A penny gets you tuppence. What do you say?" He didn't wait for their reply. Flashing them the pea again, he moved the cups, watching the sailors as they watched his hands. Once he had them both hooked he stopped and made the offer.

"Middle," grumbled the sailor on the left, in a heavy Russian accent. He slapped down his penny and lifted the cup to reveal the pea.

"Very good!" said the young man, matching the sailor's bet. "Penny gets you tuppence." Retrieving his cup, he did the dance again, leaving the sailor's coins where they were. The bet was made before the sailor could say no. "Find the ball and win it all. Tuppence wins a groat," he said, lining up the cups once more.

The two sailors conferred, never taking their eyes off the cups. "She is right," said the Russian, lifting the cup.

"Correct!" said the young man, matching the sailor's bet again. "You're a natural, my friend. I tell you what, how about we up the ante? A groat wins a shilling, but a shilling wins you half a crown."

The young man gave them his most disarming smile, but the Russian just shook his head. "Nyet," he said, sweeping up the small pile of coins. "Have enough for next round. Is plenty."

"But... a groat gets you a shilling," called the young man, as the two sailors staggered off. "That's enough for two rounds! And a pie!!" But it was too late, they were gone. "Damn it," John cursed softly. He really thought he had those two. And now, instead of being well up, he was thruppence down. That was not the way this was meant to go.

Over on the other side of the road, a small crowd had gathered. Billy Quick, a nefarious little so-and-so if ever there was one, had snagged himself a well-heeled mark. The gentleman was about the same age as John, with blonde hair down to his shoulders, a purple velvet top coat, and a fuzzy orange hat that really made him stand out among the grubby greys and dreary blacks of everyone around him. He seemed to be enjoying Billy's well-practised game of three card monte, and to have no idea that he was about to get taken for all he had.

Pocketing his cups, John popped the dried pea in his mouth as he wandered over to watch the show.

"Sir, I confess myself amazed at your perceptions," gushed Billy Quick, flashing the gentleman a tobacco-stained smile. "Tell me, have you played before perhaps?"

The young gentleman laughed. "Not at all! First time, in fact."

"Well, sir, you are a natural. A natural I say!" Billy lined up the ace and two eights on the table before him. "Perhaps sir would like to up the ante a bit, give me a chance to win my money back? Say... a florin? Or half a crown even?"

"What the hell? Why not a full crown, eh? I'm feeling rather lucky, don't you know."

Billy Quick took a sharp intake of breath, looking pained. Scratching at his stubbly chin, he pretended to think about it. "A crown you say? Well, I wouldn't normally go that high, sir, not for nobody. But you seems like a trustworthy fellow, and I do likes you, soooo... Oh, what the hell. Why not? Five shillings a turn it is." Flipping the three cards face down, Billy Quick started tossing them one over the other. "Back and forth and back we go. Where's the ace? Nobody knows."

His hands moved much faster than they had before. It took the young gentleman by surprise. He had to focus to keep track of the ace as it bounced around. So intent was he on following the cards he seemed to miss the move he should have been looking out for. But John didn't.

Lining up the cards, Billy made the offer. "So, do you have it sir? Do you know where the ace is?"

The young gentleman seemed torn. His hand hovered over first one card, then another, and as it caught the light John saw that it was made of metal, very fine, with gold filigree down the fingers and barely a seam visible at any of the joints. It looked expensive, with an intricate internal mechanism, judging by the way its fingers danced lightly in the air. If the young gentleman wasn't careful Billy Quick would have it off him by the end of the night.

Eventually, the young man's metal hand came to rest on the first of the three cards. "I wouldn't if I were you," said John. The young man turned to look at him.

"No?" he said, with a coy smile. "You think perhaps the centre card maybe?"

"Nope. Not that one either."

"Stay out of this, Sinister," growled Billy, glaring at John.

"Then I should put my money on number three?" said the gentleman, touching the third card lightly.

"If you like," said John. "But to be honest, unless you can bet on what's up his sleeve I'd keep my money in my pocket if I were you."

The gentleman looked a little too shocked.

"You mean the game is rigged? Well I never!"

"Now just a minute!" Billy protested. "I run a square game me. You ask anyone."

"Then prove it," said John. "Let the gentleman turn over all three cards, by himself. If there's an ace on the table, not only will *he* give you a crown, *I'll* give you a crown as well."

Billy Quick huffed and puffed, his face turning bright red. "I don't have to stand for this, y'know." He gathered up the three cards before anyone could lay their hands on them. "I run a respectable game me, and I don't need no tuppence ha'penny cup-man coming the large one and accusing me of all sorts of things. I 'as me pride." And with that he stormed off across the docks.

John and the gentleman watched him go. "You didn't have to do that," said the young gentleman. "I saw what he was up to."

"I know you did," said John. "But I wanted to. I've owed him one for a long time now."

"Really? What for?"

John shrugged. "Haven't the foggiest to be honest. But I do."

The young gentleman chuckled. "Well you haven't changed. It's good to see you again, John."

"And you, Henry. Been a while."

"Over a year I'd say. You keeping well?"

"As well as can be expected," said John, glancing over his friend's shoulder. "And what about you? Everything ship shape and Bristol fashion? Legs okay and all that?"

"My legs? Whatever could be wrong with my legs?" Henry glanced down at his feet to make sure they were still there, then looked up to find Billy Quick barging his way through the crowd towards them, accompanied by two of the biggest bruisers the young man had ever seen. "Oh, I see! Maybe we should—" But John was already halfway down the road before he could finish his sentence.

Henry, very wisely, decided to follow suit.

"There you go," said Henry, pinning the badge to John's lapel. "You are now officially a member of The Scion Club. Congratulations."

"Yeah, thanks," said John unconvincingly. He inspected the crossed wrench and shovel that Henry had just lumbered him with. The embossing was nice, but he wasn't sure how he felt about wearing the old school emblem once more. His jacket still had a dark patch on the pocket where he'd ripped the badge off the day they graduated.

"Actually, I'm surprised you've never come in here before. You're allowed, you know."

"I know, but what would be the point? Even if I did come in I'd never be able to afford anything. I mean, look at this place." John gestured towards their surroundings, marvelling, not for the first time, at how the other half lived.

With its oak-panelled walls, plush carpeting, armchairs as deep as a philosophy lecture, and bar full of drinks the likes of which most people had never even heard of, the Scion was the epitome of what a private members' club should be. You could hide out there all day and no one would ever know. And even if they did they would never tell. Discretion was a cornerstone of the club's mentality. Discretion, elitism, and huge wads of cash.

The Scion was a club for the old boys and girls of Howard Aglet Grammar School, Hammersmyth's most privileged centre of learning. It was their home away from home, their haven from all the riff-raff, social climbers, hangers-on, and debt collectors of the world. It was a place for Old Hags and Old Hags only, which explained why John was getting so many funny looks. The sight of someone like him – an obvious member of the Great Unwashed – in the club bar, wearing a club pin, was causing quite a stir.

"So when did you get back?" said John, leaning nonchalantly on the bar for everyone to see.

"Oh, I don't know. A couple of months ago maybe? I left India at the start of the year, came back via Egypt. Took my time, saw a few sights along the way. Giza, the Pyramids, that sort of thing."

"And how was India? Did they teach you how to levitate and stick your foot behind your head and all that?"

A cloud passed across Henry's face. He looked away. "India w as... a little different than I was expecting. I mean it was fun, for a while, but the novelty soon wore off. Some of my friends over there got a little out of hand. Ended up in prison some of them. Almost took me down with them, too. It was... unpleasant, at times, if you know what I mean?"

John did. The far edges of the Britannic Empire were home to some of the best, most inventive, most courageous people you could ever hope to meet, as well as some of the worst. It didn't take much to fall in with the wrong crowd, and heaven help you if you did. A bad investment, an ill-conceived wager, the wrong word to the wrong person at the wrong time, it was all too easy for a man to end up behind bars. And that's if you were lucky. Jail wasn't the worst thing that could happen to you. In the dark recesses of the unknown places, people had been known to disappear altogether.

"You've got a new hand, I see. Very nice."

"Do you like it?" said Henry, holding up his metal appendage for them to admire. "I picked it up in Paris just before I got back. Lost the other one in a game of cards. I thought I had a good hand, but his was better. Then he took *my* hand to settle the debt, the swine."

"Classy. Although I must say, this one does seem like an improvement on the one you had before."

Henry wiggled his fingers to show how dexterous they were. The way the prosthesis moved, you'd almost think it was a real hand inside a metal glove. "Yes, wonderful, isn't it? Much better than that mechanical claw thing I used to have. With this I can mix a cocktail, deal a hand of cards, or dance with a pretty lady easy as—" He snapped his fingers with a resounding clang to prove his point. "And at the end of the day, what more do you need?"

"What indeed."

"And what about you, John? What have you been up to while I've been away?" Henry tried to sound optimistic with his inquiry, but John could tell what he was thinking. John was still wearing the same coat he'd had at school, with its mismatched buttons and much-mended lining, still had on the same black cap, the same hand-me-down shoes, and he still held his trousers up with the red

Printers' Union sash he'd found among his father's things because he still couldn't afford a proper belt. It was clear to see that life was not going according to plan for John Sinister. But then again, when did it ever?

"Oh, y'know, this and that. The usual, I guess. Work's been a bit thin on the ground since school. No one's offered to take me on anywhere. It seems I'm a bit over qualified for manual labour, but not connected enough for managerial work. I've been odd-jobbing it mostly, doing what I can when I can to keep my head above water."

"Well that's a waste of talent if ever I heard it," said Henry.

"You'll get no argument here, pal," said John, polishing off his drink. Henry silently ordered them two more as he gave John an appraising look.

"Tell me, John, how would you feel about coming to work for me?"

"For you? Doing what exactly?"

"Well, I've been helping out down at the airship factory, and—"

John choked on his drink. "Hold on! You're not telling me Henry Chard has a job, are you?"

Henry laughed. "Hell no. Well, not as such anyway. No, I've just been messing about in the workshop now and then, inventing, experimenting, that sort of thing. Father keeps trying to get me into the office but that is more Peter's domain. I can't be done with all that paperwork. Although, as it turns out, perhaps I probably should be."

"How so?"

"Well it seems there's something going on behind the scenes. Something... decidedly untoward."

"'Decidedly untoward'?" said John. "Decidedly untoward how?"

"I've no idea, which is where you come in. I'd like to take you on as an apprentice."

"Me? But I don't know anything about building airships."

"And you wouldn't have to. It's an apprenticeship. Besides, you wouldn't be there to build airships. You'd be there to find out what, if anything, is really going on down there."

John shook his head. "I doubt I'm the right man for that kind of job either."

"Nonsense," said Henry. "Remember when Professor Letchworth lost the key to his office? *You're* the one who found it hanging in the tree outside the girls' changing rooms."

John shrugged. "That was easy enough to work out when you took into account when he lost it, the kind of man he was, and when the girls used to do their drill exercises."

"Yes, he really was a dirty old letch, wasn't he?"

"That's why they sacked him in the end. He got caught using the school telescope to spy on the headmaster's wife when she was in the bath."

"No! I had no idea."

"No one did. They hushed it up. But when you're friends with the night porters you find out all kinds of things."

"See, that's exactly what I'm talking about. I need someone who can find out things. What do you say? I'll pay you ten bob a week until you find something, plus whatever you get for the apprenticeship. Now you can't say fairer than that, can you?"

No, you can't, thought John. Ten shillings for a week's work was a very tempting offer indeed.

He glanced at Henry's eager face. Part of him suspected it was a pity offer, a way to give money to his poor friend. And if it was then Henry had pitched it just right. Ten bob was just the right amount that it didn't seem like charity. And then there was the story, 'Something *might* be going on and only *you* can find out what.' That part was so transparent it was downright plausible.

Plus, it was intriguing. John hated to admit it, but he hadn't had a good bit of intrigue in a while now.

"Alright, you're on."

"Excellent! Excellent. Thank you, John. I really appreciate it. I mean it's probably nothing, and fingers crossed that is the case, but knowing you're looking into it is a real weight off my mind."

"Mine too, if I'm honest. I mean, I get by alright, but it'll be nice to contribute a little more to the pot for once. I think my sister's tolerance for having me on her couch is wearing a little thin."

"Oh yes, I forgot to ask, how is Jane? And her little girl, um...?"

"Emily. She's fine, thanks. They both are in fact. Emily's five now, if you can believe that? Cannot sit still to save her life. I'm telling you, it's exhausting." Henry chuckled at the thought. "And what about your lot? How's your brother? And your father? And the, er... rest of the family?"

Henry grinned. "How's Mary, do you mean?" John blushed. "She's fine, as are the rest of them. Quite literally fighting fit, I'm sorry to say. Talk about exhausting."

John smiled, then fell silent. So did Henry. There was an unspoken question in the air, one that didn't need asking. Both men had lost their mothers whilst at school, but it wasn't something they ever talked about, not then, and not now. Really, what was there to say?

"Why don't you come to the house tomorrow," said Henry. "We could go over what's going on at the factory. And I'm sure Mary would love to see you."

"I'd like that very much," said John.

Henry winked at his friend. "Yes, I bet you would."

"Oh, y'know what, Henry, go stick it where the sun don't—"

"Good God, Lefty! Is that you?"

John's heart sank as another blast from the past sent a chill down his spine. He turned reluctantly to find Spencer Shelby the Third in the doorway of the bar.

John had gone to Howard Aglet's on a scholarship, and whilst few of his contemporaries had enjoyed his being there, they'd at least had the good grace to leave him be most of the time. But a handful of them – mainly the Chess Club, for some bizarre reason – had taken special exception to having this Hardship Oik at *their* school. They'd done their best to make life as miserable as possible for John, and leading their efforts every step of the way had been Spencer Shelby the Third.

John sighed from the very bottom of his heart. He had hoped, after he left school, that he'd never set eyes on Spencer Shelby the Third ever again.

He wondered if Spencer was still upset about that time he beat him and his friends at chess? Probably, if history was anything to go by. Spencer wasn't the type to let something like that go. He was the sort to hang on to a grudge, doling out his petty revenge when you least expected it – which consequently made him the sort of person you wanted to shove head first into a vat of hot porridge.

As Spencer sauntered over, shooting his cuffs and adjusting his tie as he went, John spotted something thin and straggly clinging to his upper lip.

"My God! What's that on his face?"

Henry laughed. "I know. Awful, isn't it? He hates it."

"Then why doesn't he shave it off?"

"He can't. He's not allowed."

"What do you—"

"Well, Lefty! Look at you." Spencer Shelby gave John a friendly slap on the back, harder than was strictly necessary.

"Hello, Spencer," said John. He couldn't bring himself to add 'Nice to see you', even to be polite.

"What are you doing here? I wouldn't have thought this was your kind of thing."

John knew he shouldn't ask. "Really? And why's that then?"

"Well, I mean…" Spencer blithely indicated John's entire being, as if that explained everything.

"Alright, Spencer, don't be a Dob," said Henry.

"Why? What did I say? Did I say something?"

"Just leave off, alright."

"Oh come on, I was only messing about. John knows I was kidding, right, John?" Spencer slapped him on the back again, hard, and John had to resist the urge to punch him in the throat.

"That's alright, *mate*," said John, with the hint of a smile. "Spencer was just having a little fun, weren't you, Spencer? You can't take his play too seriously." He shrugged. "I never have."

Spencer locked eyes with John. "Well quite," he said, with a fixed grin. "We're all friends here, after all."

"That we are," said John, polishing off his drink in one giant gulp. "Anyway, Henry, I need to get going. Lovely to see you again. What time do you need me tomorrow?"

"How about eleven? We can have an early lunch then go on from there."

"Sounds good. I'll see you then."

John turned to Spencer. He should just walk away, it would be the smart thing to do, but he couldn't resist one last dig for old times' sake. He let his gaze come to rest on Spencer's ridiculous peach-fuzz moustache. "Goodbye, Spencer. It was fluffy to see you again."

"What? What did you say?"

"Lovely. I said it was lovely to see you again," said John, glancing repeatedly at Spencer's top lip.

"Yes, goodbye, Lefty. You take care now," said Spencer, giving in to a strange compulsion to scratch under his nose. "Please, do be a stranger."

John watched Spencer's moustache as he passed it by, in case it went for him. Spencer clenched his jaw, a vein popping out on his forehead. "Impudent little upstart," John heard him hiss as he walked away. "Who the hell does he think he is?"

John gave a half smile as he headed for the door. *Well that was fun*, he mused. *Now, time for a proper drink.* He needed one after that little encounter.

Heading down the stairs to the front door, John passed some more of the old Chess Club as they headed up. He caught their side glances and feigned indifference, but he couldn't be bothered to acknowledge them. He'd bandied words with enough idiots for one night.

CHAPTER 2

SATURDAY

If cities were people, Hammersmyth would be the sort who got up early, worked hard, spent most of the day in a foul mood, then went to bed late after having drank too much on the way home. By the time the sun came up, its streets were full of harried servants, barking costermongers, shop workers, tradesmen, and captains of industry, all rushing about their day full of Business and Purpose – activities to be thought of with the capital letter very much in place. Steam-driven omnibuses and horse-drawn carriages filled the air with the chug of their mechanical engines and the clatter of their steel-rimmed wheels, drowning out the dawn chorus before it even had a chance to begin. The Saturday market was in full swing, arguments had already broken out in Freedom Square over who had right of way, and somewhere to the south two policemen had the odious task of fishing a mangled corpse out of the river. In other words it was very much Business As Usual.

In Hammersmyth it was generally agreed that if you weren't up and about by the time the cathedral bell struck six then you were nothing more than a shiftless layabout.

John Sinister awoke some time around nineish. Actually, to be precise, he awoke for the second time some time around nine. He was first awake when his niece came bounding in looking for him.

His niece, Emily, liked puddles, big holes, and jumping off things. She also liked showing people things she'd picked up in the street, although not always. Sometimes she picked things up at the park as well.

"Unca John! Unca John! Lookit what I found yesserday. It's a frog, Unca John!" Sleeping on your sister's couch might not cost any money, but it still had a price.

"That's great, Em. I'll look at it later, yeah? Uncle John's a bit tired still."

"Yeah, but look. He's all slimy and that. See? Inn'e funny?"

"Come on, Emily. Leave your uncle alone. He's had a hard night." The words 'by the smell of him' remained unsaid, but they both knew they were there. John's sister, Jane, ushered her daughter from the room, before contemplating the mess that was her brother.

"Time to get up, John," she said. "The day's a-wasting."

"Mmmnhguhnur," said John from underneath his pillow.

John must have still been a bit drunk when he woke up the first time, because when he woke up the second time his head felt like someone had buried an axe in it, blunt end first. It took crawling to the outhouse, introducing the porcelain throne to what was left of last night's dinner, and splashing some cold water on his face, before he could even conceive of staggering out into the daylight.

John spent the morning on a park bench at the top of Paradise Hill. It was his favourite spot to while away the hours until the sun went down. You could see the whole city laid out before you – its factories and forges, its museums and seats of learning, its grand central train station, the roof of which was still in need of repair – and the view you got of the transatlantic airships turning their slow, majestic circles in the sky were practically unparalleled.

He chewed on a breakfast of cinnamon-spiced pumpkin seeds and honeyed almonds – about all his stomach could handle at the moment – whilst his thoughts turned to what he and Henry had discussed the night before.

What could be going on at the airship factory to have him so concerned? Henry was not a worrier. He was as easy going as they come. For him to think something was up probably meant that something was. But what?

A squirrel jumped up onto the end of the bench and sat there eyeing up John's breakfast. "What do you think?" said John, depositing a few seeds on the bench next to him. "Do you think the Air Line is in trouble?" The squirrel ran up, grabbed a seed, then retreated rapidly to feast on its bounty, something which John took to be a confirmed maybe.

Everything John had read about the Transatlantic Air Line said that it was going great guns. There didn't seem to be any trouble on the horizon. "Unless someone's got it in for them?" said John to the squirrel. "Or their creator, perhaps?"

Opinion of Donald Chard, Henry's father, was mixed to say the least. The most successful industrialist the world had ever seen, you didn't have to go far to find someone who would gladly slap him in the mutton-chops given half the chance. He may have been the man who'd made the omnibuses run on time, but he was also the man who'd rebuilt the courts and financed a new jailhouse, two achievements the citizens of Hammersmyth had rather ambiguous feelings about. And he'd shut down the Ram's Head Brewery because he didn't like the smell (or so people said). People were much less ambiguous about that little manoeuvre. But the one thing he'd done that they could all agree on, the thing he was most proud of, the thing they were all most proud of, were the airships.

Donald Chard's 'Pond Hoppers' were a wonder of the modern age. Gleaming white cylinders that glided through the air like albino sky whales, they'd cut the journey time to the Americas by half whilst simultaneously making the trip far safer for all concerned. The oceanic shipping lanes were a plague of hazards, not least of which was the kraken – giant, squid-like creatures with massive tentacles, razor sharp beaks, and a voracious appetite for wood, canvas, and terrified mariners – and though no kraken attack had been reported for a couple of years now, why risk it when you could float high over the seas, unafraid and unmolested, out of reach of the kraken's hungry grasp?

"No, you're right," said John, putting an almond on the bench beside him. "Even the people who hate Donald Chard wouldn't mess with the airships. People love those things." John and the squirrel chewed things over. "Unless it's a rival, of course. Someone trying to steal the technology. Or one of the shipping companies out to get their own back for his ruining their business. I could see that happening, especially around here." He turned to the squirrel. "What do you think? Theft or revenge? Espionage or sabotage?" The squirrel flicked its tail, hedging its bets. John nodded. "Yeah, I'm with you. Probably best not to speculate, eh?"

Depositing a few more seeds on the bench before he left, John made his way down into town, to catch the train up to Turning Hill.

Down in the police morgue, a detective and a coroner stood contemplating the body from the river over a steaming mug of hot cocoa.

"Have you confirmed it's him?" said the coroner.

"Not yet," said the detective, blowing on her drink. "The boss is doing that now." She took a tentative sip, burning her lip. "I wonder why he did it."

"Ours is not to reason why, Detective," replied the coroner.

The doors of the morgue burst open and the detective's boss marched in, his face like thunder. The detective quickly hid her cocoa behind her back.

The detective inspector was brandishing a thick leather-bound book. "It's him alright," he grumbled. "Says so right here in the Who's Who?"

"Well I'll be damned," said the detective.

"You know what this means, don't you? I'm going to need you to do a proper write up on this one. We're talking interviews, diagrams, the works."

"But—"

"But what?"

"It's just I've got so many other cases to be getting on with. Can't one of the other guys do it?"

The detective's boss leaned over her. He was a big man. He cast a big shadow. "No, one of the others cannot do it, because the others are *senior* detectives and you are a *junior* detective, and the junior detective does the paperwork, got it?"

The detective's gaze dropped to her feet. "Yes, boss."

"And besides, you've got the best handwriting, and we need this one to look neat."

"Okay, boss."

"Just be sure to dot all the i's and cross all the t's. And don't forget the diagrams. The higher-ups love it when there's diagrams."

"You got it, boss."

"And don't look so bloody miserable about it. *I'm* the one who has to go tell the family that their precious little boy has gone and offed himself."

"Yes, but maybe not in those exact words," offered the coroner.

As he left the station John realised that he hadn't been up to Turning Hill, where all the rich folks lived, in quite a while. Without Henry to visit there'd been no need. He could have called on Mary of course, they were friends too after all, but even he knew that wasn't the done thing, not for a man in his position.

Turning Hill Station sat at the back end of Chard Manor, a good twenty minute walk from the main entrance to the Chard family's massive estate. Fortunately for John there was a back door into the estate on the other side of the road, next to the omnibus shelter. Unfortunately for John it was locked. That was annoying. He didn't have the money for the omnibus, and he really didn't fancy the long walk to the front gate, not this early in the day (if ever). Thankfully there was an alternative, one he and Henry had used many times over the years.

Scrambling atop the omnibus shelter, John jumped across onto the estate's high wall, gently lowering himself down the other side into the grounds of Chard Manor. Or at least that was the plan. But as he negotiated with a tree on the other side a branch hit him in the face, he lost his footing, the world slipped sideways, and he landed face down in what he hoped was a pile of leaves on the other side of the wall.

"Well that's just great," he grumbled, pushing himself upright. "Like I wasn't dirty enough already."

Dusting himself off, John went looking for the cinder path that led from the back gate up to the main house. Following it through the woods, he eventually emerged out onto the back lawn of Chard Manor.

John had always liked Chard Manor, even if it did creep him out a little. He liked the higgledy-piggledy nature of the place. Years of revamps and renovations had turned a once average country house into a haphazardly stacked pile of architecture, held together by a ridiculous amount of pipework. A convoluted web of copper crawled all over the house, like out of control metal ivy, delivering the glory of steam to every room in the place. It was this that John didn't like. Not the piping as such, but the way it would vent unexpectedly, hissing water vapour from every orifice in one big disgruntled sigh. It gave the impression not only that the building was alive, but that it was rather annoyed about the fact, too.

The local kids used to climb the walls of the estate to get a look at 'Mr Chard's Steam Castle'. Convinced it was haunted, they would dare each other to go and tap three times on the brickwork to see if they could wake the demons within. Few would, of course. Why risk being dragged to hell when you had your whole life ahead of you? But for those with guts enough to go for it, a lifetime of bragging rights awaited, and many an argument had been settled with the words, 'Yeah? Well *I* tapped the castle when I were a kid. Has *you*?' before now.

It's funny the things folks'll do to convince themselves they're brave, thought John. *People can be so superstitious sometimes.* Crossing the lawn he went down the side of the building, absent-mindedly rapping on the wall three times as he made his way round to the front of the house.

John's knock at the front door was answered by a perfectly-pressed butler's uniform, containing a tall, sinewy, bald-headed man. Regarding John down the full length of his vulpine nose, the man gave the most eloquent sniff. "Can I help you... sir?"

John smiled. Whilst all head butlers were notorious for being more snobby than the families they worked for, the Chards' head butler had it down to a fine art. He went by the name Hercules, and his contempt for the poor was more obvious than the unbelievable shininess of his incredibly shiny shoes. "You sure can, mate. I'm here to see Mr Chard."

The butler raised an incredulous eyebrow. He took in John's shabby clothes, his unpolished shoes, and the fact that he appeared to have been dragged through a hedge backwards, and came to a swift yet inevitable conclusion. "I'm afraid Mr Chard is unavailable to casual callers at this time," he said, reaching for the door. "Now if you wouldn't mind vacating the premises, the house is rather—"

John's hand hit the door to stop it from closing. "Actually, pal, I think you'll find he's expecting me," he said, firmly.

"Are you quite sure about that, sir?"

"Absolutely."

Sniff. "Very well, sir. If you would follow me, please."

Inside, the house was quiet. Subdued, almost. For a moment John thought he could hear someone crying in one of the rooms to his left, although it may have been the steam pipes chuffing. It was hard to say.

The entrance hall was much as he remembered it, with its grand, sweeping, double-curve staircase and its black and white chequerboard floor. The life-sized terracotta warrior on the first-floor balcony was new though, as was the piece of art below it, in between the two staircases – a metal sculpture of the top half of a man in what looked like a butler's uniform, sat atop a large wooden plinth. John wandered over to have a closer look.

"WELCOME, WELCOME! PLEASE, DO COME IN. MAY I TAKE YOUR COAT?"

The contraption burst into life, its arms flailing as it lunged at John. Grabbing him by the collar, it tried to wrestle the coat off his back.

"ARE YOU WELL TODAY, SIR? HAVE YOU COME FAR?"

"What the—" John beat on the machine's arm, trying to break free. He pulled at its fingers but they held on tight.

"DID YOU SEE THE CRICKET THE OTHER DAY?"

John slipped. Hanging by his neck he started to choke. Then, without warning, the machine let go, John tumbling to the floor in one big undignified heap. He looked up to find Hercules the butler standing over him with what would have been an amused expression on his face, if he had any idea what being amused felt like.

"Please don't stand still, sir. It only encourages him."

"What the hell is that thing?" John gasped.

"A 'Robobutler', apparently. The very latest in automaton technology, or so I have been led to believe. One of Mr Chard's more... experimental inventions, although not one of his more reliable ones, I'm afraid. Best to steer well clear I think, sir. The damn thing's liable to scrag anyone that comes near it. Now, if you would follow me, please."

The butler led John down a short hall to what turned out to be a large study.

"If you would wait here, I will inform Mr Chard of your... presence."

As the butler left, John couldn't help but notice that he'd failed to take his coat. Clearly he didn't expect him to stay for very long.

John looked around. He was in Donald Chard's study. The room was full of everything you might expect from a successful industrialist. The bookshelves were laden with technical manuals for things like airship buoyancy and steam-powered locomotion, not to mention a great many sketches and blueprints for all kinds of fanciful machines. Every bit of wall space that wasn't bookcase was taken up with either civic commendations or photographs of Donald Chard in his signature rolled-up sleeves and black waistcoat, shaking hands with the great and the good of Hammersmyth society. Including, in one of them— Good God, was that the Queen?!

It certainly was, smiling and laughing like they were old friends. Which, come to think of it, they probably were. After all, Donald Chard wasn't only famous for his airships and omnibuses; he was the man who'd kick-started the Great Steam Revolution. His creations were the rock on which the Britannic Empire had been built. It made sense the two of them would be the best of friends. Without Donald Chard and his hyper-steam – a method of making and storing steam that did away with the need for individual boilers, allowing you to charge your devices from one central boiler unit instead – Britannia's vast empire wouldn't be half the size it was today.

Catching sight of Donald Chard's desk, John casually let his feet wander in its general direction.

As a rule John wasn't one to pry. He respected another man's privacy, especially when that man was someone like Donald Chard. But since Henry had brought up the prospect of something going on with the airships, and what was on the desk looked kind of airshippy, he felt like it was his duty to take a quick gander to see what was what.

He'd just begun leafing through the paperwork when a loud, pointed, "Ahem," came from the other side of the room. He spun around, ready to apologise, but there was no one there. Just a dark grey tabby with yellowy-green eyes over by the fireplace, sat watching him in an intense way that he found quite unnerving for some reason.

"What are you looking at?" he growled.

The cat kind of smiled, tilted its head to one side, and said, "Meow?"

John frowned. A strange thought popped into his head. *Was that a meow, or did that cat just* say *meow?* He wasn't quite sure. And the more he thought about it the less sure he became. He watched the cat, waiting for it to say something else, but it soon became clear from the look on its face that it had no intention of giving him the satisfaction.

Turning his back on the cat, John carried on his perusal of the desk. It was covered in paperwork, like the great man had been in the middle of something and had been called away. There were scribbled notes everywhere, written in some kind of code, next to what looked like the plans for a new type of airship. John leant in closer so he could get a better look. Yes, it was an airship, bigger than the ones that had been built so far, with twin balloons, and a much larger gondola able to carry five times as many—

Thump!

"Nyah!" yelled John, as the dark grey tabby landed on the desk next to his head. He leapt back, his hand flying to his chest like some society lady who'd just caught sight of her husband's sock garters. All things considered, it was not his finest moment. The cat wasn't interested though. Ignoring John, it walked to the middle of the airship plans and sat down, giving him its best 'What do you think you're looking at?' look as it came in to land.

John stared back at the cat. This thing was starting to get on his damn nerves. He was sorely tempted to push it off the desk, see how it liked that. He'd like to see the look on its face then. Not that he was into hurting cats, you understand. He liked cats for the most part, but this little sod was asking for it.

John was deep into his cat-flying-through-the-air fantasy when the study door opened and in walked Donald Chard.

John couldn't snap to attention fast enough.

"Mr Sinister, how do you do? So very good of you to come." Donald Chard strode up and shook John's hand – a short, sharp, up and down action that nearly yanked his arm out of its socket.

"Oh! Er, Mr Chard. Yes, hello. How do you do?" John tried to keep the tremor out of his voice, but it wasn't easy.

"I hope you are well, sir?"

"Yes, yes. Very well, sir, thank you," John squeaked.

"And your sister, Jane? How is she?"

"She's fine too, sir, thank you for asking."

"Good. That's good. Family is important you know. Really, very, quite... important." John watched in bemused silence as the barrel-chested industrialist shrank before his very eyes. The looming presence that could fill a room vanished, like a candle snuffed out in the wind, leaving behind a hollow vessel, awash and adrift on the vagaries of life.

Wandering over to the fireplace, Mr Chard went and stood next to the cat, which had moved itself onto the arm of the chair. Stroking its head in a distracted manner he stared into the coals of the fire, his thoughts a million miles away. He had a drink in his hand, a large one by anyone's standards. Taking a long, sloppy swig, he sucked the remnants out of his bushy moustache before wiping his mouth with the back of his hand. "I wish I could say I remember you well, Mr Sinister, but I'm afraid my work has kept me distracted from my children's lives over the years. I used to leave that sort of thing up to my wife to take care of."

"That's quite alright, Mr Chard. You're a busy man. Everyone knows that."

"Yes, busy. Too busy it would seem." His mind drifted once more. John saw it happen. The faraway look, the half-mumbled words, one minute there, the next minute gone. It was quite disconcerting. "My dear Louise never thought much of Henry's friends from school. A bunch of self-important little so-and-sos she used to call them, full of all the bad habits of their parents. But not you, Mr Sinister, she liked you, something I would consider a great compliment. My Louise always was an impeccable judge of character."

"That's kind of you to say, sir. I liked her very much also. She was a fine woman, very fine indeed."

"That she was, that she was," said Mr Chard, a sad smile flashing across his tired face. "You were at Howard Aglet's on a scholarship, were you not?"

"I was, sir, yes."

"And I seem to remember something about you taking on the entire Chess Club and beating them all? Seven consecutive games, if I'm not mistaken?"

"Not exactly, sir, no. It was seven simultaneous games, but I didn't win them all. I won four and lost three which, according to the rules of the wager, counted as a win over all."

"Most impressive. Most impressive indeed. Tell me, was it skill, luck, or something else?"

"Skill, sir. It was skill. But not at chess. At least, not entirely." John waited for the inevitable follow up questions, but Donald Chard wasn't really listening.

"Henry always did enjoy a good game of chess. He didn't care if he won or lost, he just enjoyed playing for the fun of it, something which I confess I always thought of as a weakness. How can a man win if he has no ambition? But, at the same time, what price victory if it costeth a man his soul. Perhaps finding the joy in life, taking pleasure in the little things, is in fact the greatest skill of all."

"It's certainly an interesting question, sir," said John, glancing around the room. "Um, where is Henry, by the way? Will he be down shortly, do you think?"

Donald Chard stared at him. "You mean to say you don't know? You haven't heard?"

"Know what, sir? I haven't heard anything."

"Henry is gone, Mr Sinister. He has been taken from us."

"Taken? I'm sorry, I don't—"

"Dead, Mr Sinister. He is deceased. My son Henry is dead, sir."

John's mouth fell open. "Dead! Henry's dead? My God! When? How?"

"He was found this morning in the river, somewhere near the sewers. They say he drowned late last night."

"Drowned! I don't believe it. Henry would never drown. I mean– What on earth would he be doing in the river? How did he get there? Does anyone know what happened?"

Donald Chard turned to stare into the fire. "I own shares in the sewage works, you know. Bought them a while back. Seemed like a good investment at the time," he said, his voice trailing off as he got lost among the coals.

John took a half-step forward. "What happened, sir? Please, tell me."

Mr Chard gave the briefest of shrugs. "They can't say for certain. The policeman who was here suggested that Henry may have jumped in the river of his own accord. Apparently there's a history of such things. I believe he called it 'tombstoning'."

John was surprised. He'd heard of tombstoning, of course. It was a tradition among the students of Howard Aglet's, where they celebrated their graduation by leaping off Gravesend Bridge. It was incredibly dangerous, and not something John had ever been tempted to try. He had no interest in being that stupid. The thing is, neither did Henry.

"I'm familiar with the term, sir, although I find it hard to believe that Henry would ever do such a thing. He considered jumping off a perfectly good bridge to be the height of lunacy, and said so on many occasions."

"I'm sure you're right, Mr Sinister. I'd certainly like to believe my son was smarter than that. But since the only alternative appears to be"—he almost couldn't say it—"suicide, then I have to believe that this is what the police say it was, a drunken stunt gone wrong."

There was a third option, a more unsavoury one, but John kept that one to himself.

Surrendering himself to the armchair by the fire, Donald Chard took another sloppy swig of whisky. "Truth be told, I did not know Henry well, Mr Sinister, not that I know Peter or Mary any better, for that matter. I have been a poor father and I know it. Louise was the heart of this family. She was the glue that bound us all together. Without her our family died. And I, for my sins, I let it."

There were tears in Donald Chard's eyes. John wanted to go and comfort the man, to let him know that he was not alone, but he knew that he couldn't. They were too far apart, the distance between them too great. Try as he might, even the best of intentions could not cross that divide.

"Mr Chard," said John finally, "I cannot speak for your entire family, but I do know that Henry had a great deal of respect for you. He knows you did the best you could, and he admired how you held the family together all these years. The Chards are a strong-willed bunch. Keeping them on the straight and narrow is a challenge, I'm sure." He allowed himself a small smile. "I know I couldn't do it."

"Thank you," said Mr Chard, just about managing to return his smile. "That's kind of you to say." Then he wept softly, no sound, just a stream of tears rolling down his face. John had to look away, finding interest wherever he could. It's an uncomfortable thing to see such a strong man so broken, if only for a moment.

"I should go," said John. "I have intruded on your grief long enough. If there's anything I can do please don't hesitate to ask. I am at your disposal, sir."

Donald Chard nodded absently, but he could not speak. John took that as his cue to leave.

He beat a hasty retreat towards the front door, feeling a sudden need to be outside as soon as possible. The air in Chard Manor was thick with pain, and it was stifling. But as he reached the entrance hall he heard it again. Not the steam pipes chuffing, as he'd first thought, but the sound of grief coming from an open door on the other side of the hall.

John tried to walk on by, to get out of there, but he couldn't help himself. Crossing the hall, he pushed open the door and entered.

In the manor drawing room, sitting in the middle of a huge ornate sofa, John came across the lone figure of Miss Mary Chard. She was perched on the edge of her seat, chewing on a fingernail as she stared off into the distance. He had to knock on the door get her attention, which gave Mary quite a start.

"Oh, John. What are you doing here? I, um... Sorry. Please forgive me." Turning away from him, she wiped her tear-stained face with a white lace handkerchief.

"No, Mary, please. It is I who should beg forgiveness. I didn't mean to intrude."Mary gave him a wan smile. "No, that's quite alright. Some company would be nice. Please, won't you sit?" She moved down the sofa, pulling the folds of her yellow dress out of the way.

"I heard about Henry, Mary. I'm so sorry. It must be quite a shock for you. How are you holding up?"

"Oh, alright I guess. It's hard to think that yesterday he was here and today he's not. I can't quite believe it's true."

"I know what you mean," said John, wishing he could think of something more comforting to say.

"The last thing I ever said to him was 'We're out of boiled eggs'," said Mary. "I mean, can you imagine? As last words go it's pretty pathetic, don't you think?"

John smiled. "Oh, I don't know. I think if Henry were here he'd think that was absolutely hilarious."

Mary smiled back. "Yes, he probably would, wouldn't he?" She made an effort to pull herself together. Wiping her eyes once more, she tucked some stray blonde hairs back behind her ears before turning to face John. "I must confess, I'm surprised to see you here. You haven't been up to the house in such a long time." Seeing John stumble for an answer Mary raced on. "Not that it isn't wonderful to see you," she said, placing her hand on top of his. "It's very kind of you to come and see how we are."

John didn't know what to say. His brain had stopped working. He'd never held hands with Mary before. It was discombobulating to say the least. (They *had* held hands once, that time they got caught bunking off Latin, but he didn't think being chased through the cloisters by the day porter really counted – and if it did then they'd have to come up with a new name for whatever it was they were doing now.)

"Mary, I must confess, I only found out about Henry a moment ago, speaking to your father. I ran into him last night and he invited me to lunch. I had no idea he was gone until I got here."

Mary stared at John for what felt like forever, then she burst into laughter. "Oh Lordy, John, you haven't changed have you? So honest. So dependable. And so silly. I have to say, whatever the reason for your being here, it *is* good to see you again."

"And you, Mary."

And then her hand was gone.

"So tell me," she said, "what have you been up to since school?"

"Oh, y'know. This and that. Nothing special really." Nothing at all really. "What about you?"

"Well," said Mary, with a slight smile, "until a few months ago I was in the United States."

"Were you really? How exciting."

"Oh it was, John, you have no idea. Once father set up the Transatlantic Air Line I simply couldn't resist popping over to see how things were done on the wild frontier. And it was quite an experience, I can tell you."

"Life changing I'll bet?"

"And how, as our American cousins would say. I met some amazing people, people who really opened my eyes to the possibilities of life. And I learned so much, you wouldn't believe."

"Sounds wonderful."

"You're darn right it was. Such a shame I had to come back really. Life in the Manor isn't quite the same as it is out there. Over there, if you don't make yourself useful they've got no use for you. Here all I'm expected to do is sit around looking pretty. It's... very different."

"Well," said John, "it's hard to sit around *not* looking pretty when, well..." He trailed off, his cheeks flushing red. Mary chuckled.

"Oh, John, you can be such a cornball sometimes."

She grabbed his hand again. Twice in one day! John's mind went blank. "Oh, I– That is, I mean—" What the hell was a 'cornball'? Mary laughed again, squeezing his hand. John was at a loss.

"I should probably get going," he said, feeling like a wretch for saying it. "I have... an appointment to get to."

Mary's face fell. She withdrew her hand.

"I see," she said. "Well, if you must?"

"I'm afraid I must," said John, standing.

Mary stood with him. "But you will come again, won't you? It *has* been lovely to see you, despite the circumstances. I would so hate to lose you again."

"Of course I will, Mary. I'll come as soon as I can. I promise."

Before he left, John glanced back at the lonely figure sitting on the couch. He felt a pain in the pit of his stomach, which might have been drink related, but was probably something else. As he closed the drawing room door, a voice behind him made him jump.

"Mr Chard would like to see you, sir." It was Hercules the butler.

"Me?" said John. "He wants to see me? Whatever for?"

Sniff. "I'm sure I have no idea, sir."

Donald Chard was at his desk, a completely different man to the one John had left moments ago. He was writing a letter, a stern look etched upon his face. A man in his element, this was the man John Sinister remembered. Strong, confident, a shaper of worlds and a builder of empires.

"Please have a seat, Mr Sinister. I'll be with you in a moment."

There was a wing-backed armchair opposite the desk. John sank into it slowly.

Donald Chard continued writing. The room was silent save for the crackling of the fire and the scratch, scratch, scratch of his pen. John looked around. All the plans and diagrams had been cleared away. The room had been sanitised for his benefit, like Donald Chard knew he'd been snooping before. Or maybe he just assumed that he had. Either way it was a bit insulting, even if it was totally justified.

Something hit the back of his chair. John looked up to find the cat staring down at him. He tried to ignore it, but he could feel its eyes on him, burrowing into his soul. It was unsettling to say the least. He was trying to think of a subtle way to knock the cat off the back of the chair when Donald Chard finished what he was doing, blotted his letter, and looked up.

"Mr Sinister," he said, steepling his fingers. "I have concerns about my son's death, concerns I believe you share. The manner of his death does not fit with who he was as a person, I think you'll agree. Good God, a knife fight with a midget would make more sense than this bridge jumping nonsense."

"I can't say I'm entirely with you on that point, sir, but I do take your meaning."

"Good. Because I want you to look into it for me."

"Look into what, sir?"

"Henry's death. I want you to do some digging around, see what you can find."

"Digging around, sir?"

"That's what I said, isn't it? I want you to investigate, to see what you can dig up. If there's something fishy going on I want to know about it."

"But surely the police—"

"The police? Pah! The police have made their minds up already. They are convinced that, for whatever reason, Henry died by his own hand. Any investigation they do now will only be to reinforce their own theories. No, Mr Sinister, I do not expect much from the police, which is why I wish to engage you."

"But I'm not a detective, sir. I'm not even very good at the crossword puzzle in the local paper. What can I do to help?"

"You knew Henry. And you know these so-called friends of his. You can go places and ask questions the police couldn't, or wouldn't, think to."

"Really, sir, I wouldn't know where to start with something like that," John protested, but Donald Chard wasn't listening. He'd opened a drawer in his desk and was busy unlocking something.

"This is for you," he said, tossing some money onto the desk. "That's ten pounds, for your services, with more to come if you need it. That should be enough to get you started, don't you think?"

Indeed it would. Ten pounds was a couple of months' wages to some people, and a year's rent to others. It was more money than John had seen for a long time, and Donald Chard kept it lying around in his desk drawer just in case. It really was a different world. "That's... very generous of you, sir. But where would I start?"

Mr Chard held up a finger as he reached across to the wooden box sat on the end of his desk.

The radiophone was one of the few modern devices not invented by the boffins at Chard Mechanical, but it was one Mr Chard had taken very much to heart. He'd had them installed in all of his airships, and he was in the process of having them installed all around town. All the richest houses had one already, they were the latest thing, but he was having them put in hospitals, police stations, places of business, anywhere you might need to contact in a hurry. There was even talk of putting them in boxes on the street, although most people couldn't see the point in that.

He lifted the receiver and tapped its cradle. "Yes, this is Donald Chard. Get me the police headquarters, right away, please." He waited. "This is Donald Chard. I need to speak with Detective Inspector Murtaugh. — Now, God damn it! This is important." John shifted uncomfortably in his seat. "Murtaugh? A man called Sinister is coming to see you. He speaks for me. Give him any and all assistance he requires, is that understood? — When? Let's see. Are you busy now? — Lunch be damned, man! My boy is dead, or did you forget that? — Yes. Good. Thank you, Detective." He hung up the radiophone and handed John the letter he'd written. "There you are. Detective Inspector Murtaugh has agreed to help with your enquiries. But if he, or anyone else, gives you any trouble show them this." John read the letter carefully. It was brief, and to the point. Basically it said, 'The man holding this letter works for me, and you better give him any assistance he requires or else!' It scared the bejesus out of John, so he couldn't imagine being on the receiving end of it. "It should open any doors you find closed to you. But if that doesn't work come speak to me and I'll see what I can do."

"Um, thank you, sir."

"You report directly to me, is that understood? Tell no one what you are doing unless absolutely necessary, and if you have to keep a record of anything do so in code. You never know who is watching."

Donald Chard stood and held out his hand. John leapt to his feet only to find he had the letter in one hand and the wad of cash in the other. Stuffing the money under his arm he shook Mr Chard's hand.

"Good luck to you, Mr Sinister. I expect to hear from you *very* soon, is that understood?" He pulled John closer and looked him dead in the eye. John simply nodded. "Excellent. Now if you'll excuse me I have matters to attend to. Hercules will see you out." Mr Chard headed for the door.

"Yes, right. Very good. Um, sir?" Mr Chard paused at the study door. "Last night Henry said something about trouble at the airship factory. He had suspicions of some sort that something was going on over there?"

"Yes, that. Don't you worry about that. That is nothing. You just find out what happened to Henry. That is your only concern from now on."

"Right. Got you. Very good, sir. As you wish."

John stood there bewildered, as Mr Chard left the room. He looked from the money, to the letter, and back to the money, trying to remember when exactly he'd agreed to take the job. He heard what sounded like a snigger, but when he looked round all he saw was the crackling fireplace and that damned cat again, sat there watching him with a kind of half-smile on its furry face. Keeping an eye on the cat, John folded up the money and the letter and put them away, just as the study door opened again and in walked Hercules the butler.

"If you would follow me please, sir, I will escort you out."

John left, wondering what the hell he was going to ask the police the next day.

As the study door clicked shut the cat smiled and shook its head. "What a numpty," it said, chuckling to itself.

John was still pondering his impending encounter with the police as he left the front gates of Chard Manor (with everything that had gone on he thought it best to leave the respectable way this time). Deep in thought, he didn't see two men exit the bushes.

FLASH!

"Hell's teeth!" he cursed. Thieves! Stumbling back out of reach John braced himself for the attack. When it never came he blinked away the blurriness to find two men standing before him. Both were shabbily dressed in ill-fitting suits, and neither of them looked like someone you'd trust even if *their* life depended on it. There was the faint whiff of printer's ink about them, something his father used to smell of when he came home from work. The tall one carried a camera that had seen better days, whilst the short one held a ragged notebook and the tiniest stub of pencil in his fat, filthy hands.

"Evenin', sir. 'ope we didn't startle you none. Wilfred Bumbleton, Hammersmyth Gazette. May I ask who you are, and why you were up at Chard Manor? Are you a doctor perhaps? We heard Mr Chard was a bit ill, like."

"What? No. Go away." John went around the two men, but Mr Bumbleton wasn't giving up that easily.

"Tragic thing, young Henry Chard being taken like that. He was Mr Chard's heir y'know. Who's his heir now, do you fink? Who's gonna run Chard Mechanical after Donald Chard's demise? There must be a will, I suppose. Or is there? Is Mr Chard well? It must be a right strain for him, losing his first born like that. 'as 'e got long to live, do you fink? Is he dyin' or what?"

"What? No. Of course not. Don't be daft."

"So you deny Mr Chard is ill then?"

"No. I never said anything of the sort."

"So he *is* ill!"

"What? Look, I'm not saying anything alright. It's not for me to—" He watched Mr Bumbleton busily scribbling notes down. "I have to go," he said quickly.

John walked away as fast as he could, Mr Bumbleton waving him off with a smile on his face. "Thankee, sir. Thankee very much."

In his study, Donald Chard sat staring into the open fire, the grey cat draped along the back of the chair above his head.

"You think he'll find anything?" said the cat.

"Let us hope," said Mr Chard. "The situation as it stands is intolerable."

"He went through your desk y'know. When you weren't here."

Donald Chard stiffened. "Did he now." He gave a sharp nod. "Good. I'm glad. We need a man who is willing to stick his nose in where it does not belong. Perhaps he will get the answers that we seek."

"Perhaps," said the cat, stretching out into a more comfortable position. "But I wouldn't count on it."

John arrived at Wainwright's Yard with a brown paper package tucked under his arm. He'd done a full shopping spree on his way there, buying himself a new navy coat, some black trousers, a crisp white shirt, leather shoes, the whole works. Now that he had a bit of money in his pocket he thought he should dress like it too. The brown paper package held his old clothes, because one does not simply throw out ones old things just because they were starting to look a little care worn. Besides, his mother had made his old jacket herself, by hand. The material had cost her a month's wages, but she'd been so proud of him getting into Howard Aglet's she'd spent the money gladly. And she'd put so much care and attention into making it that his badge was the only one that had stayed on his entire time at the school. How could he ever get rid of it?

He did like his new duds, but they were taking some getting used to. Everything was too clean, too new, too squeaky. He felt shiny and he didn't like it.

Wainwright's Yard was a dark, imposing building. It was all grey stone and grey slate, with thick sound-proof walls and high windows so that you couldn't see what went on inside. It was not somewhere you went by choice, not if you could help it, and if you did you made sure someone knew where you were so that they could come looking for you if, for whatever reason, you should fail to return.

Inside Wainwright's Yard, a tubby desk sergeant sat on a tall stool, behind an even taller wooden podium. The man looked down at John as he approached, not that he had any choice in the matter. Down was the only option available to him.

"Can I help you, son?"

"Yes, I'm here to see Detective Inspector Murtaugh."

"Are you now? And do you have an appointment?" He was suspicious, as all policemen naturally are.

"Indeed I do. Donald Chard arranged it for me." John had the letter in his pocket but he didn't want to bring it out just yet. He wanted to see how far the name alone got him first.

The desk sergeant looked doubtful, but he didn't get where he was today by thinking for himself. Leaning forward, he whistled loudly into the brass speaking tube attached to his desk.

"Yes, Sarge?" said a disembodied voice.

"Constable Williams, I got a mister..."

"Sinister," said John. The sergeant raised an eyebrow.

"A Mr Sinister here to see Detective Inspector Murtaugh. Says he's got an appointment. Let the inspector know, would you?"

"Will do, Sarge."

Mission accomplished, the desk sergeant got himself comfortable again. "The inspector should be with you shortly, Mr Sinister," he said, nodding towards a cushion-less stone bench on the other side of the room. "You can have a seat over there while you wait."

"Wonderful," said John, eyeing up the uncomfortable looking bench with little enthusiasm.

John's bum had gone numb. Half an hour he'd been kept waiting, and probably on purpose. The local coppers could be a petty bunch when they wanted to be. He was just thinking about saying something to the desk sergeant when a side door burst open and a young woman marched in.

She looked like she wanted to hurt someone, and despite being quite small – barely as tall as the desk sergeant's desk, in fact – she looked more than capable of doing a thorough job of it. *Heaven help anyone who gets in her way*, thought John. *They're about to have a very bad day.*

She spoke to the desk sergeant, who happily pointed in John's direction. The young woman marched over. "Mr Sinister?"

John jumped to his feet, pins and needles shooting down his legs. "Yes. Detective Inspector Murtaugh?"

"Do I look like a fat old man?"

No, thought John. *No you do not.* "Sorry, I—"

"Come with me, please," she said, storming off back the way she'd come.

John hurried after her, just about managing to keep up despite the distinct lack of cooperation from his legs.

Through the side door, the young woman led John down a long corridor lined with rooms, most of which stood empty save for a small wooden stool and a bucket. The few that had their doors closed clearly contained some miscreant being helped to a full confession by one of Hammersmyth's finest, judging by the unpleasant sounds coming from within. John tried to ignore what he heard as they passed them by, but every now and then a nasty wet crunch would set his teeth on edge. It was fair to say that, despite recent attempts to modernise the metropolitan police force, there were still plenty of coppers left for whom the right way and the hard way would always be the same thing.

Like a lot of women these days, the short-haired young woman storming ahead of John had on trousers, charcoal grey with a jacket to match. A fairly recent phenomenon, this trend away from dresses had confused John at first, until he'd asked his sister about it. She'd responded with one simple word, "Pockets". After that John had kept his stupid questions to himself.

Finally, when they were nearly at the back of the building, they arrived at the young woman's office. It looked more like a boiler room at first glance. Half of it seemed to be pipework, criss-crossing the room at various heights, with one big pipe that ran the length of the back wall at head height, on which a metal coffee pot had been precariously balanced. You could barely move without bumping into something. Whoever had managed to squeeze a desk in there, they were a genius.

The young woman slid in behind her desk and climbed into her seat; climbed, because she had to go over the arm of her chair to get her legs in. The desk was piled high with paperwork, somewhere amongst which was a small brass plaque that read 'Detective Hardigan'. There was a small wooden stool opposite the desk, like the ones in the interrogation rooms, but John was in no rush to sit on it. He'd heard what happened to the people who sat in one of those chairs.

The detective noticed him hovering and frowned. "Well? Sit down then," she snapped, pointing at the stool. Eager to oblige, John did what he was told. Perching himself on the little stool, he glanced around surreptitiously for any nearby buckets.

"I'll be honest with you, Mr Sinister, I could do without this," said the detective. "I've got enough on my plate without having to babysit some busy-body here to stick his nose into police business. I mean I get it, everybody wants answers. Rich, poor, they all want to know why. But we haven't the time nor the resources to take them all by the hand and guide them through the investigation, and I don't see why Donald Chard should get special treatment just because he knows people in high places."

"Y'know what, I totally agr—"

The office door opened and a large, gruff-looking man barged his way in. His clothes were too small for him ten years ago, never mind now, and his moustache was so unkempt it covered his entire mouth. He had a pipe in one hand, a mug in the other, and he seemed surprised to find the small room occupied.

Detective Hardigan jumped to her feet, banging into her desk. John jumped up with her, banging into some pipework.

"Ah," said the man, "you must be Mr Sister? How do you do? I'm Detective Inspector Murtaugh." He jammed the pipe into his mouth and held out his thick hand.

"Sinister, Inspector. John Sinister. Pleased to meet you."

"Sinister. Quite right, quite right. My mistake. Well, welcome to Wainwright's Yard, Mr Sinister. I hope we can help you with whatever it is you desire." *Now there's a thought*, John mused. "Although I must be honest, I'm not sure that your presence here will change anything. This whole business appears to be a clear cut case of death by misadventure, if you ask me."

"That may well be, Inspector, but you never know. I knew the deceased, he was a very good friend of mine, and I can tell you that tombstoning was not his style."

"Really? Then we have to consider the possibility of suicide then."

"He wasn't the suicidal type either."

"Believe me, sir, they all say that. No one is suicidal, until they are."

"If it was suicide then where's the note?"

"Who can say? Blown away, stolen, washed downstream, it could be anywhere. But I can promise you that if there is one, we'll do everything within our power to find it."

"Yes, I'm sure you will," said John.

He tried not to sound sarcastic, he really did, but he couldn't help it. It was just how he was built. Detective Inspector Murtaugh fixed him with a steady gaze. Without breaking eye contact he reached out for the coffee pot and filled his mug, only looking away to return the pot to its rightful place.

"Yes, well, I'll leave you in the capable hands of Miss Hardigan. I'm sure she can answer any questions you might have."

He opened the door.

"Detective."

"What?"

"Detective Hardigan," said John, reaching down and tapping the brass plaque on the desk lightly. "Says so right there."

Detective Inspector Murtaugh said nothing, but the end of his pipe quivered as he bit down hard on the mouthpiece. Detective Hardigan very wisely found something of great interest on the ceiling to stare at.

"Quite so, Mr Sinister. Quite so," the detective inspector growled. "Now, if you'll excuse me, I have work to do. Please give my regards to Mr Chard when you see him next."

John smiled warmly. "I'd be happy to. Good day, Inspector."

As the door closed John turned back to find Detective Hardigan watching him closely.

"Have a seat, Mr Sinister," she said, in a much less angry tone than before. "Now please, if you would, tell me about your friend, Henry."

"Well," said John, making himself comfortable. "I knew Henry from school. We were at Howard Aglet's together. I was there on a scholarship." Why did he feel the need to tell her that? "I had a little trouble fitting in, and he was one of the few there who'd talk to me. He even invited me over to his house, where I got to know the whole family."

"Which explains how you came to be here."

"In a roundabout way, yes."

"So tell me, was there anything at home causing him any difficulty?"

John hesitated. Should he mention Henry's concerns about the factory? He probably should. But he didn't think his employer would like that very much. "Not that I know of. No more than any other family at least. But I can't say for certain. We hadn't seen one another in quite a while."

"How come?"

"Oh, he was away, then I was away. I was up north looking for work."

"Any luck?"

"No, not really. It seems I know too much to carry bricks for a living but not enough to tell people where to put them. It's a bit of a double bind that I can't seem to do anything about." More details he didn't need to offer. Detective Hardigan was certainly good at getting people to open up.

"So you met up again recently?"

"Yes. The night he died, in fact. We went for a drink at the Scion Club during which Henry invited me to lunch at the house."

"And was there anything at the club that night, or in your friend's demeanour perhaps, that struck you as either odd or suspicious at all?"

John thought for a moment. Could Spencer be involved? Probably not. Although it was tempting to throw him under the omnibus anyway. "No, nothing I can think of."

"What time did you leave the club?"

"I left around eight and went to my local for a pint. I don't know what time Henry left, but I don't think he was planning on staying very long."

"And you've no idea where he went after the club?"

"No, none. You'd have to speak to his friends about that."

The detective grabbed a pen. "Who are his friends?"

"Well, I saw Richard and Julia Rosemont arrive, along with Thomas Whitby-Smythe and Melissa Oakhampton, but the one you want to talk to is Spencer Shelby the Third."

The detective looked up. "Spencer Shelby the Third? As in Shelby Construction? Those Shelbys?"

"The one and the same."

The detective hesitated, clearly unsure whether questioning a Shelby was a road she wanted to go down. But then, to her credit, she wrote the name down anyway, along with all the others. "Well, it looks like I'll have to speak to the club staff to confirm all this. Whatever happened, happened between eight pm and seven am. That's when the body was found. Mr Chard appears to have drowned, but despite what my boss thinks, I prefer to wait for the coroner's report before coming to any definitive conclusions."

"I wonder, would it be possible to speak with the coroner at some point?"

"I'm not sure, but I can ask if you like. Although, you should know that he's a bit of a prickly customer, even to those who have friends in high places."

"That's alright, Detective. I'm a people person."

The detective smiled. "Yes, so I've seen already."

They considered each other for a moment.

"Tell me, Detective, are you sure Henry went into the water at Gravesend Bridge?"

"As sure as I can be, yes."

"But he could have gone in the water anywhere between the bridge and the sewer, couldn't he? Why are you so sure he went in at the bridge itself?

"Because the river is surprisingly predictable when it comes to currents and corpses. If he'd gone in along the side we'd have found him washed up on one of the riverbanks. For him to be found down by the sewer in the middle of the river means he would have had to have gone in via the bridge. And if he'd gone in north of the bridge he never would have made it that far. Trust me, that's just something I know from experience."

"I see," said John, taking it all in. "And who was it that found the body, may I ask?"

"A local woman walking her dog."

"Any other witnesses?"

"Not that I know of."

"What about at the bridge? Any witnesses there?"

"That I can't tell you. I've yet to go up there and ask around. I'm kind of on my own on this one and, as you can see, I've got a load of other cases to be getting on with as well." Detective Hardigan indicated the many piles of paperwork on her desk.

"Well lucky for me I've got nothing but time," said John. "Would you mind if I asked around, to see what I can come up with?"

Detective Hardigan shrugged. "Be my guest. Although I must insist that if you come up with anything interesting you let me know right away, is that understood?"

"Oh, absolutely, Detective. You'll be the first to know," John promised. And to his surprise, he actually meant it too.

From Wainwright's Yard John limped home to change. His feet were absolutely killing him and his new jacket smelled funny. There was no way he could spend the entire day like that. Donning his old jacket and shoes he hung his new jacket in the back yard and stuffed the shoes with balls of rolled up newspaper, before heading out again.

John stood outside the front door of the Scion Club resisting the urge to knock. He was a member now, he didn't need to knock, but when faced with such a large, imposing black door his working-class heritage had a tendency to rear its ugly head. Checking that his member's pin was in place, he pushed on through.

The lounge of the Scion Club at lunchtime smelled of port, game, and unrestrained privilege. John's mouth watered as he realised he hadn't had anything substantial to eat all day. Maybe he should avail himself of the club's bill of fare before he left. He could probably just about afford it now.

He spotted Henry's friends in a snug just off the bar. They were hunched round a table whispering urgently at one another. So engrossed in their conversation were they, they didn't spot John's approach.

Richard Rosemont seemed to be holding court, with his sister Julia and her best friend Melissa Oakhampton listening intently to everything he said. The clown of the group, Thomas Whitby-Smythe, was also hanging on his every word, whilst Oswald Crunk, their 'bit of rough' (He was new money, you see, the pirates in his family being slightly less deceased than the pirates in everybody else's) simply nodded his approval whenever he thought necessary.

Spencer Shelby the Third was not with them. John hated to admit it, but he was quite relieved about that.

It didn't look like any of them had changed much since school, except maybe for Whitby-Smythe, who seemed to have leapt on the craze for aviation wear as only someone with more money than sense ever could. Whilst the rest of them looked very smart in their tailored suits and fine dresses, his get-up of a fur-lined leather jacket, leather flying helmet and goggles, and white silk scarf flung casually over one shoulder, made him look like a little kid playing dress up – if that kid had a beer drinker's paunch and was starting to go prematurely bald.

Oswald Crunk spotted John in the doorway of the snug. Sitting up, he cleared his throat loudly, nodding in John's general direction with all the subtlety of a drunken uncle. Richard Rosemont turned in his chair to find John standing right beside him. For a moment no one spoke. John glanced round the table. Was that guilt he saw? Or fear? Or something else? Whatever it was, Richard Rosemont was the first to recover his composure.

"My word, Lefty. It's been a while. How the devil are you?"

"I'm fine, Richard, thanks for asking. And it's John these days, not Lefty. We're not at school anymore."

"Really? Are you sure? You appear to be wearing the same clothes you did at school." Some of the table laughed.

"What's the matter, Lefty?" crowed Thomas Whitby-Smythe. "Can't mummy afford to buy you a new outfit? *A-haw-haw-haw-haw!*" He looked around, fully expecting the others to join in, but most of them remembered, and they at least had the good grace not to. Whitby-Smythe's laugh faltered, turning into an embarrassed cough before tapering off completely.

John gave a vicious smile as an old, familiar, slow-burning anger flared up inside him. "May I?" he said, pulling up a chair before anyone could object. Folding his arms he sat back, taking the time to consider them all one by one.

"Look, what do you want, Sinister?" said Richard Rosemont. "We're kind of in the middle of something here."

"Really? And what's that then?" said John.

"Never you mind. That's none of your concern. Now, can we help you with something or what?"

"Yes, I think perhaps you can. I don't know if you've heard, but I have been commissioned by Donald Chard to look into the circumstances surrounding Henry's death."

"Do you mean... an investigation?" said Julia, sitting forward.

John smiled at Julia. He tried not to, but he couldn't help himself. For a few weeks one summer the two of them had had a bit of a dalliance – a semi-secret fling that ended as mysteriously as it had begun – and the memories of that time could still override his common sense when they wanted to. "That's right. An investigation." This caused a ripple among the group. "Now, you lot were among the last to see Henry alive, so I was wondering what you could tell me about that?"

"Tell you about what?" said Richard Rosemont. "Are you trying to imply we had something to do with his death?"

"I'm not trying to imply anything, Richard, but I would appreciate it if you could tell me what you know about last night. Like, what you did? When the last time everyone saw Henry was? That kind of thing."

"Would you now? And if we refuse?"

John sighed. "It doesn't have to be this way, y'know."

Richard Rosemont smiled. "Oh, but it does."

"Oh for God's sake, Richard! Give it a rest, won't you?" snapped Julia. "John, the truth is we don't know what happened to Henry. He went off without us, after we all went dancing. That was the last any of us saw of him."

"And you don't know where he went?" said John. Julia shook her head.

"He probably went to Caesar's," said Melissa Oakhampton. "That's where you'd usually find him when he wasn't here or at work."

John's ears pricked up. Caesar's Coffee and Chocolate Emporium was Hammersmyth's most notorious gambling den. A favoured haunt of the dodgy and the dissolute, it was just the sort of place Henry would go for a bit of fun.

"Did he go to Caesar's often?"

"All the time," said Melissa.

"To gamble?"

"Well he wasn't going there for the hot chocolate," laughed Oswald Crunk, much to the amusement of Whitby-Smythe.

John almost laughed too, because whilst Caesar's was as famous for its games of chance as it was for people getting their fingers broken, they also did the best hot chocolate John had ever tasted – although whether that was still the case he couldn't say for sure. He hadn't been back to Caesar's since a very dubious winning streak had seen him heavily advised to 'go gamble somewhere else from now on'.

"Henry had a problem," Melissa continued, ignoring Oswald's interruption. "He liked taking risks. It was bad before, but ever since he got back from India..." Melissa gave an imperceptible shrug, her gaze dropping to the table. John's heart went out to her. The most human of the entire Chess Club, she had carried a torch for Henry for as long as John could remember, and whilst nothing had ever come of it, he was well aware that if Henry had ever decided to settle down, she was the one he would have liked to have settled down with.

John turned to Julia. "Which dance club did you go to?"

"We went to that new place over by Freedom Square. Constance Abernathy's Dance Academy."

"And how long were you there?"

"Not long. Only about an hour. We had to leave early because *somebody* couldn't behave themselves." Julia glared at her brother, but he feigned not to notice. "That was when Henry went his own way and the rest of us went back to ours for a nightcap."

"The rest of you. So, you five?"

Julia nodded. "That's right."

"And what about Spencer? Where was he during all of this?"

"Spencer? Oh! He, um—" Julia glanced around the table.

"He was with us the whole night," said Richard Rosemont, practically daring John to contradict him.

"Really?" said John, trying to keep his sarcasm in check. "You're sure about that, are you?"

Richard Rosemont scowled at John. "You know what? I don't think I like your tone, Sinister. In fact it's damned impertinent if you ask me. I think perhaps it's time you were on your way, before anyone says anything they might come to regret."

"Do you now?" said John. "And what, pray tell, is it you think you might come to regret saying, Richard?"

"Now see here, Sinister," exclaimed Thomas Whitby-Smythe, jabbing his finger across the table at John. "No one is going to answer any more of your damn questions, got it? So you can just naff off, do you hear? Unless you want me to come round there and give you a damn good thrashing, what!"

John grinned back at Whitby-Smythe. It was hard enough to take the man seriously at the best of times, never mind in that ridiculous outfit. "Alright, Wing Commander," he said. "Keep your goggles on. I'm going."

John stood, replacing his chair back where he'd found it. "If any of you can think of anything that might be important please do let me know. You can contact me via the Chard family," he said, glancing around the table. He didn't really expect to hear from any of them, but he thought it was worth a shot anyway.

"Don't hold your breath," replied Richard Rosemont, idly inspecting his fingernails as though bored with the whole conversation.

With a weariness he hadn't felt since grammar school, John headed for the door. Making his way down the stairs, he considered his next move. He would have to visit the dance academy to verify their story. That would be easy enough. But he was also going to have to go to Caesar's and ask a few questions, and that was not something he was looking forward to. They might not be too happy to see him back there. He and Nero had not parted on the best of terms.

I mean, it's not like I owe the guy any money or anything, John mused. *And I never actually scammed anyone did I?* Not really. At least, not in a way that anyone would notice. Plus, it was only a few questions. Nero would be alright with that, wouldn't he? He was a reasonable man, after all.

John wondered if saying it over and over again might make it true. He certainly hoped so. At least concentrating on the possibility was preferable to thinking about all the terrifying, painful, and downright nasty ways it could go instead.

He decided to pop by the pub on the way there. A little Dutch courage, that's what he needed. Just a quick snifter to see him through. No one could begrudge him that, could they?

The Big Guy entered the stables to find his skinny associate sitting on a wooden crate, diligently whittling the skin off a large piece of ginger.

"What you up to?"

The Skinny Man grinned. "I'm gonna teach old Doris there a lesson in manners," he said, pointing out an old grey horse he had tied up in the corner of one of the stalls. He'd positioned a couple of barrels next to her, pinning her against the wall, and placed a bag over her eyes so she couldn't see. "I reckon a bit o' ginger where the sun don't shine will learn her not to kick buckets at people, don't you?"

"Not really," said the big man. "Anyway, there's no time for that now. The boss wants us ready to go. He's got somethin' he needs us to take care of."

"Sure thing. Just gimme a sec. I'm almost finished."

The Big Guy walked over and plucked the piece of ginger out of the Skinny Man's hand.

"Hey!"

"Now means now," the big man rumbled. "You know the boss don't like to be kept waitin'." He watched the other man's knife out the corner of his eye, just in case, but he didn't seem in the mood to use it for once.

"Yeah, right. Whatever you say, big fella."

Wandering over to a table full of horse tack, the Skinny Man began sorting out all the bits and pieces he needed. "Any idea what the boss wants us to do?" he said over his shoulder.

"Yeah. Apparently there's some geezer he wants us to find."

"Yeah right, 'find'. And then what?"

"Find and take care of, I suppose."

"Excellent," the other man said, examining the pointy end of a hoof pick thoughtfully. "So where is this guy then?"

"No idea. That's how come we gotta find him, eh?"

"Hang on. So we don't even know where this geezer is?"

"Or what he looks like. All we've got is his name."

"His name! What good is a name? What're we gonna do with that, go round asking everyone if they've seen so-and-so?"

"That's kind of how these things work, yeah."

"But that'll take ages," the Skinny Man moaned. "And what if he's not usin' 'is real name, eh? What'll we do then?"

"What, like if he's using one of them soodynims or something?"

"Exactly."

The Big Guy shrugged. "I dunno. Have a nice ride out at the boss's expense, I guess."

Throwing down the hoof pick, the Skinny Man banged his fist on the table. "God damn it, I've had about enough of this."

The Big Guy didn't want to ask, but he figured he may as well. He was going to hear it anyway. "What's that then?"

"This! All this 'doing stuff' nonsense. It's no way to make a livin', is it?"

The Big Guy frowned. *Actually, that's* exactly *how you make a living,* he thought. But he could kind of see his point. It wasn't the nicest job in the world.

The big man thought about it for a while. "You could always emigrate," he said. "They're always looking for people in America. I could see you setting up a little farmstead and that, taming the savage lands, that sort of thing." *Or getting eaten by a bear, if there was any justice in the world.*

"Emigrate? What on earth are you on about emigrate? I'm talkin' about making a little money on the side so we can get out from under."

"Oh. I see. Like how, for instance?"

"Like if we played both sides, traded a bit of information here and there. We could make a good few quid if we were smart about it." The Big Guy didn't like where this was going. "I had this cousin, see, right nasty piece of work he was." *What a surprise.* "He had me help him fence some stuff he nicked. Then, when all that was done an' I'd got me cut, I went and shopped him to the coppers for another couple of bob. I made out both ends, if you see what I'm saying?"

"I see what you're sayin'. You're talking about selling out the boss." *And me along with him, by the sounds of things.*

"No, no. Not at all. I just mean there's got to be some way we can make a bit of extra cash, what wiv everything that's been going on round here lately. I mean there's bound to be someone *somewhere* who would pay to know what we know, don't you think?"

The Big Guy frowned. "I think that if the boss hears us speculatin' on sellin' him out there'll be all kinds of trouble, don't you?"

The Skinny Man shrugged in an extremely casual manner. "Suit yourself," he said. "It was just an idea. Forget I said anything." He threw his giant comrade a reassuring wink, whistling to himself as he returned to his organisation.

The Big Guy sighed. Why couldn't life be simple? Why did people have to go and complicate things all the time?

With the growing feeling that this job was no longer worth what he was getting paid for it, the big man exited the stables, tossing the lump of raw ginger on the compost heap on the way out.

John swayed a little as he approached the entrance to the alleyway. He was feeling a little 'braver' than he had originally intended. If he wasn't careful it was going to get him killed. In Caesar's Coffee and Chocolate, half-cut and mouthy was not a good combination.

Into the alleyway and down the club's stone stairs, John did his best to look relaxed and carefree, which wasn't easy considering what was waiting for him by the bottom step.

Agnes Goodenough ran the door at Caesar's. Six-foot tall and built like a brick outhouse, her black doorman's uniform bulged in all the most dangerous places. She reminded John of an onyx obelisk he once saw at the Museum of History. Both were impressively imposing, utterly immovable, and any attempt at violence on either would result in a lot of bleeding and broken bones, all of them yours. People didn't mess with Agnes Goodenough. And if they did, they never did it twice.

Her family came from the Niger Delta, on the west African coast, though you'd never know it to hear her talk. A resident of the worst parts of east London since the age of two, when she'd moved to Hammersmyth she'd brought just two things with her; a devastating right hook, and one hell of a cock-a-knee accent.

"Well I'll be! Look what the cat dragged in. John Sinister, as I live and breathe."

"Hello, Agnes. Been a while. You're looking well."

"Ever the charmer. What do you want, Sinister? Not here to gamble I hope?"

"Heaven forbid. No, I was just hoping to have a quick word with the boss if he's in?"

"Of course he's in. He's always in."

"Excellent. Then do you mind if I...?"

Agnes shrugged. "Knock yourself out, mate." She stepped aside to let him through, but as John opened the door Agnes grabbed his arm. "Hey, how's that sister of yours doing?"

"My sister?" How did Agnes know Jane? "Oh, um... She's fine, I guess."

"Great. Glad to hear it. Here, you give her my best next time you see her, eh?"

"Of course. Happy to," said John, smiling. Agnes didn't smile back. She did let go of his arm though. Resisting the impulse to rub where her massive hand had been, John went inside.

The interior of Caesar's was very much like the Scion Club. The same tasteful opulence, the same array of side rooms and discreet alcoves, the same smell of intrigue and old money, albeit a little darker and more threatening – the intrigue more than anything. Its membership was much less exclusive though. Anyone with the fifteen pounds annual fee could join, no questions asked. Money may have talked in the Scion Club, but in Caesar's it always got the last word.

John had managed to scrape together the joining fee last year, during a brief moment of affluence. It had been a lot, most of what he had at the time, but he'd thought it would be worth it. With all the gaming that went on behind its doors, Caesar's had promised to be a gold mine for a man of his talents. And it was, for a while.

He hadn't been back since the ban. What was the point? All he could do there now was spend money, and he didn't have the cash for that. Where the price of a drink in the Scion Club would make your eyes water, a drink in Caesar's would make you fall to your knees and weep.

John let his eyes adjust to the semi-darkness before wandering over to the bar. There he found the barman sitting on a stool, reading a book on his hand-held Bibliostack.

John recognised him as the one who made the good hot chocolate. "Evening, Dick. The boss around?"

"Upstairs," said Dick, not looking up from his device.

"Upstairs. What upstairs?"

Dick pointed to a dark red curtain hanging next to the bar. Pulling it aside, John came across a brightly lit, carpeted stairwell leading upwards. Slightly disturbed by the fact that, despite the number of times he'd been in there he'd never noticed these stairs before, John began the climb.

At the top of the stairs he found a lavishly decorated room full of fake columns, ornamental cornicing, and half a dozen saucy cherubs sculpted into various states of suggestive repose. Some surprisingly realistic ivy had been painted round the edge of the ceiling, trailing down the wall in places, and the newly laid red carpet was both deep and luxurious. Three long, baize-covered tables sat proudly in the centre of the room, and fussing around them, making sure everything was just so, was Nero.

A short, stocky man with an unruly mop of curly black hair, penetrating eyes, and a nose that looked like it had been broken more than once, Nero always wore black from head to toe, except on his hands and neck, where he carried an obscene amount of gold, enough to tempt even the most cautious of thieves. Not that he ever had to worry about anyone trying to steal it from him. Even a blind man could see what a bad idea that would be.

"Well now! Good evening, Mr Sinister," said Nero, lifting up a leg to half sit on the end of one of the tables. "Tell me, what do you think of my latest little venture?"

"I'm not sure. What am I looking at?"

"Hazard tables. From France. Very popular these days, and soon to be the next big thing over here if I have anything to do with it."

John had heard of Hazard. A dice game similar to what the Americans called Craps. It was all chance, no skill, and a great way to lose money.

"Very nice," he said, being sure to look suitably impressed.

"These babies are going to make me a fortune."

"I thought you already had a fortune."

Nero flashed John a wicked grin. "One can always have more, don't you think?"

"I guess so," said John. "It's not something I've ever had to worry about."

Nero chuckled. "So what can I do for you, Mr Sinister? I assume you have a good reason for being here. I can't imagine you just wandered in off the street for a quick chat."

"Straight to the point, as always. That's what I like about you, Nero." John tried for a jovial smile, but Nero's cold, hard stare killed it before it had a chance to take shape. "Yes, well, I was wondering if you could help me out with something? You see, they fished a friend of mine out of the river this morning—"

"Henry Chard."

"That's right, Henry Chard. Anyway, his family have asked me to look into his last moments for them. What he did, where he went, that sort of thing. And it turns out that, um, well, that he may have come here the night he died."

"I see. And you think I had something to do with his passing maybe?"

"What! Oh, no. No. Of course not, no. Heaven forbid. No, I was just wondering if you can remember him being here last night? Or if anything – totally unrelated to you of course – might have happened while he was here?"

Nero considered John for a long time, an uncomfortably long time, whilst John did his best not to bolt for the door.

"Mr Sinister, you know I can't talk about our clients. What goes on here depends on a great deal of discretion. If word got out that Nero couldn't be trusted, well, where would we be?"

"I don't think Henry would mind."

"No, but his friends might."

"So he was here with friends?"

"I didn't say that."

"But he was here."

"I didn't say that either."

"So what are you saying?"

"Only this," said Nero. He folded his arms. The silence stretched on. Nero smiled. John almost asked 'What?' until he realised how stupid that would be.

"Please, Nero, I'm trying to find out what happened to my friend. I'm not asking you to betray any confidences or anything. I just want to know if he was here. Was he even a member?"

Nero gazed up at the ceiling as he mulled things over. "Alright, son. Everybody gets one. Yes, your friend Henry does, or rather did, come here now and then, but I don't recall seeing him for a week or two. Not that that means anything. People come and go, and I can't keep tabs on everyone. But you can ask the guys on the way out if you like, see if they remember him being here."

"Thanks, Nero. I will do. Er, just out of curiosity, when he did come in, how did he do?"

"You mean did he owe the house any money?"

John swallowed loudly. "Yes."

Nero shrugged. "He played poorly, like all you posh boys do. But unlike most of your lot he paid his debts in full and on time. I had no problem with him."

John wasn't sure that quite answered his question, but he wasn't about to ask it a again. If he'd had any luck when he arrived it had run screaming for the door a long time ago.

"Thank you, Nero. I appreciate your help with all this. And good luck with the new venture. I hope it goes well for you."

Nero smoothed his hand along the green baize table top.

"Thanks. But with these babies, I don't need luck."

John stopped by the bar on the way out, where he found Dick the barman with his head still stuck in his Bibliostack. "Hey, Dick, you remember a guy in here last night? Purple top coat, long blonde hair?"

"Sorry, boss, I wasn't in last night."

"So who was, do you know?"

"Tom I think, but you'd have to check with Nero about that."

"Right. I see." John glanced towards the red curtain. "In that case I'll leave it for now then. No need to bother the man twice in one day, is there?"

"Whatever you say, boss," Dick mumbled, turning the page with a swipe of his finger.

John went to leave, but then he hesitated. The barman finally looked up from his book. "Something else I can help you with?"

"Yeah," said John. "Give me one of the house specials with a bit of everything."

The barman set aside his Bibliostack. "You got it, boss. One Caesar Special, coming right up."

John left Caesar's two shillings lighter, a thousand times happier, and utterly convinced that as long as there was chocolate in the world, everything would always be just fine.

"Still alive then," chuckled Agnes, as he pushed his way out the door.

"Yeah, just about," John replied. "Say, Agnes, do you mind if I ask you something?"

Agnes frowned. "You've got chocolate on your chin, y'know."

John wiped his mouth with the back of his hand. "Right. Thanks. So anyway, do you remember a guy here last night, purple top coat, long blonde hair? Would have arrived some time between ten and eleven."

Agnes thought for a moment. "Can't say that I do, guv, not that that means anything. I pay as much attention to who goes through the door as you lot do to the one who's holding it." She thought about it some more. "Mind you, that being said, I think I'd remember a purple top coat showing up. It's not the sort of thing you normally get around here."

"Alright. Well thanks anyway, Agnes," said John, heading for the stairs. "I'll see you around, yeah?"

"Hey, Sinister. Don't forget to give your sister my best now, will you?"

"Sure thing," said John. "You have my word."

"Good lad," said Agnes, tossing him a quick wink.

John did not wink back.

The one thing John knew about the rich and powerful was that they didn't like to be kept waiting. Jumping on the first omnibus he saw, he headed up to Chard Manor to make his report. He arrived to find a large group of men crowded round the manor gates. Exiting the omnibus, John stood for a while on the opposite side of the road, observing what was going on. He counted at least a dozen men milling about. Some of them had cameras, some of them had notebooks, and none of them looked like someone you'd have over for dinner, which explained the policeman stood on guard. He looked bored and annoyed, as policemen often do. John wondered if it was something they taught you on day one of police school. 'How to look like you want people to sod off and mind their own business: Lesson one – Scowling.'

There was a man sat at the omnibus stop, his eyes fixed on the goings on at the gate. A chimney sweep by the smell of him, with a pile of crushed cigarette ends at his feet, he seemed to have no idea John was there. "Excuse me, mate," said John, walking over, "but any idea what's happened?"

Startled, the man dropped his cigarette. Picking it off the floor he gave John a nervous smile. "Oh, um, I dunno, like. I think they're all journalists or somethin'. I 'eard one of 'em say that someone had died."

"Well yeah, they did. But that was this morning. What're they doing here now?" With five editions a day, the news in Hammersmyth got old fast.

The man shrugged. That kind of speculation was obviously beyond him. "Alright, well, cheers, mate."

"No problem," said the man cheerfully. He gave John another nervous smile, but John didn't notice. He was halfway over the road by then.

As John approached the gate, a familiar mass of lies and insinuation broke away from the group to intercept him. "Good morning, Mr Sinister," said Mr Bumbleton. "Lovely to see you again. Any chance of a few words for the readers of the Hammersmyth Gazette?"

"How do you know my—" John stopped himself when he saw the smug gleam in Mr Bumbleton's eye. The man had an informant among the police, didn't he? Of course he did. Who John was, and what he was up to, was probably the worst kept secret in Hammersmyth by now. He walked on.

"So, you think there's something suspicious about young Henry Chard's death, do you? What do the police say about that? Any suspects? Do you think someone is out to get the Chard family, perhaps?"

John had no intention of giving Mr Bumbleton anything he could work with so he gave him two words. Exactly two. The second one was 'off'.

The policeman by the front gate squinted at John like he was trying to decide what charges he could arrest him on. John smiled in return. "I'm here to see Mr Chard," he said.

"Yeah, right. Of course you are. Pull the other one, sunshine."

John removed Mr Chard's letter and offered it up to the policeman. "Read this."

FLASH!

"OY! What have I told you about that? Do it again and I'll take that thing off you, do you hear?!"

"Sorry, Officer," said Mr Bumbleton, ushering his photographer out of arms reach. "Won't happen again, guv, I promise."

"See that it don't," said the policeman, glaring the two men away from him. He turned his attention back to John. "And as for you, you can hop it an'all. I ain't got time for your nonsense neither."

"I understand, Officer, but I really think you'd better take a look at this first." When it became clear he wasn't going to leave, the policeman took John's letter and gave it a quick once over. "Now I think you'd better let me past, don't you, before you find yourself on permanent night duty, eh?"

As he finished the letter the policeman smiled in an almost gleeful manner. Folding the letter up neatly he handed it back to John. "Yes, sir. Of course, sir. Go right on through, sir," he said, giving a slight bow as he gestured with an outstretched arm for John to proceed.

There was a murmur among the journalists as John was let through. Heading up the driveway he risked a glance over his shoulder. The reporters were busy scribbling down notes whilst the photographers wrestled fresh plates into their cameras. And standing with his back to them, his hands on his hips, the policeman was still smiling.

John rushed on up the drive.

As he approached Chard Manor, John got the oddest feeling in the pit of his stomach. The manor house seemed to be sagging, as if it was tired or depressed or something. Little jets of steam shot out at odd intervals, making forlorn sniffly sounds, like someone who's been crying all day but has finally run out of tears. It was very strange, and kind of sad, and it made John more than a little nervous. Hurrying up the front steps, he rang the doorbell.

"Now is not a good time, sir," said Hercules the butler as he opened the door.

"Why, what's going on? Where's Mr Chard?"

The butler hesitated. "Perhaps you better come in, sir. I will see if someone is available to talk to you."

Hercules left John in the entrance hall, disappearing off into the drawing room. John listened. Though he could hear voices he couldn't tell what they were saying. As he waited he kept one eye on the Robobutler, but it appeared to be out of commission thank God.

John was about to go over and press his ear against the drawing room door when it opened and Detective Hardigan emerged.

"Mr Sinister. What are you doing here?"

"I could ask you the same thing, Detective. What on earth is going on?"

"You mean you don't know? Where have you been all day?"

"Making enquiries, of course. Why?"

"Then you're probably the only person in Hammersmyth who hasn't heard. Donald Chard had a heart attack this afternoon, in his lawyers' office."

"My God, is he alright?"

"No, Mr Sinister, he is not. Donald Chard, I'm sorry to say, is dead."

"Dead! But, how can he be dead? I only saw him this morning. He looked fine to me."

Detective Hardigan shrugged. "I don't know what to tell you. You know how these things go. One minute people are running around business as usual, and the next minute they're gone." She clicked her fingers. "Out like a light. You see it all the time in my job."

"So it was natural causes then?"

"Looks that way. Why, do you know something?"

"No. I just wondered is all. I mean, if it was natural causes, then what are the police doing here?"

"Are you really surprised? Someone as prominent as Donald Chard dies, the police turn out to keep an eye on things."

"And the journalists too, I guess."

"More often than not. Although I think most of that lot being here is down to the rumour that Donald Chard died intestate, that he was at his lawyers' making out a will when he died."

"Really? Is that possible do you think?"

"I highly doubt it. I mean I never met the man, but he didn't strike me as the sort of person to leave something like that to chance."

John had to agree with her there, but you never could tell. Some people were superstitious when it came to death. They saw making out a will as tempting fate. Perhaps Donald Chard was such a man.

"And how are your enquiries going, may I ask?" said Detective Hardigan. Have you found out anything interesting about Henry Chard's death?"

"Not yet," said John. "I'm still trying to work out how Henry ended up in the river. Sadly, it's starting to look like it might have been suicide after all. He owed a bit of money about town, which may have been a factor in all of this."

"Debt, you mean. But surely his family would—"

John grabbed Detective Hardigan's arm. "My God! The family. Mary! Where is she? Is she okay?"

Detective Hardigan nodded towards the drawing room. "She's in there, with the boss. Poor thing's quite upset."

"Detective, excuse me, but I must see how she is," said John, rushing past Detective Hardigan. At the drawing room door he knocked quickly before entering.

Mary Chard was sitting in the same spot as when John had found her that morning. Her eyes were red from crying and she clutched a lace handkerchief to her face. Detective Inspector Murtaugh stood close by, looking decidedly uncomfortable.

"Mary!"

"Oh, John, did you hear? It's so awful." She held out her hand, John taking it in his as he sat next to her.

"I just heard. How are you holding up? Is there anything I can do?"

"No, no. I mean, everyone has been so kind, but what is there to do? Really, what can anyone do?" Covering her mouth, Mary sobbed into her handkerchief.

"Don't worry. Everything will be alright. I promise."

Mary smiled briefly, but said nothing. Behind John, Detective Inspector Murtaugh gave a discreet cough. "Pardon me, Mr Sinister, but might I have a word?" He took John over to the window, out of earshot. "I was curious as to whether your investigations had turned up anything of interest?"

Nothing I fancy sharing with you, mate, thought John. "Er, no. No, nothing really. Why? Do you suspect foul play?"

"Not at all, not at all. But with two deaths in one family one does have to wonder."

"Yes, I see what you mean. Well, I'm still looking into it, but so far I haven't come across anything suspicious."

"Good. That's good to know. Please, if you do come across anything unusual you will let Detective Hardigan know, won't you?"

"Of course, Inspector. She'll be the first. Now if I may, what happened with Donald Chard? They say he had a heart attack?"

"Well, according to Miss Chard,"—they glanced over at Mary who suddenly burst into tears—"Mr Chard was fine when he left the house, but by the time he reached his lawyers' office he was starting to feel unwell. Then, all of a sudden, he simply collapsed and died." Mary let out an anguished wail. "Poor thing. This is all so much to deal with. It must be very difficult for her." John thought that the understatement of the year.

The Detective Inspector rocked on his heels, unable to decide between clasping his hands in front of him, behind him, or letting them hang down by his side. "It's so hard to know what to do in these types of situations, don't you think? Her younger brother – Peter, is it? – is on the way, but until he gets here, well, what comfort can someone like me offer?"

"If you wish to leave, Inspector, I can stay with her until her brother arrives."

Detective Inspector Murtaugh was visibly relieved. "That's very good of you, Mr Sinister. I think that might be best, don't you, you being a friend of the family and everything?"

The Detective Inspector approached Mary. "Miss Chard, forgive me, but I have some matters to attend to. Mr Sinister here will stay with you until your brother arrives, if that is alright with you?"

"Oh. Thank you, Inspector. Yes, that would be most welcome."

"Very good. Well, good day, miss. And once again, so very sorry for your loss."

Mary gave Detective Inspector Murtaugh a gracious smile, and he left. John sat down next to her again.

"Oh, John, I still can't believe it. First Henry and now father. What is going on? Is it us? Are we cursed, do you think?"

"Not at all. It's just bad luck, that's all. Damned bad luck. I know it's no comfort, but sometimes these things just happen."

"But what am I to do? With father gone who will take care of everything? There's just so much to organise, so many different companies and interests. And then there's the house! It's so big, so many rooms. How does one cope with it all?!" Mary started panting in short, sharp, little breaths as she threw her hands around, grasping for a solution. John had to grab her hands and hold them tight to stop her from flying away.

"Mary, please don't fret. I'm sure your father has people for that kind of thing. Your family's continued success is too important to too many for anyone to let it fail now."

Squeezing John's hands, Mary took a deep, calming, breath. "Oh, John, you always did have such a clever way of looking at things. I'm so glad you're here. You really are my knight in shining armour."

John blushed, his cheeks hotter than the glow of the fire. He searched for a worthy reply.

The front door slammed.

"You! Where's my sister?"

The drawing room door opened and in marched Peter Chard. For a moment, John was taken aback. With his collarless shirt, mutton-chop moustache, three-piece suit and stove-pipe hat, he was the spit of his father as a younger man. "I came as fast as I could," said Peter, rushing to his sister's side.

Mary stood to greet him, the two of them sandwiching John on the couch between them. Finding himself with an unflattering view, John did his best to look anywhere except straight ahead of him.

As Mary and Peter's embrace ended, Peter Chard seemed to notice John's presence for the first time. "Who's this?" he growled.

"Peter, this is John Sinister, an old friend from school. He's been doing some work for father recently."

"How do you do?" said John, standing and offering his hand.

"Work? What kind of work? I haven't seen your name on the company payroll."

"Well, no," said John, lowering his unshaken hand. "I was hired in a more private capacity by your father, to look into the circumstances surrounding your brother's passing."

"The circumstances? The circumstances are that Henry got drunk and fell in the river, end of story."

"Well, your father thought—"

"My father is dead, Mr Sinister." Peter sneered the name. "And with him your reason for being here. Feel free to leave at any time."

"Peter!" Mary gasped. "Don't be so rude. John is a friend."

"And this is a family matter. One which we must deal with, *as a family*. I'm sure Mr Sinister understands."

"Whether he does or he doesn't, that's no way to talk to our guest."

"No, he's right," said John. "You two need some time alone, and I have no desire to intrude. Therefore, if you'll excuse me?" Stepping between the two of them John headed swiftly for door.

Mary caught up with John on the other side of the drawing room door. "John, I'm sorry about Peter. He can be such a brute some-times."

"That's alright Mary. He's probably a little overwhelmed."

Glancing at the slightly open drawing room door, Mary moved John further into the entrance hall. "That is one word for it. I can think of many others, none of them as polite."

"Yes, I'm sure you can," said John, leaning nonchalantly against the Robobutler's wooden base.

"WELCOME, WELCOME! WELCOME TO CHARD MANOR. PLEASE, DO COME IN. MAY I TAKE YOUR COAT?"

The Robobutler lunged at John, grabbing him by the scruff of the neck. *Not this again!* he thought, as the Robobutler lifted him bodily off the ground.

"Let him go!" Mary yelled. Grabbing an umbrella from the coat rack she whacked at the automaton's arm, smacking it again and again until something important went *Ping!*, the arm dropped, and the machine's hand flew open, sending John tumbling to the ground.

John lay on the floor gasping, watching in awe as Mary gave vent to all her fury. Wielding the umbrella like a two-handed broadsword, she beat the Robobutler with all her might, whilst the Robobutler, to its credit, kept smiling and offering its assistance no matter what.

"Thank you. Can I—" *Whack!* "Can I—" *Thump!* "May I be of ass– ass– ass—"

Hercules, the human butler, appeared from a side door. Step-ping in between Mary and his nemesis, he took charge of Mary's umbrella. "Allow me, miss," he said. Turning on the Robobutler, he resumed the relentless whacking in her stead.

Mary stumbled back, panting. Wiping the loose hairs away from her face, she looked down at John. "Oh, John. I'm sorry. I—" She ran into the arms of her brother, Peter, who guided her back into the drawing room. John tried to call out to her but all he managed was a weak croak and a coughing fit.

Seeing that the coast was clear, Hercules slipped in behind the Robobutler's dais. Opening up the machine's back panel he jammed the umbrella deep into its inner workings. The Robobutler jerked and shuddered as all kinds of unpleasant noises emanated from its back end. Reaching out one final pleading hand it slumped forward, like a puppet without strings, its dying breath a hiss of steam, a single oily tear rolling down its flat, lifeless cheek.

Hercules the butler emerged triumphant from behind the dais. Straightening his jacket, he turned his attention to John.

"I trust you can see yourself out," he said, with a small, satisfied smile. Exiting the entrance hall, he left John in a bemused pile on the floor.

"Now what?" said a voice.

"Now I go home and take a bath," said John. "Nothing more for me to—" He looked around. Where did that come from? There was no one else about. Just that damned cat, standing there watching him with that vague look of contempt it always seemed to have.

"Who said that?" he ventured.

"Have a guess, genius."

He looked over at the cat. Did it just speak? No, that can't be right. Cats can't talk. But its mouth moved, didn't it? Or was that a trick of the light? Yes, that had to be it. Exhaustion and hunger were playing tricks on him. There was no way the cat just said something. He must be imagining things.

But then again, if it wasn't the cat, then who was it?

The cat cocked its head to one side. "That's right, the cat can talk. Deal with it," it said.

John scrambled to his feet. "You can talk," he managed.

"That's right, I can talk."

"But... You can talk."

"Evidently. As can you, just about."

"You're a talking cat?"

"I feel like we've been over this. Yes, I'm a talking cat."

"Yes, but... You can talk?"

The cat sighed. He walked forward a little. "Look, if it helps, I'm not a real cat."

"You look real."

"Well of course I look real. I'm meant to look real. And in the purely existential sense, I *am* real. I'm just not a real cat."

"So what are you then?"

"I'm a self-regulating automaton running an experimental analysis engine. I'm capable of independent motion, independent thought, and I may well be the smartest creature in this house. At the very least I'm the smartest half of this conversation. Got it?"

"Er, yes. I think so."

"No you don't. I can tell by the bovine look on your face. You meat-sacks never get it first time round. But I haven't got time to lead you through the intricacies of my creation right now. My master is dead, and you are going to help me find his killer, *capiche?*"

"Ka-what? His killer? What are you talking about? Mr Chard had a heart attack, didn't he?"

"My hairy grease nipple he did. The man was fit as a fiddle. He was murdered, and I know who did it."

"Who?"

A bell rang somewhere below stairs.

"We can't talk here. Follow me."

John watched the cat as it walked away. At the front door it stopped and turned. "Come on. Don't just stand there staring like a dog that's just been shown a card trick. Let's go!"

The cat disappeared through a small flap in the front door. John, his mind still running to catch up, quickly followed.

They headed down the gravel driveway. John still had no idea what was going on, but he'd learnt long ago that the best thing to do in these types of situations – not that he'd ever been in a situation quite like this before – was to just go with the flow and figure it all out later. Things usually made sense after a while. Usually.

"So you think Mr Chard was killed?" said John.

"I *know* he was killed, I just don't know how."

"But you know who did it?"

"I do. Or rather, I know who had it done. He'd never get his own hands dirty, the devious little sod. It was his son, Peter. He's the killer. I guarantee it."

"And this is based on what exactly?"

"On the fact that I know him. I know the type. He's a sneaky, conniving, twisted little so-and-so. He's been after sole control of Chard Mechanical for years, and now he's got exactly what he wanted. It stands to reason he's behind it. He probably killed Henry, too, to get him out of the way."

"So what you're saying is you have no evidence."

"Evidence! I don't need evidence. I *know* he did it."

"I'm afraid the police are going to need a little more to go on than that."

"Which is where you come in. You're going to prove he did it."

"Me? I've no part in this anymore. My employer is dead and his family just let me go. My involvement with all this is over."

The cat rounded on John. "The hell it is! You took Mr Chard's money. You're bought and paid for, my son. You're not done until *I* say you are."

"Now hang on a minute—"

"I thought you were Henry's friend?"

"I am. Was."

"And you're completely satisfied that everything about his death is fully explained, are you?"

"No, not everything."

"And Mr Chard's death? Doesn't it seem like a bit of a coincidence, the chair of Chard Mechanical and his immediate heir both dying one after the other?"

"Well, coincidences do happen," John offered, though even he didn't believe that one.

"Ha!" the cat scoffed. "And dogs lick their balls because they like the taste. Look, mister, something stinks worse than yesterday's fish around here, and I'm not going to rest until I find out what. And if you were any kind of a man you wouldn't either."

John stared at the cat, his hands on his hips. It was annoying getting moral judgement from a cat, especially when that cat had a point. Something *was* going on. He probably should look into it a little more. Plus, he *had* been paid quite a lot up front to find out what that something was, so it kind of *was* like he had a job to do. Sure, his employer was dead and there wouldn't be any more money after this, but what he had in his pocket already should cover a few days' work at least. Maybe a week.

"So, you in?" said the cat.

"I'm in," John replied. "I'll give it till the end of the week. Beyond that we'll have to see. Deal?" Dear God, he was negotiating with a cat.

"Deal. Now, I suggest you start at the factory. If there's any evidence, that's where it'll be. Do you know where it is?"

"Every idiot knows where Chard Mechanical is."

"Yeah, but do you?" said the cat, chuckling. John recognised the sound.

"Hang on a minute. The first time I came to the house, that was you laughing at me in the study, wasn't it?"

"Got it in one, Meat. You should have seen the look on your face. It was hilarious. Quite similar to the one you've got now actually."

The cat burst out laughing, and when it became clear he wasn't going to stop any time soon, John just left him to it.

Near the front gate they stopped behind a bush, out of sight of everyone.

"I better leave you here. You don't want to be seen talking to a cat. They might think you've gone mental."

John took in the talking mechanical cat once more. From its grey fur, to its swishing tail, to the way its ears moved independently of each other, it really did look like a proper, genuine, fleas and furballs, scratch-you-for-no-reason, moggy.

"Do the family know about you?" he said.

"No. They think I'm a real cat. All part of the experiment, to see if I could pass for real."

"Well you fooled me. You certainly look real. Are you sure you're mechanical?"

"You'd rather be having this conversation with a real-life talking cat?"

"No, it's just... Oh, I dunno."

The cat seemed to feel a pang of sympathy for John's predicament. "Look, I'll prove it to you, alright. Kneel down and look deep into my eyes." John, intrigued, did so. The cat got right up to him, nose to nose. "Ready?"

"Ready for what?" said John.

The cat whacked him in the face, hard. John tumbled over backwards, clutching his cheek. The cat's front leg wasn't so much an iron fist in a velvet glove, more like a metal paw in a furry mitten. John still wasn't sure exactly what this thing was, but whatever it was, it was definitely man-made.

"Satisfied? Or do you need more convincing?"

"No," said John, rubbing his jaw. "No, I'm good."

"Good," said the cat, walking off. After a few paces it stopped and turned. "The name's Dexter, by the way."

"John Sinister," John replied.

"Yeah, I know," said the cat over its shoulder, as it set off again back towards the house.

Climbing to his feet, John prodded at his battered cheek. He really hoped Dexter hadn't left a mark. He didn't want to have to explain to his sister why he had an angry paw print on his face when he got home.

As he arrived at Chard Mechanical, John realised that he still hadn't eaten anything since breakfast. He should have gotten something outside the main station but he'd been a bit distracted. Meeting a talking cat will do that to you. Who would have thought that the untimely passing of Hammersmyth's most prominent citizen would be the second-most bizarre thing to happen to him today. Robobutlers were one thing, but a walking, talking, mechanical cat, that was something else. Sadly though, his sustenance would have to wait. You couldn't get a pie this far out of town to save your life.

John looked up at the wrought iron lettering above the factory gates. "The Chard Mechanical Corporation," he announced to the world for no good reason (some signs just ask to be read out loud).

Despite the sign, and this being where most people were referring to whenever they talked about Chard Mechanical, this was not the company's true home. Most of what they did, including the hyper-steam side of things, was up near Telford, where the Chards originally came from (and where John had spent most of the time on his travels looking for work). They'd only moved down to Hammersmyth to get their airship division off the ground, so to speak.

When Donald Chard bought the Slater Blimp and Airship Corporation everyone thought the man had gone mad. Back then airships were dinky little things cobbled together from the hulls of old cutters, with balloons made from scrap canvas and paste. They were only good for short trips up and down the country, with the odd jaunt to the continent when the weather was right. More of a novelty item than anything else, they had no real commercial applications. Donald Chard had changed all that. His airships were purpose built, and ten times the size, as different from their predecessors as using a fountain pen was to scratching letters in the dirt.

John could see one of the transatlantic airships in the field beyond the factory, the crown of its envelope and the peak of its tail-fin cresting high above the factory roof. If he had time he'd have to pop round and have a look at it on his way out. He'd never seen an airship up close before, and who knew when he'd get the chance to again? Besides, Emily would never forgive him if he didn't. She loved the airships even more than he did.

"Are you gonna stand there gawping all day?"

John looked up to find Dexter sitting on the factory wall. "What're you doing here?"

"I came to keep an eye on you, didn't I?"

"Wonderful," said John. "How'd you get here so quick?"

"I flew. In that," said Dexter, nodding towards the airship.

"Wow! Really?"

"No of course not, you dozy sod," said Dexter, pushing himself to his feet. "I hitched a ride with our murderer, didn't I?"

"Peter Chard's here? Damn. I was hoping he'd still be at the house. I was planning on snooping around a bit before speaking to him."

"That's alright," said Dexter, jumping off the wall and into the yard. "I can have a look around while you talk to Peter."

"Really? Do you know what you're looking for?"

Dexter snorted. "Do you?" he said, with a tilt of the head. John searched for a witty comeback, because 'No, not really.' wasn't quite up to the job. "Look," said Dexter. "I've been sat on Donald Chard's lap for the better part of a year, learning everything about everything and a lot more besides. When you're a cat there's really not much else to do. If there's something wrong with what's going on I'll know about it. Trust me."

John didn't, but he didn't seem to have much choice either. "Fine. You have a look around, while I go and speak to the big man."

"You got it," said Dexter, slipping off behind some crates.

John watched him go, wondering if life could get any more strange. He suspected it could, but he really hoped that it wouldn't. "Right," he said. "Let's go see what had Henry so worried, shall we?"

Approaching the airship factory, John was in awe at the scale of the thing. A veritable cathedral of iron and brick, its buttressed walls stood a good hundred feet high – not as tall as a finished airship, but tall enough to hold its fully inflated balloon whilst it was under construction. The two huge sliding doors along its front stood slightly open, but John headed for the smaller, human-sized door near the corner of the building. Inside he found a small office housing a desk, some filing cabinets, a bench for visiting dignitaries, and an elderly woman busy making tea. She had a copper kettle in one hand, a silver teaspoon in the other, and she seemed to have lost the thread of what she was doing. All brown wool and determination, with a perfectly coiffed helmet of wavy grey hair, she was every bit the quintessential Little Old Lady. Just being near her gave John the urge to go help her with her shopping.

Weeping with quiet dignity as she bravely marshalled tea-leaves between caddy and pot, she didn't hear John enter. He was about to make his presence known when he spotted a plate of biscuits balanced precariously on the edge of the old lady's desk. Sidling up to it he slipped a couple into his pocket before clearing his throat to get her attention.

The old lady jumped, rattling the lid of the teapot she was holding. "Oh! I'm terribly sorry. I didn't hear you come in. Please, forgive me. I... Oh dear. Now where can I...? Oh dear." She ranged about, looking for somewhere to put the teapot. Finally she opted for the small pot-bellied stove in the corner, jamming it on next to the kettle.

Her back still to John, the old lady fished a crumpled handkerchief from the depths of her cardigan sleeve and gave her nose a noisy blow. Taking a moment to make herself presentable – checking her hair, straightening her cardigan – she eventually turned to give John the official company greeting.

"Welcome to Chard Mechanical," she said. "How may I be of assistance today?" She moved behind her desk with a grace that only years of comportment lessons could provide, sinking into her chair like a duchess sitting down to dinner. John almost felt compelled to bow.

"Please forgive me," he said. "If I am intruding I can come back later."

"No, no. That's quite alright. I—" Her facade began to crack, the tears rising once more. She reproduced her damp hankie in preparation. "Oh, I'm sorry, sir. What must you think of me? It's just... Have you heard? Such terrible news. Our founder, Donald Chard, is dead."

"Yes I heard. So tragic. And so unexpected, eh?"

"Yes I know! Truly it is. I still can't believe it myself. I mean, how could this have happened? How?"

Tears rolled down her face as fast as she could wipe them away. John went to the corner of the room and poured her a cup of tea. Placing it in front of her, he rested a gentle hand on her shoulder. "I put in two sugars, to help keep your strength up."

"Oh, bless you, sir. You are kind."

"Not at all. These things can be a real shock sometimes. You must have known Mr Chard well?"

"Oh, I did. Twenty years almost. Such a lovely man he was. So kind and thoughtful. Never forgot my birthday. You don't get many bosses like that these days."

"No, indeed you don't."

"I was his personal secretary right up until he handed the company over to young Peter to run. I almost retired when that happened. If Mr Chard hadn't asked me to stay on for a bit to help keep an eye on things, I would have done, too."

"Keep an eye on things?"

The secretary leant in towards John and dropped her voice to a whisper. "To keep an eye on young Peter mainly. I mean he tries, bless him, but he hasn't got the head for business his father had."

"I see. So Donald Chard had retired from Chard Mechanical. I had no idea."

The old lady was aghast. "Retired! Donald Chard would never retire. He just... went off to do other things, that's all. But he was still in here every week, making sure everything remained on the up and up. He may not have been running things, but Mr Chard was still very much in charge, you mark my words."

"So, as someone who saw him every week, you'd know if he was ill or not?"

"Ill? Mr Chard was never ill. Mr Chard was fit as a fiddle all year round. I don't know how he did it but the man was a bull. A bull I tell you!"

"And did he leave a will, do you know?"

The secretary squinted up at John. Leaning back, she gave him a quick head to toe. "Who are you, sir, if you don't mind me asking? You're not a journalist, are you?" She said the word 'journalist' in the same way most people would say 'debt collector' or 'mime artist'. John was sure to look suitably indignant at the very idea of such a thing.

"Good Lord no. I'm a friend of the family. I was hired by Mr Chard to look into the death of his son, Henry. And now I've been asked to look into Donald Chard's death as well." He told her the truth because some people you lie to, and some people you don't.

"Hired. By who? The family?"

"Exactly! By Peter Chard in fact. Which is why I'm here. I came to discuss it with him." Well not much you don't, anyway.

"So he's expecting you?"

"That he is."

"Then you'd better go on up then, hadn't you?"

"Up?" said John. "Don't you mean through?"

The secretary gave John a curious look. "You haven't been here before, have you, sir?"

The back door to the reception didn't lead to an office, as one might expect, but to an old iron staircase out on the factory floor. The staircase went up the side of the building to about half way up the back wall, where it turned left, following the back wall the rest of the way up until it reached a large metal box hanging impossibly among the rafters at the very top of the building.

John's knees wobbled just to look that high. He wasn't expected to go up there was he?

"Don't look so worried, dear," said the secretary, Mrs Crabtree (she had insisted upon a formal introduction before proceeding any further). "It's not as high as it looks. Or as dangerous. Honestly, no one has fallen off in ages. Just keep moving and don't look down, that's the trick. Keep moving and don't look down. But mostly don't look down."

She gave John a reassuring smile that did nothing to reassure him whatsoever. Placing one hand on the bannister – there only was the one, the other side being the wall – he placed his foot on the first step. The metal grate felt loose and unreliable, like a spinster aunt at a wedding reception who's had too much sweet vermouth. As he shifted his weight onto it, it creaked and groaned in a most alarming way. If said auntie had him trapped in an upstairs room and was promising to show him a thing or two John couldn't have been more frightened.

"Go on, dear. You get up there. I'll be along shortly with the tea."

Well that does it, thought John. *If she can do it with a tea tray I can certainly do it without one.* Taking a deep breath, he fixed his gaze straight ahead and began to climb.

As it turned out, the stairs were a lot sturdier than they looked. Sure, every one he stood on gave a funny little squeak or rattle, and the odd one shifted about more than it probably should, but on the whole they appeared to be well made and in no rush to go anywhere. *Score one for Hammersmyth's forgers*, thought John. *They've done us proud once again.* Of course, all that being said, John was more than happy to reach the platform at the half way point.

Taking a moment to munch on his pilfered biscuits, he looked out over the factory floor. From this great height he could see everything.

A dozen men were working on a new airship. Like the upturned ribcage of a giant metal whale, the ship's framework grew out of the ground, curving up to meet itself at an invisible point some-where near the top of the building. To its side, curved iron spars were being bolted together ready for hoisting into place, whilst over in the far corner, away from all the heavy lifting, someone had started work on the ship's gondola. It was just a box without walls at the moment, little more than a wooden framework, and it looked like it had been that way for quite some time.

John had expected more activity somehow. For such a big com-pany making such big machines he had thought they would need a much bigger workforce. A dozen men seemed like nothing really, not for such a monumental task. But, then again, they no doubt knew what they were doing. Perhaps a dozen men was enough, and it was only the size of their work, and the place in which they did it, that made their efforts appear small.

Speaking of effort, John couldn't put it off any longer. Turning his attention back to the staircase he began his ascent up the back wall, to the nesting place of the Lesser Spotted Boss Man bird.

John didn't know what to expect when he went through the office door, but he certainly wasn't expecting what he found.

Peter Chard's office had all the warmth and luxury of a cosy gentleman's study. There was rosewood panelling on every wall, most of which had plans and diagrams pinned to it, and a beautiful Persian rug that covered the entire floor. The wall behind the door held two bookshelves, between which was sandwiched an actual fireplace. How it didn't burn through the floor and drop into the factory below was anyone's guess. And at the far end of the room, behind a desk so unbelievably large it was impossible to imagine how they got it up there, sat Peter Chard. Lost in a world of ledgers and invoices, paperwork spread over every inch of his desk, he didn't seem to notice John enter.

There was a window to John's right, which looked out onto the field behind the factory. Through it he could see the airship he had spied earlier getting ready for take-off. Spooling up its engines, it slipped its moorings, the magnificent machine drifting slowly skyward as it turned to face the factory. He watched its nose tilt up as it rose to clear the building, enjoying a close-up view down the airship's entire length as it sailed overhead. As the airship's gondola came level with the window John waved to a tall man in an impressive looking hat which he took to be the ship's captain, and got a crisp military salute in return. He smiled. Wait till he told Emily when he got home. She'd be so jealous.

"For God's sake, Mrs Crabtree, will you just leave the tea and get out. You're letting all the heat out."

John looked over to find Peter Chard still deep into his paperwork. "Forgive me, Mr Chard, but I—"

Peter Chard's head snapped up, and as he caught sight of John, a look of fear flashed across his face. "What the hell? Who let you in here? I– Wait a minute, I know you. You were at the house today, weren't you?"

"Indeed I was, Mr Chard. John Sinister, as you may recall."

The look of relief that came over Peter Chard quickly gave way to anger. "What the devil are you doing here? I dismissed you, as *you* may recall."

"Indeed, you did," said John. "But fortunately I don't work for you, so I don't have to do what you say."

"No, you worked for my father, who is dead. And since you now have no employer, you now have no job. Or is that too difficult a concept for you to understand?"

"As a matter of fact, Mr Chard, I do have an employer. Someone who has asked me to look into not only your brother's death, but your father's as well."

"A new employer. Who? My sister?"

No, your cat, said John in his head. Out loud he said, "That I can't tell you, I'm afraid."

"Well I don't care who it is. I'm a busy man. I don't have time for the likes of you, so get out." Peter Chard returned to his paperwork, angrily scribbling notes as he pointedly ignored John's presence.

John took a few steps forward. "You must be very busy to be back at work so soon. I'd have thought you would want to be at home, comforting your sister."

"Perhaps I would, but I have a company to run. I've no time for grief."

"Spoken like a true businessman. Your father would be so proud."

Peter Chard snorted. "Not any more he wouldn't."

John took a couple more steps forward. "So how is business anyway?"

Peter Chard was stunned. "I beg your pardon?!"

"Only it looks a bit quiet out there. Not a lot going on. I mean, I'm no expert, but I would have expected something a bit more... industrious."

"How dare you!" said Peter Chard, leaping to his feet. "Who the hell do you think you are, coming in here, asking me such things? The impertinence of it. I should thrash you where you stand."

"Look, there's no need to—"

There was a massive spanner in Peter Chard's hand. Where he got it from John didn't see. He imagined a secret compartment in the enormous desk, where the spanner lived until it was needed. Another of Donald Chard's clever innovations no doubt. His final negotiating tactic, when all else failed.

"Get. Out," Peter Chard growled, gripping the spanner tight.

John, his eyes firmly fixed on the huge lump of iron, backed out of the room slowly. Sometimes it's hard to tell whether a man is bluffing or not, and sometimes it's easy. Very, very easy.

Leaving the factory by its big double doors, John went looking for Dexter. He wasn't on the factory floor, and a quick scout around the yard showed that he wasn't there either. That just left the small workshop to the side of the main building. Approaching the workshop he heard a strange noise coming from the field next door – a swishing, swooping, whacking sound that reminded him of school for some uncomfortable reason. *Now what could that be?* he wondered. *Kind of sounds like—*

John dove for cover as something loud and metal flew at his head. Landing in the mud, he rolled over to gape up at the bizarre contraption barrelling through the air above him. Someone had bolted a lounge chair to a steam engine, surrounded it with an ornate metal frame, topped it off with two sets of airship propellers, and then made it fly. Probably the little man in the leather helmet and goggles trying to pilot the thing, the one frantically pushing pedals and pulling levers, his arms and legs going in all directions like he was doing battle with a baby kraken. It looked like hard work, keeping the machine aloft, but he was doing it alright. And he seemed to be enjoying himself too. John could see the grin on his face from here.

Clinging to the back of the man's chair, and looking much less happy to be there, was Dexter.

The machine circled around John before coming to a stop in mid-air. Lowering itself to two feet off the ground, it crabbed sideways across the grass towards him. Then it jinked, hopped, and gave a splurt, before falling to the ground with a teeth-rattling thump. Its blades slowed and the noise died down until eventually the entire contraption came to a shambolic halt.

Lifting himself off the ground, John approached with caution.

The little man was already out of the machine and working on the controls when John got there. Dexter was sitting on the pilot's seat, next to an open toolbox.

"Er, hello?"

The man spun around. He had his goggles down around his neck, and in the two goggle-shaped holes on his grimy face John was surprised to find a young Japanese man staring back at him.

"Hello!" said the man, a little too loudly. "What you think? You like? She handles well, yes?"

"I guess so," said John. "Though to be honest I don't know what to think. What is it?"

"This my Whirlygig. She next thing in flying, if I can get her to behave. She still not big fan of landing. She wants to be off, up in the air!" The man laughed and threw his hands up, admiring his invention with the same look a doting father gives their mischievous child.

John had to admire his handiwork. Now that it had come to rest he saw the rotor blades were shaped like huge sycamore seeds, with a long, curved front edge that turned back on itself in a big loop. He'd seen sycamore pods whirring down to the ground many times. It never occurred to him that they might whirr up as well.

"It all about the angle," said the man, seeing where he was looking. "If you tilt the blade it pushes air down, and that pushes machine up. My idea. Very clever."

Normally arrogance grated on John, but the man didn't appear to be boasting. As far as he was concerned he was just stating a fact. And John had to admit he did have a point. It did sound very clever. "Why are there two sets of blades?"

"To stop her spinning away. Blades go in opposite directions, cancel out spin on chassis. Whirlygig stay pointing in one direction... most of the time."

The pilot adjusted something and pulled on a lever. It didn't move. He made another adjustment and tried again. Still nothing. "*Chikushou!*" he hissed, tossing his spanner into the toolbox. Fishing a rag out of his back pocket, the man wiped the grease from his hands.

"Hey, that your cat?" he said, pointing at Dexter.

"Er, yeah. Kind of."

"Do he talk?"

"Talk? No. Of course not. What makes you say that?"

"You sure? Because I swear I hear him talk."

"No. You can't have done. Cats don't talk, do they? That's crazy."

Dexter and the man both burst out laughing. "See!" said Dexter. "I told you. Didn't I tell you? Look at his little face. How priceless is that? Meat-sack, this is Nomko. He's the man who keeps Chard Mechanical ticking over. He fixes all the airships, keeps the omnibuses running, and, more importantly, he's the man who made me." Nomko and John shook hands.

"You're not from round here are you?" said John, surreptitiously wiping the remnants of Nomko's greasy handshake on his trouser leg.

"Very observant. No, I from Japan."

"And how did you end up here, if you don't mind me asking?"

"Not at all. I came over for big exhibition a few year ago, where I meet Mr Chard. He offered me job as Chief Engineer so I stay. Been here ever since."

"Wow. You must have really impressed Mr Chard for him to offer you a job like that?"

"Yes. He had a stand, all these steam machines. One of them stopped working so I fix for him. He very impressed, give me job on the spot."

"I see. So you were an engineer back in Japan?"

"No. I was sort of... acrobat. I came over with dance troop. But I always very good with machines. They break, I fix. Easy-peasy lemon-squeezy."

As Nomko went around the whirlygig gathering up his tools, John could see the dancer in him. He moved with confidence and grace, which was strange to see in a man of his calling. Most of the engineers John had met were lumbering, methodical men.

John remembered visiting the Japanese Exhibition when it was on; several times in fact. He'd found the living village quite fascinating, with its beautiful yet strange looking houses and its traditional workshops full of craftsmen and artisans. He couldn't remember seeing any dancers though. There'd been all manner of entertainment available within the grounds of the Buddhi Temple – wrestlers, musicians, shadow puppets, fire jugglers – but no dancing he could think of. Or at least nothing he recognised as dancing anyway.

He did remember Mr Chard being there though, showcasing the many inventions he hoped to sell to the Japanese now that trade routes had been opened up. It was strange to think of Nomko being called upon to fix one of his machines. You would have thought the great man able to take care of that himself, should the need arise. But if that truly was the case, and Nomko had been able to fix something Mr Chard could not, then it was no surprise he had offered him a job. He'd have been a fool not to.

"So you're the one responsible for this annoying little ball of fur, are you?"

Nomko laughed. "Yes indeed. Dexter is my pride and joy. He made from all the latest technology. Titanium actuators, micro-compressor valves, gyroscopic balance system. He quite the modern miracle." Nomko petted Dexter, the cat purring as it rubbed its head against his hand.

"That's great," said John. "But did you have to make him so..." He pulled a 'y'know' kind of face and Nomko chuckled.

"Not my fault," he said. "I only teach Dexter basics. He do rest himself. It his experimental analytical engine, you see. It learn as he goes."

"A learning engine? I've never heard of such a thing."

"It new idea. One of a kind. Very clever. It one of the things make Dexter so unique."

Dexter couldn't have looked smugger if he tried. "Alright," he said. "That's quite enough admiration for now. How did it go upstairs with boyo? Did he confess?"

"Not as such, no. He wasn't really up for answering a lot of questions."

"Ha! Neither would you be if you'd killed your own father."

"What is it you say?" said Nomko. "You think Peter Chard kill his father?"

"Of course," said Dexter. "Don't you?"

"Not really, no. He may be bit of a *iyana yatsu*, but he still an honourable man. I can not see him killing Mr Chard."

"What about you, Meat? Anything out of the ordinary going on in there?"

"Not as far as I could tell. Business seems on the up and up, what there is of it. It did seem awfully quiet, I thought."

Nomko nodded. "Yes, it is so. Do not tell anyone, but company not doing well. It get by, but still, could do better."

"Tell him about the break-in," said Dexter.

"What break-in?"

"Someone break-in a few days ago," said Nomko.

"Really. What did they take?"

"Nothing," said Dexter.

"Nothing?"

"Nothing," replied Nomko.

"Then how do you know there was a break-in?"

"Because someone in my workshop. They move my things. When I get up in morning, automotive engine not where I left it."

"What's an automotive engine?"

"Invention, like whirlygig, but different. Run on wheels."

"And how do you know it was moved?"

"It my workshop. I live there. I know when things move and when not."

"You live there?"

"Yes. Sleep in cot in back. Very comfy. Very cheap."

"But if you live there how come you didn't hear them break-in?"

"Because I in airship all night, fixing engine. I too far away to hear."

"And what about the night watchman? How come he didn't hear anything?"

"No night watch. He fired weeks ago to save money."

"Smart move, right?" said Dexter.

"Genius," said John. "So did you call the police, have them look into it?"

"We did. Waste of time. They not care because nothing was taken. But someone in my workshop. Move my stuff! I no happy about that."

"Nor should you be, mate," said Dexter.

"When was this break-in?" said John.

"Break-in was last night."

"Last night? The same night Henry was killed."

"Yes, that is so. Poor Henry. He good friend to Nomko. He help with automotive engine. Have some good ideas. Very clever. Very creative. It so sad that he is gone."

"That it is, mate. That it is," said Dexter.

The group fell silent as they remembered their fallen friend, their thoughts turning to moments lost, never to come again.

Nomko ended the silence by plopping his flying helmet back on his head. "Okay, I must go. Have much to do. It nice to meet you, Mr Sinister."

"Likewise," said John, shaking Nomko's greasy hand.

"And you, Little One. You stay out of trouble, yes?"

"I can't make any promises," said Dexter, winking.

Nomko laughed. Scratching Dexter behind the ear, he leant down and kissed him on the forehead before walking off across the field. Watching him go, Dexter turned back to find John grinning at him from ear to ear. "Don't get any ideas," he warned. "Only he gets to do that."

"Believe me," said John. "I wasn't."

"Good. So what do we do now?"

John caught the 'we' but he decided to let it slide. "Now I think we need to talk to the coroner, see if they're happy with the cause of death. Also, we need to have a proper look around the factory, see what's really going on in there. I forgot to say, but Peter Chard looked worried when I saw him. We need to know what he was worried about."

"And how do we do that?" said Dexter.

"You heard Nomko. There's no night watch anymore. We can come back later when there's no one about and have a good snoop around."

"Right. Well if that's the plan then you need to take me home first."

"What? Why?"

"Because I don't have enough steam to stay up all night, that's why. I need to recharge."

"Can't you find your own way home?"

"How? I don't know where it is. Or where *I* am for that matter. I've never left the house on my own before. Besides, you need to come up to the house. There's something I need to show you. Someone sent Mr Chard a note before he died."

"A note? What did it say?"

"I, um..." Dexter scowled. "Look, just come and see for yourself, ok? It won't take long."

John sighed loudly. "Fine. Come on then," he said, turning to leave.

"Er, you'll have to carry me," said Dexter.

"What? No way. You can walk. You've got more legs than me."

"I can't. I told you, I'm low on steam. I might not make it all the way there."

John glared at Dexter. "Okay, fine!" he hissed through gritted teeth. "Have it your way."

Scooping up the cat, John tucked him under his arm. Dexter was heavier than he was expecting. It was like carrying a sack of potatoes. A warm, furry, smart-arsed sack of potatoes.

As he carried Dexter across the field, John thought he heard him chuckling to himself. "Did you say something?" he said, making it quite clear from his tone that the answer better be no.

"What? Oh, no. No, nothing," said Dexter, hacking and coughing unconvincingly. "Got something stuck in my throat is all."

The air in the train compartment was thick with tension. John sat at the end of one bench with his arms folded, staring resolutely out the window. Dexter sat at the other end of the opposite bench, pretending to be asleep. They'd barely said two words to each other since leaving the factory. That had been a wise move on the omnibus, and in the train station – only old ladies and vicars can get away with having long conversations with their cats – but now it was starting to get personal.

More than once someone had come by, been tempted by the compartment's empty seats, only for them to take one look at its inhabitants and move on. The moody atmosphere leaked out through the cracks around the door, and no one with an ounce of sense wanted to get in the middle of whatever this geezer had going on with his cat.

At Turning Hill, John didn't offer to help Dexter out of the train. He simply held the carriage door open and waited, whilst Dexter hopped down and walked out of the station without a backward glance.

John found Dexter on the street, sitting waiting for him. "We should probably go in the back way," he said. "I don't want to run into all those journalists again. They'll only start asking questions."

"Whatever you say," said Dexter, setting off across the road. John trailed after him.

They found the back gate open, which was a relief. John did not want to have to get the both of them over the back wall. Heading up the cinder path, John started thinking about the stories in the papers. "Hey, you know you said you were sat on Donald Chard's lap for the past year. Did you ever see him with a will or anything like that?"

Dexter gave a moody shrug. "I dunno. I don't know what one looks like, do I?"

"It would have had 'Last Will and Testament' written at the top, and it would have started off 'I, Donald Chard, being of sound mind and body...'."

"Okay."

"So?"

"So what?"

"So did you see anything like that?"

"I dunno."

"What do you mean you don't know?"

"What do you mean what do I mean?"

"I mean either you did or you didn't."

"Fine! Then I didn't."

"But..." John gave Dexter a sideways glance. "What's going on with you?"

"There's nothing going on."

"Clearly there is, so what is it?"

"Look, just leave it, alright."

"Why? What is it? Why are you so—"

"Look, I can't read, alright! I never learnt how. So there. You happy now? You got it out of me."

"Okay, okay. Sorry. But it's nothing to get worked up about, y'know."

"Huh. Easy for you to say. You can read."

"Well, yeah, I guess so. But, I mean, it's not your fault they never taught you to read, is it? They probably didn't think you'd ever have to, on account of your being a cat and all."

"No, it *is* my fault. They tried to teach me but I just couldn't get it. It was the letters, all those funny shapes, they got all mixed up in my head. And the words, the words wouldn't sit still. No matter how hard I tried I couldn't understand any of it."

John and Dexter walked on in silence for a bit, but a different kind of silence to the one before. Leaving the back woods, they found themselves in Chard Manor's Healing Garden.

Henry's mother, Louise Chard, had been one of the most eminent herbologists of her time. If you were sick she invariably had a cure for what ailed you. Her healing garden was regarded as the largest, most comprehensive collection of medicinal plants in the country.

John had always found Mrs Chard to be a fascinating woman. She could make the cultivation and preparation of household anti-inflammatories sound like the most interesting thing in the world. He had respected her greatly, and had always been happy to help out in the garden whenever she needed a hand (they used to have to threaten him with the cane to get him outside when he was at school). The fact that Mary used to be out there most of the time as well, helping her mother, was purely coincidental.

"Y'know," said John, "I knew this guy once. Lovely fella. Smart as anything. Couldn't read to save his life. Got himself a job working the railways when he was a boy. Said he could do all the mechanical stuff just fine, but when it came to the timetables he couldn't make head nor tail of them. So what he did every night, he got his mum to read them to him and he memorised them, each and every one. By the time he'd finished that man knew the departure and arrival times of every train in and out of Hammersmyth, including week-ends, bank holidays, and the ones that run different on Wednesdays for no good reason. It was quite a feat and no mistake.

"Ended up assistant manager at Hammersmyth Central Station he did. Doing quite well for himself last I heard."

Dexter looked up at him. "Yeah?"

"Yeah. It just goes to show, there's more than one way to skin a cat. Metaphorically speaking that is."

"Yeah, I guess."

The two walked on.

As they approached the back lawn they heard hushed voices somewhere amongst the shrubbery. At the edge of the lawn, behind a large topiary bird, they came across Mary Chard and Spencer Shelby the Third standing closer to one another than John would have liked.

Where she was standing, amongst a confluence of flower beds, bushes, and trees, Mary was trapped, Spencer blocking the only way out. He didn't look to be threatening her in any way, but when Mary looked over and saw John coming he saw the fear in her eyes. "John!"

Spencer spun around, a scowl appearing on his freshly-shaven face. "Lefty! What the hell are you doing here?"

"That's funny. I was just thinking the same thing?"

"I came to offer my condolences of course. Mary's father died today, or hadn't you heard?"

John looked to Mary. "Are you alright?"

"Yes, I'm fine thank you, John." She looked like she believed it almost as much as he did.

John held out his hand. "Perhaps I could borrow you for a moment? There's something I'd like to ask you."

"Actually, we're not done talking," said Spencer, stepping between the two of them.

"Actually, we are," said Mary, barging past Spencer to go and stand by John. "Thank you for coming, Spencer. I appreciate your concern."

Spencer just about managed to force himself to smile. "Of course, Mary," he said, with a slight bow. "And you will consider what we discussed?"

Mary snorted. "I can assure you I will think of nothing else."

"Then I take my leave," said Spencer, bowing once more. With one last glare at John, he turned towards the house.

"Hang on a minute, Spencer," said John. "I want a word with you."

Spencer seemed to find the idea amusing. "Oh really? About what exactly?"

"About the night Henry died."

"Ah yes, I heard about your clumsy interrogation of Rosemont and the rest. How embarrassing for you. And for them also. Such an undignified way to go about things. And now you wish to subject me to the same treatment. Well, all I can say is, good luck with that."

He turned to go. John didn't have time to think. "I know you were the last person to see Henry Chard alive."

Spencer stopped. "Now who on earth told you that?"

No one. It was a complete shot in the dark. "I want to know what you two discussed before you parted ways, that's all. What did you talk about?"

"We didn't discuss anything. Whatever you heard, someone's telling you porkies, old boy."

"Don't you want to know what happened to Henry?"

Spencer smiled like a cat eyeing up a mouse. "Goodbye, Lefty. Always a pleasure," he said, walking away.

"The more you avoid my questions the more it looks like you've got something to hide," John shouted after him.

Spencer spun around.

"Why you impudent little toad! How *dare* you talk to me like that? I don't answer to the likes of you. People like *you* answer to *me*, got it? Or do you need a damn good thrashing to get that through that thick head of yours?" Spencer marched towards John only to find Mary in his path.

"Spencer, that is enough! Get ahold of yourself. How dare you start this nonsense, today of all days."

Spencer seemed surprised. Taking a step back he summoned up enough decency to be ashamed of himself. "My apologies, Mary. I'm sorry you had to see that."

"I think perhaps it's time you were on your way, Mr Shelby."

"Yes. Of course." He gave another quick bow. "Good day to you."

John and Mary watched him leave, John breathing a sigh of relief as he disappeared from view. Crikey, he hadn't had this many people threaten to give him a 'damn good thrashing' since his school days. Admittedly, it was a lot of the same people, but still, it showed he must be doing something right.

"Lands sakes, John, that wasn't very smart. You know what a hot-head he is. He might have hurt you, or even worse. The man has no control."

"I know. I'm sorry. I can't help it. He just winds me up something rotten."

"Yes, well, let's forget about him shall we?" said Mary, taking his arm. "Come, walk with me a while."

They headed towards the house. John looked around for Dexter but he was nowhere to be seen. He must have gone off to recharge.

"John, I want to apologise again for my brother's behaviour earlier. He can be a bit of a bully sometimes, especially when he's a little overwhelmed. I'm sure he didn't mean to be as insulting as he was."

"That's alright, Mary, no apology necessary. I've suffered far worse, as you may have noticed. The trick is to hear the things you want to hear and ignore all the rest."

"Indeed. Speaking of which, I notice that you're still asking questions about Henry, despite what my brother said."

"Yes. I feel like I owe it to your father. And to Henry for that matter. It wouldn't be right for me to just walk away now."

"That's understandable, I guess."

The two walked on in comfortable silence. Mary steered him toward the rose garden, guiding him between the fragrant bushes in whichever direction took her fancy.

"So how are you doing?" said John. "I mean, really? Has it all sunk in yet?"

Mary gave a long, heartfelt sigh. "I don't know, John. Probably not. I mean, Father and I had such a difficult relationship, I can't even say if I miss him or not. I only know that he's not there. Do you know what I mean?"

"Not exactly, if I'm being honest. But I can imagine."

"It's so strange to think that for years I blamed him for Mother's death. Hated him even, him and his stupid inventions. I've wished him dead a thousand times. But now that he's actually gone..."

John nodded. That part he understood. Louise Chard had died riding one of Donald Chard's experimental omnibuses. The boiler had exploded killing her instantly, and putting Mr Chard in the hospital for weeks. Mary had been devastated. She and her mother had been very close. So close in fact that she'd refused to visit her father in hospital, lashing out at anyone who dared suggest that she should. "Why should I go visit my mother's murderer?" she'd barked at John the one time he'd been foolish enough to offer his opinion. "He can rot in hell for all I care!"

Turning onto the back lawn they continued their slow stroll up to the house.

"Tell me, what are you doing tomorrow?" said Mary.

"I don't know yet. Why?"

"Well, I have this obligation I must take care of, and I was wondering if you'd like to accompany me?"

"I... don't see why not. What sort of obligation? Will I have to wear a special hat or something?"

Mary chuckled. "Only if you want to. No, it's this little shindig the family is sponsoring, over at Kelham Red Racecourse. Father would have gone but, well, now it falls to me to go in his stead."

Mary's gaze fell to the floor. John placed his hand on hers. "Do you have to go?" he said. "Perhaps it would be best to cancel, given the circumstances? I'm sure people would understand."

"No, I can't. It's too important. It must go ahead, and the family must be represented or people will take note."

Even in her grief she's a Chard through and through, thought John. "And you want to be seen there, out in public, with someone like me?"

"Why not? If I must attend it may as well be with someone I... like." Mary smiled, looking deep into John's eyes. But then her smile faltered. "However, if you don't want to go I understand. All you have to do is say."

"What? No. No, I'd love to go. Really I would. In fact, I would be honoured."

"Excellent. I'm so glad. Thank you, John." They arrived at the back door of the house. "Forgive me, I must skedaddle. But do leave your address with Hercules and I'll send a carriage for you in the morning."

"A carriage! Well, well, you are spoiling me."

"Absolutely, if I can," said Mary, squeezing his hand as she kissed him on the cheek. Disappearing through the back door, she left John in a bit of a daze.

"Hey, Guvverpoy."

John looked down to find Dexter at his feet. "What did you say?"

Dexter dropped the scrunched up ball of paper he had in his mouth. "I said, 'Hey, Loverboy.'"

"Right," said John. "Is this the note?" He picked up the ball of paper. It was a square of cream vellum, good quality, with a torn edge along the top. The writing was in black ink, in a flowing hand, and all the words were spelt correctly. He read out the contents. "'Dear sir, I have information regarding your son's death. Meet me tomorrow morning at eight at the centre of Waterdown Woods. Come alone.' And did he plan on going do you know?"

Dexter shook his head. "Didn't even entertain the idea. Just screwed up the note and tossed it in the bin."

John nodded. Folding up the note he slipped it into his coat pocket.

"So what time you picking me up tonight then?" said Dexter.

"You don't have to go, y'know. I can take care of it if you need to recharge or something?"

"Don't you worry about me, my son. I'll be right as rain in a few hours."

More's the pity, thought John. "Alright then, how does sunset by the back gate sound?"

"Works for me, Casanova." Dexter headed for the boiler room. "I'll see you then. Try not to trip over your tongue on the way out."

John looked for something non-lethal to throw at Dexter, but by the time he'd discovered a pine cone in one of the flower beds the cat was already gone.

John tried to think about the case on his long walk to the front gate, but his mind was all over the place. Every time he started getting his meagre facts lined up Spencer popped into his head, then all he could think about was slapping that stupid grin off his stupid face once and for all. John tried not to hate anybody. Like his mother always said, hating someone was like drinking poison and expecting it to kill the other person. He'd tried to let go of his anger towards Spencer many times over the years – many, many times – but he couldn't help it. Every time he saw the man he just wanted to beat him senseless with his own shoes.

The most annoying part of the whole thing was how much it clouded his judgement. He had a gut feeling Spencer was involved with Henry's death somehow, but he didn't know if that was because he actually was, or because he was jealous of Spencer's relationship with Mary (whatever that may be). He didn't think they were courting, but from what he saw they were certainly more than just good friends.

But if Spencer was involved, what would be the point? What would he have to gain from killing Mary's father and brother? Money, of course. With them gone Mary was in line to inherit a fortune, and if Spencer was to marry her all that wealth would be his. But was that really motive enough for murder? Spencer already had access to vast amounts of cash. What could he do with 'more' that he couldn't already do with 'loads'? Unless it was Chard Mechanical he was after? A marriage between Shelby Construction and Chard Mechanical would make them the largest, most influential corporation in the Britannic Empire. Now there was something worth killing for.

John tried not to think about Mary's impending inheritance, or about the fact that he appeared to have a date with Mary tomorrow. Was it a date? It felt like a date, but he didn't want to go making a fool of himself by making any assumptions. He was particularly inept at these sort of social cues, and he was very wary of reading more into a situation than was actually there.

The weird thing was she'd never shown any romantic interest in him before. So what was different now? She'd changed since school, that much was clear. She was quieter now, less angry, more subdued even. But had she changed so much that John was now her type all of a sudden?

Perhaps he'd changed. Perhaps he'd become the kind of man she was interested in? It was difficult to tell. He didn't *feel* any different. But, then again, what would a change in personality feel like?

John just knew that whatever was going on, he needed to remain calm. There were a million ways it could all go wrong, and only a few ways it could go right. He had to keep his wits about him and not get too excited – something which was easier said than done when somewhere in the back of his mind a little boy was doing cartwheels all over the place.

At the gate, the horde of journalists had surprisingly vanished. With deadlines looming they'd no doubt gone off to write their masterpieces ready for the evening edition. John would have to pick a paper up on his way home tonight. It would be interesting to see what so-called facts they decided to present to the world.

On the road, the eternal question presented itself, omnibus or Shanks's Pony? He had the money for the omnibus, but he'd been spending a lot recently. Maybe he should save a bit of cash and walk. It'd be good for him too. And he could certainly do with the exercise.

As he pondered his choices, John gazed across the road at the omnibus stop. His friend the chimney sweep was there again, smoking away, watching the front entrance of Chard Manor.

Watching? Yes, he was, wasn't he. Always in the same place, all hours of the day, a mass of cigarette ends at his feet. What else could it be? He wasn't waiting for an omnibus, that's for sure. The chain-smoking chimney sweep had some kind of an interest in Chard Manor.

The man spotted John staring. He looked around, trying to work out what he was staring at, until he realised it was him. Crushing out his cigarette the man made a show of standing and stretching, giving John one last look before wandering off down the road, his hands in his pockets, his pace leisurely. He whistled to himself as he walked, kicking at the pavement as he tried to appear as nonchalant as possible.

John crossed the road. Passing the omnibus stop he followed the man, taking his time so as not to spook him, but still walking fast enough to start gaining ground. The man looked over his shoulder. He saw John and sped up. John sped up, the man sped up – both still walking, but only just. They looked like two men trying to maintain their dignity as they rushed to catch the last train home.

The road ran alongside a six-foot high brick wall that belonged to the house opposite Chard Manor. It ended at a corner a hundred yards up the road. Reaching the corner the man cut right, disappearing from view. John jogged to catch up, but when he turned the corner the man was already well away, hurtling full pelt down the road, arms and legs pumping hard.

John gave chase.

He used to be a good runner at school. Not fast, he was never fast, but good over long distances. He had stamina, and that had put him ahead of the more athletic students more than once. But that was a lot of late nights and quite a few fish suppers ago. Ten seconds into the run he was starting to feel it. He wouldn't be able to keep this pace up for long. Thank God the other guy was a smoker. He looked done in already.

John started to gain ground. Seeing this, the man lunged for the wall beside him, somehow managing to scramble himself over the top. John followed, tumbling into a mass of thorny brush on the other side. Battling his way through the undergrowth he emerged onto a perfect sea of emerald green.

It was the most magnificent lawn John had ever seen. Not a weed in sight, not a blade out of place. Perfectly level from one side to the other, it was pristine grass-work of the highest order. But there was no time for admiration. The man was on the other side of the lawn already, his hob-nail boots gouging great muddy ruts in the lawn's perfectly manicured surface. John gave chase, following the man's tracks into the mass of shrubbery on the other side of the lawn. There was an angry shout from somewhere behind him but he ignored it.

Barging through the undergrowth, branches tugging and pulling at his clothes, John tried to go in a straight line but it was impossible. He got pushed this way and that by the thick foliage, soon losing track of where he was. Pushing through a wall of holly he tumbled out into a small clearing. He'd lost the man, and if he kept charging about the place he was going to lose himself too. Holding his breath John listened, hoping for a clue as to which way to go. He closed his eyes and tilted his head, thinking that would help for some reason.

Snap!

Someone was in the woods behind him, just the other side of all the holly. John crept towards the noise, keeping the thick foliage between him and them until the last possible second.

Bursting through the undergrowth, John skidded to a halt as he came face to face with the business end of a double-barrelled shotgun. It was pointed right between his eyes, and its owner was very, very angry indeed.

"Who the hell are you?! What're you doing here?!"

"Whoa! Take it easy. I'm nobody."

"Nobody! NOBODY! Have you seen the state of my lawn?!"

"The state of your what?"

"MY LAWN, MY LAWN. My magnificent lawn!"

"What? No. I didn't– What?" John found it hard to concentrate with a gun barrel quivering inches from his nose.

"You didn't? You didn't?! But you did, didn't you? Indeed you did. Fifteen years I've been cultivating that lawn. Fifteen years of seeding, fertilising, aerating, levelling off. Almost lost it to crab grass six years ago, but I got her back, didn't I? You're damn right I did! Fifteen years of work and you destroyed it in a matter of seconds!"

"Look, I'm sorry. But—" The gun barrel became more agitated.

"Sorry! SORRY! I'll show you sorry. I should shoot you right now, bury you in the compost heap. I could use you to fertilise the lawn. That'd show you, wouldn't it?! Oh, indeed it would. That would be *real* justice!"

"Wait! Let's talk about this."

The gun barrel lifted up, level with John's forehead.

"I tell you what, a shotgun in the face certainly focuses your attention."

"I imagine it does," said Dexter.

"I thought I was done for. I really did." Every time he thought about that gun barrel rising up, John felt sick. Even now, hours later, he still felt lucky to be alive.

"So what did you do?"

"Well, once it became apparent I wasn't about to die I was able to focus on the man holding the gun. Turned out it was some old fella, eighty-odd if he was a day. He didn't look like the lord of the manor so I assumed he was the gardener."

"Makes sense. He did seem to have some strong opinions about the local plant life."

"Indeed. Anyway, I apologised to him as sincerely as I could for destroying his damned lawn, which seemed to calm him down a bit, then he frogmarched me back over there and made me spend the next hour replacing divots and rolling out the damage that had been done." Dexter laughed. "And I tell you what, fair play to the man. He could barely hold that big old blunderbuss of his up by the end, but he kept it on me the whole time. I was more afraid he'd shoot me by accident than on purpose."

"Then what happened?"

"Then, when I was done, me and the old fella went to his shed and had a brew."

"He made you a cup of tea?"

"Yeah. He got out a couple of deckchairs and we sat there in silence, drinking our tea and admiring the lawn."

"How bizarre."

"No, not as bizarre as it sounds. Not at the time anyway."

"And what about the guy you were after?"

"Gone. No idea where. Don't even know why he ran. But he had something to hide, that's for sure."

"Well from what you said it sounds like he'll be back. I'll keep an eye out for him."

"Good idea," said John, stretching out his legs one at a time.

John and Dexter were sitting at the top of some steps, in a doorway opposite Chard Mechanical. As far as they could tell most of the workers had left hours ago, as had Peter Chard, but someone was still there. There was a light on in one of the windows, and the factory gates, although closed, had not yet been locked.

"Do you think it's Nomko in there, pottering about?"

"In the main building? I doubt it. He does most of his work in the workshop on the side."

"But he'll be around somewhere, right?"

"He usually is."

"Will he hear us snooping around, do you think?"

"Probably not. He'll either be so engrossed in his work he'll have no idea we're there or he'll be asleep, in which case an earthquake wouldn't shift him. That man could sleep through anything."

"But what'll we do if we run into him? Will he blab to Peter Chard if he sees us?"

"No idea, but let's not put him in that position, eh? He doesn't need the aggro."

"I'll do my best," said John.

"See that you do," said Dexter.

A chill wind blew down the street. John and Dexter pushed themselves a little deeper into the doorway.

Dexter glanced across at John. "Can I ask you something?"

"Sure. Go for it."

"Back there at the house, why did Shelby the Turd call you Lefty? Is it because of your name?"

John smirked. He didn't know if Dexter had heard Spencer's school nickname from Henry, or if he'd come up with it all on his own, he was just happy that it lived on.

"No, he's not smart enough for that. He thinks it's a clever play on words. I'm Lefty because I'm never right. As in always wrong, get it?"

"Really? Wow, that's disappointing. For some reason I was expecting something cleverer."

"Indeed. That's Spencer for you. One crashing disappointment after another." Dexter nodded. "I tell you what though, it starts to grate after a while. I mean, I know that's the point, and I try to ignore it, but you can't help yourself can you? That's why I challenged the Chess Club in the end, to try and put an end to it."

"Oh yeah, I remember Mr Chard mentioning that. You beat them all at once, right?"

"More or less. But yeah, as a group I beat them."

"How did you do that, by the way?"

John shrugged. "Easy really. I—" Across the road the light in the factory went out and the door to the reception opened. "Here we go," said John.

A knitted haystack stepped out into the cold moonlight and shuffled its way across the yard. "It's Mrs Crabtree, poor thing," said Dexter. "Bless her for working so late. I swear that whole place would fall apart without her."

John looked down at Dexter. "Y'know what, that may well be the nicest thing I've heard you say about anyone, ever."

"So? I can be nice when I want to be. Besides, Mrs Crabtree was always nice to me whenever I came visiting with Mr Chard. She used to put a saucer of milk down for me next to the stove, in case I was thirsty. Not that I could drink it of course, I don't need food or water. But I would pretend to, to make her happy. It was the least I could do. I think she misses her old cat something rotten."

At the gate, Mrs Crabtree struggled with the heavy new chain bought to replace the old one, but eventually she got it through the bars and around the uprights, locking it into place with the steel padlock. With a nod of satisfaction she trundled off down the road to catch the eight-thirty-two omnibus home.

John and Dexter waited until she was out of sight before crossing the road.

"Well we ain't going through there," said John, inspecting the lock.

"You need to start thinking more like a cat," said Dexter, hopping up some crates and disappearing over the wall.

John went after him. It was easier than it looked. He fairly skipped over the wall and down into the yard, though he did manage to miss the last crate, stumbling the last few feet onto the ground.

"Well done, Meat-sack. Very dignified."

"What? I landed on my feet, didn't I? Hey, perhaps I was a cat in a previous life."

"Huh. Don't flatter yourself."

Crossing the yard, John looked towards the workshop. It was dark and the door was closed. Nomko must have been in bed already. Either that or he was out for the night, not that they'd seen him leave.

The door to the reception was locked, as were the big double doors.

"Now what?" said Dexter.

"Now we do something cats can't do," said John. "Use tools." He produced a pen knife from his jacket pocket. Climbing on top of a small crate, he went to work on the window latch above the reception door. Popping it open, John got ready to climb through.

"Hey! Aren't you going to lift me up or something?" said Dexter.

"Lift you up? Can't you just jump through?"

"Yeah right. From what exactly?"

"Oh for God's sake," said John. Reaching down he grabbed Dexter by the scruff of the neck.

"Ow! Watch it. That's me you're grabbing."

"You'd rather I reached underneath and fiddled about a bit?" said John. Dexter didn't reply.

John deposited the sulky cat on the windowsill, from where he jumped down into the reception. Scrambling up after him, John somehow managed to get himself through the window, landing with a thump on the other side of the door.

"Where's the damn light?" he said, stumbling about the room. After knocking into every piece of furniture he could find, the lights suddenly went on by themselves.

Dexter was sitting on the reception desk, his paw on the lever of the self-lighting desk lamp. "Y'know what, mate, the only tool around here is you."

John couldn't think of a witty response. "Just start looking, will you? See what you can find."

"Whatever you say, Meat," said Dexter. "You start on the paperwork, I'll have a sniff about, see if anything smells funny."

John got behind the desk whilst Dexter went around the room sticking his nose into every nook and cranny and taking a good whiff. *My God, he is!* thought John. *He's literally sniffing for clues.*

The paperwork on the desk may have been as neat and organised as it was possible for it to be, but it was still a load of old gobbledygook to John. It may as well have been in ancient Greek for all the sense it made. There were lists of assets, incorporation papers, and what looked like some deeds outlining the transfer of ownership, but beyond that he had no idea what it all meant.

"How's it going?" said Dexter from the other side of the room.

"Terribly. How about you?"

"Well, they've got a bit of a mouse problem, but other than that I got nothing. I reckon the really good stuff will be up in Peter Chard's office. If we're going to find anything, that's where it will be."

"Er, yeah. Right. Peter Chard's office. Up the big stairs, yeah? The ones—"

"In the factory. Yeah. Those ones."

Oh joy, thought John.

On the other side of the reception door the factory was pitch black. John could barely see his hand in front of his face, never mind the staircase.

"I can't do this," he said.

"What? Why not?"

"It's too dark. I can't see."

"Didn't you bring a lamp?"

"Why would I bring a lamp?'

"To see where you're going in the dark of course. My God, have you never broken in somewhere before?"

"I... No. Not really. I mean once, at school, but that doesn't really count."

"Right. Well think of this as on-the-job training."

"But, er... But won't it be locked? His office, that is."

"It will, yes. But I know where he hides the key."

"Yeah, but– I mean—"

Dexter sighed. "Suck it up, Meat, because there's no getting round it. We need answers, and they're at the top of those stairs."

"Oh hell," said John, staring up into the darkness.

If he squinted he could just about make out the staircase, it's shadow being slightly darker than the other shadows on the wall. He could see his final destination just fine though. There was a window on the landing outside Peter Chard's office, and the moonlight coming through it illuminated the office door, enticing him up in no way whatsoever.

John turned to where he thought Dexter was last. "Are you alright on your own, or do you want me to carry you?"

"I'm good," called Dexter from half way up the stairs. "I can see fine in this light. Got very sensitive eyes, me."

"Well la-di-dah," said John under his breath.

"Pretty sensitive ears, too," said Dexter. "Just so you know."

"Wonderful," said John loudly. "I'm happy for you."

Dexter chuckled. "Come on, Meat. The longer you wait the harder it'll get."

"I'm coming, I'm coming. Don't rush me."

Somewhere in the darkness John heard the sound of padded paws on metal. Taking a deep breath, he began to climb.

If John thought going up in the daytime was nerve-wracking that's only because he hadn't considered the delights of going up at night. Every creak and groan was the staircase threatening to come off the wall, plunging him into a bottomless pit a thousand miles deep. He tried concentrating on the steps in front of him but it was too dark for that, so he instead focussed on the landing up ahead.

But rather than give him comfort that merely reminded him how high he was, and how far he had to fall if he didn't pay attention.

Reaching the halfway point was little solace. He stopped to catch his breath, and maybe calm down a little, but his heart was having none of it. Its plan for the situation seemed to be to have a heart attack and be done with it. At least that way it wouldn't have to climb any more of these damn stairs.

"Get a move on," Dexter called from the office landing. "I haven't got all day."

Cursing in his head, John started up the second flight of stairs. That cat was really starting to get on his nerves. With each step he came up with a new and colourful way to describe Dexter, none of them complimentary, and by the time he'd reached the landing he'd actually expanded his vocabulary somewhat (He wasn't quite sure what 'minking' was yet, he just knew Dexter wouldn't like it.).

"Well done. I almost died of old age waiting for you."

"And what a shame that would be," said John. "So where's this minking key at then?"

"On the lintel above the door," said Dexter, making a mental note to find out what minking meant later on. Retrieving the key, John opened the door.

It was brighter in the office than it was in the factory. The window to the outside let in plenty of moonlight. Or perhaps John's eyes were just getting used to the dark. Either way it made finding the desk lamp a lot easier.

John sat at Peter Chard's desk. There were two accounts ledgers laid out before him, both full of names, dates, and amounts, and both in an unexpectedly neat and flowing hand. Whoever their accountant was he had impeccable penmanship. Next to the ledgers was a scattering of invoices and receipts, all for different things and different amounts, and all made out to different people.

"So what have we got?" asked Dexter.

"More of what was downstairs," said John. "With the added bonus of some accounts as well."

"And is any of it of interest to us?"

"I don't know. I mean, I'm no accountant, but there does seem to be a lot more minuses than pluses, which confirms what Nomko said about the company being in trouble. But apart from that..." John's eye was caught by a piece of paper with writing on, half hidden beneath one of the ledgers. He fished it out.

"What's that?" said Dexter.

"It says 'The Peculiar Tools Company', followed by a long list of dates and amounts which total to... Wow!"

"What?"

"Which total to one heck of a lot of money."

"And what does it mean, do you think?"

"I don't know. But if it's of interest to Peter Chard then it's of interest to us. And look what he's written at the bottom. 'Lost?', with a big circle around it."

"So? They're making a loss. It happens sometimes."

"Yeah but it doesn't say loss, it says lost. Like it's something he wants to hide maybe."

"Interesting. Why would it say that?"

"I have no idea. But what I want to know is, is this one of *his* companies, or is it an outside contractor?"

"Well let's take the list with us, see what we can find out."

"No. We have to leave everything as it is. We don't want anyone to know we were here."

John went through the rest of the paperwork but nothing else stood out to him. It was just more of the same boring paperwork he'd looked at downstairs. He tried the desk drawers but they were all locked.

"Is there a key to the desk?"

"Probably."

"Do you know where it is?"

"No idea. Why? Didn't you bring any lockpicks?"

"Oh let's not go through that again," said John, heading for the door.

"Whatever you say, chief."

Clumping down the invisible staircase, John let his irritation carry him to safety.

Scrambling back through the reception window, John landed on the other side. Taking a moment to reposition his underwear and tuck his shirt back in, his eyes were drawn to Nomko's workshop.

What were the thieves-who-didn't-nick-anything up to in there? What was their interest in the automotive engine? In fact, what was an automotive engine in the first place? And how was it tied in to all this, if it even was at all?

"I'm going to have a quick peek in the workshop," said John. "I won't be long."

"What? No! You can't. That's Nomko's. You can't go in there."

"It's alright. I'm just going to have a look, see what's what."

"But Nomko's in there. What if he hears you?"

"I thought you said he could sleep through anything."

"I know what I said," hissed Dexter, "but it ain't right. What if he wakes up and sees you, what then? Nomko's a good guy. He'd have to say something. You can't go putting him in that kind of a position."

"Oh don't be so dramatic. I'll be quiet, I promise. All I want is a quick peek."

"A peek at what? Look, whatever's going on here, it's got nothing to do with Nomko. Trust me."

"I just want to see this automotive engine he told us about. It might be important."

"Huh. I doubt it."

"Well I'm going anyway."

"Fine! Suit yourself," said Dexter, storming off across the yard.

At the workshop, John was surprised to find the door unlocked. Pulling it open he panicked a little when he saw a light still on, until he heard the snoring. Opening the door further, he risked sticking his inside.

Nomko was nowhere to be seen. From the sound of the snoring he was at the back of the room, behind several layers of over-burdened shelves. John could make out a little shed back there, Nomko's bunkhouse presumably. The lights inside the shed were out and the door was closed, making the volume of his snoring all the more impressive. That little guy really knew how to sleep. The light John had seen came from a lamp on a workbench that had been left burning.

The front half of the workshop was flanked by two large work-benches, every inch of which was covered in the kind of things men meant when they talked about something's 'inner workings' – complicated fiddly little devices that did intricate and important jobs. But they weren't what caught John's attention. That honour went to the machine in the middle of the room, the big, shiny, four-wheeled contraption that simply had to be the automotive engine.

About the size of a large carriage, only longer and thinner, it reminded John of an omnibus, although this thing only had room for two passengers, including the driver, as the back half was taken up by an enormous engine connected directly to the rear wheels by a complex set of gears and pistons.

The wheels themselves were too big for the machine. They made it look all gangly and hard to control, which explained the heavy bumpers that had been fitted front and back. But it also looked fast, faster than an omnibus at least. Such a big engine on such a small machine, it had to have quite a turn of speed. If someone really had taken her out for a spin John couldn't blame them. He desperately wanted to have a go himself.

Pushing the workshop door closed, John went looking for Dexter.

He found him sitting on the wall by the gates, trying not to look huffy. "Don't look so worried," said John, climbing over the wall. "Everything was fine."

"Great. I'm so happy for you," said Dexter, jumping down to the street beside him. "Are you going to take me home now or what?"

"Can't. It's too late. There's no train this time of night. You'll have to come back with me to my place. I'll take you back in the morning." Dexter was quiet. "Is that okay? Have you got enough steam to last until then?"

Dexter scowled up at John. "Don't you worry about me," he said. "I'll be fine." Marching off down the street, his tail in the air, he didn't look to see if John was following him or not.

John didn't have the heart to tell him he was going the wrong way. Or, at least, not the right way. Not exactly. They'd still get home, eventually, but Dexter's route was definitely the long way round.

John set off after him, resigning himself to the longer walk. It was easier than trying to get him to turn around. He was pissed off enough already as it was.

CHAPTER 3

SUNDAY

John awoke when something hard and furry batted him in the eye.

"What the hell?!" he protested, throwing up his hands to protect his face.

"Wake up, Meat. There's work to be done."

John carefully opened his other eye to find the scowling face of Dexter staring down at him.

"For God's sake. What's your problem?"

"You! You're my problem. Now come on, move it. There's things to do, people to see. Let's go!"

John was tempted to point out the irony of a cat complaining about laziness but he couldn't be bothered.

Dexter leapt to the ground as John dragged himself upright. Padding to the centre of the room, he stood watching with barely concealed contempt as John tried to deal with the fact that it was morning.

John had managed to drag on his pants and was doing up his trousers when he heard the front door slam. Emily came charging in, followed by her mother, a bunch of peacock feathers clutched in her muddy hand.

"Unca John, look what I– KITTY!!!"

Dexter tried to run but he didn't stand a chance. He hadn't gone two steps before little Emily scooped him up in her arms and gave him an almighty hug, rocking from side to side as she made overjoyed 'Mmmmm-mmhh!' noises. John had to stifle a laugh. The look on Dexter's face was priceless.

Emily was unbelievably happy, her mother less so. "Wonderful. Another stray cluttering up my home. And where did he come from, pray tell?"

"Oh. I, er...."

"Whass'is name, Unca John?"

"His name? Um..." John grinned. "His name's Fluffycakes, I think."

"Fluffycakes! Oh, I wub Fluffycakes. Eh'oh, Fluffycakes. I wub you." Dexter glared at John like he wanted to set him on fire.

"Actually, his name's Dexter. And you need to be careful with him, Em. He's very delicate."

"Okay, Unca John," said Emily. She put Dexter down, the cat charging out of reach the second his feet touched the floor.

"Emily, why don't you go get Dexter a saucer of milk from the kitchen?" said Jane.

"Okay!"

She ran off. Jane, hands on hips, turned her attention to John. "He's not staying."

John held up his hands. "Don't worry. I'm just cat sitting for a friend. They had to go away suddenly, but they'll be back tonight. You won't have to see him again after today."

"Good. I've got enough to deal with round here without adding stray animals to the mix." The forcefulness of her protest was diminished by the way she knelt down to tickle Dexter behind the ear.

Emily returned with a saucer filled to the brim with milk. She carried it slowly, with extreme concentration, being careful not to spill a single drop. Placing it in the middle of the floor she sat down next to it and waited, an excited look on her grubby, grinning face.

All eyes turned to Dexter.

The cat seemed to let out a sigh. Walking reluctantly over to the saucer, Dexter sat down next to it and started lapping at the milk, delighting little Emily who began stroking him from head to tail with a great deal of care and attention.

John left them to it. He followed his sister into the kitchen where she'd started preparing breakfast. Whilst she whipped up a load of scrambled eggs on toast, John set about making the tea.

"You got back pretty late last night," said Jane. "What were you up to?"

"Oh. Um... Working. I was working. I've, uh, got a new job."

"Working? Wow. That's great. Odd hours though, eh? Your boss must be a bit of a hard-case, keeping you out that late. Is he tough to deal with?"

John filled the teapot, keeping his back to his sister. If she got a look at him she'd know he was hiding something, she always did. "He can be a bit difficult sometimes, but I'm getting used to his little quirks." He found a couple of clean cups and began doling out the sugar.

"Well don't worry. I'm sure he'll be a lot easier to deal with now that he's dead."

"Yes, I imagine that—" John's teaspoon paused mid-air. "Who told you I was working for Donald Chard?" A newspaper landed on the table in front of him.

John's picture was front and centre, the one of him talking to the policeman outside the gates of Chard Manor. He had his hand out, offering the policeman Mr Chard's letter. It all looked very official, like he was handing out orders. It was a good photo, perfect for the front page. He was in it, and even *he* wanted to know more.

The headline below was full of intrigue too:

CHARD FAMILY MYSTERY DEEPENS

The ever-inventive Mr Bumbleton had pegged him as a Private Detecting Agent, searching for the 'lost will of Donald Chard' (something John had to admit he quite liked the sound of). There was no talk of anything suspicious going on, no speculation about either of the two deaths, just lots of rumours of a family in turmoil and a business on rocky ground after the loss of its founding father.

"Something you want to tell me?" his sister said.

"Actually, yes. Yes there is."

John told his sister everything that had happened so far. Or at least almost everything. He had to leave a few things out. Dexter and the break-in were no-go areas, as were a lot of the more dangerous elements. He didn't want her to worry unduly. But still, once he'd finished he'd told her a good eighty percent of what was going on. Well, maybe seventy-five. Or possibly seventy. But certainly no lower than that.

By the time he was done making up a plausible reason for being out late last night – a stake-out of the factory with absolutely no going inside whatsoever – Jane had her worried face on. "You be careful, John. You know how these rich folks are. They take care of themselves first, and no one else second. People like you and me, we're expendable to them."

"Don't worry. I know what I'm doing."

"With all due respect, John, when do you ever know what you're doing?"

The kitchen door banged open and Emily tottered in, a very unhappy Dexter clasped firmly in the warmth of her loving embrace. He was defeated, a broken cat, completely resigned to whatever this little girl had planned for him next.

"Mum, can we keep Dexter? Pleeeeeease."

"No, we can't. He belongs to someone else. Right, Uncle John?"

"Right. Sorry, Em, but he's got to go back to his owner." Emily looked crushed. John could see the tears waiting to explode forth. "But maybe we can get you your own cat... or... something?" He trailed off under his sister's withering glare.

"Oh! Can we, mum? Can we gedda cat?!"

"No we can't. There are enough mouths to feed around here as is, including yours, young lady. Now put that cat down and sit. It's breakfast time."

Emily reluctantly let go of Dexter, the cat bolting up onto a chair in the corner of the room from where he could keep a sharp eye out for the next humiliation.

Dexter was lucky, he only had to suffer one more extra-long hug from Emily before she left with her mother to go to school.

He was up on the kitchen table as soon as the front door closed. John showed him the newspaper.

"Looking good, Meat."

"I'd argue with you, but who'd believe me?"

"So what does it say?"

"Oh it's just more speculation about the rumour that Donald Chard died without a will."

"And you don't think it's possible?"

"It could be, but I can't see it myself. He was smarter than that. However we should probably check it out, just in case. You never know, stranger things have happened." Dexter nodded as John considered the mechanical cat for a moment. "So what's the score with you and food?"

"What do you mean?"

"Well I saw you drink the milk, but you said you don't have to eat, so how does that work?"

"What can I say? I've got an internal storage system, so I can pretend if I really have to. The worst part is getting it back out again later. I don't have an exhaust port, so it all has to come out the same way it went in."

"Ugh! So you don't have a—"

"No, I don't. I have a charging port instead. That's where I plug in to recharge my steam."

"Crikey," said John, sitting back in his chair and leaning ever so slightly sideways. "That's... unusual."

"To you, maybe."

"So where is it? Under your tail or something?"

"Yeah, it's– Hey! Pack it in."

John jerked upright. "What? I wasn't looking. Honest."

"Sure you weren't," said Dexter, shuffling his back end as far from John as he could.

"So, hang on. If it's so nasty regurgitating the things that you eat, why eat them in the first place?"

Dexter shrugged. "I dunno. Helps me blend in, I guess? And it makes people happy. They get all funny if you ignore the stuff they give you."

"It makes them happy?" A look of delight spread across John's face. "Oh my God! You like Emily."

"What? No!"

"Yes you do. You like her. The big tough kitty has a soft spot for little girls."

Dexter glowered at him. "Are you done yet? Can we go? We need to go talk to the lawyers, sort this will nonsense out."

"Yeah, sure. We will. But later. I've got to meet up with Mary first, remember?"

"Oh come on, we don't have time for that."

"Yes we do. And if we didn't, we'd make time, got it?"

Dexter shook his head. "Honestly, you meat-sacks and your mating rituals. It's ridiculous. No wonder you never achieve anything. Think of all the things you could accomplish if you didn't spend half your time being led around by your—"

"Hey, that's enough! This is happening, so deal with it. Or don't, I don't care. In fact, feel free to find your own way home. I'm sure that'll be easy for a smart cat like you."

John and Dexter stared at each other until, with a dismissive snort, Dexter jumped off the table and went back to his chair in the corner, where he descended into a profound sulk whilst he waited for John to finish his breakfast.

The carriage Mary sent for him was the finest John had ever seen. The padded leather seats were spring-loaded, ironing out all the lumps and bumps of the road, the window curtains and wall coverings were both silk, judging by the feel, and there were actual flowers in the wall vases. No one put flowers in their vases, not even the Queen (probably). The whole set up reeked of luxury, which was why John was glad he'd taken the time to dress for the occasion.

He had on his new suit and jacket, his shiny new shoes, and he'd even washed and combed his hair, leaving his black cap at home so that he didn't mess up all his hard work. He hoped Mary appreciated the effort, because Dexter sure didn't. On the bench opposite, the mechanical cat was giving John the stink-eye something rotten.

"Are you going to be like this all day?" said John.

Dexter turned to look out of the window, making a point of ignoring him, so John decided to do the same. Upsetting the cat seemed to be easier than giving a dowager Duchess an attack of the vapours. If he spent all his time worrying about Lord Stroppy's mood-swings he'd never get anything done.

The carriage pulled up outside Kelham Red Racecourse.

The Kelham Red had been the most famous racehorse in all of Hammersmyth in its day. A rusty-coloured thoroughbred that flew over the fences, it won the Smithy Stakes three years in a row, and had been on course for a record fourth win when it fell, broke its leg, and had to be put down. Everyone had loved that horse, mostly because it won them a lot of money. That's why they'd named the racecourse after her a year later, as a mark of respect. Quite how that respect extended to having the horse stuffed and put on display in the racecourse's entrance hall was a bit beyond John, but he tried not to think about it. It was what the people wanted apparently, so who was he to argue?

John was very familiar with Kelham Red Racecourse. He used to go there all the time back when he had an iron-clad, fool-proof system for beating the ponies. That had lasted about a month. He'd given up betting on horses and taken up poker when he decided he preferred winning over losing.

It was an odd place for a date, which made John wonder once again if it was indeed a date. There wasn't even a race on today as far as he knew, although something was going on in there. A steady stream of people all dressed in their Sunday best were making their way through the track's triple-arched entryway.

John and Dexter followed the crowd through the dark entrance hall. It echoed to the sound of tinny music, and there was candyfloss and popcorn on the air. Emerging out into the light, they discovered a steam fair in full swing in the centre of the racecourse. Brightly painted carousels, gyrating swing-chairs, and rocking pirate ships competed with one another for people's attention, their pipe organs and player pianos plunking out a litany of unrecognisable tunes whilst atop each stand and stall animated mice, automated rabbits, and more than one mechanical cat beckoned the passing punters to 'Come on in!', 'Have a go!' and 'Win a prize for the pretty lady!' their smiles fixed and humourless, their eyes glassy and dull.

"Look at them," sneered Dexter. "They're hideous. Honest to God, who'd make such a thing?"

"Oh I dunno. That cat on the merry-go-round is kinda cute. Why don't you go over there and say hello? You never know, you might get lucky."

"You're not funny, y'know."

"Lighten up, Dexter. I—"

John spotted Mary in the enclosure below, making her way towards him. She had on a fine white dress that looked absolutely stunning, with some long white gloves, a white lace parasol, and a wide-brimmed hat to finish off the look – which, of course, was also white. John couldn't take his eyes off her.

She must have been at the steam fair having a look around before the race began. It was unlikely she was down in the enclosure placing any bets. Not only was she not the type, but from what John could see there wouldn't be much point. There only seemed to be one race scheduled today, three riders, with some fairly even odds. No one was going to be making a fortune today, although there were plenty inveterate gamblers in the enclosure who seemed eager to try.

Dexter saw the way John was looking at Mary and grinned. "Why don't you go over there and say hello? You never know, you might get lucky."

"Oh, ha ha," said John. "Listen, you need to make yourself scarce. She might wonder what I'm doing here with the family cat."

"Not a problem. I don't fancy watching you make a fool of yourself anyway." Slipping off between the legs of the crowd, Dexter headed for the steam fair.

John became incredibly nervous all of a sudden. His butterflies had butterflies, his heart was going like the clappers, and he couldn't stop his palms from sweating. *This is ridiculous*, he thought. *I have to get ahold of myself.* Closing his eyes he took some deep, calming breaths. He felt his heart rate slow, his body relax, his mind begin to settle, until eventually he started to feel like himself once more.

When he opened his eyes, Mary was standing right in front of him.

"Yah!" he squealed, his hand flying to his mouth. Mary burst out laughing. "Sorry," said John, lowering his hand.

"That's quite alright," said Mary. "So you made it then?"

"Yes indeed. Thank you for the carriage. It was lovely."

"Did you like it? Oh I'm so glad. Yes, I do like that one. So elegant, don't you think? I thought it was high time we got some use out of it. Father never did take it out much, which always seemed such a shame to me."

"Well it certainly does the job," agreed John. "So, are you going to tell me what's going on? Are we here to see a horse race or something?"

"Ah!" said Mary, with a knowing smile. "Come with me and I'll tell you all about it."

Mary led John into the stands above the entrance hall. Its ornate rows of seats were full of the great and the good of Hammersmyth society, sipping champagne and chatting while they waited for the fun to begin. Nodding a few hellos as they climbed the steps, Mary led John to a private box up at the back of the stand. It held two plush, oak chairs, a selection of canapés, its own bottle of chilled champagne, and a personal butler who bowed deeply as they entered the box.

"Please, have a seat," said Mary. "Would you like a drink?"

"No, not for me thanks. I'm trying to cut back."

"I see. Some fruit juice then, perhaps? Damson and rhubarb? Or maybe some pineapple?"

"Sure. Whatever's going is fine with me."

"And I'll have the same," said Mary, addressing the butler. With a small incline of the head the man showed his understanding, and left.

"Well, this is fancy," said John.

"I know. Terrible, isn't it? I can't stand these public displays of wealth myself, but sadly, it has to be done. If you don't flaunt it, people think you haven't got it."

"I wouldn't know," said John. "I've never had enough of it to worry about... it."

Mary smiled. "Thank you for coming, John. I do appreciate your being here."

"Not at all. It's my pleasure."

Mary took a deep breath, filling herself with the outside world. "It's so good to get out of the house. You can't imagine what it's like there at the moment. Those darn journalists are all over the place. They keep sneaking onto the grounds, peeking in windows, like they're going to uncover a scandal of some kind. It's enough to drive you mad."

"I can imagine. But don't worry. I'm sure they'll leave once the will has been read."

"I don't understand. Why would that make a difference?"

"You mean you haven't heard the rumours?" No, of course she hadn't. People like Mary Chard didn't read the local chip wrapper. "Apparently there's a rumour going round that your father died intestate, that he was at his lawyers' making out his will when he passed."

"Oh for heaven's sake! Is that what it is? How ridiculous. I thought these people were just ghouls. I didn't realise they were morons as well."

"So your father did make a will then?"

"Of course he did. Years ago."

"Did you ever see it?"

"I– Well, no. Not exactly. But he told us about it. He said he was going to make one... after mother died."

Mary lapsed into silence so John decided to change the subject. Unfortunately, he didn't realise what the new subject would be until the words came out of his mouth.

"I was surprised to see Spencer yesterday. Does he come round often?"

"What? Spencer? Um, no, thank God. Hardly ever, in fact. Yesterday was something of an anomaly."

"Really? Because I thought—" This time John heard the next sentence in his head and managed to stop himself. If only he could have stopped himself sooner.

"Thought what, John?"

Well, there was no going back now. "It's just I thought the two of you looked quite intimate for two people who hadn't seen each other in a while, that's all."

"Yes, I see," said Mary, a guilty look in her eye. "Yes, well, that's probably because Spencer and I were seeing each other for a little while, not so long ago."

"Oh," said John, his face nowhere near as expressionless as he thought.

Mary gave an imperceptible shrug. "It was when I was summoned back from the Americas. I did it as much to annoy father as anything else. His dislike of anything to do with the Shelbys was the only thing guaranteed to get under his skin. I was angry, and I was acting out, and Spencer... Spencer was just the easiest way to do that.

"It didn't last long, and it ended months ago, but still, it's humiliating to think that it ever happened in the first place. I... I hope you understand?"

"Mary, you don't have to explain yourself to me."

"But I do! Of course I do. I don't want any confusion between us, John. I have no interest in Spencer, or anyone else like that. Not anymore. I'm looking for someone kinder, and more genuine." Mary reached out and took John's hand. "Someone who can make me laugh every now and then."

She squeezed his hand, looking deep into his eyes, and John panicked. "Did I ever tell you how I beat the Chess Club at chess?" he blurted.

"Oh yes, your famous victory. No, you never did tell, and I always did wonder. Seven simultaneous games of chess. However did you do it?"

"Well, I realised as soon as I made the bet that I was never going to beat the entire Chess Club, especially not all at once. Despite appearances they had some pretty decent players. Thankfully though, they let me set the rules, which meant I could kind of... cheat, a little bit.

"I took the six best players they had and divided them up into three pairs in my head. I made three of them white, and three of them black, then I memorised the opening moves from the three white players, so that I could play those moves against the three black players on the other side of the room. Then I remembered *their* opening moves, and played those moves back against the first three.

"You see, I never actually played *any* of them. All I did was remember their moves, and then mirror those moves across on their designated opponent's table. It looked like I was playing six games at once, when in reality one half of the group was playing chess against the other."

"Gosh! That's amazing. So you were always going to have an equal number of wins and losses across the six games, because half of them were bound to lose against the other half."

"Exactly."

"But what about the seventh game? Who were they playing?"

"That was the tricky one. That one I had to play straight. So I pitched myself against the weakest player they had, who, as it happens, was Spencer. As long as I beat him I'd win the bet. Thankfully, he's far worse at chess than I am. I beat him easily, ending up with four wins and three losses which, as you know, meant I won against the group overall."

Mary clapped her hands in delight. "Goodness, John. How very clever of you. How audacious! I never would have guessed. I mean, I always knew you were smart, but this..."

The look on her face had John in raptures. Basking in the glory of her smile he couldn't be happier. The triumph of the moment was so great he could almost hear trumpets in his head. No, wait a minute, he really *could* hear trumpets. Where on earth was that coming from?

Down on the track, a dozen liveried trumpeters had lined up to announce the start of the race. John and Mary turned their attention to the start line to see today's runners and riders trot out.

John was surprised. He'd been expecting horses, and although horses were what he got, they weren't quite the horses he was expecting.

Dexter wove his way through a forest of legs, trying not to get trampled on.

He'd never been around this many people before. It was disconcerting. He'd lived his entire life in the manor house, and no one ever came there. Oh, you got the odd dinner party or business meeting, but Dexter could stay out the way of those easy. This thing, this steam fair, was an entire world of moving limbs that didn't care that he was there at all. The only way to navigate this mess was to dart from cover to cover hoping he didn't accidentally get hit in the head along the way.

It didn't help that the people attached to those moving limbs were often distracted by all the dancing foxes and waving bunny rabbits. Dexter avoided looking at the steam fair's automata, especially the cats. They made him uneasy. Is that how people would look at him if they knew? Like some novelty item there for their amusement. The very idea set his teeth on edge. Dexter had no problem with people not liking him, you couldn't like everyone, but he hated the idea of not being thought of as real. He couldn't think of anything worse than to be dismissed or ignored, to be treated like you didn't matter. To him it was worse than hate.

Thank God Sinister didn't do any of that. The man might be a tool, and utterly infuriating, but at least he talked to Dexter on a level, treated him like an equal. Sure, he didn't do what he was told most of the time, which was annoying as hell, but at least he listened.

Anyway, what did it matter what other people thought, *he* knew he was real. So what if he was steam powered, or that he wasn't as agile as a meat cat? He could still do almost everything else they could do, and more. In fact in many ways he was better than a 'real' cat. At least he didn't shed on the furniture (well, not much anyway). And if he couldn't climb a tree, well that just meant he didn't get stuck all the time, didn't it?

Dexter heard something that stopped him in his tracks – a loud, mocking, malicious laugh that made his lubrication run cold. Ducking under a tablecloth he headed towards the sound, weaving his way through table legs and boxes of toys to come out into a small clearing among the steam fair's enclave of games of skill and chance.

There he was, the biggest tool of them all, Spencer-bloody-Shelby the Third.

Spencer was standing at the coconut shy, tossing a wooden ball in his hand while the shy's attendant dutifully replaced its three coconuts back on their respective sticks. The attendant, a stocky young man in overalls and a flat cap, looked livid, and Spencer was loving it.

"Three more," he said. "Three more and she's mine."

"Yes, sir," said the attendant. "That would indeed seem to be the case."

There were a number of prizes strung up around the coconut shy, all with different numbers on them, the best of which was a large stuffed bear in a bow tie with the number '9' pinned to its chest. That seemed to be the one Spencer was going for, from the looks he kept throwing at it. It looked imported, and expensive. No wonder the stall owner was worried.

Stepping in front of the last coconut, the attendant took a little longer fixing it in place than he had the other two. "Now remember, sir," he said, stepping to one side. "They has to be all in a row, like. Miss one and you's gotta start again."

Spencer grinned. "I remember. Don't you worry about that."

Dexter gnashed his teeth together. God how he hated Spencer Shelby the Third. He'd never met a human he despised more. The man wasn't just mean, he was deliberately cruel. And the way he treated cats was downright deplorable.

They'd only met the once, although met was probably too strong a word for it. Dexter had been walking through the library at Chard Manor, minding his own business, when a massive compendium of steamships had slammed into the wall above his head, frightening the life out of him. It sent him scurrying for the door, the sound of Spencer's mocking laughter ringing in his ears. That was why Dexter had hidden when they ran into him in the garden yesterday, he didn't want to find out what Spencer would decide to throw at him next.

The impact broke a vase, the book bouncing off the wall and into a nearby table. That brought everyone out. Caught in the act,

Spencer had blamed Dexter, and he would have gotten away with too if Dexter had been any other cat. But later on, in Mr Chard's study, Dexter had been able to tell the big man exactly what had happened.

The next day, Mr Chard had banned Spencer Shelby from the house. The vase had been a gift from the Japanese Ambassador, like that damned terracotta warrior that loomed over the entrance hall. An incredibly rare and expensive piece of porcelain, it was just the excuse Donald Chard had needed to get 'that Shelby boy' away from his little girl. Truth be told he hadn't even liked the thing, but he'd liked Spencer Shelby the Third even less, so when he turned up the next day like nothing had happened, Mr Chard had taken great pleasure in tearing him a new one before sending him on his way.

That had been fun to watch, almost as much fun as what was unfolding before him right now. Dexter could see what was coming, even if Spencer Shelby couldn't.

Spencer sent the first two coconuts flying, his aim strong and true. But when the ball hit the third one there was a loud *thunk*, the coconut barely shifting position as the ball bounced off into the side of the booth.

"What the hell?!"

"Oh, I'm sorry, sir. Looks like you caught the stand on that one. Such a pity. Still, it was a good effort. Better luck next time, eh?"

"Caught the stand? What rot. I hit it and you know it."

The attendant shrugged. "But you can't have, sir. See, the coconut is still in its place. If you had hit it, it would have fallen over, wouldn't it, sir?"

The attendant exuded innocence, as if butter wouldn't melt, and finally Spencer saw it. "It's a fix!" he said. "It has to be. You've done something to it, glued it or something?"

"Now, sir, there's no need to be like that. This is a square game, you ask anyone."

"Hogwash. The game is rigged and I'll prove it." Spencer put a foot on the counter, ready to leap across, only to find the business end of a pick-axe shaft pressed against the centre of his chest.

"Please, sir," said the attendant softly. "Let's not make a scene, eh? It would be an awful shame for anybody to get hurt over a game of coconuts." Shelby glared at the attendant, actually weighing up his limited options, before finally coming to his senses and lowering his leg. "There's a good gentleman. Now, to show there's no hard feelings, have this here, with my compliments." He offered Spencer a scrawny little coconut from the Knock-One-Win-One box.

Spencer didn't even consider his prize. Straightening his jacket, he locked eyes with the attendant. "You're gonna get yours one of these days, mate. You mark my words."

The attendant smiled. "Don't have to, mate. I got mine already."

Spencer looked fit to burst. Marching off into the crowd he shouldered people out of the way, sending chestnuts and candyfloss flying as he went.

Watching him storm past, Dexter couldn't have been happier. *What a lovely day it was turning out to be after all,* he mused, as out of nowhere the sound of trumpets filled the air.

With a great deal of hissing, clanking, and jerky motions, the three runners made their way to the start line.

"Oh I see," said John, everything finally falling into place.

The horses were all mechanical.

Finding a replacement for the horse would be the next big thing, and everyone with a workshop was working on it in some way or another. It took up a lot of people's time and money, and whilst some thought it impossible, others knew that if they could crack it the rewards would be astronomical. Imagine a horse that never got tired, always did what it was told, and didn't require feeding, brushing, or cleaning up after it all the time. People would pay good money for something like that. And if it put a few farriers and soil-men out of work, well at least the streets would smell a bit nicer.

Today's competitors represented three very different ways of tackling the mechanical horse problem. The first on the track was only half a horse for a start. It had two legs at the front, to pull itself forward, but a pair of cart wheels at the back where its rear legs should have been (which struck John as cheating, but was not against the rules apparently). It seemed stable though, and reasonably quick, although getting it to turn looked a bit difficult. It plodded about on the start line, shuffling back and forth as it tried to get itself in the right position.

The second one was more horse-like, except for the fact that it had six legs. Almost as long again as an average horse, its back was a mass of gears, pistons, and levers, all flinging about at once in an effort to keep the six legs moving with some kind of coordination. It was an accident waiting to happen, and John was glad he wasn't standing anywhere near it. That thing was going to kill somebody.

A ragged cheer went up as the last horse came out. Clearly the crowd's favourite – probably because it looked most like an actual horse – it had four proper legs, a head that bobbed up and down, and a tail that swished about for no good reason. Its two creators, little men with big moustaches and pointy-toed, knee-high boots, whipped off their huge wide-brimmed hats to wave enthusiastically to the crowd.

"Good Lord. Where did you find those two?" said John.

Mary laughed. "Our two cowboys, do you mean? They came over last week on one of our Pond Hoppers. There are great strides in horse mechanisation being made in the Americas, you know. Our two friends down there are keen to show us limeys how it's done."

"I see. And which one is yours?" said John.

"None of them. Chard Mechanical isn't competing."

"Really? You're not working on a horse of your own? I'm surprised."

"Oh we are, kind of, but our approach is a little different."

"How so?"

Mary smiled. "I can't tell you that, John. It's all very hush-hush. Let's just say that trying to recreate an actual horse is nigh on impossible, as you're about to see. We have taken another path."

John thought of the automotive engine. "I don't get it, though. Why would your father sponsor this competition if he didn't think it a possibility?"

"Because you never know, one of these might actually work, and then where would we be? By offering a prize, our competitors are working for us without their even knowing it. They put in the hours, assume all the risk, and if they succeed they've pretty much already agreed to sell us their invention for a fixed price."

"Wow, I never thought of it like that. I have to say, that's pretty clever."

"Thank you. I thought so."

"It was your idea?"

"Indeed it was."

Down on the racetrack a bell rang and the crowd fell silent. The three horses were lined up, ready to go. The race official raised his starting pistol into the air, fired a single shot, and they were off! Sort of.

The three horses staggered over the starting line like drunks heading for the bar. There were no riders. All three of them had controllers walking behind them, pulling levers and tugging reins to keep them on the straight and narrow. Bit by bit they built up momentum, the crowd whooping and cheering when it looked like they were going to have an actual race on their hands. Their optimism didn't last long, however.

The six-legged horse was the first to fall. Its multitude of limbs started firing off all at once, bouncing it around all over the place. It flipped over the guard rail and landed on its back, its legs flailing helplessly in the air like some giant upturned beetle.

The cart horse pulled into an early lead, trotting forward with confidence until one of its legs froze in mid-air. Then it just ran around in circles for a while before finally coming to an ignoble halt with its face in the dirt, engulfed in a cloud of steam.

Slow as it was, the cowboys' horse was the most competent. It moved like a real horse, building up speed as it passed its two competitors. The crowd went wild as it crossed the half way mark, looking like it would make it all the way to the end. But then a loud bang and some grinding of gears, followed by a lot of smoke and the horse toppling over sideways, signalled the end of the mechanical horse race.

All told the whole thing lasted less than thirty seconds.

"Ah well," said Mary. "There's always next time, I guess. Although I do feel sorry for our cowboy contingent. They came such a long way for this."

Down on the track, the two Americans stood over their fallen creation looking like they either wanted to cry or to put a bullet in the damn thing. John suspected that whichever one they chose, there'd be an awful lot of whisky drunk later that night.

Realising how thirsty he was, John was pleased to see the butler returning with their drinks. The man had managed to rustle them up some pineapple juice, a rare treat which John made sure to savour, parched though he was.

Tucking her feet up onto the seat of her chair, Mary leant in towards John. "So tell me, how goes the investigation?"

John gave a bit of a shrug. "Oh, y'know. Slowly but surely. These things take time. You know how it is."

"Oh come on, John, don't be shy. Why don't you tell me what you have and let's see if we can't catch this critter, eh?"

"Alright," said John, reluctantly. "Well for a start there's your brother, Peter."

Mary's eyebrows shot up. "Peter! Why on earth would Peter have anything to do with what happened to Henry?"

"To get control of Chard Mechanical."

"But he already has control."

"Yes but for how long? With Henry back how long before your father tried to put him in charge?"

"But that's—" Mary thought for a moment. "No, I see what you mean. Foolish though it would have been, Henry was his first born, and father always was very traditional about that sort of thing." John said nothing. "But no, I can't believe it. Not Peter. He may be a bit of a grump, but he doesn't seem the type to kill anyone."

"Okay. Then let me ask you something else. Have you ever heard of The Peculiar Tools Company?"

Mary looked off into the distance. "Peculiar Tools? No, I don't think so. I'd remember a name like that. Why do you ask? Who are they?"

"I don't know. It's just a name that's come up. I'm trying to find out who they are."

"Well I can't help you, I'm afraid."

"That's fine. It was a bit of a long shot anyway."

Mary shook her head slowly. "I'm sorry, but I can't believe Peter is involved. You must be mistaken. Is he your only suspect? Is there nobody else you've been looking into?"

"Well there is someone, but I don't want to alarm you. It might be nothing." That, of course, alarmed Mary more than anything.

"Why? Who is it? Is it someone I know? Is it someone in the house? Do you suspect one of the staff?"

"What? No, no. Not at all. It's just..." He was going to have to tell her. "Look, there's this man, alright. I've seen him outside the gates of the manor a few times. I don't know why he's there, but I got the feeling he's watching the place, so yesterday I went to have a word with him. Unfortunately he took off before I could get anywhere near him, so that didn't work out quite how I hoped. I chased after him but he got away."

"Oh my God! There was someone at the house?! Who was he? What did he look like?"

"I don't know. He's a young guy, dark hair, northern accent, smokes a lot. Ring any bells?"

"No, not at all. And you say he was hanging around outside the gates?"

"Yes. At the omnibus stop over the road."

"At the omnibus stop?"

"Yes."

"Could he not have been, you know, waiting for an omnibus? The staff from the other houses use that stop all the time."

"He– Yes, he could have. That's true. But then why did he run when I chased after him?"

Mary gave John a pitying look. "You *were* chasing after him, John. I mean, if a strange man chased after me I'd probably run away too. Wouldn't you?"

"I—" *Yes*, thought John. *Yes, I probably would.*

"Whatever he's up to, I'm sure it's not worth worrying about."

"I'm sure you're right," said John, decidedly unsure that that was indeed the case.

Gazing out across the track, Mary chewed on her fingernail, lost in thought. The sudden silence was too much for John. "And then there's Spencer of course."

Mary looked at John like he was mad. "Spencer! Why on earth would he want to hurt anyone?"

"I don't know exactly, it's just... There's something about him I don't like. He seems like he's up to something."

Mary broke into an unexpected grin. "Why, Mr Sinister, I do believe you're jealous."

"What? No. That's– I mean, I can't– I mean—" John felt his face burning. He looked away; to the track, the floor, the sky, anywhere but Mary's eyes. It was horrible. She just wouldn't stop smiling at him.

John broke out into a cold sweat. He had to change the subject, fast! "What do you think about your father having a heart attack the same day Henry was found dead?" he heard himself say.

Mary frowned. "What do you mean?"

Yes, what *did* he mean? "I mean the owner and the direct heir of one of the largest corporations in the empire both die on the same day. Bit of a coincidence don't you think?"

"You think the two are connected? That father died die of natural causes after all?"

"I don't know. It's just... It's a possibility that has arisen."

Mary looked away and John felt awful. She had enough to deal with without him throwing the circumstances surrounding her father's death into doubt as well. Maybe if he retracted the question she'd forget he'd ever asked it? Then they could go back to being... whatever they were to each other.

Mary seemed to come to a decision. "You can't tell anyone about this, John, not anyone! If it ever got out..."

"I won't tell anyone. I promise."

"No one outside of the family knows about this, not even our lawyers, but father had a weak heart. He'd been ill for months. The doctors kept telling him to take it easy but he wouldn't listen. He refused treatment, refused to slow down. He seemed to think that he could just power through like he always did and everything would be alright. It was so infuriating." John nodded but said nothing. "We used to argue about it all the time. It was so frustrating, trying to get him to see sense. It drove me up the wall."

"No one gets us as riled up as family, eh?"

Mary chuckled. "Ain't that the truth." As quickly as it came, her smile faded. "That's why I wasn't surprised when he collapsed. We've been expecting something like this for a while now. Not that that makes it any easier to deal with. I mean, I know nobody lives forever, but we could have had a few more years at least, if only he'd listened."

John heard the catch in her throat and saw the tear in her eye. Slipping his hand into hers he gave it a reassuring squeeze. "Thank you, Mary. That's helpful to know, it really is."

"Good," said Mary, placing her other hand on top of his. "I'm glad." She smiled again, and for John all was right with the world once more.

Over at the steam fair a commotion broke out. John and Mary heard shouts and saw people running. On one side, where the prize stalls were, a steady plume of smoke rose into the air.

"What's going on over there?" said Mary, craning her neck to see.

John got to his feet. "I don't know," he said. "It looks like one of the stalls is on fire."

"Goodness. Whatever could have caused that?"

"No idea," said John, retaking his seat.

As they sat and watched the unfolding chaos, the occasional crack of an exploding coconut reverberated around the racecourse.

"So, Loverboy, how did it go? Did you get a good sniff? You two lick each other's mouths out like you lot like to do?"

"What? No. Don't be disgusting. We just talked."

John and Dexter were sitting on the top deck of an omnibus, enjoying the view from the front as it trundled its way into town.

"What about you?" said John. "See anyone you fancy at the fair?"

"Ha-ha. Very funny. So what did Miss Chard tell you?"

"Not a lot really. I think she thinks that what happened to Henry is exactly as it seems, more or less. And that her father's heart attack is not the big surprise everyone thinks it is."

"And what do you think about that idea?"

"I'm hoping that the coroner has come up with something, because it could go either way for me right now."

"Fair enough," said Dexter. "It pays to keep an open mind, I guess."

The omnibus stopped to let people on. They were at a stand opposite the Scion Club's road end. John glanced down the road in time to see the club door open, and for Nero to step out into the street. What the hell was he doing there? He wasn't an Old Hag. Nero turned and spoke to someone inside the doorway, smiling and shaking hands with whoever was there before walking off down the road.

John watched the open door. He saw a flap of fabric as someone donned their coat, but just as they stepped out into the street the omnibus set off again, the unknown figure disappearing behind the awning of a sweet shop before John could make out who it was.

Now what was all that about? he wondered.

Ten minutes later, the omnibus arrived outside Wainwright's Yard. John and Dexter disembarked.

"Right. You stay out here."

"No way," said Dexter. "I'm going in with you."

John shook his head. "You can't."

"Why not?"

"Because they're not going to let me in with a cat under my arm, are they? And they're certainly not going to take me seriously, even if they do."

"Don't you worry about me, my son. You won't even know I'm there. Just hold the door open a bit when you go through and I'll sort myself out."

John folded his arms and waited, but Dexter didn't take the hint. He seemed determined. "Okay, fine," said John. "But if you get caught you're on your own."

At the police station's double doors, John paused to check the time on his pocket watch. Only when he felt something furry slip past his leg did he let go of the door to continue inside.

There was a different desk sergeant on duty, a bulldog of a man whose feet barely reached the stool's foot rest. "Well now, sir. And what can I do for you?" he said as John approached.

"I'd like to speak with Detective Hardigan, please," said John, offering up his winningest smile. It was wasted on the desk sergeant.

"She'll be pretty busy. Who should I say is calling?"

"Tell her it's her favourite busy-body. She'll know who you mean."

The desk sergeant paused with his hand on the speaking tube. "I'm going to need a name, sir, if you don't mind. This isn't a social club."

"Oh. Of course. The name's Sinister, John Sinister."

With as little grace as he could possibly manage, the desk sergeant relayed John's request down the speaking tube, the constable on the other end sounding as enthusiastic about helping as the desk sergeant was. "You can wait over there," said the desk sergeant, pointing out John's favourite bench at the back of the room. "She'll be out when she's ready."

"Wonderful," John replied.

Thankfully John had less of a wait this time than he'd had on his first visit. He'd only had time to consider every object of interest in the spartan room twice – he hadn't spotted Dexter yet, although his money was on the potted plant in the corner – before Detective Hardigan arrived.

"Mr Sinister, what can I do for you?"

"I'm so glad you asked, Detective. I'd like to speak with the coroner if I could, please?" The detective pulled an unhappy face. "You did say on my first visit that it was a possibility."

"What I said was that I'd ask, but that's not the point. Why do you want to see the coroner?"

"I wanted to know if he thought there was anything odd about Donald Chard's passing. To see if he suspects foul play or not."

"Do *you* suspect foul play, Mr Sinister?"

"Always, Detective Hardigan. But I want to see if *he* suspects foul play. That is his job after all."

The detective pursed her lips. "Very well. But I warn you, our coroner is not as warm and fuzzy as I am. He might not want to talk to you."

Detective Hardigan led John into the back rooms of Wainwright's Yard once more. She was a little confused by the way he rushed ahead to hold the door open for her, lingering after she'd gone through only to rush to hold open the next one, but not enough to comment on it. It wasn't the weirdest attempt at chivalry she'd ever seen. In fact, it was kind of sweet.

Half way to her office, she led him down a spiral staircase into the building's basement. It was dark down there, and chilly, and it had an unpleasant smell. John tried to place it but all he could come up with was a strange mixture of bleach, death and hot chocolate.

It made him sick, scared and hungry all at the same time. Annoyingly, he couldn't see anything to throw up in.

Down a dank corridor, sparsely lit by guttering gas lamps, they came across the police morgue.

If John thought the smell in the corridor was bad he was unprepared for the morgue itself. It hit him as he pushed open the swing door, an unpleasant cloud of odour that shot right up his nose and parked itself so deep in his sinuses he could smell it in his brain. He tried covering his nose and mouth with his sleeve but it was no use, the stench was already in there.

Detective Hardigan tried not to smile but she was enjoying herself too much. "Bracing, isn't it?"

"I'll say."

"Don't worry, you get used to it after a while."

John doubted that very much, but what choice did he have? As soon as he felt something move past his leg he let go of the morgue door and dove right on in.

The morgue was a large room, with small, high windows at street level to let in the light, and terracotta tiles on the walls and floor because they were easy to mop clean. Four large wooden benches stained with blood sat in each corner, and all of them were currently occupied. Thankfully each bench's occupant was covered with a white sheet. John didn't think he could handle it if they weren't. As it was, there was an arm dangling down from the bench to his right, which was more than enough dead for him to deal with right now, thank you very much.

The coroner, a tall, robust man in his late fifties, was at the back of the room hunched over some poor soul's lifeless torso, his hands stuck in places where hands really shouldn't go. Extracting something red and sticky from the torso's abdomen he weighed it on a nearby scale. Seemingly happy with the results, he looked up to find Detective Hardigan coming towards him. Whilst the two of them talked John waited on the other side of the room – partly out of politeness, but mostly because this was as close to a cracked ribcage as he ever wanted to get.

Giving his hands a quick wash in the sink, the coroner followed Detective Hardigan over, drying his hands on his once white apron as they walked.

"Doctor Semble, allow me to introduce John Sinister. Mr Sinister, Doctor Adrian Semble, our coroner."

"Please to meet you, Mr Sinister," said the doctor, offering John his recently bloody hand with a sly grin.

John looked at it, at the coroner, then at the detective, who also had an amused look on her face. *So, it's like that, is it?* he thought. *Charming.* Grasping the coroner's hand, he shook it firmly. "And a pleasure to meet you, Doctor Semble. I've heard great things."

"Oh I doubt that. It's rare my work gets much attention. But I appreciate the attempt at flattery."

"You are most welcome," said John, making a conscious effort not to wipe his hand on his trouser leg.

Detective Hardigan gave a small, satisfied nod. "Right, well, I've got work to do, so I'll leave you boys to it, if that's alright?"

"Absolutely, Detective," said John. "And thank you. As always it was lovely to see you again."

"Alright, Sinister, save it for the posh nobs. Some of us work for a living around here." And with that she left.

"So, Mr Sinister, what can I do for you?"

"Did Detective Hardigan explain that I have been hired by the family to look into the deaths of Donald and Henry Chard?"

"She did. Did she explain to you that I am a very busy man?"

"Not in so many words, but with that in mind I'll be brief. Is there anything about the deaths of Donald and Henry Chard that troubles you in any way?"

"Not at all. One drowned, the other suffered from heart failure."

"And are you sure of that? Did you do a full, erm... examination?"

"Autopsy. No, not a full one." Dr Semble walked to the back of the room, talking over his shoulder as he went. "Henry Chard had water in his lungs, and Donald Chard's heart shows definite signs of damage,"—he pointed to the red mass resting in the silver scales next to the open body—"confirming assumed cause of death in both their cases. When that happens a full autopsy is not deemed necessary. The facts fit the investigation, so it's case closed as far as I'm concerned." He retrieved a mug of cocoa from beside the sink and took a good long swig.

John's attention was focussed solely on the doctor, and definitely not on the body next to him. Now that he knew it to be Donald Chard it made being close to it so much worse than before. "So you've no intention of looking any further then?"

"Why should I? Without proof of criminal activity I'm not required, nor am I inclined, to look any further. It would be a complete waste of my time. So, unless you have some proof of criminal activity that you'd like to share, Mr Sinister?"

"I don't, no. But you have to admit it's highly suspicious. Two deaths in the same family in the same week."

"I admit it's strange, but it does happen. It's a coincidence, nothing more."

"I don't believe in coincidences."

"And I don't believe that everything happens for a reason. Look, forgive my being blunt, but unless I'm asked to do so by the higher ups, there's nothing you, a private citizen, can say that will make me waste my time performing a more detailed autopsy on either of these two men."

"Oh yeah?" said John, holding up a wad of cash. "Would a tenner change your mind?"

As he exited the police station, John paused at the front door to fiddle with his shoelace. Once Dexter was out he went and joined him by the roadside.

"Nicely done in there," said Dexter. "Let's hope he comes up with something."

"Yeah. Fingers crossed, eh?"

"So now what? Where do we go next?"

"Now we head to the solicitors. I want to get this will business sorted out once and for all."

There was something imposing about the offices of Holberton, Hutchison and Murphy. Perhaps it was the columns that ran the full height of the three storey granite facade, the iron railings along the front to keep the hoi polloi at bay, or the impenetrable black door atop the impressive double-sweep stone staircase, but whatever it was, John felt very small standing before them (which, he had to concede, was quite probably the point).

"So what's the plan? You going to slip in behind me like before?"

"No, not this time. They've got a dog in there, a yappy little thing that'll go mental if I go anywhere near it. I'm going to have to go up round the back. Look, don't you worry about me, I know where I'm going. You just get yourself in and I'll see you up there."

As Dexter trotted off round the side of the building, John took a moment to make himself presentable before heading up the stairs into the lion's den.

In a small dark room that smelled of animosity and stale sweat, John came across a harassed-looking legal clerk with wiry black hair sitting hunched over a large roll of vellum. He kept mumbling to himself, stopping every now and then to count on his fingers, whilst on a piled up blanket in the corner of the room a scruffy little dog with even wirier hair lay with its legs in the air, yipping away softly as it dreamed of the glory of the chase, of battles to be fought, or quite possibly just of lunch.

The clerk spotted John in the doorway. "Can I help you, sir?" he asked in a nasal whine that suggested he'd really rather not.

John stuck out his chest in a way he thought made him look important. "Indeed you can, my good man. I'm here to see Mr Holberton."

"Mr Holberton? Mr Holberton is in Manchester, sir. Has been for weeks."

Damn it! He'd rolled the dice and lost. And on a three in one chance too. "Sorry, did I say Holberton? I meant Hutchison. I'm here to see Mr Hutchison. My apologies. I always get those two mixed up." Fingers crossed he's not in Manchester as well.

"Mr Holberton and Mr Hutchison are as alike as chalk and cheese. How could one ever confuse one for the other?"

"Well, they both begin with H don't they?"

The clerk's eyes narrowed. "Do you have an appointment, sir?"

"Er, no. Not exactly. But—"

The clerk pushed back his chair, the noise waking the dog. Spotting John, it scrambled to its feet, dropped its head, and let out a low, suspicious growl. "I'm sorry, sir, but without an appointment I'm afraid that—"

"I do have this though," said John, reaching into his pocket. His hand landed on his bill fold but he thought better of it. The man didn't look the type. Instead he removed Mr Chard's letter and handed it to the clerk. "Perhaps you could give this to Mr Hutchison. I'm sure he will want to see me."

The clerk received the letter like it might burst into flames at any moment. "Very good, sir. I will see if Mr Hutchison is available. Please wait here." He headed for a narrow staircase in the corner of the room. "And if you could refrain from touching anything whilst I am gone I would very much appreciate it."

John stuck his hands in his pockets and gave the clerk a reassuring smile. It didn't seem to work. The clerk begrudgingly made his way up the stairs, his eyes on John the whole way.

Don't touch anything indeed. Like he would want to touch anything in there. On the desk, John's eyes fell upon the clerk's pen protruding from its inkwell. It was a nice pen, a very nice pen indeed, silver with an intricate floral engraving. A gift no doubt from somebody special.

With a quick glance at the stairs John reached for the pen. He heard a low, menacing growl. Looking to the side he found the little dog watching him, its teeth bared, its top lip quivering. He pulled back his hand and the growling stopped. Locking eyes with the dog he reached out again, the dog growling until he pulled his hand back out of reach of the pen once more. *Well, this is a fun game,* thought John.

He jabbed a finger at the pen. The dog went *rrrr!* He did it three times fast, the dog growling *rrrr-rrrr-rrrr!* John smiled. It was hard to take such a little dog seriously. *What would it do if I actually grabbed the pen?* he wondered. There really was only one way to find out.

He reached slowly for the pen, the little dog growling louder the closer he got. He kept going, inching ever closer. The dog's growl increased in intensity. By the time John's hand was over the pen the little dog was on its feet, teeth bared, leaning forward ready to strike.

John started to lower his hand...

"What are you doing?" came a voice from the stairs.

John spun around, clasping his hands behind his back. "Nothing! Nothing at all."

The clerk, whose view of the desk was obscured, looked from John, to the dog, and back to John. "Mr Hutchison will see you now," he said finally. "If you would follow me, please?"

Following the clerk, John glanced at the dog on his way up the stairs. Expecting a growl, he found it licking itself instead, their encounter completely forgotten already.

Ah well, to the victor the spoils, he mused.

At the top of the stairs was a landing with three doors. The clerk led John to the middle door where he knocked twice.

"The gentleman, sir," said the clerk, stepping aside so that John could enter. John was impressed. The way he'd pronounced the word 'gentleman' said more about the Britannic class system then an entire treatise on the subject ever could.

"Thank you, Wilberforce. That will be all," said the gentleman by the window. The clerk retreated, leaving the door slightly ajar.

The man standing by the window was statuesque in every conceivable way. Well over six-feet tall, he was square shouldered, straight backed, chisel featured, and unbelievably stoic. He looked like he should be on a plinth staring off into the distance, thinking noble thoughts.

His office, a true extension of the man within, was practical, organised, and not a place for nonsense or tomfoolery. There was little decoration save for a family photograph on the desk, and a child's drawing of a horse pinned to the wall next to no less than three framed law degrees.

"Do have a seat," said the man without turning. "An interesting document you have here," he said, brandishing John's letter. "Worthless of course, since its signatory is now deceased, but interesting nonetheless."

"I wouldn't say worthless, Mr Hutchison. It got me here, didn't it?"

Mr Hutchison turned. A coy smile played at the corner of his mouth. "Yes, I suppose it did." Walking to his desk he sat down, handing the letter back to John. "So, what can I do for you on this fine morning, mister...?"

"Sinister. John Sinister. I was hired by the late Donald Chard to look into the circumstances surrounding his son Henry's death."

"Yes, he told me about that. But I don't see how I can help. I hardly knew the boy."

"Well, since Mr Chard's passing I have also been engaged to look into his death as well."

"Have you now? Engaged by whom, might I ask?"

John caught a flash of movement by the window, where he saw Dexter's tail appear briefly before dipping out of sight. "I'm afraid I'm not at liberty to divulge that information. Let's just say a friend of the family, shall we."

"How mysterious," said Mr Hutchison, raising an eyebrow. "I am intrigued." Sitting back in his chair, he interlaced his fingers in front of him. "Well, fire away, Mr Sinister. Let us see where this journey takes us, shall we?"

"Right. Well, let's start with an easy one, eh? You were Donald Chard's solicitor, were you not?"

"One of them, yes."

"Who else was there?"

"My two partners of course, Mr Holberton and Mr Murphy."

"Of the three, who knew Donald Chard the best?"

"I guess that would be me."

"Excellent. So was it you who met with him the day he...?"

"It was."

"And did he—" A chilling thought occurred. "Hang on, is this the room he died in?"

"It is. In that very chair, in fact."

The compulsion to stand was overwhelming, but John forced himself to stay in place. "So what happened, if you don't mind me asking?"

"Not at all. I believe it's common knowledge by now. Mr Chard came to see me because he had a number of business matters he wished to discuss. He was feeling ill when he arrived, which he put down to rotten eggs and a bumpy carriage ride, but as our meeting progressed he became increasingly unwell. He started to have trouble breathing, becoming quite red in the face, before collapsing into what I can only describe as uncontrollable convulsions. I summoned Wilberforce to try and help the man but it was no use, Mr Chard died within a matter of seconds. There was nothing anyone could have done." Despite his flat, business-like delivery, John saw great guilt and sadness in Mr Hutchison's eyes.

"That sounds like a horrible thing to experience, Mr Hutchison."

"Indeed it was. Although it was infinitely worse for Mr Chard, I can assure you."

"Well, quite," said John, shifting uncomfortably in his seat. "Um, forgive me for asking, but you said Mr Chard had trouble breathing before falling into some sort of convulsions. Now, I'm not a medical man, but I've seen someone have a heart attack before, and I don't remember any convulsions at the time."

"I cannot speak to that. I am not a medical man either. All I know is what I saw, and what I described is what happened, I can promise you that."

"Of course. Now if I may, what business did you discuss with Mr Chard before he died?"

"I cannot tell you that, Mr Sinister. That is privileged information."

"Your client is deceased, Mr Hutchison. Surely his privilege died with him."

"As did his authority. Yet you have your letter, and I have my legal obligation. I will not surrender it on what I conceive to be a technicality."

"Alright, then let me ask you this; did Mr Chard leave a will?"

"I cannot tell you that either."

"Oh come on, Mr Hutchison," snapped John.

Mr Hutchison sat forward, placing his hands flat on the desk. "Mr Sinister," he said. "I'm telling you the same thing I've told every policeman, journalist, and business associate of the Mr Chard that has come knocking on my door of late, I can answer no specific questions about my client's legal situation without his express permission, which, I'm sure you'll agree, is going to be a little hard to obtain now."

"Well..." said John, reaching for Mr Chard's letter.

"Nice try. But not good enough I'm afraid."

John shoved the letter back in his pocket, doing his best not to start swearing. This legal stuff was a brick wall of privilege and obligation. How was he ever going to find out what he needed to know?

Seeing the consternation etched upon John's face, Mr Hutchison took pity on him. He sat back, interlacing his fingers in front of him once more. "What I will say is I would find it *extremely* unlikely for a man in Donald Chard's position *not* to have a will, if you catch my drift?" He raised his eyebrows, giving John a very meaningful look.

"Yes, I see," said John, mulling the statement over.

"Good," said Mr Hutchison, with a curt nod. "I'm glad. Because Donald Chard was a close personal friend of mine, Mr Sinister, as well as a client. If there *is* anything untoward about his death I want to do everything I can to help find out what that is. But you have to ask the right questions, do you understand?"

"Yes, I believe I do," said John, nodding slowly.

He sat and thought for a moment. Behind him the door to the office creaked open, and the downstairs dog came shuffling in. "So tell me, if a businessman, someone like Donald Chard for example, *were* to make a will, I assume it would be quite a complex and comprehensive document?"

"Indeed it would."

"And would it lay out not only their intended heir, but also successive heirs, should the intended heir be deceased at the time of their passing?"

"From a fall into an icy river, for example."

"For example, yes."

"It would. In fact such a provision would be quite standard, in a case such as you describe."

"And might such a provision follow the traditional line of succession, from the eldest to the youngest child?"

The dog, having sniffed at John's leg and deciding thankfully not to mark it as his own, began shuffling around the room, sniffing at other things.

"It might, it might. Though not always. If the youngest son, for example, was already intimately involved with said business, he might 'jump the queue', as it were."

"I see. Very interesting. Very interesting indeed," said John, a little distracted. He had half an eye on the dog, and half an eye on the window, as the two moved ever closer together.

"That's not to say, of course, that anyone would be left out in the cold, as it were. Such a businessman, a man like Donald Chard, would make sure his family were well taken care of. *All* of his family, Mr Sinister. Each one of his children. Anything less would be shameful in his eyes."

The dog stopped walking and fixed its attention on the window above. John watched it closely. "Of course, of course. There's no doubting Donald Chard was a good and honourable man."

"Well I wouldn't go that far," said Mr Hutchison. "But anyway, who's talking about Donald Chard? I thought we were discussing general legalities, not one man's specific situation."

The dog growled up at the window.

"Oh absolutely," agreed John. "Very general. Nothing specific."

Dexter popped his head up to see what was going on and the dog went insane. Leaping and barking, it tried to scramble its way up the wall, its claws scrabbling at the pristine layers of paint and plaster.

"Dear God! What on earth has gotten into him?" exclaimed Mr Hutchison.

"I think it was a pigeon," said John. "Or a, um, mouse maybe." Mr Hutchison stood to have a look. "Whatever it is, I think it's gone now," he added quickly.

"It's a cat. Damn thing. Go on, get away from there! Shoo! Shoo, I tell you!"

Walking to the window with a rolled up newspaper, Hutchison pushed it open in time to see Dexter's back end jump to the roof of a neighbouring building and disappear behind a chimney stack. At his feet, the dog saw nothing. It kept yapping and leaping about all over the place, determined to see off the intruder no matter the cost.

Despite the newspaper in his hand, Mr Hutchison didn't have the heart to hit a defenceless animal. He called downstairs for Mr Wilberforce, who came and removed the barking ball of fur with much apologising and a great deal more difficulty than a beast of that size should have offered – proving once again that with motivation and determination, stature is no barrier to any endeavour.

"I'm sorry about that, Mr Sinister. Liebling is normally such a placid creature. But he does get worked up on the subject of cats, I'm afraid."

"He and I both, Mr Hutchison, believe me."

"If there's nothing else I can help you with, I do have a number of matters to attend to."

"No, that should do me for now," said John, standing. "Except to ask if you know anything about The Peculiar Tools Company? Possibly as a subsidiary or client of Chard Mechanical maybe?"

"As I've said already, I cannot discuss the Chard family business. Although I will tell you that the name is unfamiliar to me. Not that that means anything, of course. Mr Chard was more than capable of handling basic contracting matters without the need for my assistance."

"I see. Thank you, Mr Hutchison," said John, offering his hand. "Perhaps I can call on you again should I have any more, um, general legal queries I need clearing up?"

"Absolutely, Mr Sinister. Any time. I found our discussion most interesting."

"As did I," said John, shaking the man's hand. "As did I."

Out on the street, John found Dexter licking his wounds.

"Are you alright?"

"Kind of. I landed funny when I came back down."

"I thought cats always landed on their feet."

"Once again, I'm not a real cat," said Dexter, craning round to try and look at his own tail. "Here, do me a favour will you? Have a look and see if you can see anything wrong back there?" Dexter sat and cocked up a leg so that John could inspect his undercarriage.

"I can see all kinds of wrong," said John, "but no damage as far as I can tell."

"Good. Thanks. So, how did it go? I didn't catch it all. Did you get what you wanted?"

John relayed what he'd been told, namely that with Henry and Donald Chard out of the way, Peter Chard looked set to inherit the company.

"You see! I told you that man wasn't to be trusted. And now we have proof. So, when do we get him? When do we go to the police?"

"Whoa. Hold your horses. We haven't got anything yet. We're going to need a lot more evidence before we can go to the police."

"Oh for heaven's sake! So what now then? What do you want to do?"

"I want to go talk to Peter Chard, tell him what we know. Y'know, shake the tree a little, see what falls out."

Dexter looked at him funny. "Are you sure that's such a good idea?"

"Yeah. Why?"

"Well, you're not the biggest guy in the world. I'm not sure you could take him."

"What do you mean? I... I'm not going to strong-arm him or anything. I'm going to talk to the man, to rattle his cage, see if he lets something slip. Shake the tree is just an expression."

"Oh. I see," said Dexter. If mechanical cats could blush Dexter would have been a beetroot. "Well... as long as we get him I don't care how we do it. I just hope you're up to the job is all."

As Dexter stormed off to hide his embarrassment, John wondered, not for the first time, what it was he had against Peter Chard that made him dislike the man so much.

John decided to spring for a Hansom cab to get to Chard Mechanical. After the morning they'd had, he figured Dexter would appreciate the opportunity to put his feet up for a while, conserve a bit of energy. And he wasn't exactly averse to the idea himself either.

Wandering into the factory's front yard, John and Dexter heard shouting coming from Nomko's workshop.

"Just get it done, alright! Or you're through. D'ya hear me?!" Peter Chard charged out of the workshop, leaving a tirade of Japanese expletives in his wake. Marching towards his office, he spotted John moving to intercept him. "Oh, for God's sake! What do you want now?"

"Just a quick word, if I may?" said John.

"Not interested," said Peter Chard, holding up a hand to fend John off as he walked right past him.

"Are you sure? It could be of great benefit to you."

"I doubt that very much," Peter Chard scoffed over his shoulder.

"I just came from your father's lawyers' office," said John. Peter Chard stopped walking. "He had some interesting things to say about your father's will."

"Such as?"

"Such as who benefits from your father's death, things like that."

Peter Chard snorted. "That's no mystery. Henry would have– Oh I see. With Henry gone I'm next in line to the throne, is that it?"

"Something like that."

"So now you think I killed my own brother and father to get control of all this!" He waved his arms in disgust at everything around them.

"It's a powerful motive, wouldn't you say?"

Peter Chard looked at John like he'd just insisted that two plus two equals lemon. "It may have escaped your attention, but I already have control of Chard Mechanical, for all the good it does me. Why on earth would I kill two people for something I've already got?"

"Because with Henry back how long would it be before Donald Chard handed his beloved company over to his first born son?"

Peter Chard burst out laughing, actually throwing his head back and grasping his belly to stop his sides from splitting. It was a bit showy, but it did give John pause for thought. "Oh my God," he said, wiping away an imaginary tear. "That's hilarious. You really haven't got a clue, have you? Look, not only did Henry have no interest in running the family business, he was *incapable* of running the family business, something my father knew all too well. He was no threat to me. My brother was a bum, Mr Sinister, plain and simple. Only good for drinking, whoring, and running up large debts. In fact, if you're really interested in finding his killer – if indeed killed he was – then that's where you should start, at that club of his."

"The Scion Club?"

"No, not that place. The other one. Caesar's Coffee and Chocolate. He was always in there throwing money away. Money he didn't have. If anyone wanted him dead it was probably them."

"Nice try, but I've already been there. They had no beef with Henry. According to them he always paid his debts."

"Henry paid nothing. *I* paid off his debts, to avoid a scandal. Or at least I did until a few weeks ago. That's when I decided enough was enough and cut him off."

"You stopped bailing him out?"

"I did. For his own good, I might add. He never would have stopped gambling otherwise."

"So he'd stopped gambling then?"

"Honestly, Mr Sinister, I don't know and I don't care. My brother was a liability, a bad investment from day one. His loss is not something I'm going to lose sleep over any time soon."

John didn't like how this was going. Time to up the stakes a bit. "Did you cut him off because the company is in trouble?"

Peter Chard stepped towards John, balling his fists. "Who told you that?"

"A little bird."

"Well it's a lie, I tell you, a damned lie! You should be careful, Mr Sinister. A man could get himself in a lot of trouble going round spreading rumours like that."

"Is that a threat, Mr Chard?"

Peter Chard smiled a very nasty smile indeed. "I don't make threats, Mr Sinister. It's a waste of time. I just take care of problems. Now, if you don't mind." Turning on his heel, Peter Chard went inside the factory.

Dexter came out from behind a packing crate. "Well, that was interesting."

"Indeed it was."

"Do you think he meant everything he said, about Henry and all that?"

"Actually, I do. He seemed too worked up to lie. Or to lie convincingly at least."

"So what do we do now?"

"Now? Now I need to have another talk with Nero, to see what he has to say about all this." John was as enthusiastic about that idea as he was about sticking important parts of himself into a meat grinder.

"Sounds good. You gonna shake his tree too?"

"Er... no. No, I think I'll settle for asking politely and hoping he doesn't kill me." There was a loud crash inside the workshop, followed by more Japanese profanity. "Tell you what, why don't you go see what's up with Nomko while I pop inside and have another quick word with Peter Chard. There's one thing I need to clear up with him before we leave."

Dexter squinted up at John. "Are you sure that's such a good idea? He seems a bit... agitated, at the moment."

John looked towards the factory. "No, probably not. But you don't ask, you don't get, right?"

"If you say so, mate," said Dexter, fairly convinced that the only thing John was about to get was a punch on the nose. "It's your funeral."

John entered the reception of Chard Mechanical prepared to tackle the company's gatekeeper, Mrs Crabtree, only to find Mary Chard standing by the secretary's desk, accounts ledger in hand.

"John, what are you doing here?"

"Oh, hello, Mary. I was just, um, chatting with Peter outside, and I wanted to ask him something else quickly, if that's alright?"

"I see. Well that explains his foul mood, I guess."

"Not entirely my fault," mumbled John. "So, what are you doing here? You didn't say you were coming by earlier."

Mary glanced over at Mrs Crabtree, who was very definitely busy with some invoices and absolutely not listening to everything they said. Taking John by the elbow Mary moved him as far from the secretary as the small room would allow.

"I came to see if I could help out at all," she said. "All hands on deck, that sort of thing. So what is it you wanted to talk to Peter about?"

"Oh, um..." John couldn't see any way of not telling her. "It's just it turns out Henry had a bit of a gambling problem, and that Peter is the one who has been paying off his debts since he got back. Or at least he was until recently. I needed to find out when exactly he cut Henry off, that's all. It might be important."

"I see. Well I'm not sure Peter is in a sharing mood right now."

"No, probably not," agreed John. "Perhaps there's something in the ledger that could tell us?" he said, pointing to the book Mary was carrying. "Would something like that even appear on the books? Can we check, maybe?"

Mary closed the ledger and clutched it to her chest, folding both arms across it. "There's no need. I know when it was. It was two weeks ago."

"Really. How do you know?"

"I know because Henry's gambling is not the big secret everyone seems to think it is. Two weeks ago I heard father and Peter arguing about it at the house. Peter was sick of throwing good money after bad. He said it was time to put an end to it. Father was against it, of course, but when Peter explained it was the only way for Henry to face up to his demons, and maybe get some help, he reluctantly agreed."

"And did it work? Did Henry stop gambling?"

"Oh I don't know," snapped Mary. "Look, John, is it not time to stop all this? All this snooping around, poking your nose into things? It's upsetting a lot of people, myself included. Maybe it's time to let sleeping dogs lie, don't you think?"

John was taken aback. "I... I'm sorry. I'm not trying to upset anyone."

"I know you're not, but all this talk of murder and intrigue, it's not very nice, is it?"

John shrugged. "Not everything in life is nice, Mary."

Mary's gaze became cold and hard. "Don't patronise me, John. I am not an imbecile."

"I'm sorry. I didn't mean it like that. I just... All I want to do is find out the truth."

"I know you do. We all do. But maybe it's best to let it go, for all our sakes. Yours, as well as mine."

John stared at the ground, unable to look Mary in the eye. He wanted to do as she asked – he'd do anything for her, he really would – but it wasn't as simple as all that. Henry was his friend, his best friend, possibly his only friend. How could he walk away knowing there might be someone out there who was responsible for his death? It just wasn't possible. He'd never be able to live with himself if he did.

"I'm sorry, Mary, but I can't. Henry was a good friend to me. I owe it to him to see this thing through."

"You have to do what you have to do, I guess," said Mary, turning away. It crushed John inside.

"Look, I tell you what. If the coroner doesn't come up with anything I'll stop, I promise."

Mary frowned. "The coroner? I thought he'd already decided it was an accident."

Now it was John's turn to look away. "He did. I, er, persuaded him to do some more tests."

"I see," said Mary, giving John a look of disappointment that cut to the very heart of him. She let out a deep, heartfelt sigh. "Well, I better get on, I suppose. There's lots to do. These books are in a bit of a mess."

John almost said 'I know' but he managed to catch himself. Instead he said a rather weak, "Of course. Please, don't let me keep you."

Mary went to go, but John couldn't leave it like that. He had to try and salvage the moment somehow. "Uh, Mary? Perhaps later, if you're not busy, we could maybe have dinner or something?"

Mary avoided his gaze. "That's... sweet of you, John, but I think I'm going to be here quite late. There's a lot to sort out."

"Of course. No, that's okay. I understand. Some other time maybe?"

Mary looked at John in a sad way that he couldn't quite fathom. Stepping close she gave him a gentle, lingering kiss on the cheek. "Goodbye, John. You take care of yourself."

John managed to smile back, but he couldn't think of anything to say.

Leaving the reception, John tried to put the whole thing out of his mind, knowing full well he'd be replaying that conversation over in his head for days to come, trying to work out what he'd done to make Mary so mad.

Outside, John headed for Nomko's workshop. He could still hear things being flung about, although with not as much vigour as before.

As he approached the workshop door Dexter emerged, a lop-sided grin on his face. "I tell you what, if you only understood Japanese," he said, shaking his head.

"So what's up with Nomko?"

"Well, from what I can gather Lord Peter wants this automotive engine of theirs finished by the end of the week. He's got some big presentation coming up or something. It means Nomko's going to have to go and pick up some parts he needs from the manufacturer in Streebly tonight, which in turn means riding all night if he's going to be back by morning." In the workshop Nomko threw something heavy at the wall. Dexter gave a dirty chuckle. "Poor sod. I think he had a date lined up for later."

Lucky him, thought John. "Couldn't they send someone else for the parts?"

"No, it has to be him. He needs to inspect them, make sure they're okay."

A metal bucket flew out of the workshop and went cartwheeling across the yard, closely followed by a furious Nomko pushing what looked to John like an angry penny farthing. It had a thick rubber wheel at the front, two smaller wheels at the back, and an unfeasibly large engine to drive it forward. A padded seat curved almost the entire length of the frame, from the low engine mount between the rear wheels up to the backwards bullhorn handlebars at the front, with saddlebags attached either side packed with Nomko's tools.

"What the hell is that?"

"That's Nomko's three-wheeled bike. He calls it his trilocipede."

"I– That's– I'm not sure that's how those words work," said John.

Dexter shrugged. "Who cares? It sounds good and he likes it. What does it matter if it's right or not?"

"Don't let the dictionary people hear you say that."

"Huh. Let 'em come. I ain't scared."

They watched Nomko climb aboard his creation. Straddling the trilocipede, he knelt on a couple of knee pads, jamming his feet into two stirrups that looked worryingly close to the ground. Donning his leather flying helmet and goggles, he zipped his jacket up tight before lying his full length face down along the padded seat.

"So it's a powered bike then, is it?"

"And then some," said Dexter, chuckling.

Flicking some switches on the side of the machine, Nomko yanked on a lever. The trilocipede came to life, juddering menacingly – its engine making a low, burbling noise like a cornered animal that was about to strike.

"You might want to step back a bit," said Dexter, moving out of the way.

"Why?" said John, wisely following suit.

"Well put it this way, if you thought the whirlygig was unstable you ain't seen nothing yet."

Nomko released the clutch and the trilocipede was let loose, it's huge front wheel squealing angrily as it fought to find purchase. Lurching forward, the machine skittered across the yard, its back end whipping back and forth as Nomko tried desperately to hold it in a straight line. Barrelling through the front gates it skidded off down the road, Nomko clinging on for dear life.

"Bloody hell," said John. "That thing's lethal."

"True," said Dexter. "But she'll get you from A to B fast enough, and no mistake."

"I've no doubt about that."

"So," said Dexter, "I see you're still in one piece. Did you find out what you needed to know?"

"I did. It seems Peter stopped paying off Henry's debts a couple of weeks ago, meaning that if Henry kept gambling, and kept losing, he could have been in a lot of trouble by now. Serious trouble even." John gave an unhappy sigh. "I really am going to have to go talk to Nero again."

"Sounds good. Let's go," said Dexter.

"Actually," said John, "I was thinking it might be better if you stayed here."

Dexter squinted up at John suspiciously. "And why's that then?" he said.

"I want you to keep an eye on Peter Chard. Now that he knows we're on to him he might do something stupid to give himself away."

The cat grinned. "Sounds good to me," he said. Then his smile slipped slightly. "Um, how long do you think you'll be?"

"I dunno. A couple of hours maybe. Why?"

"It's just that I've got to get back to Chard Manor to recharge. I haven't topped up since yesterday evening, remember?"

"But you'll be alright for now, yeah?"

"I'll be fine," said Dexter, brushing off John's concerns with a swipe of his paw. "So long as I get back by the end of the day everything will be hunky dory."

"Well you don't have to worry about that," said John. "We'll get you sorted out before the sun goes down. I promise."

John headed straight for Caesar's this time, no detours. He wanted two things from this meeting; to get it over with quickly and to come out of it with all his bits intact, and to do that he was going to need his wits about him.

He found Agnes on the door again. She seemed in a good mood. At least she managed a half-smile when she saw him coming down the stairs.

"Well now, Mr Sinister. Twice in one week. We are honoured."

"The pleasure's all mine, Agnes. Is he in?"

"He is, but I wouldn't go in there if I were you. He's not in the best of moods."

John, who had been reaching for the doorknob, pulled up short. "Oh. Really? Why's that then?"

"No idea, Johnny-boy. He didn't say and I didn't ask. I find it's best to leave him be when he's all worked up. Safest thing all round really."

John's hand hovered over the doorknob. "I really need to talk to him. Just a quick word mind, nothing major. He'd be alright with that, wouldn't he?"

Agnes shrugged. "Hey, if you want to go in there it's up to you, but don't say I didn't warn you." She pulled open the door since John didn't seem like he was going to do it himself. "You'll find him in the upstairs hall, practising."

"Practising? Practising what?"

Agnes smiled. "You'll see. Just make sure you make plenty of noise on your way up. We don't want any nasty surprises now, do we?"

"Er, no, I guess not," said John, unsure who was in line for a nasty surprise, him or Nero.

Heading through the club, John stomped his way up the back stairs, making plenty of noise as instructed. Up ahead he heard a *whoosh-thwack!* followed by a lot of words he didn't recognise but whose meaning was abundantly clear: 'Bugger off and leave me alone,' they said, 'or else.' He stopped walking. There was another *whoosh-thwack* followed by another tirade of profanity. *Maybe I should leave it for now?* he thought. *Nero really doesn't sound up for visitors at the moment.* But he knew that if he didn't go now he wouldn't try a second time, so, with as much bravery as he could muster, John stomped the rest of the way up the stairs.

Something fast and pointy shot past his nose end. Tripping over his own feet John fell straight down, landing on his backside with a teeth-rattling thump.

"Damn it, Sinister! What the hell do you think you're doing? I nearly took your damn head off!"

Nero marched past John, longbow in hand, glaring down at him as he went. At the other end of the room John saw the reason for all the colourful language. There was an archery target set up, with lots of arrows around its outer edge and not one anywhere near the centre. It was a pretty poor showing by anyone's standards. A beginner could have shot better. There were even a couple in the wall behind the target, one of which had penetrated a carved cherub in a most unfortunate spot. Nero had to pull hard to get the arrow loose, pulling away intimate bits of cherub along with it.

Nero marched back to the other end of the room. "What do you want, Sinister? I'm busy." Picking himself up and dusting himself off, John swiftly got out of Nero's line of sight.

"Sorry to interrupt," he said. "I just wanted a quick word, if that's alright?"

"Is this about that Henry Chard nonsense again?" said Nero, nocking an arrow and pulling back on the bow.

"It is, yes."

"I heard his father is dead now too, is that right?"

"Yes, that's right."

"And now here you are to ask me some more questions. That is unfortunate." Nero let fly, the arrow shooting across the room to lodge in the edge of the target. He snarled at his own incompetence, before nocking another arrow. "I hope you're not here to accuse me of having something to do with Donald Chard's death as well. I never even met the man."

"No," said John quickly. "No, not at all. I just wanted to clear something up about Henry's gambling, that's all." For some reason he expected Nero to say something then. The uncomfortable silence stretched on whilst Nero drew and sighted the bow.

"Well, get on with it then," Nero barked over his shoulder. "I haven't got all day."

"Yes. Right. Well, um, the last time I was here you said that Henry Chard always paid his debts on time. But he didn't, did he? The money came from his brother, Peter Chard."

Nero let fly, his arrow deflecting off the target to go clattering into the back wall. Pursing his lips, Nero shook his head slowly. "So what's your point? The debts were paid, everybody's happy. What does it matter where the money came from?"

"Because Peter Chard stopped paying off his brother's debts a couple of weeks ago. He cut him off completely, in fact, in an effort to get him to stop gambling."

"So?"

John's mouth went dry. "So... was he still gambling?"

Nero nocked another arrow. "Probably. You know what people are like."

"I'd like to know for certain."

"And I'd like a new gaming license, one that covers Hazard tables, but we don't always get what we want, now do we? Look, I don't know what your pal Henry was up to in the weeks before he died. I can't keep tabs on all my clients all the time."

"I find that hard to believe."

"What you do and don't find hard to believe is no concern of mine," said Nero. He loosed off his arrow, this one going well wide. Silently, deliberately, he nocked another.

John figured it was time to roll the dice, see what happened. "Did Henry Chard owe you any money?"

"I thought we went over that on your previous visit."

"We did. And you avoided answering the question, as I recall. Much as you're doing now in fact."

Nero looked over at John. "I'm not sure I like your tone," he said. "It's going to get you in trouble one of these days."

Some people are smart. Some people know better than to poke the bear. Some people, on the other hand, go looking for the biggest stick they can find. "Who did you meet at the Scion Club this morning?"

Nero lowered his bow. "Now that really *is* none of your business," he said, turning to face John. The half-drawn bow hung loosely in his hands. He wasn't exactly pointing it at John, but he wasn't exactly *not* pointing it at him either. "Y'know, I do hope you're not planning on becoming something I need to do something about, Sinister. Because there's a pig farmer over in Heath Row who owes me a favour, and it would be nothing for me to take you over there and introduce you to his prize sows. They're quite something. Voracious appetites. Will eat anything you put in front of them. Honest to God, half a dozen hungry hogs can strip a man of his flesh in a matter of minutes. Believe me, I've seen it happen. And not just his flesh, but his clothes, shoes, belt, bones, the lot. It's quite remarkable. You know how they say you can eat every part of a pig except the oink? Well a pig can eat every part of a man except the eek."

Nero held John's gaze for what felt like forever, then in one fluid motion he turned, drew, loosed, and shot an arrow dead centre in the middle of the target. Without a word he nocked another arrow and drew again, ready to take another shot.

"I think perhaps it's time you left, don't you?"

"But I—"

"*Goodbye*, Mr Sinister."

Outside the club – once he'd stopped shaking – John weighed up what he'd learnt.

Nero was right, people rarely change. It was likely Henry was in debt to somebody when he died, the question was how much and to who? Possibly Nero, but Henry could easily have owed money elsewhere as well. If there's one thing these rich boys didn't have any difficulty doing it was running up a tab.

His friends might know, although whether they'd tell him or not was another matter? Still, there was no harm in asking. Whatever happened, it was unlikely to be as bad as the conversation he'd just had. Probably.

A fog had rolled in by the time John reached the Scion Club. It was cold and damp and it chilled him to the bone. He was glad to get inside, even if his relief was short lived. The Scion was deader than a church on Cup Final day. None of Henry's friends were in, and they hadn't been for a while by all accounts.

Outside, John decided to swing by Gravesend Bridge on his way to pick up Dexter. It was about time he visited the scene of the crime, to pay his respects if nothing else. Turning up his collar against the worsening cold, he headed off down the road.

Across the street from the Scion Club, two men stepped from the shadows of a shop doorway. After a brief yet animated discussion – involving lots of angry, and somewhat obscene, hand gestures – one of the men was dispatched at a jog down a side street, whilst the other sauntered off up the road after John.

The fog had thickened by the time John reached Gravesend Bridge. Stood at one end he could only just see across to the other side. It was not ideal investigating weather but what could you do? He was here now, so he'd just have to make the best of it.

He considered the looming bridge for a moment. One of the oldest in Hammersmyth, it had been built back when the world was all horse-and-cart and nobody was in a rush. Its central arch was higher than the two either side, giving it a considerable hump in the middle – although the two either side were nothing to be sneezed at either. Whilst a leap from any part of the bridge might charitably be called 'a very bad idea', a leap from the central span was just plain suicide. No way Henry would have leapt off of his own accord, even if he did feel he had something to prove.

John walked up and down each side of the bridge. He saw nothing along the south side, not on the wall nor in the gutter, but on the north side up near the apex he found that some of the brickwork was a little loose. Considering how low the wall was, about hip height, it was conceivable for a person to have bumped up against it, for one of the stones to have slipped, and for said person to go tumbling over the edge into the icy water below. Not likely, mind you – they'd have to have been damn unlucky for that to be the case – but conceivable nonetheless.

John peered over the edge of the bridge, imagining what it would be like to fall from that height. The year he'd graduated, only one person had been dumb enough to give tombstoning a try – little Teddy Dobson. Looking to make a name for himself he'd flung himself into the void with hope in his heart and a smile on his face, neither of which had lasted very long. Everyone heard him change his mind halfway down, the meaty slap when he hit the water, and the agonising scream when he broke the surface. Dragged from the river with tears streaming down his face and his arm hanging limply by his side, the sight of him being carted off to hospital had been more entertainment than most of them had bargained for. They'd all left after that.

He did make a name for himself though. From that day forth any time anyone did, was doing, or was about to do, something stupid, telling them 'Don't be a Dob' was usually all it took to get them to stop.

Kneeling down, John saw there was a scrape on the brickwork at about knee height – a long thin line cut deep into the mortar. *Now what could have made that?* he wondered. Something hard and heavy, moving with enough force not to be bothered by a brick wall. A small cart maybe, or possibly an omnibu—

There was a man standing at the far end of the bridge. More accurately, there was a man standing at the far end of the bridge watching John, and making no attempt to hide it.

John stood and faced the lone figure. It was too dark and too foggy to make out anything other than shadows and shapes, yet something about the way he stood there, unmoving, unafraid, put the willies up John something rotten. He kind of looked like the man John had chased outside Chard Manor, although so would anyone at this distance, in this weather. Not that it mattered really. Whoever he was, John had no intention of making his acquaintance. God gave you two ends of a bridge for a reason, and John had every intention of using the other end of this particular bridge very quickly indeed.

He turned his back on the man, only to find another man standing on the other end of the bridge. Well, this was awkward. The other man was bigger than the first, wider, heavier. He looked like he could flatten John with one hand if he wanted to. He wasn't actually trying to be menacing, but he really didn't have to. Being there was quite enough.

John turned back the other way. If it was a choice between the man mountain and the other guy it was no contest. Except the other guy now had a meat hook in his hand, a vicious looking implement John didn't like the look of one bit. He didn't know what the man planned on doing with it, he only knew he wouldn't like it when it happened.

The two men started walking towards John, slow and steady, all the time in the world. John, keeping calm – once you panic, you are lost – checked his pockets for weapons he knew he didn't have. The men moved closer. He tried pulling loose one of the bricks on top of the wall, but despite appearances they were jammed in there tight. Stepping to the middle of the bridge, walking backwards to keep both men in sight, he tried to come up with a plan.

The two men moved out into the centre of the road with him as they continued their slow advance. They were about twenty yards away now. John looked from one to the other. Perhaps he could rush one of them. He might make it past, although more likely is that they would land a blow, or catch his jacket, and then he would be done for. He felt the panic rise now. He could call for help but what would be the point? There was no one around to hear. And even if there were, his shouts would be drowned out by the river crashing far below him.

The river.

What choice did he have?

As the two men rushed him John bolted for the wall. With a wild leap he sailed headlong over the edge of the bridge, dropping through the air into the dark, icy river below. The force of the water hit him hard, like falling into concrete. It pushed the air from his lungs and sent his mind into a spin. He scrambled to the sur-face just in time to see a bridge support rushing towards him. He slammed into it, and an agonising pain shot up his leg, exploding in his brain. He screamed, rancid water filling his mouth as he was dragged back under. Clawing his way to the surface, coughing and retching as he gasped for air, he caught his shoulder on a rock, the turbulence of the water turning him over and pushing him back down again. He lost track of which way was up. Flailing about, he searched desperately for fresh air, but there was only water. His lungs were on fire. It took all his strength not to open his mouth and simply suck in a load of whatever was there. He tumbled over, breaking the surface as the river threw him sideways, slamming him head first into a large rock.

There was a blinding flash of light, John's body went limp, and with unexpected relief, he slowly felt the inky blackness take him.

CHAPTER 4

MONDAY

For a brief moment when he awoke, John felt quite serene.

In the river, as the darkness came, he'd completely given up, let go, released control in every conceivable way – and it had been divine. No stress, no worry, no fear or anxiety, just the flow of the river and the simplicity of wherever it may take him. It was pure liberation, devoid of fear and regret. He'd been in the moment for perhaps the first time in his life, and as he gradually came to, the last remnants of that liberation remained, taunting him with their simplicity as the world began creeping its way back into his conscious mind.

He was in a hospital bed. That was a good start. Beds were good. Better than the bottom of the river at least (although technically, that would be a bed too, right?). Keeping his eyes closed, he did a quick mental check of all his bits and bobs. Everything seemed to be in place. He wiggled his fingers and toes and nobody complained too much. But there was a dull throb in his right hip, and when he moved his leg a searing pain shot through his pelvis and down his leg, causing him to gasp. That wasn't good. It felt like serious damage, like something was missing or broken down there. It was hard to tell what. Reaching a hand under the covers he felt around, taking stock. His legs and hips seemed to be intact, albeit extremely battered and bruised, and between his legs he was relieved to discover that the family jewels were all present and correct as well.

"When you're quite finished, Mr Sinister, I'd like a word." John opened his eyes to find Detective Hardigan sitting on a stool at the end of his bed.

"Detective Hardigan. How delightful to see you again," said John, extracting his hand from beneath the covers. "Delightful to see anyone in fact, now that I come to think about it. I have a funny feeling I had a bit of a lucky escape."

"I'll say you did."

"Perhaps you would be good enough to fill in some of the details for me? My memory of recent events is a little hazy."

"Well, to begin with you're in St Hubert's. You were brought here last night when some old fella walking his dog found you floating in the river by the sewer outlet."

That explained it, John realised. Why his mother was on his mind all of a sudden: it was the smell, he knew he recognised it. A heady stench of sickness and chlorine that lingered in the air and got on the back of your throat. He'd never forget the hospital his mother had died in, and smelling its cold, unforgiving miasma once more brought all the old memories flooding back. He recognised the sickly green walls, draughty windows, and creaky iron beds that infected every room of the place. Seeing them again after all these years made him want to throw up.

"God knows what you were doing in the river, but I'm guessing from where we found you that you were thrown in somewhere near Gravesend Bridge?"

"That is correct. Although I went in the river of my own accord, just so you know."

"You did? Well that was stupid. Whatever could have possessed you?"

"I had incredible motivation, believe me."

"What sort of motivation?"

"One with hands like jack-hammers, and another with a meat hook."

"I see. So someone was trying to kill you?"

"It seems so, although who knows? All I can say is I had no intention of waiting to find out."

"Any idea who they were?"

"Not really. One of them kind of looked like this guy I chased the other day, but I can't say for certain. It was too foggy to tell."

"What guy?"

John told Detective Hardigan about the chain-smoker outside Chard Manor; what he looked like, when he'd seen him, and how he'd chased him into the grounds of a neighbouring house only to lose him in the woods. He left out the bit about the lawn. She didn't need to know about that.

Detective Hardigan wrote everything he said down. "And you've no idea what this man was up to?"

"None at all."

"What do you *think* he was up to?"

"Beyond having an interest in Chard Manor, I couldn't say."

"Why would this man want you dead?"

"I couldn't tell you."

Detective Hardigan lowered her notepad to look at John. "You're not being very helpful, Mr Sinister."

John shrugged. "I'm sorry, Detective. What can I say? I don't know what I don't know."

"Alright, then let me put it another way. Can you think of anyone else who might want to hurt you?"

John took a deep breath, blowing out his cheeks as he exhaled. "Well, there's Peter Chard for a start." Detective Hardigan raised an eyebrow. "I've been working on the theory that he killed his father and brother to get control of Chard Mechanical. It's entirely possible he thought I was getting too close and hired a couple of goons to take me out. He seems the type."

"I see," said Detective Hardigan. "Anyone else?"

"Well, there's Nero. He's a, er... chocolatier, among other things."

"Yes, I'm well aware of Mr Nero and his activities," said Detective Hardigan. "How does he fit into all this?"

"I think Henry owed him some money, although I can't say for certain."

"Really? He must have owed him a lot for Nero to kill him for it."

"I don't think he meant to kill him, if indeed he did. He probably just wanted to scare him a bit and it went wrong somehow."

"I see. Well, we can look into that too, which will be a lot of fun I'm sure," said the detective. "So, is that everything? No one else who might want to put you out of their misery, so to speak?"

John couldn't help himself. "There's also Spencer Shelby the Third. He was in a relationship with Mary Chard until recently. He might have done away with Donald and Henry Chard to get to her. And her money."

Detective Hardigan frowned. "That's pretty thin, Mr Sinister."

Of course it was thin, he knew it was thin, but if it sent the police to Spencer's door then he was all for it. "It's a possibility I've been working on," he said with a shrug.

Detective Hardigan reluctantly made a note of the name. "Sounds like you've been making friends all over the place."

"It's a gift," said John blithely.

"Well your 'gift' seems to be bad for your health. Hopefully you'll leave the investigating up to us from now on."

"I still have an obligation to my client, Detective."

Detective Hardigan put away her notebook. "Suit yourself, Mr Sinister. Personally, I'd rather not have to look into your untimely death as well. Even if waiting to see who tries to kill you next would probably save me a lot of legwork in the long run."

"Why, Detective Hardigan, I didn't know you cared."

"I don't. Believe me," she said, standing. John pushed himself more upright, wincing at the pain in his leg when he moved. Detective Hardigan watched him try and get comfortable again. "I'd tell you to stay out of trouble, but with that leg I suspect I don't have to. You're not going anywhere any time soon." She made her way to the door. "I'll let you know if I find anything. In the meantime get some rest, Mr Sinister, for all our sakes."

John smiled with absolute sincerity. "For you, Detective, anything."

John left the hospital five minutes after Detective Hardigan. He wasn't trying to be heroic, he just figured that if the people who'd tried to kill him heard that he was still alive they might try again, and if he stayed in St Hubert's they'd know exactly where to find him.

That and the smell. He couldn't stand the smell.

He made it as far as the main entrance with his gammy leg before he had to sit down. Getting on his manky trousers, which were all hard and crinkly from dried-up river (as well as God knows what else) had been difficult enough, but getting down the corridor and out of the building had nearly wiped him out. Thank goodness there was an omnibus stop right outside the hospital. At least he wouldn't have to walk all the way home.

Hobbling through his sister's front door, John let his jacket fall to the ground. Shuffling down the hallway he followed the smell of soap powder into the kitchen. There he found Jane with a washboard against her chest, scrubbing skivvies in the kitchen sink.

"There you are, I've been worried sick," she said without looking up. "So what did you get up to last night? Drinking and gambling, I'll be—" She spotted the shambolic figure hunched in her doorway. "My God! John. What's happened to you?"

"I had an argument with the river," he said, with a reassuring smile. "The river won."

"What? You fell in the river!" Mary dried her hands on her apron as she went to help him. "What on earth did you do something like that for?"

"I was trying not to die at the time. Look, can we talk about this later, I need a bit of a lie down? I'm feeling a bit..." John waved his hand in the vicinity of his head.

"Of course we can. Here, let's get you through to the other room."

With one arm for his sister and one arm for the wall, John made it to the couch. Collapsing onto it, he lay there whilst Jane pulled off his boots and gently lifted his legs up off the floor. Tucking a blanket in around him, she pressed her palm to his pale, grubby cheek.

"I'll get you some tea," she said. "Be back in a sec."

When she was gone John freed his arms and reached under the couch for his travel bag. Rooting around in it he found the small wooden club – about the same shape and size as a policeman's truncheon – that had seen him safe more than once on his travels looking for work. Slipping it under the cushion beneath his head he suddenly felt a lot safer.

It was always best to be prepared. If they were still after him then his attackers could come for him at any time. He would have to remain vigilant, to stay aware of his surroundings. There was no telling when or where they might strike again.

When Jane returned with the tea she found John fast asleep, a small wooden club lying on the floor beside him.

Crouched on the window ledge, Dexter eyed up the jump. It wasn't far, only a few feet, but considering the massive drop if he missed, nearly the full height of the airship factory, he was understandably nervous. Unlike your average cat, he did not have nine lives to play with.

Dexter would be the first to admit that even though he was better than a meat cat in lots of ways, agility was not one of them. He had balance, thanks to his internal gyroscope, but when you're mostly made of heavy metals, leaping nimbly from place to place was not something that came naturally. He could jump, of course he could jump, it just took a bit more concentration on his part that's all.

He was sitting in the window of the landing outside Peter Chard's office. His goal was the block and tackle rig sticking out the side of the building, a couple of feet to his left. The door to Peter Chard's office was closed, and whilst he could hear a little of what was going on if he pressed his ear up against the wood, he wanted to see what was happening as well. And if he jumped onto the tackle support and walked to the end he'd get an unobstructed view of everything Peter Chard was up to, provided he did it next to his desk that is.

He needed to stop faffing about. The longer he sat there the worse it got. With a quick whispered prayer to the cat gods – "Nuts to this." – Dexter jumped from the window to land perfectly on the wooden support. "As if there was any doubt," he said, smiling to himself.

Walking to the end of the protruding beam, he settled down to watch whatever nefarious activities Peter Chard got up to.

An hour went by, quite possibly the most boring hour of Dexter's short life. All Peter Chard did was look at bits of paper, occasionally scribbling something down with a disgruntled look on his face. He didn't count out any ill-gotten gains, didn't call anyone to arrange anything dubious, didn't issue any orders to have someone 'taken care of', he just shuffled paperwork, drank tea, and sat with his head in his hands looking dejected. All told, it was turning into a thoroughly disappointing stake-out.

He did make one call on the radiophone in that time, but only to shout at someone about gaskets and fittings, which Dexter considered a serious misuse of a quite excellent invention. Donald Chard had explained to him at length one day how the radiophone worked. He'd shown him how to make a call, explained how the sound was converted into radio waves, and how it was converted back at the other end. Dexter had found it quite fascinating. A wonderful piece of technology, worthy of respect, and here Peter Chard was using it to abuse people for no good reason. It was criminal.

It was nice to see Peter Chard looking so stressed though. That was fun. Dexter didn't think of himself as someone who succumbed to the pleasures of schadenfreude, but for some people he was willing to make an exception. Peter Chard was one of the those people, and the reason for that was quite simple; Peter Chard liked to kick cats.

It wasn't just cats, Peter Chard was the type to lash out at the world when he didn't get his own way, but it was the cats that bothered Dexter. He'd seen him one day, from one of the upstairs windows at Chard Manor. There'd been a lot of shouting and slamming of doors, and then Peter Chard had come storming out, crunching his way angrily across the gravel driveway looking for a fight. What he found was one of the local strays wandering across the drive, not a care in the world. A sweet little short-haired grey with cute ears and kind eyes that only ever wanted to make friends with people. Unfortunately, it tried to make friends with Peter Chard.

The meat-sack had taken a swing at her, tried to boot her out of the way. Thank God Shorty was quick on her feet. She'd dodged his flying kick and was away into the bushes in no time, nearly putting him on his ass when his boot connected with nothing but fresh air.

Dexter had got a right laugh out of that. As far as he was concerned, cat kickers deserved everything that was coming to them. After all, it didn't take much effort to be nice to cats. A quick scratch behind the ear and a leg to rub up against and they were good. All it took was a little self-discipline. Hell, even Mary Chard, who could also fly off the handle at the drop of a hat, was nice to Dexter when he was around.

If Peter had problems at the factory, then good. Couldn't happen to a nicer bloke. He felt a bit sorry for Nomko and Mrs Crabtree though. They were good people, they didn't deserve to be working at a failing company. But as for Peter Chard, he couldcouldcould—

Whoa! What was that? He'd glitched. He hadn't done that in ages, not since the early days. Dexter did a quick internal scan and found that his steam was low, less than a quarter of full capacity. He needed to recharge. He hadn't gone this long without recharging since... He couldn't remember ever having gone this long without recharging. He normally charged up every night to be safe. To be this low was not good. He really needed to get back to the manor to sort himself out.

Where was that fool Sinister? He should have come for him last night. Not that he was surprised he didn't. He was, after all, just another unreliable meat-sack.

Dexter had spent last night in Nomko's. He thought the engineer would have come back this morning, but he didn't. There must have been some delay with the parts he'd gone to get. Okay, well, that was a while ago. Maybe he was there now. Only one way to find out really. Leaping back through the window, Dexter trotted down the iron staircase, through the factory, and out into Nomko's workshop.

Dexter did a full sweep but there was no sign of him. He still wasn't back yet. The bed was as he'd left it, the kettle was cold and, most importantly, the boiler hadn't been switched on. There's no way that would be the case if Nomko had been anywhere nearby. He needed steam almost as much as Dexter did.

Dexter eyed up the boiler's connectors. Even if he could get the thing fired up there was no way he could connect himself to recharge. Back at the manor house Donald Chard had set up a special rig so that Dexter could connect himself each night. Here it was all loose hoses and screw-in joints. He might be able to get a hose into his charging port, with a bit of contortion and a lot of luck, but he'd never be able to lock it into place. He didn't have the thumbs for it.

He wasn't worried though. He had enough steam for now, probably enough to last him until tomorrow even, if he used it right. As long as he got a full recharge by the end of the day he'd be fine.

Nomko would be back soon, he was sure of it. And if not, then Sinister had said he would come for him – he'd promised, in fact – so there was no need for concern. He had options. Everything would be fine. There was certainly no need to panicpanicpanic—

Uh oh.

Chapter 5

Tuesday

Jane gently shook her brother awake. "Rise and shine, sleepy-head," she said. "Time to get up."

"Wassup? Woz goin' on?" John rubbed his eyes with the heel of his hand. "Sorry, I must have dozed off. Guess I needed a bit of a nap, eh?"

"A nap? You've been asleep for hours," said Jane.

"Hours? What time is it?"

"Around eight."

John looked at the sunlight coming in through a crack in the curtains. "At night?"

"In the morning, stupid. You slept through the night."

"But that's,"—he counted it out on his fingers—"eighteen hours! How could you let me sleep for eighteen hours? Why didn't you wake me?"

"Because you needed the rest. Why? What's the problem?"

"There's just... somewhere I have to be, that's all." He thought of Dexter, alone at the factory. Would he still be there? Would he be okay? Surely Nomko would be back by now. He'd take care of him, wouldn't he?

"You're not going anywhere, not with that leg you're not. Besides, you have a visitor."

Jane went to the window and flung open the curtains, filling the room with blinding light. Blinking away the sleepiness, John's eyes slowly came into focus to reveal the figure of Agnes Goodenough looming over him.

My God! he thought. *She's come to feed me to the pigs.*

John spotted his club lying on the floor. He lunged for it but it was too far away, too much of a stretch, and as his fingers closed around the handle a paralysing pain shot through his hip, locking him in place. On the other side of the room, Agnes Goodenough chuckled.

"Settle down, tough guy. I came to talk." Easing him back onto the couch, Agnes plucked the club from his unresisting hand.

Jane was mortified. "John! I'm surprised at you. Agnes is our guest."

Agnes waved away her concerns. "That's alright, Jane. I understand. I'd have done the same if I were him."

"Well that's very kind of you to say, but still..." She gave John a withering look. "Anyway, Agnes, please have a seat, won't you? Can I fetch you anything? Some tea perhaps?"

And then the most amazing thing happened. Agnes Goodenough smiled.

John was mesmerised. He'd never seen Agnes smile before. Oh he'd seen her smirk, and grin, and look on with wry amusement, but he'd never once seen her offer up a genuine smile. Not a real smile, a smile from the heart, the kind you save for someone you really like. It was beautiful, it lit up her face, and her face lit up the room.

"That would be lovely, Jane, thank you."

Jane smiled back. "Coming right up."

Agnes's smile followed Jane all the way out of the room. When she turned back she found John watching her closely. The smile vanished. "What's your problem?"

"What? Oh, nothing. Nothing," John busied himself sitting up and getting comfy. "So, er, to what do we owe the honour? You said you came here to talk?" He said the word 'talk' like it was an alien concept.

"That's right," said Agnes, sitting herself down in the biggest armchair in the room. It was just wide enough for her hips, but the arms were too low for her to rest comfortably, so she had to let her hands dangle in-between her knees instead. "Nero had a visit from the police last night. Now, you wouldn't know anything about that would you?"

"Er... no. No. Nothing at all."

"You're a terrible liar, Sinister."

John felt a little faint. "Is he mad?"

"Well he ain't happy, put it that way."

"Should I be worried?"

"Given your propensity for making friends, probably. But not where Nero is concerned."

"Really?"

"Yeah. I mean, I wouldn't show my face round Caesar's any time soon, if at all in fact, but apart from that you've got nothing to worry about."

"Wow. I have to admit, I'm a bit surprised."

"Why's that then?"

"Well, you'd think putting him in the frame for murder would get a bit more of a reaction, to be honest."

Agnes shrugged. "Normally it would, but he's got other things on his mind right now. Plus, in this case, there are what you might call mitigating circumstances."

"Which are?"

"He didn't do it."

John pulled a face. "Yes, well he would say that wouldn't he?"

"He's not saying that. *I'm* saying that. Nero's not involved. Not only is there no profit in offing your friend, there was no reason to neither. Your friend was square. He didn't owe the club nothing. Hadn't been by in weeks, in fact. I asked."

John couldn't believe what he was hearing. "But I asked Nero that before and he wouldn't say. Why didn't he just tell me that in the first place?"

"Who knows? Maybe he didn't know. Maybe you didn't ask politely enough. Maybe he thought it was none of your business. The reasons don't matter. All that matters is that whatever happened to your boy, it had nothing to do with us."

"Says you."

Agnes scowled at John. "You need to get over yourself, mate. This is a courtesy call. I don't need to be here, I don't owe you an explanation, and I certainly got no reason to lie to you. But if you don't believe me that's fine. It's no skin off my nose either way."

John shifted uncomfortably in his seat. Agnes's glare was hard to bear. He tried to speak, to make it better, but he couldn't find the words. Like everyone else, John found apologies hard to come by. It was a relief when his sister finally returned with the tea.

Agnes jumped up to clear some space on the sideboard, so that Jane would have somewhere to set down the tray. Peering up at the offering, John saw that his sister had pulled out all the stops. She'd dusted off the good china, had put the sugar in a bowl and the milk in a little jug, and she'd even managed to rustle up a plate of macaroons, which he was a little annoyed about. He didn't know they had macaroons. He'd been craving macaroons all week, and now he knew why. He must have smelt them baking one day.

Jane was mother, pouring out the tea and handing it round. Then she offered them all a biscuit – guests first, of course – before taking one for herself. Finding a stool, she joined them for their impromptu tea party.

Agnes looked hilarious balancing a tiny teacup in one massive hand whilst she delicately clutched a macaroon between thumb and forefinger in the other. John started to laugh, then he remembered he liked his head where it was, so he quickly choked back the giggle, covering his bizarre spluttering with a loud slurp of hot tea. Jane gave him another withering look.

"So, Agnes, lovely though it is to see you, I know this isn't a social call. I believe you and John were in the middle of discussing something and I interrupted. Please, do continue."

"Thank you, Jane. Actually, I've said what I needed to say, more or less. The only thing left to add is this; if you want to find out what happened to your mate you need to talk to those idiot friends of his, if you haven't already, and ask them about that little club of theirs."

"The Scion Club? What has that got to do with anything?"

"No, not that, the other one. What was it they called themselves now? Something stupid. Oh yes, that was it, the Hell-Bats. They called themselves the Hell-Bats."

John choked on his drink, hot tea shooting out of his nose. He started to cough, Jane leaping up to rescue her china from certain disaster whilst he fumbled in his pocket for a handkerchief. A cup in each hand she turned to Agnes, utterly bemused. "I don't understand," she said. "Who are the Hell-Bats?"

"Where did you hear the name Hell-Bats?" croaked John.

"Your boy Henry used to bring his friends round Caesar's now and then. I heard one of them talking about it one night. Sounded like a load of posh-boy nonsense to me, but they got shushed up pretty quick so I figured it might be important. Why, do you know what it is?"

"I do, sort of, only it doesn't make any sense. The Hell-Bats don't exist anymore."

"You sure about that?"

"I was, yes. But now..."

"Sorry," said Jane, "but who are we talking about?"

"Right," said John, sitting up. "It's like this. The Hell-Bats were this gang at school, way before I went there." He turned to Agnes. "I went to Howard Aglet Grammar School," he explained.

"Good for you."

"Not quite. You see the school was originally set up by the industrialist Howard Aglet to educate the children of his workers, only it did so well it wasn't long before all the rich people wanted to send their kids there as well. Now you can imagine what that was like. The poor kids hated the rich kids for taking over their school, and the rich kids hated the poor kids because they showed them up every day.

"You see the rich kids didn't want to learn anything. Why would they? They were all set to inherit a fortune. But they didn't like to be made fools of either, so they started giving the poor kids grief, and thus the Hell-Bats were born."

"So the rich kids started the Hell-Bats, yeah?"

"No. The other way around. The poor kids started the Hell-Bats as a way of fighting back. They couldn't do anything to the rich kids face to face, they'd get expelled, but they could bide their time and get them later on when no one was looking. They'd mask up and lie in wait, then, whenever someone on their list came by, *whack!*, justice was served. You've heard of the School of Hard Knocks, I take it? Well this is where the phrase comes from."

"Nice," said Agnes, smiling.

"Not so much," said John. "When the faculty found out, all the poor kids were expelled, every last one of them. Not that there were all that many left by that point. Howard Aglet's became just another private school for the upper classes, and the poor kids had to go back to getting their education on the streets like before."

"But if that's the case how come you went there then? You ain't rich."

"Howard Aglet's likes to let in one scholarship each year, to feel like they're still doing their bit for the community, and I was the lucky soul who got in."

"Huh. I bet that was fun."

"You've no idea," said John.

"So I was right. It is a load of posh-boy nonsense after all. But if all this finished years ago, what was your mate and them going on about in the club then?"

"No idea," said John. "I mean it sounds like they've resurrected the Hell-Bats, but why? They can't be out to fight the status quo. They *are* the status quo."

"Why don't you ask one of them and find out?"

"Because I doubt anyone is going to confess to being a member. Not without some kind of proof anyhow."

"So get some proof."

"And how do you suggest I do that?" said John.

"Well," said Jane. "It sounds like this club of theirs is a way for them to get away with doing things they're not meant to be doing, like the poor kids at Howard Aglet's. So why don't you start with the police, see if there are any strange, unexplained crimes that have happened recently? Whatever they've been up to they're bound to have left a trail."

"That's true," said John. "Good idea. I need to go speak to Detective Hardigan." He started struggling to his feet.

"John, for God's sake! You can't go out like that. You're in no fit state."

"I can and I will. They killed my friend, Jane. I can't let them get away with that."

"And they almost killed you, remember? What happens if they try again? How are you going to defend yourself?"

John took in his torn and mangled body and sat back down again. "You make a good point."

"Sounds like you need protection," said Agnes.

"Is that an offer?"

"Good God no. But I can put you in touch with a couple of geezers I know who'd be up for it, if you like?"

"Are they as tough as you?"

Agnes smiled. "No one is as tough as me."

"Then why would I hire them?"

"Because I'm not available."

"Would ten shillings make you available?"

Agnes shook her head. "I'm afraid not, mate."

"What about a pound? Would that change your mind?"

"I don't think so."

"Two pounds?"

"I said no."

"Three?"

"You're getting on my nerves now, Sinister."

Jane leaned forward and placed her hand on Agnes's arm. "What if we said please? Please, Agnes, will you help my brother out?"

"Damn it," Agnes protested. "That's not fair. Why you gotta ask me like that?" Jane gave her an apologetic smile, and Agnes groaned unhappily. "Five pounds," she said. "Not a penny less. Someone's tried to kill you already. If you want my help it's gonna cost you five pounds."

"Done!" said John.

"I think I have been," said Agnes, shaking John's hand reluctantly.

"Wonderful. Thank you, Agnes," said Jane, squeezing Agnes's arm. "You're an angel." John wasn't sure, but he thought he saw Agnes blush.

"So, when do we start, boss?" said Agnes.

John shrugged. "Right now, I reckon."

"Oh no. Surely you've got time for another biscuit before you go?" said Jane.

"That's up to the boss, it's his gig."

John was torn. He wanted to crack on, and he really needed to see about Dexter, but he was damn hungry too. "I tell you what," he said, "you throw in some hot, buttery toast and you got yourself a deal."

Barrelling his trilocipede through the factory gates, Nomko skidded to a halt in a cloud of dirt and dust. He made weary noises as he dismounted, stretching the kinks out of his back as he staggered across the cobbled courtyard. He'd been up all night with the artificers in Streebly, trying to get the parts he needed within acceptable tolerance limits. It had been a nightmare of a job. But finally, after hours of painstaking tweaking and adjustments, he'd got them just how he needed them to be.

Yawning and rubbing his eyes, Nomko stumbled into his workshop. It took him a moment to realise something was wrong, but when he did he dropped the finely-tuned parts he was carrying onto the workshop's hard concrete floor.

"No again," he groaned, looking at the empty space where his automotive engine should have been.

Marching through to his living quarters he dug out his personal radiophone and battered the receiver. "Hello? Put me through to police. Yes it emergency!" Sitting on the end of his bed he waited to be connected. He didn't see the tail sticking out from under his bed, or hear the faint click-click-clicking of a tiny steam engine clinging on for dear life.

John and Agnes made their way up the street towards Wainwright's Yard, John leaning on his mother's old cane for support.

Truth be told he didn't need it. Yes his leg still hurt, but the long rest had done him the world of good. He could probably walk on his own if he had to. But Jane and Agnes had put the kibosh on him taking his club for protection – "You don't need a club, you've got me next to you, innit." – so he'd insisted on the cane to have something heavy in hand, just in case.

Outside the station, Agnes pulled John to a stop. "Right, I'll be out here when you're done, yeah?"

"You're not coming in with me?"

"You're having a laugh, mate. I've been in there before, too many times, in fact. There ain't no way I'm going in by choice."

"But what if something happens?"

"Nothing's going to happen."

"It might."

"Oh don't be such a baby, you'll be fine. The place is full of policemen. No one's going to come after you in there." Agnes reconsidered. "Unless they're the ones who are after you of course, in which case you're screwed. But, if that *is* the case, then there ain't nothing I can do to help you. So..."

John didn't know what to say. He hadn't thought about that as a possibility. The idea was extremely troublesome, although it did make sense. If you were going to kill someone as important as Donald Chard, having the police in your pocket would be a wise thing to do.

Agnes, seeing John glaze over, snapped her fingers in front of his face. "Chop-chop, my son, time's a-wasting. You've only got me until five, remember? Can't stand around gawping all day." Agnes still had work to get to tonight. She had a sweet gig going at Caesar's, and she wasn't going to mess that up no matter how much John paid her.

Distracted by a plethora of new, unpleasant possibilities, John hobbled up the steps of Wainwright's Yard. He had to wait less than a minute before Detective Hardigan came to collect him this time. It seemed nearly getting yourself killed got you the VIP treatment around here.

"Sinister, what the hell are you doing here? You should be in hospital."

"Thank you for your concern, Detective, but I'm fine. The doc said it looks much worse than it is. Other than a bit of bruising I'm the picture of health."

Detective Hardigan eyed up his cane, and the drawn look on his face. "Yes, I can see that. So what can I do for you this time? I assume you have another request for me?"

"Actually, Detective, it's what I can do for you that matters. Tell me, do you have any unsolved cases on your books?"

"Loads. Why?"

"Well I might be able to solve a few of them for you. Today, in fact."

"I highly doubt that, but the prospect alone will get you a cup of tea. Why don't you come through? Let's get you sat down before you fall down."

In Hardigan's office John gladly lowered himself onto her tiny wooden chair.

"First things first," said the detective. "Before you ask there's no news on who might have helped you into the river the other night. No witnesses have come forward, and without a witness we really don't have much to go on."

"That's alright, Detective. I didn't expect you to have anything so soon."

"We've spoken to the three suspects you mentioned, Peter Chard, Nero, and Spencer Shelby the Third – who is quite a piece of work, thank you very much – and they all have alibis for when it happened."

"Well of course they do. They're not the sort to do their own dirty work, are they?"

Detective Hardigan forestalled any further comments with a raised hand. "They also found the suggestion that they might have it in for you to be fairly laughable. I mean none of them seem to like you very much, but they don't seem to dislike you enough to do anything about it either. I got the impression that you're just a stone in their collective shoe. A minor irritation, nothing more."

"Well that's disappointing, I must say. I thought I was a bit more annoying than that," said John. "And what about the man I chased? Any sign of him yet?"

"Not a dicky bird, I'm afraid. No one has seen hide nor hair of any mysterious man outside the gates of Chard Manor before or since your little dip in the river. He's long gone, if he was ever there to begin with."

"He was there, Detective. I chased him, remember?"

"Sorry. Slip of the tongue. Anyway, like I said, we've got nothing so far. Unless you're about to tell me something to change all that?"

"Er, no. Sorry. But that's not why I'm here."

"Then why *are* you here?"

"Well, a possibility has come to light that may go some way to explaining what happened to Henry Chard. I'm here to see if the idea's got legs or not, which is where you come in. Tell me, what sort of open cases do you have at the moment?"

"Let's see. Besides these two deaths that won't go away,"—Detective Hardigan gave John an accusing look—"and your own personal bit of fun, I've got a bag thief working King Street; a dentist who prefers stealing teeth to fixing them, especially if they've got a gold filling in them; and a guy who got run over by an omnibus. And that's just over the last few days. Oh, and there was a break-in at Chard Mechanical last night that apparently didn't happen."

"Not another one. What do you mean didn't happen?"

"I mean they reported a break-in this morning, then called back a short while later to say never mind, forget about it, everything's fine. The thing we thought was missing isn't missing after all. What do you mean another one?"

"It's just that Chard Mechanical appears to be a real hotbed of non-crime. They didn't have a break-in on Friday as well. Out of curiosity, did they mention what they thought had gone missing?" *The same automotive engine that wasn't stolen Friday night, perhaps?*

"They didn't, and I didn't ask. To be honest, once they withdrew their complaint I stopped listening. I've got enough on my plate without chasing down fantasy break-ins. I only mention it because I thought it might be of interest."

"Indeed it is, Detective, but unfortunately it's not the kind of thing I was looking for. I was thinking more along the lines of something a little more... quirky."

"Quirky?"

"You know, strange, unusual, weird. A bit odd."

Realisation dawned for Detective Hardigan. "Oh, I see. You want the cuckoo cases. Well why didn't you say so? Those I can do. In fact, I've got a couple that are probably right up your alley. Let me see..." The detective rooted through the piles of paper on her desk, extracting a couple of files. "Here we go. A break-in at the Museum of History two weeks ago, and a fortnight before that someone broke into the zoo and shaved off a lion's mane."

"Someone shaved off a lion's mane?"

"Half shaved actually, on the right-hand side. We found the clippers and the rest of the mane in the enclosure. From the looks of things they bottled it half way through and did a runner. My guess is the lion woke up before they could finish the job."

"And what about the Museum of History?"

"That one someone got into the Egyptology exhibition. They moved some of the exhibits, tried on some of the outfits, that kind of thing. They didn't nick anything so we haven't bothered with it that much. We figured it was just a bunch of kids messing around."

"Yes, well, you're right about that. Mental children, at least."

Detective Hardigan was all ears. "You know who it was?"

"I have my suspicions, but I'd like to look into things a little further before naming any names, if that's alright? Any objections to me sticking my nose in a bit?"

"Knock yourself out. I've all but given up on these two to be honest. Any fresh information would be greatly appreciated. But if you find anything you come straight to me, got it? I'm the law around here, not you."

"Cross my heart and hope to die," said John.

"Well, let's call that plan B shall we?"

There was a knock at the door. A young constable entered. "Case for you, Detective. Just came in."

Detective Hardigan gave a weary sigh.

"Thank you, Tommy," she said, taking the file and looking it over.

"No problem," said Constable Tommy, giving the detective a look that she missed completely but John didn't. "Happy to help." He hovered by her desk, hoping for something more, but Detective Hardigan was too busy reading to notice.

Reluctantly, Constable Tommy left the room, pulling the door to with a forlorn click. *Poor lad*, thought John. *He's got it bad.*

As she scanned the file, an amused smile spread across Detective Hardigan's face. She looked up at John. "Well now, Mr Sinister, it seems like we've got a third cuckoo case for you. And from the looks of things it's the best yet. It seems that last night a person or persons unknown broke into Willard's Wonderful World of Waxworks and Automata and, quote 'messed about with the royal family exhibit' end quote."

"Messed about with? Messed about with how?"

"Let's just say that the Queen is now wearing trousers and her husband, the Prince Consort, isn't."

John's imagination ran wild. "I must confess, I'd like to see that."

"As would I," said Detective Hardigan, closing the file. "Tell you what, you meet me outside Willard's at noon and I'll take you in with me, provided you promise to keep your mouth shut and to not touch anything?"

John hadn't actually been angling for an invitation, but he wasn't about to argue now that he had one. "Great! Good. Yeah, sounds good. Hey, maybe I can buy you lunch afterwards as a thank you or something?"

Detective Hardigan seemed to consider this, and him, for what felt like a very long time. "Alright. But only if you change that scruffy jacket of yours. I won't be seen out with a man who looks like he slept on a park bench last night." John's new jacket had got pretty messed up when he'd gone in the river, so he'd had to revert to his old coat while his sister gave the other one a good wash.

"Sure thing. Of course. Whatever you say, Detective," said John smiling (because he didn't know what else to do). What the hell just happened? Did he just ask Detective Hardigan out on a date?

John insisted Detective Hardigan left him to find his own way out. Partly it was so that he didn't unintentionally ask her to marry him on the way to the door, but mostly it was so that he could sneak downstairs to have a word with the coroner before he left.

He found Doctor Semble up to his elbows in some poor soul – a misshapen lump of a man whose internal organs seemed to have made a dash for freedom. Physically he was kind of all over the place. The phrase that immediately sprang to John's mind was 'flat as a pancake'. Or quite possibly, 'Oh crepe!'

"Ah, Mr Sinister. Good that you are here. I was about to send you a message. I have the results of the autopsies you, *ahem*, suggested."

"Oh yes," said John, deliberately not looking down at the mangled face looking up at him. "So what did you find?"

"Henry Chard died as I said before, from drowning. His lungs were full of water."

"I see," said John, a little disappointed.

"He did however have significantly more physical injury than one might expect of a drowned man. He had a fractured skull, a dislocated shoulder, lacerations to his chest, and a broken leg, snapped at the knee, consistent with a blow from the side delivered with extreme force."

"Force from what? Something on the river bed perhaps?"

"I don't think so."

"Are you sure? A man can get tossed about pretty good in a fast-flowing river. Believe me, I know."

"It's a possibility, certainly, but I'd say it's more likely something hit him rather than he hit something else."

"Really? So you're saying it was deliberate."

"Either that or an unfortunate accident. For example, if he had been found on the side of the road like our friend here,"—Doctor Semble indicated the flattened body between them—"I'd have concluded he'd been struck by an omnibus, as was he. But, as it is, all I can say with any certainty is that the wounds are very similar and that they probably occurred on dry land."

"I see," said John. "And what about Donald Chard? Did you find something there also?"

"Ah!" said Doctor Semble, reaching for his notes. "Now there you really have put the cat among the pigeons. It seems that despite the evident damage, Donald Chard did *not* die of a heart attack as I first thought. The truth is much stranger. He asphyxiated. Donald Chard suffocated to death."

"Suffocated? You mean he was strangled?"

"No, no, not at all. The muscles in his throat went into spasm, closing off the windpipe. Once that happened death was inevitable. The poor man didn't stand a chance."

"Dear God, that's awful," said John. "What a nasty way to go. But how could something like that happen? Was it deliberate, or is it something that could have happened naturally?"

"There are any number of possible causes, both natural and man-made. It will take some time to run the necessary tests to know for sure."

"We don't have time, Doctor, lives may be at stake. Can't you guess?"

Doctor Semble bristled. "I don't guess, Mr Sinister. You will just have to be patient. The answers you seek will come soon enough."

John could tell the doctor wasn't going to budge. Like a drowning man clinging to a life raft, he had his procedures and he was sticking to them. He'd made a mistake, offered up a wrong cause of death. He would not be rushed into making another. "Very well," said John. "Thank you, Doctor. I look forward to hearing from you soon."

John left, giving the mangled corpse one last involuntary look on the way out. Life was tough sometimes, it surely was, but in many ways it could be much, much worse.

"You alright?" said Agnes. "You look a little green around the gills."

"I'm fine," said John, taking some deep breaths. "Come on, we've got some people to see."

"Right you are. So where to first, boss?"

"First up is Chard Mechanical. Apparently they didn't have a break-in last night. I want to find out what wasn't stolen, and who didn't take it."

Agnes and John stood in the yard of Chard Mechanical, where for once the sun was out. Shafts of golden light broke through the clouds, hitting the factory in dramatic fashion as if to say, 'Here, Great Works Be Done!' John thought it was a bit much, but for Agnes it was just as it should be.

"So this is where they make the airships?" she said, with a hint of awe.

"That's right."

"Brilliant. I love those things."

"Really? I didn't think you'd be into stuff like that."

"Why not?"

John's mind ran into the brick wall that is every unconsidered assumption. "I– I don't know. I just didn't."

"Well I am. I love everything about them. The design, the engineering, the way they move through the air. Honest to God, if I had my way I'd just sit and watch them float about all day."

"Yeah? Shame there's not any in at the moment. You could have had a close-up look."

"Yeah, well. You can't have everything now, can you," said Agnes.

They crossed the yard and entered the factory via the big double doors, John keeping an eye out for Dexter along the way. All the way across the factory floor Agnes was like a kid in a toy shop. She couldn't take her eyes off the airship that was under construction, even after they began their ascent up the rickety staircase. John on the other hand had more pressing concerns. The staircase rattled and shook with each of Agnes's heavy footsteps, brick dust and lumps of mortar trickling from the wall fixings as they passed each one by. It was disconcerting to say the least. They say that men find religion on the battlefield, but it was on that short climb to Peter

Chard's office that John made peace with the Almighty once and for all.

At the top, he barged into the office without knocking. Partly he hoped to catch Peter Chard doing something naughty, but mostly he just wanted to get back onto relatively solid ground.

Peter Chard was sitting at his desk, his head in his hands. "Oh for God's sake! What do you want?" he said, sitting back and folding his arms.

"Just a moment of your time if I could, Mr Chard."

"I've wasted enough of my time talking to the police thank *you* very much. I haven't got any to waste on the likes of you."

"Yes, I heard about the break-in."

"Actually I was referring to the accusation of attempted murder."

"Oh right, yes." With all the recent developments John had forgotten all about that.

"As for a break-in, I don't know what you're talking about. Now if you would please leave!"

"No break-in? That's funny, because I heard different."

"Well you heard wrong."

"Really? Are you sure there's nothing missing? A prototype automotive engine perhaps?" The colour drained from Peter Chard's face.

"Who told you about that?"

"I imagine you've sunk quite a lot of money into its development. Quite a lot of other people's money too by the looks of things." John glanced at the paperwork on the desk, Peter Chard pulling it towards him like he could hide the truth. "If it were to go missing I expect it would be disastrous for you, especially with that big presentation you've got coming up."

"I-I-I—" Peter Chard deflated. Releasing the papers, he buried his face in his hands. "My God, we're done for," he whimpered. "Chard Mechanical is ruined."

John and Agnes exchanged a look of surprise. "Ruined? What do you mean ruined? What about the airships? I thought they were going great guns."

"Are you kidding me! Those damn airships are haemorrhaging money hand over fist. It's a miracle they've managed to stay afloat as long as they have." *No pun intended,* thought John. "And what with the kraken attack last month—"

"Hold on. What kraken attack? I never heard anything about that."

"And nor should you have. It cost us a lot of money to keep that quiet."

"But I thought the airships flew too high to have to worry about krakens."

"Normally they do, but when the weather is bad they sometimes have to go a little lower than is strictly advisable."

"Well I never. I had no idea."

"Yes, that's kind of the point. We kept it quiet because if we ever let on that we were in trouble that lot out there would eat us alive. You've no idea what it's like trying to keep a company like this going. It's all smoke and mirrors. 'You have to maintain a facade of profitability until it becomes a reality,' that's what the old man used to say. 'Appear successful and success will follow.'"

"Fake it till you make it," said Agnes.

"Exactly. Words my father lived by. Our whole estate is in such monumental debt, yet he flashed money around like there was no tomorrow." John remembered Donald Chard's drawer full of ready cash. It had looked impressive because it was meant to look impressive.

"So I'm guessing you're not the one that told the police about the break-in?"

"No I did not. *I'm* the only one trying to keep a lid on this whole thing. And I thought I had too, until you showed up. Listen, you can't tell anyone about all this. Not about the prototype, the airships, the debt, none of it. If word got out how much trouble we were in it would finish us. Please. You have to keep it to yourself."

John thought of Henry. So this is what he'd been worried about. The entire house of cards was on the brink of collapse. Then he thought of Mary. Did she know? Probably not. If Henry didn't know it was unlikely they'd have told her either. He looked at Peter Chard. The poor man was hanging on by a thread. He didn't have the heart to push him any further. "My lips are sealed," he said.

Peter Chard looked to Agnes, who gave an uninterested shrug. "I got no beef with you, guv."

"Good," said Peter Chard, sinking back in his chair. "Thank you. Thank you both." He seemed to relax, the act of sharing releasing his heavy burden, if only for a moment. Then, all of a sudden, he sat forward again. "You know what, a thought occurs. What if I was to hire you to find the prototype for us?"

"Me? Why me?"

"You're a detecting agent, aren't you?" Behind him, John heard Agnes snigger. "Isn't that why you're here?"

"Well, yes, in a way. But with all due respect, Mr Chard, it doesn't sound like you can afford me."

"You're right, I can't pay you up front. But I can pay you a lump sum if you find the prototype and get it here in time for next week's presentation."

"I don't know. Something like that could be... expensive."

"I understand. How does twenty pounds sound?"

Agnes whistled softly, clearly in favour of saying yes, but John hesitated. He didn't really want to get involved. It sounded like a right pain, and he had enough on his plate already. "I don't think I can help you, Mr Chard."

Even though she was standing behind him, John felt Agnes gawp in disbelief. Peter Chard, undeterred, went in his pockets and pulled out a handful of notes and some loose change. Dropping it on the desk he counted it up. "I've got about four pounds on me," he said. "It's yours if you help me out. Plus another twenty five on delivery. That's the best I can do." John looked at the measly pile of cash on the table. "Please, Mr Sinister. I've nowhere else to turn. I need your help. What do you say?"

It was the please that did it. "I say it sounds like you've got yourself a deal, Mr Chard," said John, gathering up the cash.

"Crikey, Sinister, I didn't realise you were raking in that kind of dough. I'd have asked for way more money if I'd known."

"It's a fairly recent phenomenon, believe me. Besides, you heard the man, I don't make a penny extra unless I deliver the prototype, and the chances of that are slim at best." Heading down the iron staircase, John tried to ignore the way they shuddered.

"So where do you start with something like that?"

"You start at the beginning, I guess. The scene of the crime." Leaving the factory by its big double doors, John and Agnes made their way to Nomko's workshop.

The workshop looked different in the daylight. Sun streamed in through the skylights revealing odd contraptions on every shelf, bench, and spare bit of floor they could find. Glancing round the room, John saw a model of an iron ship floating in a large bath tub, a backpack with a long hose and some bellows that you appeared to operate with your feet, a deconstructed player piano next to various bits of a mechanical man, and, in the far corner, a pile of replica horse legs sat gathering dust. There was also a large, conspicuously empty space in the centre of the room, in the middle of which, in a pair of greasy blue overalls, sat Nomko, seemingly oblivious to the world. His legs were crossed, his eyes were closed, and his hands were folded loosely in his lap.

"Wow. Look at all the great stuff," said Agnes, inspecting what appeared to be a device for peeling potatoes.

Nomko opened his eyes.

"Ah, Mr Sinister. How nice to see you again."

"Call me John, please," said John, helping Nomko to his feet. "And it's nice to see you again, too. How have you been?"

"I am not good, John, not good at all. My heart is heavy with grief. My baby, as you can see, is gone." Nomko looked forlornly at the empty space.

"Yes, I heard about that. That's why I'm here. Mr Chard has hired me to find your, um, baby, and get it back for you."

"This wonderful news, but I do not see how it can be done? No one see anything and no one know anything. I have asked."

"Why don't you tell me what happened."

"I do not know. I in Streebly at time. I not return until this morning. That when I find engine gone. I do not know when she is taken. I call police, then I call Mr Chard and he go crazy. Tell me no one should know. Tell me I a fool. Tell me not to tell anyone else. I tell *you*, that man is a real *mendouna yatsu*."

"I'm sure he is," said John. "But anyway, what is it you think happened? Who could have taken the engine?"

"That I do not know. I wrack my brain over this but no one is there. I think maybe a rival may have taken, to slow Nomko down, but if so why bother? Why not set fire to her? That would work, also."

"Maybe they wanted it for themselves, to copy your designs. You are the best in the business."

"That true. Many people want Nomko design. But if so they very stupid. They leave plans behind." He pointed to some rolls of paper on one of the work benches. "Also, they must know we have patent on everything. If they make design like ours Chard Mechanical would destroy them in court. We may be run by a crazy man, but we have best lawyers money can buy."

"So who the hell could have taken it?" said John.

"No idea. But whoever it was, they can not have gone far."

"No? Why not?"

"Because I still working on engine when I leave. It not put together right. She run fine for a while, but then *boom*, she blow gasket. Not run anymore."

"So she's likely to be broken down somewhere nearby, you reckon?"

"Somewhere, yes, but maybe not so near. She drive some miles before she go wrong."

"Okay, good. Thanks, Nomko. That's good to know." John glanced over at Agnes, who had wandered off during their conversation, distracted by the workshop's many wonders. He leant in closer so as not to be overheard "Um, Nomko, have you seen Dexter around? I was meant to meet him here yesterday but I got delayed."

Nomko suddenly became very serious. "Yes. I see him. Come with me."

The little shed where Nomko lived was both cramped and cosy in equal measure. There was a small army cot against one wall, with a chest at its foot piled high with dirty clothes. A bench along the opposite wall held a selection of tools, a jug and basin for washing in, and a photograph of an old Japanese couple next to a small wooden shrine decorated with flowers. The room smelled funny, but not in a bad way, and it was lovely and warm thanks to a small pot-bellied stove sat between the head of the bed and the bench. Two rows of shelves around the top of each wall held more manuals and scientific papers than John had seen in his entire life.

A hose ran in through the shed's open window. It snaked its way across the floor to the bed where Dexter lay motionless, a rubber hose up somewhere rubber hoses don't normally go.

"I find under bed. He has been recharging for few hours now."

"Is he okay?"

"He will be, but it close. He almost completely out of steam. You know when he last recharge?"

"I don't really. Saturday afternoon or early evening I think."

Nomko's mouth fell open. "Two and a half day? He not recharge for two and a half day! My God, he lucky to be alive."

John was slightly bemused. Whilst he could appreciate a man showing concern for his creation he thought 'lucky to be alive' was probably laying it on a bit thick. "How long before he's fully recharged?" he said. "I need to talk to him."

"I must check gauges. One moment, please." Nomko went outside. John heard a clank and a hiss, followed by the steam engine winding down. Nomko returned. Disconnecting Dexter's hose, he stepped back and waited.

Nothing happened.

"He's not moving," said John.

"Really? Good job you here to tell me that," said Nomko. Kneeling next to the bed, Nomko felt underneath Dexter's chin. He opened the cat's mouth and peered inside, then he put his ear against Dexter's chest. "Hmm."

Clenching his fists together, Nomko whacked Dexter in the chest as hard as he could. The cat bounced off the bed and came screaming into life, shooting off round the room like his tail was on fire. Anything that got in his way was sent flying as he darted from bed to bench to the highest shelf he could find, where he sat cowering behind a stack of papers, wide eyed and terrified. "What the hell was that?!" he cried.

Nomko held his hands up. "So sorry. Gears were stuck. Nomko had to knock loose."

"You knocked something loose alright," said Dexter. "Give a cat a little warning next time before you—" Dexter spotted John. "YOU! Where the *hell* have you been? You said you'd be back for me. I *trusted* you, and look what happened. I almost ran out of steam! Do you know what that means for a someone like me? *Do you*?!"

"Hey, take it easy," said John. "I've had a rough time of it too, y'know. Do you see the cane? I'm lucky to be alive."

Dexter made his way down off the shelf. "What happened, someone let you down?"

"No. Someone tried to kill me."

"Well that's perfectly understandable," grumbled Dexter as he jumped back onto the bed.

"Anyway, you're being a bit dramatic aren't you? I mean, so what if you ran out of steam? You're a machine. Couldn't we just, y'know, wind you up, set you going again?"

Dexter looked fit to burst. "Wind me up. WIND ME UP! How can you say such a thing? I can't believe it! Of all the stupid, arrogant, ignorant things to say. I can't– I mean I just—" He paced up and down the bed, throwing evil glares at John as he flexed his claws against the bed's flimsy cotton sheets.

Nomko swiftly got in between the two of them before things got out of hand. "Actually, John, that not so. Dexter is unique. His brain special. It took many tries for us to make work, and when it did we not sure why. And we not able to recreate. If Dexter ever stop he may not go again."

"See," hissed Dexter, sitting with his back to John so that he could have a good pout.

"Alright," said John. "I get it. My mistake. But if running out of steam is so dangerous, then why didn't you make it so that he could last a bit longer between charges?"

Nomko seemed annoyed by the suggestion. "Dexter last long time for machine his size. If was today would maybe make different, but at time was best could do with what we had. He still Nomko's greatest achievement, but if you think can do better than Nomko then you welcome to try."

Dexter stalked to the end of the bed. "Look, this debate on how special I am is all well and good, but I—" He looked towards the workshop. "Someone's coming."

Agnes appeared in the doorway, a big grin on her face. "This place is amazing. I can't believe all the great stuff you've got. And some of the inventions are brilliant, just brilliant."

Nomko bowed to Agnes. "Thank you, miss. You are most kind."

"Say, Nomko," said John, "why don't you show Agnes your whirlygig? I'm sure she'd find it fascinating."

"What's a whirlygig?"

"It one-man flying machine I make."

"What, like a small balloon?"

Nomko smiled. "No. Come and see." He led Agnes back into the workshop, leaving John and Dexter to enjoy their awkward silence.

Sullen looks were exchanged. Nobody wanted to go first.

"Right," said John eventually. "We need to talk." He sat on the end of the bed next to Dexter. Dexter in turn moved down the other end of the bed, sat with his back to John, and began cleaning himself. John sighed. "Look, I'm sorry, alright. I'd have come back sooner if I could have."

"Yeah, right."

"Hey! Don't give me that. I would have. I don't leave my friends hanging." Dexter snorted his disbelief. "Anyway, how was I to know how dangerous it was for you? You never said anything."

"Why should I? It's none of your business."

"It's my business if you're relying on me. If I'd had all the facts I'd have done things differently. It's not my fault if you don't trust me, is it?"

"Oh that's right, if something goes wrong blame the cat. Broken vase? Dead bird on the doorstep? The cat must have done it. Typical meat-sack, everything is always somebody else's fault!"

"Look, I'm sorry you've had a scare, but—"

"A scare? A scare! Who said anything about being scared? I wasn't scared."

"Fine. Whatever you say," said John, rubbing his eyes. This was getting them nowhere. "Look, do you want to hear what's been happening with the case or not?"

"Very well," said Dexter, turning to face him. "Let's start with this whole walking stick thing you've got going on. You said you almost died? That sounds like a fun story."

"Oh, it was all kinds of fun," said John. "Two guys came after me on Gravesend Bridge. I had to jump in the river to get away from them."

"Really," said Dexter, not sounding too sympathetic. "That must have been very scary for you."

John nodded. "It was," he said. "Very."

He fell silent. Dexter walked down the bed and sat next to him. "Why do you think they were after you?"

"I have no idea. Clearly someone thinks we're getting too close to something. Although who, and to what, is anyone's guess at the moment."

"Well let's see. What's changed recently? Why would they come after you now and not before?"

"I don't know. Nothing really. I mean there's been some results from the coroner, but they came in after I went in the river, not before. They shouldn't be a factor."

Dexter sat up. "Results? What kind of results?"

"He said that Henry drowned, as expected, but that he had more injuries to his person than he should have had, suggesting foul play. And he said that Donald Chard *didn't* have a heart attack, he suffocated, although exactly how and why we don't know yet."

Dexter was on his feet. "You see! I told you something fishy was going on. Didn't I say there was something fishy going on?! You're damn right I did."

"Well, you'd know about fishy," said John, with a weak smile. Dexter looked at him sideways.

"You're still not funny," he said. "But you've had a rough time so I'll let you off. So, was it Peter Chard then? I bet it was. He's a cat kicker, y'know, that's how you can tell. Never trust a cat kicker, they're always up to something."

"Dexter, is your opinion of people based solely on how they treat cats?"

"Not solely. There are other things as well."

"Like what, for instance?"

"Well, there's their smell for a start."

"That's still a cat thing."

"And there's... their height. Like, how tall they are."

"Their height? What has height got to do with anything?"

"You wouldn't understand. It's a, er..."

"A cat thing?"

"Yeah."

"Well anyway, regardless of how he treats cats, I don't think Peter Chard is involved."

"And why's that then?"

"Because he's hired me to look into the theft of the prototype. And I doubt he'd do that if he was neck deep in– Did you know the automotive engine is missing?"

"How would I know that? I've been out of it since yesterday."

"That's what I thought. So you didn't see anything then?" Dexter gave John a look. "Okay, never mind. Anyway, I don't think he'd hire me to go sticking my nose into his business if he was going around killing people, do you? That wouldn't be very smart of him."

"Yeah well, I don't know about that," said Dexter. "He isn't all that smart to begin with."

"Alright, let's put it another way. Have you seen him get up to anything since you've been here?" Dexter avoided John's gaze. "Well?" The cat scrunched up his nose.

"No," he said begrudgingly. "He does stomp about the place shouting at people a lot, but as far as I can tell it's all business. He doesn't really seem like a murderer to me, just a bit of a dick."

"And what about the prototype? When did you see that last?"

"It was still here yesterday afternoon, when I... started running low. After that I don't know. I came in here looking for Nomko, and that's all I remember."

Dexter lay down, resting his chin on his crossed paws. John was tempted to stroke him but he thought better of it. He'd probably take it the wrong way.

"There's something else you should know about," said John. "I don't think it affects what happened to Donald Chard, but it could have something to do with Henry's death." He explained to Dexter all about the Hell-Bats. What they were, who they were, and how he thought they might be involved in the killing of Henry Chard. When he was finished, Dexter shook his head in amazement.

"Honest to God, how you meat-sacks came to be the dominant species on the planet is beyond me."

"Opposable thumbs and rampant self-interest probably."

"Probably," agreed Dexter. "So now what? What's our next move?"

"Next we look into these cuckoo cases the police gave me, see what we can find out."

"Sounds good," said Dexter, jumping to the floor. "Let's go."

John followed Dexter out into the workshop, the two of them heading outside when they didn't find Nomko and Agnes.

"By the way, who's the giant? She's massive!"

"Oh, that's Agnes. She's here just in case. You be nice to her. She can snap you like a twig."

"Don't worry," said Dexter. "You don't have to tell me twice."

Around the corner from the workshop they found Agnes jammed into the seat of the whirlygig, being taught the controls by an enthusiastic Nomko.

"So the levers control how fast the blades go, whilst the pedals control the angle. And it's the angle that determines the direction of travel?" said Agnes.

"Yes! That it exactly."

"Amazing. Absolutely amazing. You, sir, are a genius."

Nomko blushed. "You are too kind," he said, unable to look Agnes in the eye.

"So, how are you two getting on?" said John.

"Very good, thank you. Miss Agnes is quick learner."

"Only because you're such an excellent teacher, Nommy. And I told you before, it's just Agnes."

Nomko blushed even deeper, shuffling his feet. "Is easy with such an attentive audience... Agnes," he said, giving Agnes the sort of look John last saw on the face of a gangly police constable.

"Yes, well, I hate to break things up," said John, "but it's time for us to go."

Nomko turned to Dexter. "You are leaving?"

"I'm afraid so," said John quickly, before Dexter could answer him back. "Things to see, people to do. You know how it is."

Nomko took John and Dexter to one side. "I am thinking perhaps Dexter would like to stay? Have been working on something. Very clever. Very small. If work, would mean Dexter could generate own steam."

Dexter's eyes lit up. "Really? Is that possible, do you think?"

"Is possible, yes. But is very tricky."

"Is it dangerous?" said John.

"There is risk, yes," said Nomko. "Must take out old system to put new in. Is very difficult. But would not do if did not think possible. Nomko is no fool."

John turned to Dexter. "What do you think?"

"I dunno," said Dexter, lost in the possibilities. "I mean, if Nomko thinks it's a good idea then why not? Let's give it a go, eh?"

"Alright," said John. "In that case I'll leave you two to it." He walked back over to the whirlygig. "Come on, Agnes. Let's go."

"Sure thing, boss," said Agnes, climbing out of the pilot's seat.

She stood admiring the whirlygig one last time before going to shake Nomko's hand. "Thanks for showing me your wonderful inventions, Nommy. I had a great time."

Nomko took her hand and kissed the back of it, bowing deeply. "Pleasure all mine, Miss Agnes."

"You little charmer you," laughed Agnes, giving Nomko a playful shove that nearly knocked him to the ground. Nomko laughed as well, his face turning bright red.

John watched on, bemused by the possible logistics of it all. "Right, well, I'll see you later, Nomko, Dexter. I'll be back tonight to, um... catch up and all that."

Nomko bowed to John. "Indeed. Until then, my friend."

Picking up Dexter and placing him on his shoulder, Nomko headed back into his workshop, Dexter throwing John a sly wink as they walked away.

John turned to find Agnes giving him a funny look. "Did you just say goodbye to the cat?"

"What? No. Don't be daft. I dunno what you're talking about." Agnes grinned from ear to ear. "Oh shut up," said John, storming off.

Willard's Wonderful World of Waxworks and Automata was the most amazing, most magical, most fantabulous place in all of Hammersmyth, once. People used to travel from miles around to see its moving tableaus, paying their penny-a-piece to get up close and personal with all the famous explorers, historic generals, politicians, and many members of the royal family on display (because where else could you stick two fingers up at the great and the good and get away with it?). These days however they mostly just shuffled on past its broken facade expressing mild surprise whenever they realised that it was still open for business.

"Crikey, this place has seen better days," said Agnes.

John took it all in. The once bright paintwork had weathered badly over the years, and the faded lithographic posters along the front could have been of anyone, with just the odd top hat, handlebar moustache, or flamboyant ball gown to give a clue as to who they once were. Some of the woodwork was coming away and half of the bendy mirrors in the alcoved entrance were either cracked or missing. In fact, the only thing not falling apart on the old building was the brand new sign along the top, a blue placard with gold lettering illuminated by a dozen tiny gas lamps. "Haven't we all," said John, catching sight of himself in one of the broken mirrors.

"So who are we waiting for?"

"Detective Hardigan," said John, checking his watch. "She said to meet her here at noon."

"She? They've got female detectives now, have they? Well there's a turn up for the books. Is she cute?"

John shrugged. "I really couldn't say."

Agnes chuckled. "Yeah, she's cute alright." Glancing up and down the street, John pretended he didn't hear. "Did she say to meet her here, or inside?"

"Er... She didn't, I don't think."

"Then maybe we should check inside? She might be waiting for us."

Through the squeaky double doors, John and Agnes were confronted by a trio of happy workmen, all jolly in their labours with their pristine dungarees, neatly rolled up sleeves, and brand new hammers that had yet to see a forge in anger. Their frozen smiles were framed by rosy cheeks, and none of them looked like they ever had to eat scraps for dinner. They were damn lifelike though, and John and Agnes both found themselves keeping half an eye on them as they circumnavigated the display to get to the ticket counter beyond.

A tall, slim, dapper young man in a white-trimmed lilac suit and pin-stripe trousers, with wavy hair and a rakishly thin moustache that he pulled off with absolute aplomb, was leaning on the counter reading a book. Catching some movement out the corner of his eye, he whipped the book away, donned his lilac top hat, and waited expectantly for John and Agnes to approach.

John, a little unnerved by the man's enthusiasm, and seeing Detective Hardigan wasn't there, nodded Agnes back towards the front door.

As they turned to go, the young man hastened from behind his counter to intercept them. "Gentleman, lady, welcome to Willard's Wonderful World of Waxworks and Automata. Please, don't be shy. All are welcome here. In fact we have a special on today. Two for one entry for, erm, couples." The young man had an American accent, soft and lilting, and though he watched them nervously, like they were easily startled deer, his well-practised smile was both warm and genuine.

"Thanks, mate, but we're not here to look around. Or rather, we are, but not like that. We're with the police. Sort of."

"Oh thank God," the young man exclaimed. "I'm so glad you're here. Look, I've kept the royal exhibit closed like y'awl told me to, but I would really like to fix it up and get it open again quick as you like. It's our most popular exhibit. If people were to find out it was closed, well that don't even bear thinking about." The young man hurried off, depositing his hat back beneath the ticket counter as he went. He was at the red velvet curtain through to the exhibition hall before John knew what was going on.

"Er, no. We're not—" But the man was gone.

John looked at Agnes who simply shrugged. "Hey, the man wants to show us around, I say we go for it. I love a free show, me."

"But he thinks we're the police."

"That's his problem, innit," said Agnes, heading for the curtain. "Everyone makes mistakes."

John hesitated. He didn't want to upset Detective Hardigan, but he also didn't want to hang around all day waiting for her to show up either. And she had invited him along, hadn't she? Would it really matter if he went in ahead of her? No, of course it wouldn't. She was a reasonable person. She'd understand. And even if she didn't, it sure beat standing around out here on his own, feeling like a prize plum.

"Hold up!" he shouted, trotting after Agnes and the lilac man. "I'm coming."

John found the two of them on the other side of the red curtain. They were in what a large sign proclaimed to be the 'Hall Of Heroes'. The long corridor was lined with a bizarre collection of waxworks, none of which looked like they really belonged together.

The young man was in the middle of explaining who they were. "This is our collection of Hammersmyth celebrities, what y'awl might refer to as 'local people who done good'. We've got Joseph Macintosh, inventor of the multi-strike steam hammer, Mabel Muttersly, the first woman to cross the channel in a pedal-powered boat, Little Tommy Tinker, who scored a hat trick against Mudcaster in the final two years ago, and of course our esteemed benefactor Mr Donald Chard, God rest his soul."

"Blimey, you got that out quick," said Agnes. "He only died a few days ago."

"I'm sorry, ma'am. I don't follow?"

"Aren't these people all dead?"

"Of course not, why would you think that?"

"Well, Joseph Macintosh died in a kiln explosion, Mabel Muttersly drowned in her own bathtub, Little Tommy Tinker got shot in a duel with the Mudcaster goalie because he was having an affair with his wife, and we all know what happened to Donald Chard."

"Not yet we don't," mumbled John.

"Yes, I do see your point," said the young man. "However, those are somewhat unfortunate coincidences. We have waxworks of both the living and the dead here. For example, Mr Chard has been on display for several months now, ever since the rather generous donation he made to help with our refurbishments."

"Donald Chard made a donation?" said John.

"Yes indeed. Mr Chard was quite the philanthropist."

"I had no idea."

"Oh yes. Many a Hammersmyth institution owes their continuation to Mr Chard's generous patronage. His passing was a sad loss in so many ways." Clasping his hands in front of him, the young man bowed his head. John and Agnes looked at each other and shrugged. Hesitantly, John clasped his hands and bowed his head also, peeking every now and then to see when it was time to finish. Agnes thought they had both gone crazy.

"Amen," said the young man finally. "Now, if you folks will follow me, please?"

From the Hall of Heroes he led them into the Atrium of Adventurers.

"The Atrium of Adventurers?" said Agnes.

"Yes. I'm afraid Mr Willard was quite fond of his alliteration."

"Are you not Mr Willard then?"

"Oh good Lord! Where are my manners? My name is Abernathy, William Abernathy. I am the owner, manager and, for the moment, sole employee of this here fine establishment."

John frowned. Abernathy? Now why did that name ring a bell? "Pleased to meet you, Mr Abernathy. My name is John Sinister, and this is my... assistant, Agnes Goodenough."

William Abernathy placed his hand over his heart and bowed. "A pleasure to meet you both, I'm sure,"

"I must say, that's a lovely accent you have there, Mr Abernathy," said Agnes. "Where's it from, may I ask?"

"North Carolina, Miss Goodenough, born and raised. Came over on one of Mr Chard's dirigibles to seek my fortune. The Carolinas are a beautiful part of the world, but they lack opportunity for someone unwilling to profit from the toil of others. A man should profit from the sweat of his own brow and no one else's, don't you agree?"

Agnes nodded gravely. "I do, Mr Abernathy. Indeed I do."

John wasn't listening. He'd remembered where he'd heard the name Abernathy before. Constance Abernathy, of the Constance Abernathy Dance Academy, the one Henry went to the night he died. This must be her husband. If so, it was quite a coincidence. Either that, or there was something else going on here.

"Please, call me William, Miss Goodenough."

"And you must call me Agnes, William," said Agnes. And then John saw it again, another genuine smile. Not a massive one, not as big as she had for his sister, but a smile from the heart, and big enough for him to know that she liked William Abernathy.

"You are very kind, Miss Agnes, although that does not come as a complete surprise. Everyone in Hammersmyth has been quite welcoming to me and mine since we got here, up until last night that is. Speaking of which..."

"Lead on, Mr Abernathy, lead on."

At the end of the Atrium of Adventurers was a doorway marked the Royal Reliquary. Its handles had been tied together with a velvet rope.

"The Royal Reliquary? I thought reliquaries were meant for holy items?"

Mr Abernathy gave a look like he'd just bitten into a lemon. "Yes it is awful, isn't it? I'm afraid Mr Willard took some heavy license with his use of words and their meaning. When I took over the museum we even had a Phalanx of Freaks, but as you can imagine I had to get rid of that. Some things ought not be, don't you think? Which brings us to this... debacle." William Abernathy pushed open the doors of the reliquary, and a world of delight opened up before them.

John had nothing against the royal family per se, they seemed a nice enough bunch by and large, but sometimes it's nice to see people get what's coming to them, and this was definitely one of those times.

On a pedestal in the centre of the room was the entire royal family – the Queen, her Prince Consort, all the little (and not so little) princes and princesses, with their ever-growing collection of Pomeranians – and Detective Hardigan was right, they most definitely had been 'messed with'. Someone had squeezed their ample Queen into the stick-like Prince Consort's bright red jacket and trousers, whilst he stood there engulfed in her shimmering silk ball gown, a wig interlaced with flowers and pearls perched atop his pointy head. All the grown up princes and princesses had been moved into a variety of interlocking positions that could best be described as compromising (some of which John was going to have to look up later if he had the time), whilst the very smallest members of the group had gotten off the most lightly. No one had done anything untoward to them. They merely had little dogs balanced on their heads.

John clamped his lips together to keep from giggling, which wasn't easy with Agnes sniggering away beside him, but he had to try. If you're going to impersonate the police you should do so in a professional manner at least.

William Abernathy let out a heartfelt sigh. "It's alright, you can laugh," he said. "I know what it looks like."

"Sorry," said John, elbowing Agnes in the ribs. "So, er, so this was how you found them this morning is it?"

"Yes. Exactly like this. I haven't touched a thing."

"And the, er…"—John made a number of intimate gestures with his hands—"repositioning. That was them as well was it?"

"Well clearly," said William Abernathy. "Do you think we keep the Crown Prince bent over like that all the time?"

"No, of course not," said John. *Although that probably wouldn't be the worst idea in the world,* he added quietly to himself. The man could do with being taken down a peg or two.

As they talked, Agnes approached the pedestal to study the figures more closely. "William, if you don't mind me asking, are these waxworks the same as the ones outside? Only they look a bit different somehow."

"That's because they're not waxworks, they're automata. The mechanics make the bodies harder to sculpt, and we have to use a different type of wax for the faces because of all the extra heat and vibration."

Agnes's face lit up. "You mean they move? Can we see?"

William Abernathy shifted uncomfortably. "I'd rather not, to be honest. Their internal mechanisms have been tampered with. Normally they just wave, but now..."

"I'm afraid we're going to need to see them in action," said John. "For our, um, records, and all that. You understand."

William Abernathy nodded. With great reluctance he went behind a curtain hung against the wall and flicked a switch. There was some hissing as the steam pressure built, and then the automata sprang into life.

It was glorious. The Queen started throwing out an obscene, two-fingered gesture made popular at the battle of Agincourt, whilst the Crown Prince bent over to receive a kick up the royal backside from the Prince Consort. Some of the elder princesses had been turned into can-can dancers, and the dogs not on anybody's heads started going to town on themselves like it was going out of business.

"Good Lord," said John, biting his lip. Beside him Agnes had to turn her back, her shoulders quivering as she fought to contain her laughter.

"I know," said William Abernathy. "I can barely stand to look myself. I mean, how disrespectful can you get?"

"Indeed," said John. "Most *mmh* disrespectful. Er, perhaps you should turn it off now. I think we've seen enough."

William Abernathy did so gladly.

"So what do you think? Can you who find who is responsible, Detective?"

"What? Oh! Yes. Yes, indeed. I'm sure we can. Um, Miss Goodenough, perhaps you could look around, see if you can find any clues?" Agnes stared at John. "Mr Abernathy, could you perhaps turn up the house lights so that we can see better?"

Whilst William Abernathy went back behind the curtain, Agnes sidled up to John. "Look for clues? What the hell do you mean, look for clues?"

"I don't know. Walk about looking official. Yell if you see anything weird."

"Weird? Around here! You're kidding, right?"

"Just go," hissed John, shooing her away as William Abernathy returned. "Mr Abernathy, I wonder, can you tell me if there's anyone who might hold a grudge against you? A former business partner or ex-employee perhaps?"

"A grudge? Why would anyone hold a grudge against me? I'm a people person, Mr Sinister. I don't go around making enemies. Life, I find, is just too darn short."

That had never been John's experience, but he believed William Abernathy when he said it. "So how did the intruders get in, do you think?"

"Through the back door. I found it open this morning."

"So they broke in?"

"No. The door was unlocked somehow." William Abernathy held up his hand. "And before you ask, yes it was locked last night. If there's one thing I am, it's fastidious. I most definitely locked up before I left for the day."

"And who has a key for the back door?"

"I do. No one else. Oh! Except for the builders, that is."

"Builders? What builders?"

"The ones doing the refurbishments. They've been here a couple of weeks now. I gave them the spare key so that they could come and go as they please."

"I see. And who is it that's doing the refurbishments for you, may I ask?"

"The Shelby Fabrication and Construction Company."

Shelby Construction, eh? Now that was interesting. "And apart from the adjustments to the automatons, have you noticed anything else broken or missing?"

"No. Nothing as far as I can tell."

Looking down, John noticed a black scorch mark on the floor. "What's that?" he said, walking over to it.

"I don't know. I've never seen it before."

The mark was fairly superficial. Most of it came away when John scraped the toe of his boot over it. Picking up a pinch of the black powder he sniffed it curiously.

Agnes joined them. "Sorry, um, Detective, but I found nothing interestin' over there."

"That's alright," said John. "We have what we need." He wiped his fingers on his trouser leg. "Thank you, Mr Abernathy, you've been most helpful. A Detective Hardigan will be along shortly to take a full statement from you. If you could leave things as they are until then that would be much appreciated."

"Leave things as they are? But I need to make it right. Do I really have to?"

"I'm afraid so. It's procedure. I'm sure you understand."

He didn't, but he didn't have the strength to argue. "As you wish," he said wearily.

"Good. Thank you, sir." John offered his hand. "Goodbye, Mr Abernathy. I hope you and your wife are very happy here in Hammersmyth."

"I'm... sorry. My wife?"

"Yes. Mrs Constance Abernathy, the dance instructor. I assume the two of you are..."

John trailed off under the bemused gaze of William Abernathy, who suddenly burst into laughter. "My Lord! Yes. No. I mean, yes we are related, but no she is not my wife. Constance Abernathy is my sister, and I can assure you that she is still very much a miss. As am I... in a manner of speaking that is." He laughed again at his own turn of phrase, Agnes laughing with him, the two of them clearly tickled by something.

John just smiled. He liked a laugh as much as the next man, but for some reason he couldn't quite see the joke.

"What a nice man," said Agnes.

"Yes he was, wasn't he?"

"So did you get what you wanted out of that?"

"More or less. It's given me some ideas at least."

"Great. So what's next?"

"Next we get out of here before the real police show up." John did not want to have to explain their little impromptu tour to Detective Hardigan.

"No, I mean where to next? Where we going now?"

"Now? Now we're off to the Zoo, to see a man about a lion," said John.

Agnes chuckled. "Y'know what? I like working for you, Sinister. You do take a girl to the most interesting places."

Hammersmyth Zoo had a small but respectable menagerie that was well worth a wander on a warm sunny day. Its collection of exotic beasts from the far-flung corners of the Britannic Empire had, for the most part, come from the late Lord Altringham's country estate. His widow, Lady Altringham, had bequeathed his entire collection to the zoo just days after an encounter with a bad-tempered raccoon had led to Lord Altringham's untimely demise.

Her enthusiasm for getting rid of Lord Altringham's beloved animals had raised a few eyebrows at the time, but Lady Altringham could not have cared less. She had nothing against the idea of lions and llamas and buffalo and baboons, but after fifteen years of having to keep the windows closed all summer because of the smell she just didn't want them in her back garden anymore.

After explaining to the girl at the ticket office why they were there, John and Agnes were handed over to a grumpy wee Scotsman in a green zookeeper's uniform by the name of Jack.

"That's *Jack*, y'ken? No 'Jock'. Got it?"

"Got it," said John, keeping an eye on Jack's hook-ended walking stick. At six-foot long it stood a foot above its owners head, and the metal shepherd's crook on the end looked like it could do some real damage if its owner put his mind to it.

"Just so long as we're clear," he said, squinting at them both.

"Crystal, guv," said Agnes.

Jack led them through the zoo, past rows of black-barred cages full of morose marmoset and gloomy gorillas, none of whom looked happy to be there, to the star attraction at the centre of everything, the zoo's lion enclosure.

"Well, there he is. Oor Samson, the king o' the jungle. Just look at him would ye, the poor wee thing. Who would dae such a thing tae such a fine animal, Ah ask ye?"

On a flat rock in the centre of the enclosure, his chin resting on crossed paws, back legs splayed out behind him like that was where he'd fallen and he couldn't be bothered to get up, lay Samson the lion. On one side of his head he had a beautiful mane of golden hair; full, flowing, the envy of any lion. The other side was somewhat less impressive. Whoever had tried to rob Samson of his strength had made a right pig's ear of it. The hair had been hacked away in unsightly lumps, leaving him looking all mangy. It was growing back, slowly, but it still had a long way to go.

"Believe it or no, that's an improvement on what it was. Ye shoulda seen him a month ago. He would'nae come ootside fer a week fer fear o' being laughed at."

"He still doesn't look too happy about it now," said Agnes.

"Aye well, can ye blame him?"

"So what happened exactly?" said John.

"Ach, 'twas simple enough. Some scunner kem in o'er the back wall an' tried to shave aff his mane. But they chickened oot halfway through and done a runner, the cowardly wee sassenachs."

"They came over the back wall? Isn't that hard to do?"

"Ach no! It'd be super easy, barely an inconvenience. The walls're designed tae keep the creatures in, no humans oot. Wi' a lang enough ladder an' some determination a man cud get hi'sel' o'er nee bother."

"What about the night watchman? Didn't he see anything?"

Jack laughed. "Auld Willie? Are ye jokin'? He slept through the whole thing. Had nee idea summat had happened til Ah told him."

"No other witnesses?"

"Just Lancelot o'er the way, oor scarlet macaw. Yer welcome tae ask him a few questions if ye like, but ye'll get nuthin' oot'a him. Lancelot's no a grass." As if confirming Jack's assessment, the parrot gave a sudden, threatening squawk.

"What about the clippers?" said John. "Anything special about them?"

"Nope, 'twas a set af oor ain fre the back room. Cheeky buggers could'nae be bothered to bring their ain with 'em when they kem."

"Did they take anything as a souvenir?"

"A souvenir? Ah din'nae think so. But Ah reckon they would've taken the mane if they had'nae bottled it. That's what they were after."

"Maybe," said John, watching Samson scratch idly at his mane stubble. "Maybe."

On their way out they came across a brass plaque of the zoo's benefactors. Two names leapt out at John.

"I didn't know Donald Chard and Spencer Shelby the Second were patrons here."

"Och aye. They've bin donatin' us money fer years. We could'nae do it wi'oot 'em."

John read the rest of the list. The fathers of almost all the old Chess Club were on there, which is to say the fathers of everyone he suspected of being in the Hell-Bats.

"Interesting," he said. "Very interesting."

The Museum of History building was, in John's humble opinion, one of the finest structures in all of Hammersmyth. Its sandstone and slate exterior, with its arched windows and tall towers, made it look more like a castle than a seat of learning; although the fat, scaly creatures with giant claws and huge tusks that sat atop its battlements, in alcoves above its doorways, and even clung on to the walls themselves, left none in doubt as to where they were.

John loved the museum's cement dinosaurs, despite how ridiculous they looked. Or possibly because of it. They represented the finest thinking of their time, but times had moved on. The huge lizards of yesteryear were slowly becoming a thing of the past. People were talking about dinosaurs as more like birds now, if you could believe that? All bright colours and covered in feathers. A shame, as far as John was concerned. He liked the idea of the big lizards. He found them suitably scary. The idea of a giant chicken just didn't do it for him somehow.

A huge banner had been hung above the museum's front entrance.

MYSTERIES OF THE NILE

Discover King Ptoot's secret treasures

<u>EXCLUSIVE EXHIBITS</u>

Not available anywhere else

SEE THEM WHILE YOU CAN!

John smiled. The rivalry between Hammersmyth's Museum of History and the Natural History Museum in London was well known. The two of them were always trying to outdo each other, snatching artefacts out from under each other's noses with promises of more visitors, better billing, and, of course, more money. The stories in the papers of how a new exhibit came to be in the possession of the Museum of History were always good for a laugh for those who could read between the lines. If rumour was to be believed, its acquisition of the contents of the pharaoh's burial chamber had involved the grandson of the Sultan of Sunai, a trained monkey, a crocodile outfit, a hundred guineas in unmarked gold, and a desperate midnight camel ride from Cairo to Port Said-so. And although it most likely wasn't entirely true, you still had to admire that level of dedication to your craft.

As he approached the ticket counter, John tried to look as official as possible. "Good afternoon. I'm here to see a mister..." he checked the name on his hastily scribbled note, "Wibblelow? Your head of Egypt—" The word 'Egyptology' flew from his mind. "—tian things," he concluded weakly.

"Mr Weebilow, our head of Egyptology?" the girl said with a frown.

Damn his terrible handwriting. "Yes, that's right. Mr Weebilow, the head of Egyptology."

"May I ask why you want to see Mr Weebilow?"

"It's concerning the break-in a couple of weeks ago. And if you could hurry up about it that would be much appreciated, we haven't got all day. Lots of, er, police business to be getting on with."

"Oh! I see. So you're with the police?"

"Yes," said John, puffing out his chest. "Yes we are."

The girl rushed off to find Mr Weebilow. As soon as she was out of sight Agnes leant down to whisper in John's ear. "That was no accident."

"So?"

"So, you could get us in a lot of trouble for that."

"What difference does it make? We've already done it once."

"Because it's one thing them thinking you're with the police, it's another thing you telling them you are."

"I doubt that," said John. "Besides, in for a penny, in for a pound, as the old saying goes."

"And what if your girlfriend finds out?"

"She is not my girlfriend. And anyway, it's easier to ask forgiveness than permission."

"You're just full of useless platitudes today, aren't you?"

"A rolling stone gathers no moss."

"What has that got to do with anything?"

"It means don't just stand there, let's go."

The Egyptology exhibition was well signposted. The entire thing was in one big hall that ran the full height of the building. There were desiccated mummies, dog-faced statues, ancient artefacts, and elaborate dioramas all over the place. Along each wall were rows of display cases, each filled with a variety of items that John couldn't even begin to guess a use for. Some of them were empty, and some of them showed signs of repair. And in the centre of the room, surrounded by a circle of benches from which people could gaze upon its magnificence, stood the golden sarcophagus of King Ptoot the Third. Big enough to sleep a family of four (if they didn't mind getting all cosy) and intricately carved with lines of little dancing men, it looked like it weighed a ton.

"I bet that took a while to make," said Agnes.

"Indeed," said John, too busy checking out the room's security arrangements to care about the exhibit. There were two guards by the sarcophagus, and two guards by the doors, one at each entrance. Both doors looked heavy, and were probably very secure once they were all locked up. There were no windows, save for the skylights high above their heads. Someone would have to be very determined to get in that way. There were hot air vents in the floor, but even Dexter would have trouble squeezing down their narrow openings. All told, it was a pretty secure room. The only way in John could see was if someone let you in.

A little man with wild hair and a worried look on his pale, saggy face, appeared through one of the doorways and hurried towards them.

"Good afternoon. I'm Mr Weebilow. I believe you were looking for me."

"That's right. We're with the police," said John. Agnes quietly wandered off. "We've come about the recent break-in."

"Really? But that was weeks ago. I thought there'd already been an investigation? Has something changed? Are the exhibits in danger?" Wringing his hands, Mr Weebilow's eyes darted in every direction, on the lookout for thieves and vagabonds.

"Sir, please. There's nothing to be concerned about. Some new information has come to light and we just need to ask you a few questions, that's all."

"Oh. Good. Yes, thank you. Yes, I'm sure that would be fine."

"First off, can you tell me what happened here exactly?"

"Isn't it in the police report?"

"It is, yes. Of course it is. But I'd prefer to hear it from you, if you don't mind? Straight from the horse's mouth, as it were."

"Yes, I suppose that makes sense," said Mr Weebilow, with some hesitation. "Well, whoever broke in messed with everything. When we arrived the next day everything was open, all the mummies had been moved, and there was authentic replica Egyptian clothing everywhere. It was horrifying."

"They moved the mummies, you say?" The very idea sent a shiver down John's spine. "Where did they move them to?"

"We found them on the benches, sitting like they were out taking in the sights. I got the impression the intruders had sat and posed with them, although I'm sure I can't imagine why."

But I can, thought John. "Was anything taken? You've got quite a few empty cases in here."

"No, thank God. But some of the damage was quite substantial, and the restoration is still ongoing. It will be a couple of weeks before everything is back to normal again."

Nothing stolen. That made sense. "How did they get in?"

"We found a back window open. The internal doors they opened with a set of keys that they stole off a guard."

"So the guard saw who it was?"

"No, unfortunately. That particular guard, a young man by the name of Pete, was, er... pooping, at the time."

"Pooping? What, the whole time they were here?"

Mr Weebilow looked like he could smell what they were talking about. "Apparently, yes. Some kind of gastro-intestinal thing. I'm afraid I didn't delve too deeply into the details."

"And he was the only guard on at the time?"

"No, we had another man on duty. Charles. Been here for years. He was patrolling the top floor for the duration."

"Is Pete the Pooper here? I'd like a word."

"No. He doesn't work here anymore."

"He got fired?"

"Actually he quit. Said he didn't need the job anymore. Said he came into some money all of a sudden."

"Did he now?" said John. "How interesting." The facts were slowly falling into place. John knew now who he needed to speak to next.

"Um, is that all, Detective? Only I have quite a lot of work to do."

"Just one more thing, Mr Weebilow. Are Donald Chard or Spencer Shelby the Second patrons of the museum at all?"

Mr Weebilow almost seemed amused by the question. "Sir, I doubt there is a family in Hammersmyth who hasn't been a patron of the museum at one time or another. We are, after all, the best."

"So what did you learn from all that?" said Agnes, as she and John made their way down the front steps of the museum.

"It was the Hell-Bats alright. They paid a guard to look the other way, then they dressed up and took photographs of themselves with the mummies."

"They took photographs of themselves breaking in? That was dumb."

"I agree, but they needed a trophy, a memento to prove they were there. Nothing was taken, so I'm assuming photography. I found scorch marks at Willard's Waxworks that smelled like spilt flash powder to me."

"So when they broke in they took a photographer in with them? That's doubly dumb. Money only buys you so much loyalty. What if he blabs?

"She. The photographer's a she. And she wouldn't blab. She's one of them."

"You know who it is, don't you?"

"Indeed I do."

"So what do we do now?"

"Now?" said John, flagging down a passing Hansom cab. "Now we go talk to the photographer."

Dexter slowly opened his eyes to find an expectant Nomko hovering two inches from his face.

"Dexter! How you feel?"

Dexter stretched out his legs. "A little uncomfortable to be honest."

"Oh no. Why?"

"Coz I've got a strange Japanese man staring at me, that's why."

Nomko stepped back, smiling. "Apart from that, how you feel? You feel good, yes?"

Dexter stood and wiggled about a bit. He felt strange, different, like he'd just had a good night's sleep, only better. "I feel... good," he said, walking around. "Great actually. I feel... springy. Like I'm a lot lighter." He jumped up and down on the spot. "What did you do to me?"

"I take out old unit and install special mini boiler that I make. Dexter generate own steam now! No need store steam for days. No need recharge. And best of all, whole thing much lighter. Make Dexter more nimble, more like real cat."

"I'll say!" said Dexter, trotting from one end of the workbench to the other. He felt like a huge weight had been lifted, like he was floating almost. He had an overwhelming urge to run somewhere, anywhere. It didn't matter where, just so long as he got to go fast. "How long will it last? How much steam have I got?"

"Once have full head of steam, and if full of consumables, can last two, maybe three days, easy-peasy."

"Consumables?"

"Yes. Make own steam now. Will need water to boil and fuel to burn to keep going."

"Right. And how do I get those then?"

"You eat them of course." Nomko laughed. Dexter stopped pacing.

"Eat them? You mean really eat? As in take in food and keep it down, not just pretend like before?"

"Absolutely! Although Nomko recommend eating things that burn easy, like paper and wood and coal. Damp organics will work, but dry goods much better."

"Sure, sure. You got it. Eat burny stuff, nothing wet."

"No. Wet okay, but dry is better."

"Right. Gotcha," said Dexter, not really listening. He was giddy with the idea of eating and drinking and not having to cough it up out of sight later on. Finally, he was the same as all the other cats.

"Dexter have internal gauges for fuel and water. Will feel when both are low and is time to eat and drink. And do not worry about what go where. System can tell what is what and send to right place."

"Wow. That is amazing. Truly it is. Y'know what, Nomko, I've said it before and I'll say it again. You, sir, are a genius." Nomko smiled and bowed his head. "And I assume that if I need a quick top up I can recharge now and then?"

"Oh no, that not possible. This it now. Is complete, self-contained system. Is up to you to manage. If boiler get low and fire go out, that it for you, you done for."

Dexter stopped bouncing around. "Done for? As in done for done for?" Nomko nodded. "Right. I see. That's good to know. Thank you, Nomko."

"Like I say, Dexter can go two days without eating or drinking, like before. But to be safe should top up fuel and water every day."

"Not a problem," said Dexter. He was already looking around the room planning his first meal.

"Also," said Nomko, "cannot recharge because do not have recharge port anymore. Had to remove to fit new waste pipe." He sounded so pleased with himself.

"My new what now?"

"Waste pipe. So can eject spent fuel."

"You mean...?" Dexter did a squatting motion and Nomko laughed.

"Exactly! Welcome to life of real cat," said Nomko. He laughed again at the look on Dexter's face, although Dexter had yet to see the funny side. Swishing his tail he tried to imagine what ejection would feel like. In a strange way he was kind of looking forward to it. Whilst in another, very real way, he wasn't.

Nomko grabbed his flying jacket off the end of the bench and swung it around his shoulders. "Okay, Dexter be okay on his own now? Nomko has date with ironmonger's daughter. Must show up. She already very unhappy with Nomko for cancelling once before."

Dexter had gone back to his jumping around. He'd discovered that he could easily hop from one bench to another, and he suspected he could jump much, much further. "What? Oh, yeah. Yeah, no problem, mate. Don't you worry about me. Sinister will be along soon enough. You go do whatever it is you meat-sacks do for fun."

"With any luck," said Nomko, heading for the door.

"Hey, Nomko," Dexter called after him. "Thank you for this. Truly. I can't... Well, I'm honoured. It means a lot to me." Dexter bowed, and Nomko bowed in return.

"*Kochirakoso*, Little One. The honour is all mine."

John and Agnes's ride out of town was taking forever. The cab driver had complained when they'd told him to take them up to Turning Hill, but it's surprising how quickly people come around if you wave enough money at them.

John stared out the window at the passing fields for as long as he could, but he soon got bored. "Say, Agnes, can I ask you something?"

"Sure."

"It's just, you and my sister seemed to know each other awfully well. Have you met before or something?"

"Are you serious? You don't remember?" John shook his head. "You brought Jane to Caesar's that one time, ages ago. Spent all night ignoring her whilst you lost your shirt at poker. We had a long time to get to know each other then." And slowly, the mists began to clear.

It was right after John had gotten his membership. Jane had wanted to see what the inside of a club like that was like, so he'd reluctantly agreed to take her along with him. He hadn't meant to ignore her, but he was there to gamble and gamble he did; badly. Agnes was right, he'd lost everything. It had been one of his worst nights at the tables. He'd tried to wash away his defeat with booze, after which he couldn't remember getting home. He certainly couldn't remember Jane being there which, even for him, was pretty bad. "Right, yeah. I kinda remember that. Not my best night, if I'm honest."

"I'll say."

"Anyway, thanks for taking care of her. That was good of you."

"I didn't do it for you, mate," said Agnes. "You know how many actual conversations I have with people when I'm working? None. People see me, they see how I look and, well..." Agnes shook her head in frustration. "Anyway, Jane started talking to me and we had a good long chat about all sorts of things. It was really nice to have someone take an interest in me for once. Really special. Your sister is a kind, thoughtful, intelligent woman, and it was a pleasure to get to know her." Sitting back in her seat, Agnes returned to staring out the window.

John felt like he should ask Agnes something else. "Oh hey, uh…" Should he ask her about her family or something? Would that be weird? It felt weird. "Any idea what Nero was doing at the Scion Club the other day?"

"Nope. No idea. But he's been all over town chasing down this new license of his. Maybe it had something to do with that?"

"Uh, yeah. Maybe," said John. "Thanks."

Turning to look out the window, John went back to inspecting the passing shrubbery.

At the gates of a huge mansion the cab turned into a long gravel driveway. It crunched through the loose rock towards the biggest house Agnes had ever seen.

"Where the hell are we, Sinister?"

"This is Appleby House, home of the Rosemont family."

"And this is where we'll find our photographer, is it?"

"I hope so."

The cab swung a wide circle around a fountain to pull up outside the mansion's front door.

"Can you stick around?" said John to the driver. "We're going to need a ride back as well."

"I can, guv, but it's gonna cost you extra," said the driver. "For my time, like."

"Of course it is," said John, jumping to the ground. "How about a guinea for the rest of the day? How does that sound?" The cab driver perked up at that. A guinea was a good day's pay for a Tuesday.

"Sounds good to me, guv. You take as long as you want in there. I'll be here when you get back."

"How kind," said John. "And keep her handy, will you? We might need to make a swift exit."

"Whatever you say, guv," said the cab driver, tugging his fore-lock.

Agnes and John walked up to the house. "You expecting trouble?" said Agnes.

"Not exactly, but you never know. We're not here to make friends after all."

Their knock at the door was answered by the most decrepit butler John had ever seen. If he'd been any more bent over he'd have been upside down. The man looked like he was a hundred on a good day, and he was deaf as a post. The first word out of his mouth was, "Eh?"

"Good afternoon. We're here to see Julia Rosemont."

"Eh?"

"JULIA ROSEMONT! WE'D LIKE TO SEE HER, PLEASE!"

"Miss Julia?"

"YES."

"Oh right, yes. Of course. The young miss said something about... something. If you could step through to the drawing room, sir, I will let Miss Julia know that you're here."

The butler shuffled out of the way to let them through, letting them find their own way whilst he embarked upon the long journey to close the front door. John led Agnes across the entrance hall to where the drawing room was, or at least where it used to be. He hadn't been to the house in ages, but he didn't imagine the layout had changed all that much.

Agnes turned on the spot as she walked, taking in all the gold leaf and opulence, the grand architecture, and the row upon row of po-faced ancestors looking down on them with their disapproving airs. In the drawing room she got to inspect the porcelain silhouettes, painted landscapes, and other unnecessary fripperies that people always seemed to acquire when they have more money than sense.

"So this is how the other half lives, eh?"

"Yup," said John, taking great delight in plonking his unkempt self down in a plush, wingback chair.

"It's good to be the king," said Agnes.

John chuckled. It was a line from a popular musical doing the rounds at the moment called 'Up The Royals!' – a thinly-veiled satire on the Prince Regent's debaucherous ways that the Queen had tried to have quietly banned. That of course had only made it more popular, many people seeing it as their patriotic duty to come out and show their support. John himself had seen it twice already.

"I wonder what the rest of the house is like."

"More of the same," said John. "Just as expensive and just as tacky."

"You've been here before?"

"A few times. I know the family, you see. Julia and I have an 'intimate' personal history, shall we say."

"Do you now?" said Agnes. "Well then, this should be fun."

The drawing room door swung open and in swept Julia Rosemont. She looked radiant in a midnight blue silk ball gown, her hair tied up with flowers, a black lace choker around her neck. John was taken aback. Julia always did look beautiful, but today she'd really pulled out all the stops. Everything had been powdered, strapped, fluffed, and embellished to within an inch of its life, and the effect was stunning. The only incongruous aspect was the white bandage on her left forearm.

Now who are we all dressed up for? John wondered. *Not little old me, I'm sure.*

"How wonderful to see you again my dear, I—" Julia spotted John and her smile vanished. "John! What are you doing here?" Then she spotted Agnes looming nearby and took an involuntary step back. "What is this? What's going on?"

"Hello, Julia. Lovely to see you again. It's been a while."

Pulling herself together Julia strode through the room. "We saw each other only a few days ago. At the Scion Club, remember?"

"I do, yes. But we didn't really get a chance to talk did we?"

Julia Rosemont went and stood by the window, staring out across the grounds, the living embodiment of the word imperious. "And what exactly would we have to talk about?"

"Henry's death."

"Oh for God's sake, John. Henry's death was an accident. Why can't you just leave it alone?"

"Because there's more to it than everyone thinks there is."

"Oh really?" said Julia. "Like what?"

"Like the Hell-Bats, for instance."

For a brief moment Julia Rosemont's haughty gaze flickered, but she soon recovered her composure. "The Hell-Bats? Good Lord, now there's a name I haven't heard in ages."

"Haven't you though? Are you sure about that?"

"Absolutely. Not since Howard Aglet's, at least."

"What happened to your arm, Julia?"

Julia Rosemont threw her right arm across her left, trying to hide the bandage. "Nothing. I, er... I burnt it on the fire."

All three of them glanced at the drawing room fireplace. The fire guard had dust on it, it hadn't been used in so long. "Pull the other one, Julia, it's got bells on."

Julia stamped her foot. "How dare you come in here unannounced and make these baseless accusations? I won't stand for it, do you hear? I'd like you to leave. Right now, please."

John didn't move.

"Relax, Julia. I haven't accused anyone of anything... yet. But I can if you like?"

Julia hesitated, that's when John knew he had her. She wanted him gone, but she also wanted to know what he knew too. "Spencer and his cronies have resurrected the Hell-Bats. When, I don't know, but probably no more than a couple of months ago. Or at least that's when the dares began. How am I doing so far?"

"I think you're imagining things," she replied, perching herself on the end of a chaise lounge.

"Am I? Am I imagining the lion's mane at the zoo? Or the Egyptology exhibit at the Museum of History? What about the Wonderful World of Waxworks and Automata last night, where whoever was taking photographs spilled their flash powder, burning the floor, and most likely their own arm as well."

Julia said nothing, but she looked terrified. John couldn't help but relent slightly. They did have a history after all. "Look, Julia, I know what's been going on. I'm guessing that whatever happened to Henry was a dare gone wrong. Things got out of hand, someone messed up, and Henry ended up in the river. Am I right? Is that what happened?"

Julia deflated, the weight of it all too much to bear. "I don't know what happened," she sobbed. "I wasn't there. I was told Henry was tombstoning, he hit his head, and he drowned. It was an accident, it wasn't anybody's fault."

"And who told you that?"

"Spencer. He went with Henry to the bridge. As far as I know he was the only one there."

"I see. Well, thank you for telling me, Julia, but I'm afraid Spencer has been lying to you."

"What?"

"I spoke to the coroner. Henry's injuries were far too severe, much more than would have been caused by a simple fall into the river. Whatever happened to Henry was deliberate, and from the sounds of things Spencer is the one responsible."

"No! That's not possible. Spencer couldn't– He wouldn't—"

"Couldn't he? Oh, I think we both know that he could. Although precisely *why* he would I've no idea. It does seem a little needlessly cruel, even for him. However, only he can shed light on that. The only question I have left for you, Julia, is this; where are the photographs?"

"The what? What photographs? I told you, I wasn't there."

"Not from the bridge, from last night. Where are the photographs from last night?"

"I–I don't know what you're talking about." Her eyes flickered to the sideboard and John smiled. Standing, he made a beeline right for it, Julia leaping to her feet. "No! You stay out of there."

Agnes stepped forward into Julia's line of sight. "Sit down, miss. Please," she said softly. Julia went pale as she slowly sank back down.

John opened the first drawer and found nothing. He opened the second one and there they were, a small stack of photographs, maybe twenty or thirty, sitting in a nice neat little pile. He picked them out and leafed through the first few. They were shots of Spencer Shelby and Richard Rosemont next to the Queen, doing things to Her Majesty's person that she would not have found amusing in the slightest.

"These are good, Julia, you should be proud. You've got a good eye," said John, slipping the photographs into his jacket pocket.

As he pushed closed the sideboard drawer, the drawing room door behind him opened. "Well, well, well," said a self-satisfied voice. "And what do we have here then, eh?"

John turned to face the door.

"Hello, Spencer," he said. "I was just on my way to see you."

Spencer stood leaning against the doorframe with his arms folded, looking unbelievably smug as usual. Why he was always so smug, and what he was so smug about, remained a mystery to John.

"Really? On your way to see little old me? Well aren't I the lucky one."

"Oh, Spence!" gushed Julia, running into his arms. "Thank God you're here. He's been saying such horrible things."

"There, there, Julia," said Spencer, patting her on the back. "Everything's alright now."

John wanted to spit. So that was what the hair and the dress and the grand entrance were all about. It was all for Spencer's benefit. No wonder she'd looked so upset at seeing him there instead.

Julia had always had a thing for Spencer, everybody knew it. John suspected it was one of the reasons she'd gone out with him in the first place all those years ago, to try and make Spencer jealous. It hadn't worked at the time, but clearly Julia had figured out another way to get Spencer's attention.

"But he knows. He knows about the Hell-Bats, the museum, the zoo, the waxworks, everything!"

"Oh, that. I wouldn't worry about that. Simple high jinks, nothing more. No harm no foul, as our American friends would say."

"And what about Henry?" said John.

Spencer was sure to look suitably pained. "Ah yes, poor Henry. Such a senseless waste. A terrible accident, but an accident nonetheless. No one to blame for that now, is there?"

"You sure about that?"

"Absolutely."

"I think the police might disagree with you."

"Yes, I'm sure they might. However, what can they do? There's no proof, you see. No proof that any of us are involved in any of it, in any way. And without proof it's just your word against all ours."

Now it was John's turn to look smug.

"Spencer, he's got the photographs. The photographs from last night. They're in his jacket pocket."

The half-smile Spencer had been nursing since he'd arrived vanished. "Oh dear. That is a problem." He put Julia to one side and advanced towards John, holding out his hand. "I'm afraid I'm going to need those photographs back, Sinister. Right now, if you would be so kind?"

"I don't think so," said John, looking towards Agnes.

Spencer seemed to notice her presence for the first time. "Good Lord! Who's this? Is she with you? She's a whopper!"

"She's here to make sure no one does anything stupid."

"Protection? For you? How marvellous. I must say, I'm quaking in my boots. Or rather I would be, if I hadn't brought some protection of my own." Opening the drawing room door, Spencer cupped a hand to his mouth. "Oh, Lionel. Would you pop in here for a moment please? We have a situation."

They heard something heavy approaching, creaking the floorboards with every step. The door was pushed open and a giant entered the room. Almost as wide as he was tall, he had to stoop *and* turn sideways to get through the door. If he'd come at it head on he would've gotten stuck.

Spencer was back to looking smug again. "This is Lionel. Say hello to the nice folks, Lionel."

"Hello," said Lionel, reluctantly.

John's mouth fell open. He couldn't believe his eyes. Not because of Lionel's imposing physique, but because of the shape he made in the world. It was a distinctive shape, not one he'd ever soon forget. The last time John had seen a shape like that it had been on a bridge, at night, coming at him through the fog.

"I know you," he stammered. "You were on the bridge!"

"What bridge?"

"Gravesend Bridge, two nights ago. You and your friend with the meat hook."

Lionel gave the slightest of shrugs. "I dunno what you're talkin' about, sir."

Spencer was grinning from ear to ear. "Lionel, Mr Sinister has some photographs in his jacket pocket that belong to me. Be so good as to retrieve them for me, would you?"

"Very good, sir," said Lionel, walking towards John.

John froze. He wanted to run but his legs wouldn't cooperate. All he could see was the Irresistible Force coming towards him. Then his view was blocked by an Immovable Object.

Agnes came face to face with Lionel, who was both taller and wider than her. He looked down at her, she looked up at him. Neither of them moved. Then Lionel gave a short nod.

"Hello, Agnes," he said.

"Hello, Lionel."

"Long time no see."

"Indeed it is. How've you been?"

"Oh, y'know. Same old, same old. Mustn't grumble. You?"

"Can't complain," said Agnes. "How's the family? Well, I hope?"

"Very well, thanks. Little Denise just turned four. She starts school next year, if you can believe that?"

"Already? Wow, time flies eh?"

"It does that," said Lionel, nodding. "You'll have to come round one night, catch up with everyone."

"Thanks. I'd like that."

"So, what you doin' here? I thought you worked over at Caesar's?"

"Oh I do. That's still going. This is just a side gig for a bit of extra cash, y'know. What about you? Dock work dry up?"

"Nah, I'm still down the docks most days. But the money ain't as good as it was. Like you, this is just a bit on the side to earn a little extra. Always somethin' to spend your money on, eh?"

"Ain't that the truth," agreed Agnes.

John and Spencer exchanged a look of disbelief.

"Er, sorry, Lionel? I hate to interrupt this little tête-à-tête of yours," said Spencer, "but is there a problem?"

"I'm afraid there is, sir, yes. Y'see, Agnes and me go way back. Known each other for a long time we have. She came to my wedding, *and* she's God Mum to my little girl. So, with all due respect, I ain't gonna hit her no matter how much you pay me."

Spencer was gobsmacked. "But I'm not asking you to hit her," he protested, "I'm asking you to hit him."

"Same thing, sir. I hit him, she hits me, I have to hit her. It's inevitabubble."

"Inevitabubble?"

"Inevitable," said Agnes.

"Yeah, that. Thanks, Agnes."

"Oh, fine!" growled Spencer. "I'll get them myself then." He started towards John, only to find Lionel stood in his way.

"Actually, sir, that won't work either I'm afraid."

"Good God man, why not?"

"Well, you hits him, she hits you, I have to hit her... You see where I'm going with this? It's one of them vicious circle thingys."

John burst out laughing. "Oh, Spencer, I wish you could see the look on your face. It's priceless." Spencer glared at him, furious and nowhere to put it. John threw him a quick wink. "Well, this has been fun, but I think it's time for us to leave. Come on, Agnes, let's get out of here."

"Actually, sir, I can't let you do that neither," said Lionel. "Not with them photographs at least. There's such a thing as profeshunnal pride, you understand?"

Spencer laughed loudly. "Yes, I see what you mean, Sinister. Priceless indeed!"

John looked up at Lionel. "What? Well what do you suggest we do then? Stand here until one of us dies of old age?"

"No, sir. If you could just leave the photographs on the side there, you and Agnes can be on your way."

"And if I refuse?"

"I'd rather you didn't, sir. For everyone's sakes."

John shook his head in disbelief. The room fell silent whilst everyone tried to think of a way to come out of this a winner. Time stretched on, but the only plan John could come up with was 'kick him in the nuts and run', and tempting though it was, he had the distinct impression that that would only make Lionel mad.

"Oh this is ridiculous!" exclaimed Spencer. "Julia, be a lamb. Pop out to my coach and ask Charlie to come in here would you?" Julia did as she was asked. "And tell him to bring his stick," Spencer called after her. "The one he keeps for highwaymen." He turned to Lionel. "I assume you have no objection if Charlie handles things from here on in?"

"None at all, sir. Just so long as it ain't me, it ain't none of my business." While they waited, Lionel leant down to whisper in Agnes's ear. "If I was you," he said, "I'd have a word with your man there, maybe persuade him to leave the photographs and go. Young Charlie ain't a gentleman like what I am."

"Is he handy?" said Agnes

"Very," said Lionel.

"Handier than me?"

"Put it this way, he wasn't hired as a coachman because he's good with horses."

Agnes nodded her understanding. She went over to stand next to John. "Leave the photographs and let's go," she said.

"What? I can't do that. They're the only evidence I've got."

"I know, but it's out of my hands. There's nothing I can do. Trust me, if you don't leave them photographs this is going to end badly for both of us."

"But I—" John stopped talking when he saw the look in Agnes's eyes. Not fear, as such, but the closest he'd ever seen her come to it. Reluctantly, he removed the photographs from his jacket pocket and set them to one side.

"There's a good boy," said Spencer. "I knew you'd see sense eventually."

The drawing room door opened and Charlie came in wielding a pick axe shaft with a bunch of nails hammered through the end of it. John was not surprised to find that Charlie was the other man from the bridge, the one with the meat hook.

"It's alright, Charlie, you can stand down. Mr Sinister has seen the error of his ways."

Charlie made a short, disappointed sound, like he'd lost a sovereign and found tuppence. With great reluctance, he lowered his 'stick' to the ground.

"Let's go," said Agnes.

She let John go first, so she could keep an eye on Charlie and Spencer as they passed between them. Through the door and into the hall, they'd barely left the room when Spencer called out after them, "Checkmate, Lefty!"

His mocking laughter followed them all the way to the front door.

John and Agnes hurried across the driveway and clambered into their awaiting cab.

"Town. Quick as you can," said John.

"I'm gonna need an address, guv."

"Just go!"

The driver cracked his whip and the cab lurched forward, throwing John and Agnes back in their seats. Twisting round, John turned to watch the front door of the house through the back window.

"Relax, Sinister," said Agnes. "They're not gonna come after us."

"They might, if they count how many photographs I left behind." From his inside pocket he produced a single photograph. It was a picture of Spencer, brandishing the royal sceptre as he rode the Crown Prince like a pony.

Agnes grinned.

"You're a crafty one you are, John Sinister."

"Well, I do my best."

The carriage rattled down the driveway, skidding into the main road. The driver may have been slow on the uptake but he was making up for it now. Urging his horse forward, he swerved down the road, barely slowing down to take the corners. John stomached as much as he could before finally banging on the cab roof. "You can slow down a bit," he called out, feeling a little queasy. "We're alright for now."

"Right you are, guv," said the cab driver, reigning in his horse. "Er, any chance of that address now? Only there's a crossroads coming up, y'see."

"Yes. Head for the Barns Tenements. I'll show you where when we get there."

"The Barns Tenements?" said Agnes. "You're not going to the police?"

"I am, but I want to swing by home first, pick up a few things. With your pal Lionel and his mate Charlie on the loose I'll feel better with something more substantial in hand than this damn cane."

"I told you, you don't need any of that stuff, not when you've got me around. I'll take care of you."

"Yeah, but only till five, right?"

"Why, what time is it now?"

"Quarter to four."

"What, already? Damn. Time flies when you're having fun, eh?"

"Doesn't it just. Look, I know we had an agreement, but do you think you can see me as far as Wainwright's Yard, so I can show Detective Hardigan this photograph? It shouldn't take long, but it might make you a little late for work."

"How late?"

"Half an hour, maybe forty-five minutes."

Agnes thought it over. "Alright. That shouldn't be a problem. Ted's on right now. He won't mind if I'm a bit late. He owes me one anyway. But that's it, right? No more than that. Any later and Nero will have my guts for garters."

"That's it, I promise," said John, forgetting completely the old adage about not making promises you can't keep.

Dexter spent the first hour after Nomko left jumping all over the place. It was amazing how much lighter he felt, and how much better his balance was. Leaps he once would have had to concentrate on he could do with ease, and leaps he never would have considered before he could now do, even if it was a bit of a scramble sometimes.

And he was faster now, with a surprising turn of speed. He could get from one side of the factory to the other in an instant, although stopping was proving to be a bit more problematic. He'd already run into the wall a couple of times, but since there was no damage – either to the wall or himself – he wasn't all that bothered. He'd get the hang of it eventually.

At least no one was there to see him crashing about. Peter Chard was still in his office, but all the others, including Mrs Crabtree, had left for the day.

He'd even managed to catch a mouse, if you could believe that, something he'd never been able to do before. Back at the manor the mice were so quick and ziggy and good at hiding. It was infuriating. But this one! Dexter had been on him before he knew what was going on. It was an amazing feeling. The little guy had been terrified, its heart beating so fast Dexter thought he was going to die of fright right there in his paws.

But it turned out that catching a mouse presented its own unique problem, namely what to do with it after you've caught it. Play with it, sure, that was a given, but the novelty of that soon wore off. You could kill it of course, which would've been the traditional way to go, but it seemed that given the opportunity Dexter wasn't into that kind of thing. He couldn't see the point. You couldn't do anything with a dead mouse... except eat it perhaps, the idea of which turned Dexter's newly-installed stomach. Who would want to eat a mouse? They'd be all crunchy and wet, and what would they even taste like? Nothing good, that's for sure. In the end Dexter had chosen to let it go, watching it scurry away before going off to find something more palatable to eat instead.

He'd started in the bins. He'd figured that was where he'd find the most bite-sized pieces of material to try.

His culinary adventure began with a strip of paper, which was great because he could tear off little pieces to chew on. But it stuck to his teeth, and it made quite a hard lump that was difficult to swallow. The wood shavings were nice. They smelled good, and they broke apart well in his mouth. He found canvas to be a bit stringy, and whilst rubber was fun to chew on it felt weird going down. He wouldn't be eating any of that again in a hurry.

It was strange not having to cough what he ate back up, although not as strange as when the 'food' hit the boiler and he felt himself start to get warm. It was oddly satisfying, in a slightly unusual way, similar to when he used to recharge, although it brought with it a new sensation that he wasn't familiar with, a feeling like there was something else he needed to do. It took a while, but eventually he figured out that that thing was to drink something. He was thirsty! For the first time in his life. How wonderful!

The cleanest water he could find was a rain butt out in the yard. He'd lapped at it eagerly, taking in as much as he could until something told him to stop. Then the warmness had spread throughout his whole body, which was very nice, followed by another new sensation, one he couldn't quite put his paw on. He couldn't say why, but he needed to find a dark corner for some reason, and he needed to find one right now!

What he did in that dark corner didn't bear thinking about. Suffice it to say that when he emerged there was a small pile of charcoal briquettes where no charcoal briquettes had been before. It had been a challenging experience for Dexter, and not one he was in any rush to try again soon. Deciding to lay off eating for a while (and quite possibly forever) he'd gone inside to find out what Peter Chard was up to.

The ride back into town took longer than John anticipated. It was almost four thirty by the time they reached his sister's place. Enough time to get what they needed and get to the police station before they parted ways, but only just.

John took Agnes into the kitchen. Jane was there cooking dinner, whilst Emily sat at the table drawing a unicorn and a crocodile doing battle with a giant.

"Unca John, lookit what I drew. It's a—" Emily spotted Agnes looming in the doorway. Her mouth fell open and her eyes nearly popped out of her head.

"Emily, this is Agnes, a friend of mine. Agnes, this is Emily, my niece."

"Hi," said Agnes shyly, giving Emily a little wave. Emily's eyes grew even wider.

"Oh wow! Lookit your hands. They're huge!!"

"Emily! Don't be rude," said Jane. "Now you apologise to Agnes, right now."

Emily's chin dropped to her chest. "Sorry," she mumbled. Agnes smiled.

"That's alright, Emily, they are pretty big," she said, pulling out a chair. "So what's this you're drawing? I can see a crocodile, and a unicorn, and... is that me?" Emily giggled.

"I'll be back in a sec," said John, leaving them to it.

In the living room John went through his travel bag and found the lucky brass knuckles he used to carry with him on his visits to Caesar's back in the day. They had a reassuring weight to them, as did the club he put in his other pocket. There was also a knife, which he mainly used for prying small stones from his boots. He thought about carrying it, then he thought about stabbing someone and decided against it. Some people in life were killers, and some people, very much, were not.

As he sorted himself out, his mind wandered to Dexter. Should he go pick the cat up on his way to the police station? He'd probably get all stroppy if he didn't. No doubt he'd want to be there at the end, to see how it all went down. But the factory was miles away, and in completely the wrong direction. It would take too long, and there was no way Agnes would be up for it. Not that he'd be able to explain it to her anyway, even if she was. No, it was no good, Dexter would have to wait. And if he didn't like it then he would just have to lump it, wouldn't he?

Checking his pockets one last time John caught sight of his new clothes laying over the end of the sofa, as fresh and clean as the day he bought them.

In the kitchen Agnes had Emily in fits of laughter as she palmed her entire head, encircling her fingers around her skull as if it were no bigger than an orange.

"Oooooh," Jane cooed as John walked in. "Look at you all dressed up. What's the occasion?"

"There's a lady cop he fancies," said Agnes. "We're on our way to see her now."

"Haha," said Emily. "Unca John's got a girlfriend."

"I do not. Shut it, you." John pointed at Agnes. "And you, don't encourage her." Agnes and Emily giggled, whilst Jane just had a very knowing smile on her face.

"Well before you go, this letter came for you. It arrived just before you did."

The letter was on cream-coloured, headed notepaper. It read:

From the desk of Mary Chard

John, come quick! I need you urgently.
I fear I may be in great danger.

Mary

"What does it say?" said Agnes. John read the letter out loud to everyone. "That's it? That's pretty vague."

"Maybe she was in a hurry," said John, his mind already working. What kind of danger could she be in?

Jane took the letter and gave it a quick once over. "Maybe. But even so..."

"So are you going?" said Agnes.

"I dunno. I mean I probably should, shouldn't I?"

"What about the police?"

"Well we can go there after, can't we?"

"And where does this Mary Chard live?" said Agnes, knowing full well what the answer would be.

"Um... Chard Manor. In Turning Hill."

"Which is right back where we just were. Come on, John, you're not thinking. We don't have time to go there *and* to the police. I've got work to get to, remember?"

"Alright, well what about just to hers then?"

"And how long will that take? You don't know what's going on the other end. We could be there all night, and then what? I'm already missing dinner because of you, I'm not going to lose my job for you as well."

"Oh, are you hungry, Agnes? Emily and I were just about to eat. You're welcome to join us if you'd like?"

"That's very kind of you, Jane, it smells delicious, but I have to escort this one to Wainwright's Yard. Unless, of course, he decides to go on this wild goose chase instead?"

John had had about enough of this. "Hey, we don't know what's going on. Mary could be in real trouble for all you know. I mean we know what happened to Henry, more or less, but there's still Donald Chard to figure out. If someone did do for him then they could have it in for the whole family. And if that's the case then Mary may well be next on their list."

"That's a lot of ifs, coulds, and maybes," said Agnes. "You'd be better off sticking to the facts, mate. You don't want to risk it all for 'I *think* I *may* be in danger', do you?"

"But what if she is?" said John.

Agnes shrugged. "Then I guess you've got to decide what's most important to you, eh?"

From his perch outside Peter Chard's office window – So easy to get to now! – Dexter sat and watched Peter Chard poring over ledger after ledger. He made notes, checked things against other things, and generally looked unhappy about everything he found. His window was open, and every now and then Dexter could hear him muttering "That can't be right.", "Where did that go?", or "I don't believe it." Then, after an hour of this, he stood suddenly and exclaimed "My God! That's it. It's so obvious. How did I not see it before? I have to go. I need to show Mr Hutchison before it's too late."

In a fever, Peter Chard started grabbing handfuls of notes, piling up the ledgers as he filled his pockets with the contents of his desk. He kept checking he had what he needed, discarding pages of scribbles only to rescue them from the floor and re-examine them. So preoccupied was he that he failed to hear a carriage turn in through the factory gates and trundle across the yard. But Dexter heard it.

"Sinister. Finally!" he grumbled under his breath, jumping back in through the window to wait for him on the stairs. "About time you got here."

But it wasn't John who entered the factory a moment later. And Not John wasn't alone.

John worried about whether he'd done the right thing or not all the way to Chard Manor. Jane didn't think so, and clearly neither did Agnes, which was why he was in the carriage alone. Discharged from her duties, Agnes had decided to accept Jane's offer to stay for tea. John felt a lot more vulnerable without her, which was why he had one hand in his pocket, his fingers slipped through the grip of his knuckledusters.

Was he being stupid? Jane was right, it was probably nothing. But what if it wasn't? The guy he'd chased was still unaccounted for. What if he had decided to go from watching to doing? He could have Mary in his sights right now.

Agnes was right as well, he should have gone to the police with the photograph first, then gone up there. But that would have taken time, time he might not have. In the end he'd compromised (with himself) by saying he'd call the police from Chard Manor, tell them what he knew, and then give them the photograph later. They didn't need the evidence in their hand right away. A verbal account would do. That'd be enough to get them started, enough to get the ball rolling, wouldn't it?

It would have to be, it was too late now to change his mind.

As his cab pulled into the driveway of Chard Manor, John saw that there were no journalists at the gate, no policeman, and no guy by the omnibus stop over the road. The whole place was deathly quiet, the quietest he'd seen it in a long time. Sitting back, he really wished the phrase 'deathly quiet' hadn't popped into his head. Closing the fist in his pocket, he clutched his knuckledusters even tighter.

The Steam Castle itself was dark and still. There was a light on inside, by the front door, and a faint glow in an upstairs window, but other than that there were no signs of life; no sound, no movement, nothing to indicate anyone was there at all. Even its ever-present hiss of venting steam seemed muted for once, like the house was scared to make too much noise in case anyone heard. It gave John the heebie-jeebies and no mistake.

John rang the doorbell. The sound echoed through the house. He heard nothing from the Robobutler, nothing from the real butler, nothing from anything. He tried knocking, as if a different noise might have a different result, but still nothing. He tried the door handle but it was locked. John was about to ring again when he caught sight of someone peeking through the window beside the door. He heard the lock click, the heavy door creaked open about a foot, and Mary's worried face appeared in the narrow opening. "John, thank God it's you. I've been so scared." Squeezing herself through the gap she threw her arms around him, hugging him for dear life.

John was surprised to say the least. "Um... That's okay, Mary. There's nothing to worry about. Everything's alright now." He broke off the hug reluctantly. "What's going on? Where is every-one?"

"Oh. I, um, I gave everyone the day off. I thought after everything that's happened that they deserved a break." Mary looked down at her feet. "I didn't think about being in this big empty house all by myself though. I'm afraid I got a bit... overwhelmed."

"Your note said you were in danger."

"Oh God, did it? Oh, John, I'm so sorry. I shouldn't have sent that. What must you think of me? Oh, but what a darling you are to come rushing over like this. What a hero. How can I ever repay you?"

A reasonable explanation would be nice, thought John. But what he said was, "That's really not necessary."

"I know!" said Mary, brightening up. "How about some supper? I could cook you something."

As someone who was literally 'to the manor born' John was unsure how much time Mary spent in the kitchen, but she seemed so excited he felt bad saying no. "Sure. If you like."

Mary took him by the hand.

"Have you ever had grits?"

"I can honestly say I have no idea what a grit is."

"Oh you'll love it. It's something I learned to cook on my travels. Come with me."

Mary pulled him towards the door but John held back. His cab was still on the driveway, its driver watching the unexpected show with great amusement. John gave him a quick 'that'll do' wave and got a 'you bet it will' wink in return, before the cab set off on the long ride back into town.

Inside, Mary was keen to get him to the kitchen, but John had to stop her once again. "Before we do anything else, can I use your radiophone quickly?"

"What? The radiophone. Oh, er... No. Sorry. No, it's broken I'm afraid. Has been all day, in fact."

"Oh." John cursed himself for not checking before sending the cab away. Now he was really screwed. "That's fine. No problem," he said. "It can wait."

Mary led John towards the back stairs. As they passed the Robobutler she felt him shy away and laughed. "Don't worry, he's not working either. I had the damn thing turned off."

Gripping his hand tightly, Mary led John down the back stairs to the kitchen, almost skipping she was so excited.

"The Hell-Bats did all that? Are you sure?"

"Yup. Pretty sure."

"And you say Spencer is a part of it?"

"He is, along with the Rosemonts, and probably the rest of the old Chess Club, too. I don't know, I haven't gotten to the bottom of it all yet."

"Lord have mercy. That's insane."

"The word I'm going with to describe it is idiotic."

Shaking her head in disbelief, Mary ate a mouthful of food and chewed things over. John tried to join her but there was a problem; he didn't know what he was eating. It seemed that grits was some kind of gelatinous porridge made from corn, something John had only ever thought of as cattle food until now. Mary had ground it up, boiled it, added butter, a little salt and pepper, and the resulting white goo now sat on his plate, daring him to eat it.

If anyone else had made it for him John wouldn't have gone near the stuff. With as much enthusiasm as he could muster, he spooned a tiny amount into his mouth. It tasted like a sneeze.

"What do you think?" said Mary.

"It tastes..." John searched for a positive adjective that wasn't an outright lie. Mary laughed at the struggle on his face.

"It's a bit of an acquired taste," she conceded.

"Yes, I can imagine it is," said John, wondering why anyone would go to the bother of acquiring such a taste in the first place. He took a sip of beer – He hadn't wanted to drink but Mary had insisted. It was part of the grits experience apparently. – as his fork retreated to the relative safety of the 'refried beans'.

At least you knew what to expect from a bean. Beans were familiar. Beans were predictable. Beans you could trust. Or so he thought.

John didn't know if Mary had used all the chilli in the house, but it sure tasted like it. Choking down the spicy concoction, he cast a reassuring smile in Mary's direction as he grabbed himself a piece of bread to help quench the fire.

Chewing on the absolute safety of the crusty loaf, John wondered how little of this so-called food he could get away with eating without causing offence.

They were sitting in the drawing room by the front door, on opposing sofas, a small table between them. There was a fire burning which cast a warm, intimate light about the room. It was almost romantic, but for the strange feeling John got that Mary was distracted for some reason. She kept glancing at him like she had something to say, and whilst he knew what he hoped it might be, he tried not to think about it too much. Life was challenging enough without inventing things to hope, fear, desire, and worry over.

"So, how are you coping?" he said.

"Better than you, I think," said Mary, nodding at his plate.

John set the plate down and slid it away from him. "No, I meant with everything that's been going on?"

"Oh. I see what you mean." Mary set down her own plate, deliberately placing her knife and fork next to it. "Things are fine, I guess. It's strange not having Henry and Father around. You don't realise how important someone is to you until they're gone." John nodded. He was familiar with the feeling. "I've just been trying to keep myself busy, you know? That's why I'm really helping out down at the factory, if I'm honest, to try and keep my mind off things."

"Well they're probably glad of the help. You always were good with numbers, as I recall."

"That's kind of you to say, John, but I have to admit, I'm having a little trouble getting my head around it all. I mean, it's all so needlessly complicated and hard to understand, like they don't want anyone to know what's really going on."

"That's probably to keep the tax man at bay."

"No, it's more than that. I'm starting to get the impression that the company is in trouble."

"Is that so? I had no idea," said John, putting on his best poker face.

"Please don't say anything to anyone. I might be wrong. And I'd hate to start one of those horrible rumours that ruins somebody."

"Of course," he said. "I know how to keep a secret."

"I think my brother has made major errors in judgement, errors that have put everything at risk. It's the only explanation. Either that, or he's embezzling from the company."

"Peter? Embezzling? Surely not."

"One would hope not, but it remains a possibility. Not that it matters either way. The way things are I may have to take control of the company, for everyone's sake."

"Take control? That sounds rather drastic. Are you sure it's the right thing to do?"

"You think I can't handle it?" snapped Mary. "That a woman is incapable of running such a large corporation?"

John was taken aback. "No, I just meant that it sounds like a lot of responsibility. Are you sure there's no alternative?"

"What, like get married, let my husband take care of things?"

"No, I mean like talking to your brother, seeing if the two of you can't work this out together somehow?"

Mary seemed surprised. "Oh. Yes. Yes I suppose that is a possibility."

They fell silent, John too scared to say anything in case he said the wrong thing again, whilst Mary chewed on her fingernail, her thoughts a million miles away. Then Mary chuckled to herself. "Speaking of marriage, do you want to hear something funny? Spencer has asked me to marry him."

"Really?" said John, reaching for his beer. "And what did you say?"

"No, of course. I mean, can you imagine what a terrible husband he would be? With all the drinking and the gambling and whatnot. The man's a complete oaf."

"And yet you went out with him."

Mary shrugged. "What can I say? He was fun for a while. But I lost all respect for him when he grew that silly moustache. Every time we kissed the darn thing tickled my nose. I had to end it."

John laughed. "Fair enough, I can see that. As moustaches go, it was quite—" John got a horrible feeling in the pit of his stomach, and it wasn't the grits. "Um, sorry, but when did you say you ended it with Spencer?"

"A couple of months ago. Why?"

"Because he had that moustache of his for less than a month."

"You must be mistaken," said Mary, getting up to tend the fire.

"No, I'm not. I'm pretty sure Henry made him grow it as a forfeit."

"A forfeit? Whatever do you mean?"

"Well, the last time I saw Henry he let slip that Spencer wasn't allowed to shave off his moustache, an odd thing to say which I didn't give much thought to at the time. But now, thinking back on it, I think that Spencer was the one tasked with getting the lion's mane at the zoo. A task which he failed, hence his having to grow the moustache. So if you broke up with him a couple of months ago, and the zoo break-in was four weeks ago, then there's no way he had the moustache when the two of you were going out."

Mary laughed and shook her head. "Oh, John, what a lot of supposition. Where do you get it all from?" She picked up the fire poker. "I don't know what possessed Spencer to grow that silly thing, but he definitely had it when we were going out."

Mary turned her back on John and began diligently tending to the fire.

Reaching into his jacket pocket, John removed Mary's note to him. Then he found the ransom note delivered to her father and held the two up side by side. But for the torn away letterhead at the top of one, the two pieces of paper were identical; same colour, same weight, same feel. They were written in the same ink, by the same pen, and even the handwriting was similar. There really was only one conclusion.

John looked up to find Mary pointing a flintlock pistol at his head.

"Oh, John," she said. "You always were so terribly clever."

If John could have kicked himself he would have. "Of course! How could I have been so stupid? It was you all along." Mary smiled at him. "I wondered what was going on. Why you were so passive all of a sudden. I thought maybe travel had changed you, that something had happened to you over there, something bad. But I see now that you've been playing me since day one. Playing us all, in fact."

"Yes, I'm afraid that's true."

"I can't believe I didn't see it before."

"Neither can I, if I'm honest. I was actually worried when Daddy hired you to stick your big nose into things. But it turns out that you're the same as any other man. A kiss on the cheek, a squeeze of the hand, and your brain stops working just like the rest of them."

"Maybe so, but I got there in the end."

"Yes but it took you long enough, didn't it? Now, move down the couch if you would, please, away from the knife."

John moved away from his plate. He hadn't even thought about going for the knife. He was preoccupied with the weapons he had in his coat pockets, the coat which lay over the back of the sofa right next to him. Not that they'd be much use at the moment, of course. They'd take too long to get to, and neither would be very effective against a gun.

"So it was your handwriting on the company accounts. I thought it looked too neat and flowing for your average accountant."

"When did you see the company accounts?"

"I had a little look around the factory a couple of nights ago. I was curious."

"Of course you were," said Mary, retaking her place on the sofa opposite. "Yes, it was my handwriting. I've been at the factory for months 'helping out'. Fiddling the books, moving money around, getting the company ready for a takeover."

John threw his hands up. "Oh my God, I just got it. The Peculiar Tools Company! As in *peculatus*, the Latin for embezzled."

Mary laughed. "Very good, John. Silly of me, I know, but I couldn't help myself."

"I can't believe I didn't spot that before." *That's what I get for bunking off Latin so many times.* "So that's what this has all been about? Money?"

Mary's smile vanished. "No, John," she hissed. "Not money. It's about what's right, and what I deserve, and the way things should be. I did it to get what's mine!"

John became very still. His eyes were on the muzzle of the gun. It quivered with emotion, threatening to punch a hole in his chest any second. When it happened, he just hoped it would be quick.

Carriage wheels crunched on the gravel outside. John looked at Mary. "Don't get your hopes up," she said. "It's not a rescue. That'll be Spencer." They heard a coach door slam and some footsteps on the driveway, followed by the doorbell ringing. All was quiet. The doorbell rang again, followed by more silence. When it rang a third time, Mary gave a weary sigh.

More footsteps on the gravel, coming closer this time, then a knock at the window behind Mary. Spencer pressed his face up against the glass. "Sweetheart, it's me. The front door's locked. Can you open it for me?"

"Go around back. It's open."

"What?"

"I said, go around back," Mary shouted. "I'm kind of busy at the moment." She held up the gun for him to see.

"Oh, okay," said Spencer, waving even though Mary's back was turned. Retreating from the window, Spencer crunched his way round to the back of the house.

Mary frowned at John. "Don't give me that look."

"I didn't say anything."

"You didn't have to. I can tell what you're thinking."

"I don't know what you mean, Mary."

"Spencer Shelby may not be the sharpest tool in the box, but he's loyal, ruthless, he does what he's told, and he treats me as an equal. In that respect, he's leaps and bounds ahead of the rest of you."

John didn't think that being equal to Spencer amounted to very much but he knew better than to argue. He settled back in the chair, closer to the weapons in his coat pocket, and the cane he'd just realised was hooked on the back of the chair next to it.

The drawing room door opened and Spencer Shelby the Third sauntered in. "You started the party without me, sweetheart," he protested.

"I had to, darling. He figured it out."

"Did he now?" said Spencer. "Clever boy. I'm impressed. Took you long enough though."

"That's what she said," said John.

"Is it done?" said Mary.

"It's done alright. I'm sorry to report, but your brother Peter is dead. Killed himself rather than face the shame of what he'd done, it seems. I imagine that old bat Mrs Crabtree will find him swinging from the rafters some time tomorrow, when she takes him up his morning tea."

"Wonderful. Well done, my love. I'm so proud of you." Spencer beamed, lapping up the praise. John half expected Mary to pat him on the head and feed him a treat. "Now, search him. He might have a weapon on him."

Spencer beckoned John to his feet. He patted him down, putting whatever he found on the table in front of them. "Mary told me how you cheated at chess, Sinister," he said, as he went through John's pockets. "I always knew it had to be some kind of trick. I knew you couldn't be that smart."

"No. Just smart enough, eh?" said John.

Spencer went behind the sofa, clipping John round the ear along the way. He went through John's coat pockets, adding their contents to the pile on the table. The weapons he kept for himself. When he was done, he flung the coat into the corner of the room, along with John's cane.

"Where's the picture?" he demanded. John blinked. It took all his self-control not to look down. The picture was in his jacket pocket. It should have been on the table with everything else. Which pocket had it been in? Had Spencer missed it? Or could he have lost it along the way? Then he remembered. He'd changed coats at his sister's, put the new one on. He must have left the photograph behind. It was in his other coat.

"The police have it. I took it to them already. In fact they're probably on the way here now to arrest you."

"No you didn't," Spencer sneered. "Wainwright's Yard is too far in the opposite direction. You didn't have time." He might not be the sharpest tool, but even blunt instruments have their uses.

"It'll be at his sister's," said Mary. "Spencer, be a lamb and go get it, would you?"

"No! You stay away from her," said John. He took a step towards Spencer, only to find a large knife pointed at the tip of his nose.

"Calm down, John, Spencer won't harm your sister, will you, Spencer?" Spencer just smiled. "I said will you, Spencer?!"

"Of course not. I promise. Cross my heart and hope to die." Spencer used the tip of his knife to cross his heart. John was tempted to lunge and push the blade deep into his chest.

"You touch one hair on her head and that's exactly what will happen," he said.

Spencer laughed. "Look at the big man making threats. I'd worry about my own skin if I was you."

"Just know, anything you do to her, I do to you," said John softly. Spencer's smile faltered. Then he chuckled bravely. Sticking out his chin he practically dared John to go for it, and, despite the knife, John was very tempted to oblige him.

"Spencer! Go. Now," said Mary. "We're wasting time."

Spencer nodded. "Of course, my love." Stepping back, he tucked the knife into his belt. "Would you like me to send Charlie in to help keep an eye on this one while I'm gone?"

"Is that the skinny one? No, he gives me the creeps. But you can send in the big one if you like. He at least has a brain in his head."

"Ah, well, I can't I'm afraid. I had to let Lionel go, you see."

John grinned. "Why was that, Spencer?"

Spencer scowled at him. "It's not important."

"No, it really isn't," said Mary. "Just get going. And hurry back. We've got lots to do."

Spencer kissed Mary on the cheek, gave John a final murderous glare, and left. With her gun, Mary motioned for John to sit.

"Now what?" said John.

"Now," said Mary, settling herself in opposite him. "We wait."

Once Spencer's coach pulled out of the driveway, the only sound in the drawing room was the ticking of the clock and the turning of John's mind as he tried to think his way out of this mess. He had to stop Spencer somehow. He didn't believe for a second that that lunatic would leave his sister and little Emily unharmed. Or, for that matter, that Jane would let him waltz in and take whatever he wanted without a fight. Someone was going to get hurt.

Agnes might still be there, but she also might not. He couldn't rely on her to save them. And even if she was there, could she take on Spencer *and* his psychotic coachman at the same time? Probably not. Agnes was tough, but two lots of crazy beats one lot of tough any day.

He needed to call the police, get them there before Spencer. He didn't believe for a second that there was anything wrong with the radiophone. Spencer had obviously used it to call Mary after John saw him at the Rosemont's place. It was the only way she could have gotten the note to his sister's so quickly. He needed to disarm Mary, so he could get to the radiophone, and the only way he could think to do that was to get her talking.

"So what happened with Henry? Why'd you kill him?"

Mary was amused. "Do you really expect me to confess?" she said. John idly picked some fluff off his trouser leg.

"I was just hoping you'd fill in some gaps for me, for old time's sake. I mean what difference does it make? You're going to kill me anyway."

Mary thought about it. "Go on then," she said finally. "For old time's sake. What is it you want to know?"

John felt sick. *So, my dying is part of the plan is it? Very well then. From now on, all bets are off.*

"Why did Henry have to die?"

"Well as I've said already, I've been paving the way for a hostile takeover of Chard Mechanical for months now, setting Peter up for a fall whilst at the same time making myself indispensable. And it was all going swimmingly, right up until Henry came back from India.

"Daddy was delighted, of course, the return of the prodigal son and all that. He installed Henry straight onto the board of directors, despite everyone protesting that he was wholly unsuited to the role. He didn't care. He had his two boys running the family business and his little girl doing the accounts. He was as happy as a pig in the proverbial.

"Henry was a disaster, of course. A natural born dilettante, he didn't have the right mindset to run such a large corporation. What he did have though, unexpectedly, was a flair for invention. He became friends with that little Japanese fellow, and together the two of them came up with all sorts of ideas, not least of which was the automotive engine. They beavered away day and night on that thing trying to get it to work, until a couple of weeks ago they announced that they'd cracked it. They had a machine to replace the horse, and Chard Mechanical was saved. Naturally, I couldn't allow that."

Mary hesitated. "Henry wasn't meant to die. Spencer was just supposed to put him out of action until I had control of the company. But when he saw his automotive engine coming down the road towards him he took fright,"—*Imagine that*, thought John—"jumping off the bridge and killing himself instantly, the damn fool. It was... not what I wanted." Mary pursed her lips. "I *told* Spencer using the engine to run him down was a bad idea, but he insisted. He saw it in the workshop one day and he just *had* to have a go, didn't he?"

That explains the scratches on the wall at the bridge, thought John. They were the same height as the automotive engine's front bumper.

"Honest to God, John, I only wanted him out of the way for a while. I was devastated when he turned up dead, truly I was. I know you won't believe me, but those were real tears you saw me crying when you came to the house that day."

John didn't care. He was watching the gun. The more Mary talked, the more it dipped away from his chest towards the table. As soon as it was no longer pointing at anything made of him he was going to go for it. It would be hard, clearing the table with his gammy leg, but if he could get on top of Mary and get control of the gun he might have a chance. Moving his feet under him, he braced himself against the seat of the chair. The gun was almost to the table. Any second now...

"Anyway," said Mary, bringing up the gun, "with Henry gone I thought the plan was back on track. But then the next day Daddy made a revelation that kind of blew everything apart. He told us about the illegitimate brother we never knew we had."

John forgot the gun. "I'm sorry, he told you about what now?!"

"That's right. It seems that, as well as being responsible for killing my mother, Daddy dear was cheating on her as well. Somewhere between Henry and me, Daddy had a fling with his secretary, after which the child in question was born."

"Not Mrs Crabtree!"

Mary laughed. "Good Lord, no. Although, could you imagine? No, Mrs Crabtree was hired as the slattern's replacement. The person I'm referring to is some woman by the name of Esmerelda Tiggle." Mary spat out the name like it left a bad taste in her mouth. "She'd worked for my father for years, although clearly work was not all they got up to. When the pregnancy was discovered, Miss Tiggle was shipped off to our ironworks in Telford to keep her out of the way. The child, a boy, was raised in secret, and as long as the payments continued, dear Esmerelda seemed happy to keep the details of my father's indiscretion to herself. But then she did something that was most inconvenient. She died.

"In her will she left a letter telling her son who his real father was, and apparently the boy thought it would be a good idea to get in touch. He wanted to get to know the rest of his so-called 'new family', and with mother gone Daddy saw no reason for him not to do so. Can you believe that?"

John could, but he wasn't about to say so. "You didn't like the idea?"

"Of having *another* brother ahead of me in line to the throne. How could I? The things I've had to put up with growing up in this family, and then he just waltzes in and takes a slice of the action. I don't think so."

"Did you know that was going to happen?"

"Absolutely I did. My father made it clear he intended to make a sizeable provision for the little bastard in his will. That was what his trip to the lawyer's was all about the day he died. Naturally I could not allow that, so I sent him that note to keep him busy whilst I figured out my next move. Not that he took the bait of course. Tossed it without so much as a by your leave, if you can believe that."

"And so, when the note didn't work, you poisoned him instead?"

Mary was pleased. "Very good, John. Yes, thanks to Mother, our gardens are home to a number of poisonous flora, any of which would have been right for the job. I was quite spoiled for choice. I settled on Strangle Wort in the end, a nasty little plant that, in small doses, is quite excellent in combatting dizzy spells, but which can cause the throat to close up if you happen to take too much of it. You suffocate to death, to put it bluntly.

"I made a preparation which I slipped into his morning coffee. He used to have it so sweet he never noticed the unusual taste. I had thought he would die here, at home. How he got all the way to his lawyers I've no idea, although that turned out to be a blessing in disguise. Having an independent eye witness made his death look more like natural causes."

"Weren't you worried they would discuss the new will before he died?"

"Not at all. In fact I'm sure they did. But our lawyers would never reveal something like that outside of the family, and I'd already removed the draft will from my father's briefcase, so there was no evidence and nothing for him to sign. As far as the will was concerned I was in the clear."

She was right of course, Mr Hutchison had kept their secrets, although he had tried to tell John something was going on, in a roundabout sort of way. John cursed himself for not asking the right questions. He had asked if a will existed, not if there were to be any changes made to it. Then, all of a sudden, he realised something else.

"So that's what Hutchison meant when he talked about Donald Chard taking care of *all* his children. I thought it was a weird thing to say, but I just assumed he meant you and your brothers."

"You talked to Hutchison? My, my, John, you have been busy."

John caught the look she gave him, and the way she adjusted her grip on the gun. He'd been stomping through her plans all week.

She was dying to take him out of the equation. He needed to tread lightly.

"So," he said, "with Henry and your father out of the picture everything was back on track, yes?"

"It was, more or less. But there was still the question of this illegitimate brother of mine. He still needed to be found and taken care of. That is what Spencer and I were discussing when you found us in the garden that afternoon." Mary smiled a most unpleasant smile. "You know, I really ought to thank you."

"You should? For what?"

"Well, we've had people out looking for little Johnny Tiggle – yes, his name was John, just like you – but we had no idea where to start. We didn't know where he was staying, what he looked like, nothing. And we found nothing in my father's study that would help us out either. As you're no doubt aware, Daddy had this annoying habit of writing important things down in code. He was nothing if not paranoid."

With good reason, as it turns out, thought John.

"That's why I took you along with me to the races, to see if you knew anything." Mary chuckled. "Spencer was livid about that, by the way. Honestly, you boys can be so jealous sometimes. But he at least saw the sense in it. He knew you might know something useful. And you did, too! The moment you told me about some young man watching the house I knew it was him. It had to be. After that it was just a question of waiting for him to show up again, then sending Spencer out to take care of him."

John knew the answer, but he had to ask. "Take care of him how?"

"Spencer ran him over with the automotive engine. Stupid, I know. We should have just sent the boys after him, like we did you, but Spencer has a bit of a soft spot for that thing, I'm afraid. He insisted, so what was I to do?

"Of course he broke the damn thing didn't he, oaf that he is. They had to stash it someplace out in the sticks for safe keeping. Most inconvenient, as we do need it back at Chard Mechanical. But once I am named head of the company it will be miraculously discovered and brought back to the factory for completion. It really is a remarkable device. We're going to make an absolute fortune out of it."

"Fascinating," said John. "But let's get back to the part where you sent the boys after me."

"Ah, yes. Well, that's on you, I'm afraid," said Mary.

"On me?"

"Yes. You see, when you came to the factory after the race and told me that you had gotten the coroner to do some more tests I realised that you had to go. You were clearly far too dangerous to be left to your own devices."

"So you sent someone to stick a meat hook in me?"

"I did, yes. Sorry about that. But you didn't leave us much choice, did you? You simply wouldn't take the hint. Although I must say, well done in getting away from them like you did. Most impressive. Most impressive indeed."

"An act of pure desperation, I assure you."

"Most acts of heroism are, so I'm told."

John locked eyes with Mary. He wanted to get that gun away from her so badly. As if reading his mind, Mary lifted the gun's muzzle until it pointed directly at the centre of his chest.

"Anyway," she continued, "with you out of commission, or so I thought, and little Johnny Tiggle taken care of, it meant I could finally turn my attention back to gaining control of the company. And, as it turned out, the missing automotive engine was something of a blessing in disguise. Its disappearance almost broke my brother. He was relying heavily on it to save the company, you see. Without it, he had nothing. Oh, he had the designs of course, but without a proper working prototype he would never get the investors in time. I'd already seen to that.

"I *was* happy for the board to fire him and name me, the only living heir, as head of the company, but then you showed up again, didn't you, asking questions about the Hell-Bats of all things. Which, by the way, how did you find out about that?"

"Nothing is as secret as you think, Mary."

She waited for more but John wasn't in the mood for sharing. "Well anyway, if the board ever got wind I was involved in something like that, even by association, I'd be done for. They'd never put me in charge. The scandal would finish us."

"So you killed your brother because..."

"Because of you, of course. Why else? When Spencer called and told me you had one of the pictures I had to accelerate my plans a little. I brought you here with that vague, pathetic note, to stop you going to the police, then I sent Spencer to take care of Peter. With him out of the way, there'll be an emergency board meeting in the morning, and by this time tomorrow I'll be installed as acting head of Chard Mechanical. After that, making the position permanent is just a matter of time."

"That's if they don't appoint someone more suitable instead," said John.

"They won't. I've seen to that."

"Blackmail?"

"Let's call it proper planning and preparation, shall we?"

John heard a noise by the front door; not a loud noise, more like the click of a latch closing, or the sound of a lock opening. He almost missed it, if it was even there at all, and as far as he could tell Mary hadn't heard anything. He glanced briefly at the window behind Mary, but all he saw there was the dark of the night.

"I just can't believe you would do all this, kill four people, to gain control of a company. I mean, don't you have enough money already?"

"Oh, John, haven't you been listening? This isn't about money, it's about what's right, and what's fair, and about the way things should be. You see, you were right about one thing, travelling did change me. When I saw the pioneer women in the United States, standing side by side with their menfolk as they went west looking for a better life – not merely as someone's wife, or daughter, but as equals – I knew what I had to do. I was going to come back here and claim what was rightfully mine by any means necessary."

John wasn't sure how accurate an assessment that was of life over in the Americas, but he wasn't about to argue. He knew a fanatic's zeal when he saw it. "So you killed Henry, and your father, and John Tiggle,"—John counted the deaths off on his fingers—"*and* Peter, all to get what you think is rightfully yours."

"That's right."

"And you have no regrets about that?"

"None whatsoever. In fact if anyone should feel guilty around here, it's you."

"Me? What did I do?"

"Well apart from Henry, whose death was an accident, everyone else who died, died because of you. If you hadn't gone around sticking your nose in where it didn't belong most of this would never have happened. I would have control of the company, and my father, and Peter, and little Johnny Tiggle would still be alive. Believe me, John, their blood is on your hands, not mine."

John said nothing. It was a clever argument, of that there was no doubt. It probably helped her sleep at night. But it was complete nonsense. The only way for her to stop her father changing his will was to kill him, of that he was sure. And maybe John Tiggle could have been paid off, made to go away, but considering the persistent way he hung around after his father's death, that seemed unlikely. And as for Peter... Well, she had him there. If John hadn't been involved, Peter might still be alive. It was an uncomfortable fact, but it was a fact nonetheless.

For a split second, John thought he saw a face at the window, but when he looked again it was gone.

With an old man groan, John pushed himself to his feet.

"Sit down," said Mary, bringing her pistol to bear on John's head.

"My leg's gone numb," he growled. "I need to stretch it out."

"I said sit down!"

"No! Shoot me if you have to, but I can't sit any longer."

For an uncomfortable second, John saw Mary actually think about it. "Fine," she said finally. "But keep your hands where I can see them." John took a few faltering steps towards the fireplace. "And if you so much as look at that poker you're a dead man."

"Duly noted," said John, walking round behind the sofa. Now that he was standing up he found that his leg was quite sore. If he had gone for Mary he probably wouldn't have made it. Thankfully, things had changed. He had a new plan now.

Walking up and down behind the sofa he positioned himself so that the window and Mary were in one line. He could keep an eye on it without alerting Mary. "Y'know what, I don't believe it," he said.

"Believe what?"

"That Henry's death was an accident."

"Well it was, I assure you."

"I don't think so. You see, you said you only intended to put Henry out of commission for a while, yes?"

"That's right."

"But you used his own invention to run him over. I mean, how was that ever going to work? He was bound to recognise it, and then what? There was no way he wouldn't tell your father what had happened. They might not have got on, but I doubt he would have kept something like attempted fratricide to himself."

"But I wasn't driving, was I? Spencer was. The whole thing had nothing to do with me."

"Oh come off it. There's no way Spencer would have done something like that without your approval, and Henry would have known that."

"Maybe. But he couldn't have gone to Father, could he? He would have had to confess about the Hell-Bats, and his own involvement in the whole seedy affair."

"So what? You think Henry Chard, the apple of his father's eye, had anything to worry about in that department? Because I don't. Your father had always bailed your brother out in the past, and I see no reason why he wouldn't do so again. No, I think you killed Henry because you *had* to, because you knew that if you didn't, it would only be a matter of time before THE POLICE CAME KNOCKING AT YOUR DOOR!"

"What are you shouting for, John? There's no one here to help you."

"What? Oh, sorry. I get lost in the drama sometimes. Silly me. Anyway, you know how I know *for sure* you intended to kill Henry? Because he'd already been struck once before he went in the river. His leg was broken. He was out of action, as you say you wanted. So either Spencer tried to run him over again and he jumped, or someone threw him in the water with a broken leg and he drowned, but whichever way you look at it, Henry's death was no accident."

Mary considered John for a very long time. Then she sighed, giving him a sad, wistful smile as she shook her head gently. "See how clever you are, John," she said. "If only you weren't so dang decent all the time."

Mary sat forward, using both hands to steady the pistol as she aimed it at John's chest. Her finger tightened on the trigger when—

BANG-BANG-BANG!! "OPEN UP! THIS IS THE POLICE! WE'VE GOT YOU SURROUNDED. COME OUT NOW, OR WE'RE COMING IN TO GET YA!"

"What the devil?!" Mary leapt to her feet and rushed to the window.

"Sounds like the game is up, Mary. Why don't you give yourself up before anyone else gets hurt?"

"Oh, John, you're such a defeatist. No wonder you've never amounted to anything." Mary crossed to the door and checked the hallway. "Let's go," she said.

"Where to?"

"Father's study. There's a secret tunnel behind the bookcase that leads to the stables. We can use that to escape."

"A secret tunnel! You have got to be kidding me."

"Not at all. I've told you already, my father was a very paranoid man." Keeping her distance as he passed, Mary shepherded John out into the entrance hall.

John limped across the entrance, playing up his injury to slow them down. He kept looking for a weapon, something he could use to whack Mary over the head, but there was nothing. No vases, no walking sticks, no umbrell– The Robobutler! Of course. It was out of action, but it might still have an umbrella sticking out the back of it. After all, who was going to remove it? Hercules? Unlikely.

John started angling towards the Robobutler, trying to decide which was the quickest way round the back. Mary was only half watching him. She was too busy checking all the doors and windows. Wherever the police were, they weren't here yet.

Almost at the Robobutler, John got ready. He prayed the umbrella was still there. If it wasn't, he was a dead man. Three more steps and he would go for it. Two more steps. One more...

Thunk! A vicious ball of homicidal fur burst through the flap in the front door and hurtled across the floor towards them. It was all claws and teeth and crazy eyes, and it was going "NYAAAARGH!!!" in a most disconcerting manner.

"What the—"

The thing launched itself at Mary's face, sending her cartwheeling backwards into the Robobutler. Digging in its claws, it sunk its teeth into the bridge of her nose, biting down hard. Mary squealed, hitting her assailant repeatedly in the side of the head until eventually she was able to pull it free, one dug-in claw at a time. Flinging it across the room, she took aim with her pistol.

There was a lever at the base of the Robobutler, on the steam pipe that ran from the wall into the plinth. It was closed. John kicked it open.

"WELCOME, WELCOME! PLEASE, DO COME IN. MAY I TAKE YOUR COAT?" The Robobutler grabbed Mary and lifted her off the ground. Holding her gun hand tight, it pulled at her collar, trying to remove the coat she wasn't wearing. "ARE YOU WELL TODAY, SIR? HAVE YOU COME FAR?"

Kicking and screaming, Mary managed to free her gun arm. "Damn you, Sinister!" she hissed, swinging the pistol round towards John.

John intercepted the gun before it could reach him. Grabbing it with both hands, he tried to prise it from Mary's grasp, but she was having none of it. She held on with all her might, determined to put a steel pellet right between his eyes. Pushing his head back with her free hand Mary clawed at John's face, John screwing his eyes shut to keep away her probing fingers. He didn't see the giant terracotta warrior on the landing above start to rock back and forth, or the moment it tipped over the railing to come hurtling down towards them. He sure felt it though.

The terracotta warrior slammed into the three of them, smashing into a thousand pieces. There was dust and noise and pain everywhere. John and Mary were thrown to the floor as the poor

Robobutler snapped in half from the force of the impact. They hit the ground hard, John's head bouncing off the tiles as he tumbled across the entrance hall.

He came to a stop somewhere near the front door, his face pressed into a pile of broken warrior, and the last thing he remembered before passing out was the splintering of wood and a vaguely familiar female voice somewhere nearby shouting, "POLICE! NO-BODY MOVE. YOU'RE ALL– What the hell?!"

"You're quite sure they're safe?"

"Absolutely. I just got word from the guys we sent down there. They picked up Shelby and his coachman a short while ago. They're no danger to anyone anymore."

John let out a deep sigh. "Thank you, Detective Hardigan. Thank you very much."

"You're welcome, Mr Sinister."

John was sitting back in the drawing room, in what was fast becoming his usual spot. He had a tea towel full of ice against a large lump on the back of his head, and he felt like he was going to be sick. Detective Hardigan sat opposite him, notebook in hand, right where Mary had sat. Next to him on the couch was Dexter, laying against his leg, doing a poor job of pretending to be asleep. John actually heard him say the word 'snore' once or twice.

"Actually, to be honest with you, I don't think your sister and her little girl were in that much danger to begin with."

"What makes you say that?"

"Well, when the lads got there they found a very tall, very angry woman, dealing with the situation."

"Dealing with the situation? Dealing with it how?"

Detective Hardigan smiled. "Have you ever seen a washer-woman beat a stubborn stain out of a pair of underpants? Apparently Shelby and his driver were the underpants, and your sister's front doorstep was the rock she was using to beat them on."

John took a moment to enjoy the delightful image that conjured up. *God bless Agnes*, he thought. She really was good people. "I hope your boys didn't do anything to Agnes. She's one of us, y'know."

The detective seemed amused by the idea.

"Don't worry, Mr Sinister. Most coppers aren't as green as they are cabbage looking. We've got your friend in custody, but I'll have her let go when I get back to the Yard."

"Thank you, Detective. Again."

"You're welcome, Mr Sinister. Again."

John started to feel dizzy. He closed his eyes hoping that would help, but the room just kept on spinning.

"I tell you what though, it's lucky we got that anonymous tip off when we did. A little later and someone could have been killed."

"Indeed, Detective. Very lucky," said John, glancing down at Dexter. "I don't suppose Spencer or Mary have confessed have they?"

"Oh no, not at all. And they're not likely to either. The only word we can get out of them is 'lawyer'. Mr Shelby's driver on the other hand won't shut up. He knows how the game is played. The first to talk gets taken care of, and he's singing like grandma's budgerigar."

"Money doesn't buy loyalty, eh?"

"Not in my experience, no," said the detective.

The two sat for a moment whilst Detective Hardigan referred to her notebook. "So to recap, you say Mary Chard and Spencer Shelby the Third ran over Henry Chard with an experimental omnibus of some sort?"

"An automotive engine, yes."

"And then they poisoned Donald Chard and staged Peter Chard's suicide all to gain control of Chard Mechanical."

"That's correct. They also killed a man by the name of John Tiggle. He was Donald Chard's illegitimate son. You'll find him in the morgue with two broken legs and a crushed skull. Tell the coroner it's the guy he was working on when I was in there last, he'll know who you mean."

Detective Hardigan shook her head in disbelief. "I tell you what, for a couple of posh kids that's quite an impressive list of crimes."

"They're also responsible for the break-ins at the Zoo, the Museum, and the World of Wonders, all to do with this club of theirs, the Hell-Bats. But I can tell you all about that later. I'll even bring you some nice photographic evidence. But for now I need to rest."

"Of course," said Detective Hardigan, closing her notebook. "We can go over all this when you come in to give a statement."

"Thank you, Detective."

Detective Hardigan headed for the door. "And we can discuss your impersonating a police officer then, too," she said, as she pulled the door to behind her.

As the door clicked shut Dexter sat up. "And thank you, Dexter," said John. "If you hadn't called the police, Lord knows what would have happened."

Dexter snorted. "Wasn't easy, y'know. Have you ever tried working a radiophone without any fingers? You can't talk and listen at the same time for a start, no way to hold the ear piece. Then the meat-sack I spoke to at Wainwright's Yard turned out to be a right dope. Took him ages to catch on to what I was on about. Honest to God, I almost hung up on him quite a few times."

"Well I'm glad you didn't. You saved my life, mate, and no mistake."

Dexter looked pretty pleased with himself. "You might even say I was a bit of a hero, eh?"

John looked doubtful. "Yeah, I'm not sure how heroic it was pushing that giant statue down on top of us though."

Dexter simply shrugged. "What else could I do? She was gonna shoot you."

"Maybe," said John, prodding at the lump on his head. " But even so…"

"Oh stop complaining," said Dexter. "I nearly cracked my skull open too, y'know, banging on that door."

"Good job you've got such a thick head, eh?"

"Right back at ya, fella."

The two of them fell silent.

"Seriously though, you risked your life for me today," said John. "No one's ever done that for me before."

Dexter pawed at the sofa cushion. "Yeah, well, what can I say? I mean, you're my friend, right? Or at least you said you were back at Nomko's. And that's what friends do isn't it, they take care of each other? At least I think they do. I've never had a friend before. Not a real one anyway. So, y'know, I just did what anyone would do for their friend. I mean, if I was in trouble and needed help you'd help me out, right? Come to my rescue, that sort of thing?" John didn't respond. "Well, wouldn't you?" Dexter looked up to find John passed out cold, his head lolling to one side, his mouth hanging open. "Huh, charming."

Settling down next to John, Dexter closed his eyes. Somewhere in a far off room a carriage clock struck midnight. The day was done. Finally, it was all over.

John's hand slid off his leg, coming to rest on Dexter's back. Unconsciously, his fingers found the mechanical cat's head, idly stroking him behind the ear in a way that Dexter had to admit wasn't the most unpleasant thing in the world.

Like that, the two of them fell asleep, only to wake the next morning when Hercules the butler returned from his night on the town to find his front door smashed in and bits of broken warrior all over his beautiful entrance hall.

Chapter 6

A Week Later

Clinging on for dear life, John Sinister tried not to make any embarrassing noises as Nomko's whirlygig swung in low over the treetops. It had only been a week since the shenanigans at Chard Manor, and whilst his head wound was healing up nicely he still got the odd dizzy spell now and then, meaning the chances of him and the ground making a sudden re-acquaintance were a little high for his liking. Not that Nomko seemed to care about that. He sat at the controls of the machine, battling the kraken as before, the grin on his face matched only by that of Dexter, who sat on his shoulder, wearing a pair of cat-sized flying goggles, laughing wildly as he had the time of his life.

The last seven days had been a crazy time for John. The day after Chard Manor, when it had all come out, the press had had a field day. It had been all over the front page of every newspaper in town, and John had found himself Hammersmyth's cause célèbre for a while. The Detecting Agent who brought down the House of Chard. The man who risked life and limb in pursuit of truth and justice. Bumbleton and his boys couldn't get enough of it. They all fought for an exclusive with the man of the hour, and John had been more than happy to oblige them... for the right price that is.

And they'd been happy to pay, which was ridiculous because most of what they wrote they made up anyway. They could have stayed home and done that. They just wanted the odd genuine quote to throw in to make it sound authentic. It was laughable, and slightly insulting, and John might have been annoyed but for all the coin in his pocket. That took the sting out of it a little bit. Plus, if he was being honest, he'd embellished quite a few of the 'facts' himself along the way.

The press's interest in him lasted a total of three days, right up until all the Hell-Bats stuff came out. Then, all of a sudden, no one was interested in him anymore. They started chasing down the Rosemonts, and the Whitby-Smythes, and the Oakhamptons, anyone with money they thought they could embarrass. Overnight John became old news, something he first thought of as a great relief until he was out buying eggs one day, nobody recognised him, and he realised to his dismay that he missed the attention (an embarrassing realisation made simultaneously better and worse by the fact that there was no one there to notice it).

The criminal case against Mary and Spencer was going well, according to Detective Hardigan. It turned out that Spencer's driver, the illustrious Charlie, was a right nosy little sod. He knew everything about everything and was more than willing to talk to anyone that would listen to save his own skin. Thanks to him, the evidence against Mary and Spencer had soon mounted up. It was starting to look like an open and shut case but for one little hiccup, the missing automotive engine. Used in two murders, it was a key piece of evidence. Without it, all the police had was a lot of accusations, hearsay, and circumstantial evidence. Not an ideal position to be in. That's not to say their case wasn't strong, it was, but it would be a lot stronger with the engine there to back it all up.

That was why John, Dexter, and Nomko were up in the whirlygig plunging their way over the outskirts of Hammersmyth. A ground search by the police had found nothing, but John had figured they'd see more from the air. Starting where the body of John Tiggle had been found, they were flying round in ever increasing circles, hoping to catch sight of wherever they'd stashed the automotive engine. And whilst John had been right, you could see everything from up here, he was really regretting coming along for the ride.

As the whirlygig reached the edge of a small wood, John saw something big and shiny in amongst the trees. He pointed it out to Nomko who gave him a quick thumbs up before bringing the whirlygig in for a bumpy landing in the field next door.

John staggered off the machine, his legs shaking. He had to take a few deep breaths to calm himself down. Whatever else life had in store for him, he was never doing that again.

Pulling his flying goggles down around his neck, Dexter looked up at John and chuckled. "Are you alright? You don't look so good."

"I'm fine," said John, walking off towards the woods.

Where the trees met the field, the hedgerow was too thick to climb through. They had to jump a gate into the road and head a little way up until they found a dirt track that led into the woods. There, about fifty yards in, underneath a pile of broken branches and ripped up greenery, was the automotive engine. It had a long scrape along its side, one of its headlamps was broken, and they found what looked like blood on the front bumper and around the rim of the front right wheel.

"Crikey, what a way to go," said Dexter.

"Hopefully it was quick," said John.

"Hopefully. But even so."

Nomko emerged from round the back of the engine, an angry look on his face. "Engine all seized up," he said. "She cannot go. Will need tow to get her home. I go get horses, and police. You two stay here, keep eye on her. Yes?"

"Whatever you say, chief," said John.

"I may be some time. We long way out."

"Not a problem. Take all the time you need," said John. Any plan that involved keeping both feet firmly on the ground was just fine with him.

Nomko cut through the undergrowth, climbing a tree to clear the hedgerow into the field. They heard the whirlygig fire up, then watched through the branches as it rose up into the air to slide off across the sky back towards town.

"May as well make ourselves comfortable," said John, climbing into the automotive engine's driver's seat. "It's gonna be a long wait."

Dexter jumped up onto the passenger seat next to him. The bodywork of the engine wasn't all that high, but even sitting as upright as possible, Dexter could barely see over the sides.

"So I guess this is it," said Dexter. "Now that we've found the engine it'll be case closed, eh?"

"I guess so, more or less."

"It's been fun working together, wouldn't you say?"

"You've got an odd idea of fun," said John.

"You know what I mean."

"Yeah, I guess. I mean, it certainly has been interesting, I'll give you that."

Dexter nodded. "Yup, it has indeed. Very interesting. Very, really, er, quite interesting."

John glanced down at the mechanical cat. Something was going on with him. He kept looking round the engine's interior, out into the woods, up into the sky, anywhere, in fact, except at John. Then, with a quick bit of side eye and a nonchalant tilt of the head, Dexter said in as casual a tone as possible, "Did you hear what happened with Mr Chard's will?"

"What? The morality clause do you mean, where if Mary goes to jail she gets nothing."

"No. I mean, yes, but no. The other bit. How Mr Chard left everything to me, since all the other beneficiaries are dead. Like, the house, the factory, the airships, the whole shebang."

"Yeah I heard. I'm now poorer than a cat. You don't have to rub it in."

"What? No, that's not what I meant. I mean, I was going to say, you could move into Chard Manor, if you wanted to? It'd be no problem. There's more rooms than you can shake a stick at. And it's bound to be more comfortable than sleeping on your sister's couch all the time."

"Oh yeah? And what would I do there all day? Read and work on my needlepoint?"

"If you like. But I was thinking maybe you and I could go into business together. Y'know, become like real detecting agents, for real, like. A little something to keep life interesting, as it were. If you wanted to, that is?" John looked down at Dexter, but the cat still couldn't look him in the eye.

It was an interesting offer and no mistake. In fact, he'd already been approached by a couple of Hammersmyth's more notorious citizens about making a few discreet enquiries on their behalf. If he moved into Chard Manor he'd have a paid for base of operations from which to work, which couldn't hurt any. And the address did have a certain caché that might prove useful.

"Say I did move in," said John. "I'd have to be the one in charge. We take the cases I choose and do things my way, got it?"

"Well, I was thinking more like an equal partnership. Fifty-fifty and all that. I mean, it *is* my house."

John snorted and shook his head. "That's what I thought. Sorry, mate, but I can't work like that. I'm going to have to say thanks, but no thanks."

"But what about—"

"No. It's no good. Either I'm in charge or I go it alone."

Dexter turned and stared off into the distance, absolutely fuming. John felt bad, but if they were going to work together he had to set down some ground rules first. There was no way he was going to spend his time negotiating with some damned cat day in, day out. He had to be the one making the decisions.

"Okay, fine," said Dexter. "You're in charge. But my name goes first on the letterhead."

"Fine with me," said John. It sounded better that way round anyway. "Shake on it?" He offered the cat his hand and got a paw in return. With one short, sharp, shake, the deal was done.

John sat back and pulled his cap down over his eyes. So, a roof over his head, a warm bed to sleep in, no bills to pay, home-cooked meals, and the prospect of a little coin in his pocket. Things were looking up for once, and about time too. He was due a change of fortune and no mistake.

A large drop of rain landed on the end of John's nose. Then another. And another. He looked up at the darkening sky. *Great*, he thought, as the heavens opened. *Just my luck.*

The End

THE DRAGONFLY DELIVERY COMPANY

CHAPTER 1

Fluffy white clouds scudded beneath the airship's wooden hull, a moonlit layer of candyfloss atop the wine-dark sea of dirt below. They looked good enough to eat, like you could simply scoop some out of the air if you so desired. Stretching as far down as tip-toes would allow, Bert the cabin boy reached over the side to see if he could.

"Careful, young 'un," said the man at the helm. "It's a long way down if you go over."

Bert pulled back his hand. "I ain't goin' over. I knows what I'm doin'," he said testily.

The Helmsman laughed. "That's what they all say, and then slip, whoosh, arrgh, splat." Resting his chin on his hands, Bert stared out towards the horizon. "Anyway, it's about time you were off to bed, innit?" the Helmsman added. "It's getting late. We've got a full day of it tomorrow, y'know."

"But the captain said there'd be shooting stars tonight!" Bert protested. "I wants to see 'em." He would never admit it, but he had a particular wish that he wanted to come true.

"I don't care. I'm not having you fallin' asleep on the job coz you've been up all night."

"But I—"

"No buts, you little blighter. Bed, now!"

Sagging under the weight of every missed opportunity, Bert went below deck, mumbling a half-hearted goodnight to the Helmsman along the way. The Helmsman smiled. Young Bert was a good lad, even if he did have a bit of a mouth on him. He'd make a fine aeronaut one day.

Humming softly to himself, the Helmsman cast a weather eye over the ship's balloon before confirming once again that they were still on the right heading. It was a quiet night, with a steady wind. He didn't think he'd have anything to worry about. What he did have though was a gnawing feeling in the pit of his stomach. *Damn*, he thought. *I should have got Bert to bring me up some stew.* As if agreeing with him, his stomach gave a long, miserable groan.

Scanning the horizon for unexpected mountain ranges, the Helmsman tied off the wheel, before heading below deck to get himself something to eat.

Bert's head appeared through a hatch in the deck. Seeing the coast was clear, he scrambled up through the hole and hid behind a barrel, scanning the night sky intently as he crossed his fingers on both hands. He only needed to see one shooting star, just one, and he could go to bed happy, but as he swung his gaze from one horizon to the next all he saw was disappointment; disappointment as far as the eye could see. It looked like there'd be no new comic books for him the next time they came in to land.

Bert heard a thump. He turned, expecting a clip round the ear, and found a mushroom of metal hooks with a rope tied to it lying on its side in the middle of the deck. As he watched, the rope pulled taut, dragging the metal mushroom towards the side of the ship. Another bunch of hooks flew over the ship's rail, followed by a third, all three dragging across the deck until they caught on the railing and their ropes pulled tight. The ropes wiggled back and forth as one-by-one three figures climbed silently over the ship's rail. Unslinging the crossbows from their backs, they spread out across the deck, the three intruders making for the nearest hatch as they loaded their weapons.

Bert held his breath. *Sky pirates! Come to kill us all!* He had to warn the others.

As the three went below, Bert ran up onto the quarterdeck, where a brass bell hung next to the ship's wheel. "PIRATES! PI-RATES!" he yelled, ringing the bell with all his might. "THERE'S PIRATES ON BOARD!" He grabbed the rope with both hands and rang it even harder. "WAKE UP! WAKE UP! THERE'S PIRATES ON THE SHIP!"

A dark figure loomed over Bert. He looked up into the eyes of certain death as he heard footsteps running down below.

The sky pirate brought his crossbow crashing down on top of Bert's head, knocking him to the ground. A thousand stars exploded before his eyes, none of them shooting (unfortunately). Stumbling to his feet, blood in his eyes, Bert ran for his life, staggering blindly across the quarterdeck straight towards the edge of the ship. Somewhere far away a familiar voice yelled, "NO!"

Bert's world turned upside down as he tipped over the quarterdeck's low rail, the wind whipping around him as he tumbled towards the fluffy clouds below. A hand reached out. A shooting star flew overhead. Following it with his eyes, Bert made one final, desperate wish.

"We have to do *something*!"

"We *are* doing something. We've changed the routes."

"It's not enough. We need to know how they know so much. We need an investigation."

"Pah! That'll never work. No one will talk."

"We have to try!"

"Why bother? It's a waste of time."

"*You're* a waste of time!"

"Come over here and say that!"

"Oh I will, you wait and see!"

"Well?"

"Well what?!"

"Well come on then!"

The Annual General Meeting of the Venerable Society of Airships Owners, Sky Captains, and Itinerant Washerwomen was going about as well as it usually did.

The teashop they'd rented for the occasion was jam-packed with aeronauts from both sides of the fence, be they the ones who paid the bills or the ones who did all the work, with a small group of washerwomen in the corner having themselves a nice cup of tea and a chinwag and staying well out of it. It was a lot of linen trousers, flouncy shirts, and wide-brimmed hats, against a wall of three-piece suits, pocket watches, and neatly trimmed beards, separated by a bundle of jolly, smiling, soapy-smelling women who looked like they could bend steel with just the force of their disapproving glare alone. The meeting used to be held in a local tavern until it became apparent that any access to alcohol was a recipe for disaster. Even now, at just gone eight in the morning, a few of the captains were already one-and-a-half sheets to the wind, which probably explained why the gathering was descending into chaos a mere five minutes after it had been called to order.

Fortescue Frobisher, chairman of the society, breathed a heavy sigh. He didn't need this today. Pushing himself wearily to his feet, he removed his shoe and banged it loudly on the tabletop, rattling the teapots. "That's enough! Everybody settle down. This is no way to conduct business. Captain Lewis, let go of Mr Hargreaves at once! Thank you. Now, gentlemen,"—one of the washerwomen gave a discreet cough—"and ladies, despite our differences I think we can all agree that this situation cannot be allowed to continue. These so-called sky pirates have been taking a considerable slice of our collective pie for far too long now. They need to be stopped, and I have the solution." He held up a newspaper for everyone to see. A captain in the front row squinted up at the headline.

"You want to throw a tea party for all the maids in the city?"

"What? No. Not that." The chairman pointed to a small, blurry photograph of a man and a cat at the bottom of the page. "This."

The captain in the front row read the headline next to the picture. "Is this the world's richest cat?"

"Oh for heaven's sake, not the cat. The man next to it. That is John Sinister, the man who found Donald Chard's killer. If anyone can figure out what's going on, I'm sure he can."

That got a murmur of approval from everyone, even the washerwomen. Donald Chard was a legend in the aeronautic world, a hero to them all. The father of modern aeronautics, his loss had been keenly felt, and whilst having his killers behind bars was scant solace for the lack of his indomitable presence, it seemed reasonable to assume that anyone who had done right by Donald Chard would do right by them as well.

"Oh yeah?" said Captain Lewis, the man responsible for rumpling Mr Hargreaves. "And who's going to pay for all this? I'm sure a man like that ain't gonna come cheap."

"I'll pay for it out of my own pocket if I have to," said the chairman. "Although I'm sure we have enough in the coffers to cover such an investigation." He glanced at the bursar who nodded hastily.

The airship owners present seemed to like this idea very much. Their captains less so.

"Yeah, right," said Captain Lewis. "And who's going to carry him, eh? If I bring a spy on board me lads'll go nuts. They don't like having no strangers about, believe me. He's apt to get chucked overboard afore we reach the outskirts, you mark my words."

There was a chorus of agreement from the rest of the captains. They hadn't become air couriers because they liked people poking their nose into their business. There was a fine line between courier work and smuggling, a line many of them danced on a daily basis like they were doing a highland fling.

"I will take him," said a voice from the back of the room. The collected captains all turned as one.

Sitting with her feet up on a table, the brim of her feathered hat pulled down low, the lounging figure looked to be asleep but for the cup and saucer she had balanced in front of her. Tilting her head back just enough, she considered all the unwashed faces looking back at her. "I have no problem taking someone on board. *My* crew do what they are told, if they know what is good for them."

"But of course," barked Captain Lewis. "It'd be just like a woman to—"

There was a sudden squeak of chairs and the room fell silent. Captain Lewis turned slowly to find all of the assembled washerwomen giving him their *full* attention. Some of them were clutching knives, some of them tiny forks, and none of them were smiling. One was even brandishing a particularly spiky-looking rock bun like she knew how to use it, and whilst Captain Lewis didn't know what she was planning on doing with it, he was quite certain that he didn't want it happening to him.

"Enough," said the chairman. "Mrs Trowbury, put that chair down. Mrs Glossop, put that cake stand back where you found it at once! There's an easy way to settle this. We can take a vote."

An approving murmur went round the room. The captains liked this idea. There was safety in numbers. No one could make them back something if they didn't want to. If they all voted no what could anyone do? The motion didn't stand a chance. But as they glanced at Mrs Trowbury, who still hadn't put that chair down, they soon realised that this was not going to be what you might call a 'free' vote in the more traditional sense of the word.

John Sinister, Hammersmyth's most famous detecting agent (being the only one anyone had ever heard of) walked down a cobbled side street, his not-so-silent partner in their newly-minted detecting agency trotting along beside him. Dexter was the world's only walking, talking, mechanical cat. The most advanced automaton in the Britannic Empire, only two people knew of his existence – John Sinister, and his Japanese creator, Nomko. But now the time had come to let someone else in on their little secret, and Dexter for one couldn't wait to see how he would react.

"What do you think he'll do?" he said, grinning. "Do you think he'll faint? I think he'll faint."

"He's not going to faint."

"But he might do though, eh? I mean, you never know."

"He might, but I doubt it. He doesn't seem the fainting type."

"What, then? Will he swear, do you think? Fall off his chair? Something like that."

"From what I know of Mr Holberton, I think you'll be lucky to get a raised eyebrow."

"A raised eyebrow? A cat starts talking to him and you think all I'll get is a raised eyebrow? Be serious."

"I am being serious. He doesn't strike me as the kind to rattle easily. I think a raised eyebrow is all you're going to get."

"Nah. I think you're wrong. I think he'll faint."

Charles Holberton QC stared at the grey tortoiseshell tabby sitting in the chair opposite. In his nearly forty years before the bar he thought he'd seen every type of client there was, from the desperate, to the delusional, to the downright insane, but this was a new one on him. It just went to show, when you started making assumptions you made an ass out of you and umptions.

"Goodness me," he said. The cat chuckled.

"You were right," it said. "Not even a raised eyebrow."

John Sinister shrugged. "Told you. The man's unflappable."

"Well I wouldn't go that far," said Mr Holberton, his eyes still firmly fixed on Dexter. He sat forward, leaning on his desk. "You're an automaton, you say? Built by Chard Mechanical?"

"That I am."

"Fully independent? Capable of independent thought?"

"As much as either one of you, and probably more than this numpty," said Dexter, nodding towards John with a sly smirk.

"Well I never," said Mr Holberton, sitting back in his chair once more.

The past couple of weeks had been amongst the most bizarre the firm of Holberton, Hutchison, and Murphy had ever known. Not only had their biggest client, Donald Chard, the richest and most famous industrialist in the Britannic Empire, died in the very office in which they now sat, not only had said client chosen to leave his not-inconsiderable estate to the family cat, but now it seemed that the cat in question wasn't a cat at all, but was in fact an automaton, and quite the most advanced automaton the world had ever known. As previously stated, a bizarre couple of weeks indeed.

"Although I must say," Mr Holberton continued, "this revelation does shed light on some of the more unusual stipulations in Mr Chard's will."

"Such as?" asked John.

"Well, there's the emancipation proclamation for a start. Mr Chard left instructions that upon his death the cat known as Dexter was to be declared legally independent, something which I confess initially confounded me. Why would a cat need to be declared free from ownership? But now I understand. Without the declaration, Dexter would have remained the property of Chard Mechanical, and as such would have been unable to inherit the company. One cannot own property if you yourself are owned by said property."

"So... I *am* the new owner of Chard Mechanical then?" asked Dexter.

Mr Holberton scrunched up his face. "Not exactly. You see, whilst you can be declared not property, you cannot be declared a person within the law, and so cannot own anything. Chard Mechanical has been placed into a trust, which will be managed on your behalf."

"And who manages the trust?"

"Normally a trustee would have been stipulated in the will, but in this case the trustee is to be determined. Actually, the will states that the beneficiary, i.e. you, must appoint a trustee of their own choosing, a situation I had no idea how we were going to resolve until now."

"So I own everything, but I have to choose someone to speak for me, is that it?"

"Exactly."

"Will you do it?"

Mr Holberton chuckled. "Good Lord, no. As the executor of the will, and as legal counsel to the Chard estate, for me to insert myself into the middle of all this would be unwise to say the least. No, I suggest you appoint someone you trust to act as your mouthpiece. Someone who can act on your behalf, but who is unlikely to rip you off the first chance they get."

Dexter and Mr Holberton both turned to look at John, who suddenly felt his world get a lot more complicated. "Oh, come on! I don't want to run some massive company. Can you imagine what a pain that would be?"

"You wouldn't have to run anything, Mr Sinister. The general manager would do that for you. This would just be to keep all the paperwork nice and neat. Although, the two of you *will* have to find a new general manager to run things on Mr Dexter's behalf, seeing as how everyone who was previously eligible to run the company is now either dead or in jail."

"And how do we go about doing that?"

"I have no idea, but I suggest you do so sooner rather than later. Chard Mechanical is in a bit of a mess, to say the least. She needs a firm hand on the tiller before the whole thing goes up in smoke, if you catch my drift."

There was a knock at the door and Mr Holberton's clerk entered, a sour look on his already sour face. Through the door, the incessant yapping of a frantic, highly-agitated dog could be heard coming from downstairs. The company dog, Liebling, a bad-tempered, wire-haired terrier, had been locked in a cupboard for the duration of Dexter's visit, and neither he nor Mr Wilberforce were too pleased about the fact.

"A message from Chard Manor, sir, via the radiophone. For the... gentleman."

John was impressed. Much like on his first visit to the offices of Holberton, Hutchison, and Murphy, the clerk had managed to pack more contempt into the word 'gentleman' than John would ever have thought possible.

He read the message. "Well would you look at that," he said. "It seems we have another case."

Notes From The Author

JOHN'S CHESS TRICK

The trick John uses to beat the Chess Club is based upon a technique invented by the excellent illusionist and mentalist extraordinaire, Derren Brown.

In Series 1 Episode 1 of Trick Of The Mind – first broadcast in the UK on Channel 4, Friday 23rd April, 2004 – Derren Brown took on nine chess champions, including four Grand Masters, two FIDE Masters, and one International Master. He played the nine games as described in the book, by pairing off the players, memorising their moves, and playing them off against each other.

He won four games, lost three, and drew two (a win overall), which is amazing in and of itself. How he was able to predict the number of remaining pieces each player would have at the end of their game is beyond me.

See if you can work it out. You can watch the trick online, on Derren Brown's YouTube channel. And when you've done that, there are several full-length specials of his available on Netflix for you to enjoy.

If you get the opportunity to see Derren Brown live I thoroughly recommend it. It is fascinating to see the man at work, not to mention incredibly entertaining. New shows are announced on his website www.derrenbrown.co.uk.

NOMKO'S JAPANESE

Translations of the Japanese phrases used by Nomko can be found below. These are not always direct translations, but in fact show the spirit of what Nomko is trying to express. But be warned, with the exception of the last one, what Nomko is usually trying to express is something rude.

Chapter 2
Chikushou – Damn it
Iyana yatsu – Prick

Chapter 5
Mendouna yatsu – Pain in the ass
Kochirakoso – The honour is all mine

OLD MONEY

To the modern mind, used to neat little multiples of ten, nine-teenth-century old money can seem a bit, well, weird. Divided into Pounds, Shillings and Pence, there were twelve pence in a shilling, and twenty shillings in a pound. One pound was a lot of money back then, roughly equivalent to a hundred pounds now.

A cup of coffee cost a penny, and a week's groceries around two and six (two shillings and six pence). A funeral cost four pounds, a new suit eight pounds, and a full set of dentures twenty-one pounds (so you needed to take care of your teeth, before someone else did).

One hundred pounds was considered a decent yearly income for the average family (enough to hire a servant, at least). Young men from wealthy families often lived on credit in anticipation of the vast sums they were expected to inherit and/or marry into. And since almost everything was made by hand, even planks of wood, everything was worth stealing, hence the Artful Dodger's penchant for handkerchiefs, worth anywhere from six pence (cotton) to six shillings (silk) each.

The less said about the Guinea, a gold coin worth a bizarre one pound and one shilling (which kept being used by the upper classes to place a value on things long after it went out of circulation), the better.

DEAR READER

I hope you have enjoyed reading about the Dexter & Sinister, Hammersmyth's premiere Detecting Agents. I truly appreciate each and every reader that I have, and I thank you for giving this book a try. Without you, I wouldn't be able to do what I do.

If you have have a moment to leave a review for Dexter & Sinister it would be very helpful to me. The more people who go on Amazon or Goodreads to leave a review, the more likely I will be able to bring you more misadventures starring a talking cat and his human sidekick in the future.

Book two, THE DRAGONFLY DELIVERY COMPANY, promises airships, sky pirates, kidnapping, betrayal, revenge, and a Welsh vegetarian chef called Mento Jones who does battle in a leather butcher's apron and very little else. It's gonna be fun!

Thank you again, and if you really have enjoyed Dexter & Sinister, then please do tell your friends.

About The Author

Born in the north of England, a stone's throw from the Lake District, Keith studied film making at university before moving to London to work in film and TV. After twenty years of doing other people's bidding he went around the world, trained as a yoga teacher, rode a camel, and was finally able to publish his first novel, something he has dreamed of since he was eight years old, when he asked for a typewriter for Christmas.

Currently residing back in the north, when he's not up a mountain Keith can be found trying to get his foot behind his head. He hasn't managed it yet, but he'll get there one day.

keithwdickinson.com

Acknowledgments

There may be one name on the cover of a book, but it would never come into being without the support of so many others.

First up, I'd like to thank all my friends and family for listening to me bang on about airships, talking cats, and Victorian old money all this time. Your patience is much appreciated. Special thanks go out to my readers, Paul D, Vanessa T, and Matt W, whose invaluable feedback allowed me to improve the story in so many ways. And to my editor, Jess Lawrence, who helped me make Dexter & Sinister the best it could be.

I'd also like to thank Mike Smith for his awesome Dexter illustration, and Nell Wood for her excellent cover design. I could not have asked for two better artists to bring my cover to life.

www.jesslawrence.co.uk

www.facebook.com/doodlebagsIllustrations

www.nellwood.co.uk